# THE
# DARLING DAHLIAS
## AND THE
# CONFEDERATE
# ROSE

# THE
# DARLING DAHLIAS
## AND THE
# CONFEDERATE
# ROSE

*Susan Wittig Albert*

BERKLEY PRIME CRIME, NEW YORK

**THE BERKLEY PUBLISHING GROUP**
**Published by the Penguin Group**
**Penguin Group (USA) Inc.**
**375 Hudson Street, New York, New York 10014, USA**

Penguin Group (Canada), 90 Eglinton Avenue East, Suite 700, Toronto, Ontario M4P 2Y3, Canada (a division of Pearson Penguin Canada Inc.) • Penguin Books Ltd., 80 Strand, London WC2R 0RL, England • Penguin Group Ireland, 25 St. Stephen's Green, Dublin 2, Ireland (a division of Penguin Books Ltd.) • Penguin Group (Australia), 250 Camberwell Road, Camberwell, Victoria 3124, Australia (a division of Pearson Australia Group Pty. Ltd.) • Penguin Books India Pvt. Ltd., 11 Community Centre, Panchsheel Park, New Delhi—110 017, India • Penguin Group (NZ), 67 Apollo Drive, Rosedale, Auckland 0632, New Zealand (a division of Pearson New Zealand Ltd.) • Penguin Books (South Africa) (Pty.) Ltd., 24 Sturdee Avenue, Rosebank, Johannesburg 2196, South Africa

Penguin Books Ltd., Registered Offices: 80 Strand, London WC2R 0RL, England

This book is an original publication of The Berkley Publishing Group.

This is a work of fiction. Names, characters, places, and incidents either are the product of the author's imagination or are used fictitiously, and any resemblance to actual persons, living or dead, business establishments, events, or locales is entirely coincidental. The publisher does not have any control over and does not assume any responsibility for author or third-party websites or their content.

PUBLISHER'S NOTE: The recipes contained in this book are to be followed exactly as written. The publisher is not responsible for your specific health or allergy needs that may require medical supervision. The publisher is not responsible for any adverse reactions to the recipes contained in this book.

FIRST EDITION: September 2012

Library of Congress Cataloging-in-Publication Data

Albert, Susan Wittig.
The Darling Dahlias and the Confederate rose / Susan Wittig Albert.—1st ed.
p.   cm.
ISBN 978-0-425-24776-1 (pbk.)
1. Women gardeners—Fiction.   2. Gardening—Societies, etc.—Fiction.   3. Nineteen thirties—Fiction.   4. Alabama—Fiction.   I. Title.
PS3551.L2637D36      2012               2012016156
813'.54—dc23

PRINTED IN THE UNITED STATES OF AMERICA

10   9   8   7   6   5   4   3   2   1

*For gardeners everywhere,*
*who tend their plants with courage, determination, and*
*faith in a green and abundant future.*
*The Darling Dahlias and I are growing with you.*

# Author's Note

I am a fan of historical novels. I very much enjoyed working with my husband Bill on the Robin Paige Victorian series, researching the way people lived in England at the turn of the twentieth century. I also enjoyed writing the eight books in the Cottage Tales series, about the life and times of author-illustrator Beatrix Potter. The books were set in 1905–1913, in the English Lake District.

And now, with the Darling Dahlias, I have an opportunity to visit the American South in the 1930s. I'm fascinated by the period, and by a town that's small enough to walk wherever you want to go; where the local grocery and the Saturday farmers' market offer fresh vegetables, meat, milk, eggs, and honey produced by local growers; and where neighbors gossip over the back fence and listen in on the party line. Movies have just learned to talk, and barnstorming pilots are an amazing family entertainment. Kids spend Saturday mornings hoeing the garden and Saturday afternoons at the swimming hole or dangling a fishing hook in the river. This is a very different world from the one you and I live in, and I love being able to explore its nooks and crannies.

But it wasn't Eden. The Great Depression meant that breadwinners were thrown out of work and children went hungry. Banks and businesses failed, families lost homes, farmers lost farms and livestock, and many lost hope. Widespread drought turned the Plains wheat country into a dustbowl and dried up great swathes of the South's most productive land. Prohibition was in force until 1933, and bootlegging was the regional (if not the national) sport, with all the criminal activity it invited. Huey P. Long and Father Charles Coughlin preached a passionate populism that inspired the poor, tempted the middle class, and terrified the rich. Racism, both conscious and unconscious, open and secret, was rampant.

My mother remembered those turbulent years as the "hard times," and as a child, I listened open-mouthed to her stories of the challenges she faced. But she lived through those years because she believed that there could be better days ahead—as long as people worked hard, had faith, and respected and cared for one another. That's the spirit I want to reflect in these books: the belief in the enduring values of hard work, deep faith, respect, caring, and community.

I hope you find it as reassuring as I do.


A word about language. To write truthfully about the rural South in the 1930s requires the use of images and language that may be offensive to some readers—especially the terms *colored*, *colored folk*, and *Negro* when they refer to African Americans. Thank you for understanding that I mean no offense.

Susan Wittig Albert
Bertram, Texas

May, 1931
The Darling Dahlias Clubhouse and Gardens
302 Camellia Street
Darling, Alabama

Dear Reader,

Well. It looks like we're going to get another book written about us!

Which is not only a wonderful surprise, but a very good thing, in our opinion, because the story that Mrs. Albert is writing is full of some true and surprising events that many folks (especially Yankees) don't know anything about. In fact, when she asked us what she should call her book, we suggested The Confederate Rose, because . . . well, you'll see why as you get into the story.

But before you begin, we should tell you that here in the South, we lay proud claim to two Confederate roses. One is the flower that we grow in our gardens, which (as Miss Rogers will be happy to tell you) is more properly called by its real name, Hibiscus mutabilis. The other is the Confederate Rose, our very own Southern spy, who helped the boys in gray defeat the boys in blue at the Battle of Bull Run in 1861.

Now, we have to confess that some of us were surprised to learn about this Confederate Rose. And all of us were even more surprised when we discovered that our dear little Darling is home to the granddaughter of the Confederate Rose, an astonishing fact that was turned up by Mr. Charles Dickens, the editor and publisher of the Darling Dispatch, when he was doing *research. But now we know (and so will you, by the time you've finished the story), and we can lay proud claim to that, as well.*

*We're also very proud of our little garden club, the Dahlias. In case you don't know about us, we would like to tell you that our members have worked together for many years to make Darling the prettiest town in Alabama. Our club is named for Mrs. Dahlia Blackstone, who left us her beautiful house and gardens on Camellia Street, along with a weedy vacant lot that we're turning into a big vegetable garden, which is important in these hard times, because some people are out of work and others are out of money and—*

*But we don't like to dwell on things like that. Folks may not have much money, but Darling is still a pretty wonderful town, even though there may be one or two who (for their own personal reasons) want what belongs to other people and don't much care how they get it. But that's part of Mrs. Albert's story, so that's all we'll say about* that.

*Anyway, while there are a few dark and underhanded doings in this book, there are plenty of bright places in it, and bright places all around us, too. We Dahlias are not Pollyannas, not by a long shot. We are perfectly aware that there's a lot of trouble in this world. But we do like the old saying that Aunt Hetty Little has embroidered into a beautiful picture for our club wall.* We keep our faces to the sun so we can't see the shadows. *It's why we manage to stay (mostly) cheerful during these depressing times. And it's also why we plant yellow and orange sunflowers and marigolds and cosmos in among the collards and sweet potatoes and string beans and okra in our gardens.*

*We hope you will, too.*

*Sincerely,*
*Elizabeth Lacy, President*
*Ophelia Snow, Vice President & Secretary*
*Verna Tidwell, Treasurer*

# The Darling Dahlias Club Roster, April 1931

**Elizabeth Lacy,** president. Secretary to Mr. Moseley, attorney at law, and garden columnist for the Darling *Dispatch*.

**Ophelia Snow,** vice-president and secretary. Wife of Darling's mayor, Jed Snow.

**Verna Tidwell,** treasurer. Manager of the office of the Cypress County probate clerk and treasurer.

**Bessie Bloodworth,** club historian. Owner and proprietor of Magnolia Manor, a boardinghouse for genteel ladies next door to the Dahlias' clubhouse and gardens.

Club Members

**Earlynne Biddle.** Married to Henry Biddle, the manager at the Coca-Cola bottling plant. A rose fancier.

**Fannie Champaign.** The newest member of the club, Fannie owns Champaign's Darling Chapeaux, on the west side of the courthouse square, where she has a flower garden. She says that her flowers are the inspiration for her hats.

**Mrs. George E. Pickett (Voleen) Johnson.** Wife of the owner of the Darling Savings and Trust Bank and president of the Darling Ladies Club. Specializes in pure white flowers.

**Mildred Kilgore.** A collector of camellias, Mildred is married to Roger Kilgore, the owner of Kilgore Motors. The Kilgores live near the Cypress Country Club.

**Aunt Hetty Little.** Oldest member of the club, town matriarch, and lover of gladiolas.

**Myra May Mosswell.** Co-owner of the Darling Diner, co-owner and operator in the Darling Telephone Exchange, and champion vegetable gardener. Lives in the flat over the diner with Violet Sims and Violet's little girl, Cupcake.

**Lucy Murphy.** Married to Ralph Murphy and lives on a small farm on Jericho Road. Lucy just planted a peach orchard to help make ends meet.

**Miss Dorothy Rogers.** Darling's librarian and a spinster. Miss Rogers knows the Latin name of every plant and insists that everybody else does, too. She lives in Magnolia Manor.

**Beulah Trivette.** Artistically talented owner/operator of Beulah's Beauty Bower. Loves cabbage roses and other big, floppy flowers.

**Alice Ann Walker.** Bank cashier. Enjoys iris and daylilies because they don't take a lot of work. Her husband Arnold is disabled but tends the family vegetable garden.

# THE
# DARLING DAHLIAS
## AND THE
# CONFEDERATE
# ROSE

# ONE

# The Dahlias Get Down and Dirty

Elizabeth Lacy took off her floppy green straw garden hat and fanned herself with it. The late April sky was leaden gray and the young leaves on the live oak trees hung limp and unmoving in the languid Saturday afternoon air. Lizzy hadn't checked the thermometer beside the back door of the Darling Dahlias' clubhouse, but she'd bet dollars to doughnuts that the temperature was nudging ninety. And judging from the weight of the air and the way her blue blouse was sticking to her shoulders, the humidity was way up there, too. She glanced nervously toward the clouds in the west, which were tinged with a darker, more ominous purple. As she watched, a flash of lightning zigzagged from the base of the cloud.

Lizzy raised her voice to the women working in the large vegetable garden next to the clubhouse. All three of them—Ophelia Snow, Verna Tidwell, and Bessie Bloodworth—were club officers. Ophelia was the vice-president and secretary; Verna was treasurer; and Bessie was the newly elected club historian.

"Hey, everybody. Let's finish up as soon as we can. We don't want to be out here in the open when that storm hits."

Startled, Bessie put a hand to her back and straightened up, glancing toward the west. "Gracious, Liz," she exclaimed. "That looks like a lollapalooza." She frowned down at the row she was hoeing. "I guess these beans can wait. But we'd better plan on putting in some sort of trellis. Kentucky Wonders are like Jack's beanstalk. They aim for the skies. If we wait much longer, we'll have a mess of snaky green vines all over the ground."

"Those are the seeds your cousin sent you from Birmingham?" Lizzy asked. Good seeds weren't always easy to buy. The best often came from friends and family.

Bessie nodded. "She saved them from her last year's garden. Says they're the best green beans she's ever grown."

"I'm sure we can come up with some cane poles and twine for a trellis," Lizzy said. She glanced back at the clouds. "But let's work on it later. I'm not worried about getting wet—we won't melt—but I don't like for us to be out in the garden when the lightning is flashing." She was remembering poor Mr. Burdette, who had been struck dead by lightning when he walked out to the pasture to bring the cows home for milking one afternoon. Spring storms could be violent.

Bessie gave the sky another apprehensive glance. "And let's hope for no hail," she said. "I'd sure hate to see all our little plants beaten to death."

"I've just put in two more rows of okra, Liz," Verna called, coming along the path. She turned and pointed toward the far side of the garden, where an unpainted board fence and a row of crepe myrtles marked the edge of the clubhouse property. "And there's room for three more rows. By the time we get done planting, there'll be enough okra to feed everybody in Darling."

"That's the point, isn't it?" Ophelia asked. "Enough for

everybody?" Ophelia had a hoe in one hand and a rake in the other, and her round, sweet face was sweat-streaked and dirty.

"There can never be enough okra," Bessie said emphatically.

"I suppose," Ophelia said. To Lizzy, she added, "The last of the English peas will need to be picked in the next few days, Liz. They've stopped blooming, so that will be our final picking. And there are more carrots and beets to pull." She paused. "I hope everybody comes to help, the way they did last time. It's a lot more fun when we have a good turnout."

"Many hands make light work," Bessie observed sensibly, and Lizzy smiled. She imagined Bessie's brain as a massive library of adages that were filed under various headings, at least one for every occasion. Of course, as the unofficial historian for the town of Darling, Bessie had many other things filed away in her mind, such as important events in the past, historically important sites, and family trees.

Verna sniffed. "It would be nice if we would *all* show up," she remarked, with an edge to her voice.

Lizzy knew what Verna was thinking. The Dahlias had hosted a work party two weeks before, and thirteen out of the fourteen club members had attended. (Mrs. George E. Pickett Johnson was the missing person. She had offered to send her colored maid, Flossie, but Lizzy had declined. She knew Flossie and liked her, but she thought that Mrs. Johnson should come herself, not send her paid help.) Some of the Dahlias had picked and shelled peas, some had harvested lettuce and the last of the spring spinach, and some had pulled carrots, beets, and green onions. There was plenty for the Dahlias to share, as well as a big batch of fresh produce for the Saturday-morning farmers' market, where they had a table. What they didn't sell, they gave away when the market closed. Lizzie had noticed that some of the poorer folks hung around until closing time and were glad to get whatever they could.

"We'll need to organize another garden party, I guess," Lizzy said. Organizing came easily to her—the reason, she supposed, that she'd just been elected for another term as club president. "This time, maybe Mrs. Johnson will come."

"Don't forget that we also have to organize a planting party at the cemetery next week," Bessie cautioned. "Miss Rogers will never forgive us if we don't get those Confederate roses into the ground before the Confederate Day ceremony."

*"Hibiscus mutabilis,"* Verna and Ophelia said in unison, and they all laughed. Miss Rogers, the town librarian and a long-time Dahlia, always insisted on using the Latin names for plants. Two years before, she had taken cuttings from everyone's garden and propagated fourteen Confederate roses (not really roses, but hibiscus). The young shrubs were now large and sturdy enough to be planted along the front fence at the Darling Cemetery. And since Confederate Day (an important Darling holiday, as it is across the South) was coming up shortly, it was time to get the plants settled in their new home. Summer would be along soon—not a good time for transplanting.

Verna looked up at the sky and held out her hand, palm up. "Was that a raindrop?"

Lizzy grabbed the rake from Ophelia. "Come on, girls— let's put the tools away and cool off with some iced tea. Maybe the storm will blow over before we're ready to head for home."

A few minutes later, the four Dahlias were sitting around the green-painted table in the clubhouse kitchen, a pitcher of mint-flavored tea and a plate of Dr. George Washington Carver's peanut cookies in front of them. The cookies had been baked by Roseanne, the cook at Magnolia Manor, Bessie Bloodworth's boardinghouse for "genteel older ladies," next door to the Dahlias' clubhouse.

"That was good work this afternoon, ladies," Lizzy said, pouring the tea. She looked around the table, thinking how much she cherished these three friends. She enjoyed all the Dahlias—like different varieties of roses, each one had her own particular beauty, while some had a few thorns. But the three sitting around the table with her this afternoon were very special.

"That was *hard* work," Bessie said, pulling an embroidered hanky out of her sleeve and wiping her sweaty face with it. "But as the saying goes, we can't plow a field by turning it over in our minds."

Gray-haired Bessie was twenty years older than the others, but she could work as long and as hard as any of the younger women in the club. She always said she'd grown up with a hoe in her hand and okra and sunflower seeds in her pocket. Everybody valued her gardening experience, especially now that the Dahlias had decided to start raising vegetables in a big way.

Lizzy had been on the lookout for projects that would keep the club growing and working together, and the vegetable garden—a natural, really—had been her idea. The front yard of the clubhouse they had inherited from Dahlia Blackstone had once been filled with azaleas, roses, and hydrangeas, and behind the house had been almost an acre of beautiful flowers, sweeping down toward a clump of woods and a clear spring surrounded by bog iris, ferns, and pitcher plants. Mrs. Blackstone's garden had been so beautiful that it had been featured in newspapers as far away as New Orleans and Miami, and visitors from all over the state had come to Darling to see it.

But by the time the Dahlias took it over, the flowers and shrubs were disconsolate and abandoned and the garden looked as if it had completely given up hope. Determined to rescue it and restore its former beauty, the members had pulled on their gardening gloves and set to work. They repaired the trellises for the Confederate jasmine and mandevilla and cut back the exuberant cross vine and honey-suckle on the fence. They cleared the curving perennial borders so that the Shasta daisies, phlox, iris, asters, and larkspur could stretch out and bloom. They divided and replanted the Easter lilies, spider lilies, oxblood lilies, and Mrs. Blackstone's favorite orange ditch lilies. They also pruned Mrs. Blackstone's many roses—the climbers, teas, ramblers, shrubs, and the unruly yellow Lady Banks, who had spread her sweeping skirts of green branches across the back corner. ("Give a Lady Banks an inch and she'll take a mile," Earlynn Biddle always said.)

But when all that was done, Lizzy didn't let the ladies rest on their laurels. Next door to the clubhouse, on the corner, was a large vacant lot that had once been Mrs. Blackstone's vegetable garden—the perfect place to grow vegetables. They had hired old Mr. Norris and his bay gelding, Racer, to plow the ground. Racer's name was sort of a joke, because he was as slow as molasses on a cold January morning. But once the old horse made up his mind to get to work, he was all business, and Mr. Norris pocketed a few dollars every spring by plowing and harrowing the town gardens.

After Racer had finished plowing and harrowing the ground, the Dahlias got started, raking the soil smooth and marking the rows for the corn, green beans, collards, Swiss chard, okra, tomatoes, peppers, eggplants, squash, melons, cucumbers, and sweet potatoes they intended to plant. Lizzy had pointed out that the money they earned from the sale of their vegetables could go to fund other projects, such as the herb garden they were planning at the Retirement Haven, the old folks' home out on Rayburn Road, and the new landscaping they hoped to put in around the courthouse.

With that incentive, all the Dahlias were eager to pitch in and help. All, that is, except for Voleen Johnson, wife of the town's banker. Mrs. Johnson didn't like to get dirt under her manicured fingernails. She did agree, however, to take money at the Saturday market, although she wore her fanciest hat and a pair of dainty white gloves to keep the dirty coins and bills from soiling her hands.

"Hard work and *hot* work," Ophelia put in cheerfully. "Wonder if it's going to be like this all summer. I swear, it must have been ten degrees above normal all this week." She got up from the table and turned on the small electric fan, aiming the cooling breeze at the group around the table. "If it gets any hotter, I'm going to have to sit down at the Singer and run up a couple of cotton sundresses for Sarah. Mrs. Snow gave me some material for them." She gave her head a rueful shake. "That girl is growing faster'n a weed. Seems like I'm always letting her hems down another inch."

Ophelia was one of the younger Dahlias. She and Jed Snow (the mayor of Darling and the owner of Snow's Farm Supply) had two children: Sam, a boisterous fourteen, and Sarah, just eleven but taller than her mother. A dedicated mother and a talented seamstress, Ophelia made their clothes instead of buying them at Mann's Mercantile, which saved quite a lot. She was also raising chickens so she could sell eggs at the Saturday market. Of course, Mrs. Hancock, at Hancock's Groceries, would buy the eggs, but Ophelia could earn more by selling them herself. Lizzy knew that every penny counted for the Snows right now, because business at the Farm Supply was falling off, and what trade there was, was mostly on credit. The farmers didn't have much cash money for seed and fertilizer and none at all for new equipment, which meant that it was lean times for the Snows—and for all the merchants who depended on the farmers' trade.

Verna Tidwell tilted her glass and drank. "Normal," she muttered darkly, pouncing on Ophelia's word. "These days, I wonder what normal is. I'm not sure *anybody* knows. And I'm not talking about the temperature, either."

Unlike Ophelia, who had a reputation for smiling through even the most calamitous events, Verna had a much darker view of human nature. She had a habit of peering "under the rocks," as she put it, on the lookout for anything suspicious. Her prickly skepticism put some people off—but not Lizzy, who admired her friend's sharp eyes and even sharper mind. Verna ably employed her talents as manager of the Cypress County probate clerk and treasurer's office, in the county courthouse. That's where she heard the whispers about who was doing this or that or the other bad thing and what was going to happen when word of these misdeeds got to the wrong (or the right) person.

And since Verna never expected to find anybody behaving any better than anybody else, she was never disappointed or distressed when she discovered that so-and-so had lied about his property boundaries or siphoned twenty gallons of fuel oil out of the tank behind the county road maintenance building or was operating a whiskey still over on Shiner's Knob.

"Comes with the territory," she always said in a matter-of-fact sort of way. "If you don't want to smell folks' dirty laundry, you should stay out of the probate clerk's office. That's where it all hangs out."

But in the past couple of weeks, Lizzy had noticed that Verna's expression was darker than usual, and more frowning. She was unusually silent, too, and there were fewer barbed remarks. Something was troubling Verna, and Lizzy could guess what it was. In the law firm of Moseley and Moseley where she worked, she often picked up bits of courthouse gossip. She'd heard that there was some sort of trouble—serious trouble—with the county treasurer's accounts. But while Verna usually shared her personal life with Lizzy, she was always closemouthed about things that went on at the office. So Lizzy didn't ask what was going on. If Verna felt the need to talk, she'd do it—in her own sweet time.

Now, as if to endorse Verna's dark view of *normal*, there was a flash of lightning and an almost instantaneous clap of thunder so loud that it rattled the windows in the old house. All four of the Dahlias jumped.

"Sakes alive," Bessie exclaimed. "That one was too close for comfort. Wonder if it struck somewhere here in town." She shook her head. "One year, I remember, the Free Will Baptist Church was struck by lightning. Burned right down to the ground while the preacher and his flock were having a baptizing in the river. When they got back, there was nothing left but ashes."

Lizzy chuckled. This was the kind of story that Bessie always came up with. She knew more local history than anybody.

"It'll be over soon," Ophelia reassured them. "Give it fifteen minutes and the sun will be shining again. That's what normally happens around here."

"I know what normal is," Lizzy said, offering the plate of Roseanne's cookies to Verna. "It's sitting here with my best friends in the whole world, drinking tea and eating cookies, waiting for a storm to blow over."

"Afraid we'll have to wait a good long time for *this* storm to blow over," Verna remarked as she took a couple of cookies. Lizzy guessed that she wasn't talking about the rain that was beginning to lash furiously at the kitchen window. Verna was thinking about whatever was bothering her. Or about the dismal things that were happening around the country— people losing their jobs, families losing their homes, old folks losing their savings. Children going hungry, lots of people going broke. Hard times.

If that's what it was, Lizzy had to agree with Verna's gloomy assessment. As Mr. Moseley's secretary, she met plenty of folks who had gotten themselves into some kind of financial trouble and needed a lawyer to help them get out.

These days, it seemed like most people's troubles occurred because they were trying to hold on to what they had or get what they needed, and they hadn't gone about either in the right way. Mr. Moseley had recently agreed to represent (pro bono, without a fee) a fourteen-year-old vagrant from New Jersey who had ridden a Louisville & Nashville freight into town. The boy was accused of stealing five green peaches from Earl Ayers' peach orchard, out on Pascagoula Road. Mr. Ayers was extremely proud of his prize-winning peaches (most of which—as everybody in Darling very well knew—went to making bootleg peach brandy, a local favorite). He pressed charges against the boy for theft. The case looked like a winner for the prosecution, and it was expected that the thief would get at least thirty days in jail.

But Mr. Moseley had pointed out that there were usually about sixty-five peaches in a bushel of Mr. Ayers' finest early variety, and that the current market rate was one dollar and forty-two cents per bushel.

"Which means, Your Honor," he said to the judge (old Judge McHenry, who was known to have a very hard heart), "that each one of Mr. Ayers' splendid peaches—even when they are ripe and juicy—is worth just a little over two cents. Which further means that the three green peaches that poor, hard-luck kid ate and the two he stuffed into his overall pockets are worth a dime." He fished in his pocket and pulled out a coin, holding it up. "One dime, Your Honor. One thin silver dime, for five green peaches. Why, you couldn't *pay* me to eat five green peaches for a dime. For a dollar, either." He paused, scratching his head. "Way things are, though," he allowed, "I might do it if you gave me five."

A ripple of laughter had run around the courtroom. Old Judge McHenry had no doubt intended to throw the book at the boy. But he probably felt he'd look pretty silly if he did, so he directed Mr. Ayers to let the criminal work off his crime rather than going to jail.

At which point Mr. Moseley reminded the court that Mr. Ayers paid his peach-pickers a dollar a day for ten hours' work. At this rate, the boy ought to be sentenced to work for an hour. Which the youngster did, then hopped the next outbound freight.

Afterward, Mr. Ayers, highly incensed, had come over to the law office and threatened to get even with Mr. Moseley for making him look bad. That's what things were coming to these days. Lizzy thought that Verna was right: it would be a long time before this storm would blow over and people got back to normal. Which in Darling meant being nice to one another again.

"Well," Bessie said with her usual stout common sense, "storms come and storms go." She looked up at the ceiling and raised her voice triumphantly over the sound of the rain pounding on the roof. "But you can rain as hard as you want to. Y'hear? We've fixed the roof! We don't have to worry about leaks."

When the Dahlias had inherited Mrs. Blackstone's old house, the garden wasn't the only thing that had been in need of some tender loving care—and a sizeable investment of money, as well. The old shingle roof on the house had been in such terrible shape that the Dahlias kept busy emptying buckets every time it rained. And the plumbing was even worse. They couldn't flush without fear of overflowing, so they couldn't flush at all. Until they could afford to get the toilet fixed, Bessie had invited them to use the Magnolia Manor bathroom next door. Afford to get it fixed? They were delighted to have Mrs. Blackstone's house, but there wasn't a penny for huge expenditures like roofing and plumbing.

But then—hallelujah and praise the Lord!—they had

unearthed a buried cache of family silver, hidden by Mrs. Blackstone's mother to keep it from falling into the greedy hands of the damn Yankees as they stormed through Alabama near the end of the War Between the States. With the silver, they had found an emerald bracelet, a pair of pearl earrings, a diamond ring, and a velvet bag containing ten gold double eagles that were worth a great deal more than their twenty-dollar face value. The lucky find brought enough to fix the leaky roof and repair the plumbing, with some left over in what Lizzy called the club's "Treasure Fund."

Ophelia gave Verna a small smile. "Or to put it a different way," she said, "there's always a silver lining to every dark cloud. All we have to do is look for it."

"And if there isn't," Verna replied with a shrug, "you'll get a bucket of silver paint and slap it on. Ophelia, you are the very most optimistic person I have ever met." Seeing that she had hurt her friend's feelings, she softened her tone. "Not that it's bad to be hopeful, of course. I'm sorry. I apologize."

Ophelia looked down. "I do try to look on the bright side," she said, her voice thin and strained. "But sometimes it's hard." She swallowed. "To tell the honest truth, Jed says things aren't looking real good where the Farm Supply is concerned. So I'm a little concerned."

Lizzy looked at her friend in surprise. Ophelia usually kept her family finances to herself, even when others were discussing theirs. She must really be worried about the situation. But worrying didn't do any good, of course. Like other businesses in Darling—Hancock's Groceries and Musgrove's Hardware and the Kilgore Dodge dealership—Snow's Farm Supply depended on local trade. If people didn't have money in their pockets, they couldn't spend it. And if they couldn't spend it, the businesses went broke. Already, one of the two printing companies in town had closed, and places like Mann's Mercantile were cutting back on employees. Of the businesses on the town square, only the diner and the Palace Theater were thriving. It seemed that people could usually find thirty-five cents for a plate of ribs and a piece of pie or a quarter to see a romantic comedy and laugh away their worries for an evening.

"I don't reckon we're any different than anybody else in Darling, though," Ophelia went on bravely. "Everybody seems to be having trouble making ends meet these days." She straightened her shoulders and put on a quavering smile. "But we'll get through. It helps to know that we're not the only ones."

Lizzy patted Ophelia's hand, knowing what it took for her friend to confess her family's troubles. "We're always glad for your optimism, Opie," she said. "If it weren't for you, we'd probably all be as gloomy as Verna."

"I'm not gloomy," Verna protested. "I'm just realistic, that's all. I'm pragmatic. I think we should all get down and dirty with the truth. If we've got to deal with a problem, it's better to know exactly what it is than to try to cover it up or pretend it doesn't exist." Lizzy thought Verna sounded determined, and wondered if she was thinking about the thing that was worrying her, whatever it was. Maybe she would say something more.

But Verna only handed Ophelia the plate of cookies. "Here, Opie. Have another one. It'll make you feel better. Cookies always do the trick."

"Thank you," Ophelia said in a small voice, and took a cookie.

Putting down the plate, Verna narrowed her eyes. "Wait a minute," she said, cocking her head. "Did I just hear a drip?"

"It can't be," Bessie exclaimed. "We have a new roof!"

"You're hearing things, Verna," Ophelia said. "Or imagining them."

"I know a drip when I hear one," Verna said flatly. "And that's a drip."

Lizzy looked up. It was still raining but the wind had calmed a little and the thunder was moving to the east. The storm was rapidly blowing over. But there was no mistaking the *plink-plank-plunk* that they could all hear very plainly now.

Dismayed, she looked toward the stove, where the worst of the leaks had been before the roof was repaired. And there it was. A puddle of rainwater on their new blue and white kitchen linoleum.

"It's a drip, all right," she said.

As if to prove the point, three more *plink*s followed in quick succession.

"That's not fair!" Ophelia wailed. "How much did we pay Mr. Carlson to put on our new roof?"

"Enough so it shouldn't be leaking again," Verna replied bleakly.

"It never rains but it pours," Bessie said sadly, shaking her head. "I hope it's not an omen."

But it was. The Dahlias didn't know it, but things were going to get worse before they got better.

Much, much worse.

# TWO

# Verna

The storm had indeed blown over by the time the Dahlias left for home, and as Verna and Ophelia walked together down Rosemont, they were treated to the beautiful sight of gardens after the rain. Diamond drops sparkled amid the blossoms of dogwoods and crabapple and the floppy pink and white blooms of cabbage roses and peonies hanging heavy with wet.

At another time, the sight of gardens washed by a rain would have made Verna smile. But today, she had something on her mind that weighed her down and silenced her. She wished she could cheer Ophelia, too, for she understood her friend's financial worries. But she couldn't think of anything to say beyond a sympathetic, "I hope things will get better soon, for all of us."

And since Ophelia wasn't her usual effervescent self, either, the two of them walked as far as the Snows' house without saying more than a few words. Then, with a brief hug, they said good-bye. Ophelia climbed the porch steps to her front door and Verna turned left on Larkspur, walking the rest of the way alone.

Verna still lived in the small house at the corner of Larkspur and Robert E. Lee, the house that she and Walter had bought when they were first married. Her husband, a history teacher at the Darling Academy, had been killed when he absentmindedly walked out in front of a Greyhound bus on Route 12, a tragedy that left Verna a widow with no funds except her salary and Walter's little bit of life insurance. To remedy that, Mr. Earle Scroggins, the Cypress County probate clerk and Verna's boss, had encouraged her to invest the insurance payment in the stock market, which looked to be heading for a meteoric rise.

"I'll be glad to give you the name of my broker," Mr. Scroggins had said, in the patronizing tone that Verna found so irritating. "You act right away, little lady, and you'll make a killing. You'll be rich for life. Guaranteed."

But naturally mistrustful as she was, Verna suspected that no matter what Mr. Scroggins said, the market could go down just as easily as it could go up. So she had used the money to pay off the mortgage, figuring that the best insurance she could have was a roof over her head. Of course, the four-room house was small, with only one bedroom. But it was comfortable and homey. And since she and Walter had no children, its size was just right for her.

For her and Clyde, that is. Clyde was the affectionate black Scottie with whom Verna had shared her home for the past three years. He had shown up at the back door, footsore and bedraggled and begging for something to eat, and she'd fed him, bathed him, and fixed him a place to sleep under the stove in the kitchen. Within a day, Clyde had made himself perfectly at home and, within a week, had declared that he'd rather sleep on her bed, thank you very much. Now, he met her at the door, yelping with the ecstatic delight that always made her smile, no matter how low she might be feeling. She scooped him up with a hard hug, burying her face against his silky black fur while he washed her cheek with an eager tongue. Then she put him out into the fenced yard to take care of his business while she went to the bedroom to change from her sweaty gardening clothes into a green-printed wrap-around cotton housedress and sandals.

Pausing in front of the bureau for a moment, Verna glanced at herself in the mirror. Nobody had ever accused her of being the typical sweet Southern belle. She was tall and thin, her brown hair was cut in a no-nonsense style, her skin was olive-toned, and her chin and mouth were decidedly firm. She paid no attention to fashion and beauty fads, since she disliked the idea of changing any part of herself just to court somebody's approval. She had married Walter when she was too young to know any better, but he'd turned out to be a pretty good husband, all in all. After he was gone, she hadn't seen any reason to look for a replacement.

After all, why would she want another man in her life? She had her own home, a job that paid the bills and kept her brain sharp, good friends for fun, and Clyde for companionship. She even had a nice little bundle of money in the bank, thanks to an aunt she'd never met. Not being a typical Southern belle might have mattered when she was seventeen and wasn't sure whether she could take care of herself. Now, though, she saw her self-sufficiency, financial and otherwise, as an asset. At least she had something to fall back on, if—

She turned away from the mirror, not wanting to finish the sentence that was running through her mind, and went to the kitchen, where she took down the red metal Hills Bros. coffee can. She put four scoops of ground coffee into the percolator basket, filled the pot with water from the tap, and put it on the gas stove burner. While she was waiting for it to perk, she sat down at the kitchen table, took out a Pall Mall, and lit it.

She could definitely use a cup of coffee. In fact, she felt she could use something a good bit stronger this afternoon.

But Verna prided herself on being a law-abiding person, and since the law prohibited her from possessing liquor, she didn't—although her next-door neighbor, Deputy Buddy Norris, had several bottles of the local white lightning, collected from the local moonshiners as payoff for keeping his mouth shut about the locations of their stills. She had seen it in the pantry when she took a batch of chocolate cupcakes to old Mr. Norris for his birthday. But of course, half the pantries in Darling were stocked with bottles of corn whiskey, which was brewed in the backwoods along the Alabama River. Darling whiskey was fierce, fiery, and explosive. It had an excellent reputation, and the moonshiners had plenty of customers.

At the back door, Clyde whined plaintively. Verna got up and let him in, then went back to her cigarette at the table. Normally, she wouldn't be sitting down while she waited for the percolator to perk. She'd be putting the breakfast dishes away or heading out to the garden for salad greens or reading a few pages in her current library book. (She was halfway through Agatha Christie's *The Mysterious Affair at Styles*, with the detective Hercule Poirot.) Normally, Verna was the kind of person who liked to keep busy.

But nothing felt normal to Verna. Not today. And not since she had begun to smell trouble.

Some weeks ago, Verna had started to suspect that something very odd—something she didn't understand—was going on in her office. Which all by itself was odd, because Verna had a first-rate mind, a suspicious eye, and a talent for spotting something wrong when everybody else had already agreed that whatever-it-was was perfectly all right, in fact, couldn't be better. If anything had been seriously amiss, you'd think she would have noticed it already.

For fifteen years, Verna Tidwell had noticed pretty much everything that went on in the Cypress County Probate Clerk's Office, both the little everyday things that didn't matter a hoot and a holler to anybody, and the big, important things—like property taxes and elections—that mattered a whole lot to everybody. Normally, when Verna smelled trouble, she figured out what was wrong and she fixed it. Now, she smelled trouble, but she didn't know what the trouble was or how to fix it, or even whose trouble it was. This was bothering her a lot.

Sensing that Verna was not her usual self, Clyde jumped up on her lap and licked her chin, whimpering anxiously. He always knew when she was upset and tried to show her how much he cared. Verna hugged the little dog's muscular body close to her and rested her cheek on his head.

"Everything will be all right, Clyde," she said, wanting to reassure him. "Whatever is going on, I'm sure I'll figure it out—eventually."

Except, of course, that she *wasn't* sure, which all by itself was a very unsettling thing, since Verna was the kind of person who was always sure about everything. Her lack of confidence had come to a head when the state auditor had descended on the office two weeks before.

Now, normally (there was that word again), the state wouldn't bother to audit the records of the probate clerk, except in the case of an election irregularity. But Verna's office had changed in the last twelve months, and its new responsibilities were much broader than ever before.

A few months earlier, the Cypress County treasurer, Mr. Jasper DeYancy, had suddenly and unexpectedly died at his home, Sour Creek Plantation. According to the coroner, the deceased (the widely respected son of Colonel Montague De-Yancy, an acclaimed Confederate officer who fought to the last battle alongside General Robert E. Lee) had succumbed to alcohol poisoning. This was dreadfully embarrassing for Mr. DeYancy's wife of forty-one years, a sweet Southern lady who was very active in the Presbyterian Church. Tearfully, she insisted that her husband had never imbibed, did not imbibe, and would never, under any circumstance, imbibe.

But there it was, alcohol poisoning, right on the death certificate, and nobody could quarrel with that. It was widely speculated throughout Darling that Mr. DeYancy had fallen accidental victim to tainted corn squeezin's, although the more mistrustful wondered whether one of his opponents on various issues (there might have been one or two) had supplied a jug of a fatally potent brew. It was certainly true that accidents happened, since once white lightning was bottled and hauled to the nearest town, there was no way of telling who had distilled it or what exactly was in the jug. Moonshining was an exacting process (some wanted to call it a science) that required experience and good judgment, but not all moonshiners possessed either, both, or both at the same time. This sometimes resulted in mistakes and miscalculations, and since moonshine was odorless and colorless, it was all too easy to pass off the heads or tails (the highly toxic first and last few quarts out of the still) as the pure and perfect middlin's. Accidents happened, and one of them might have happened to Mr. DeYancy.

But while Mr. DeYancy had a long-standing reputation as a good and faithful servant who discharged his official duties with devoted attention, there was at least one person who wondered. Charlie Dickens was a veteran newsman who had grown up in Darling, moved away, and came back to take over the Darling *Dispatch* from his ailing father. Over the twelve months prior to Mr. DeYancy's death, Charlie had written several editorials questioning some of the policies and procedures in the Cypress County treasurer's office. The editorials were not your usual hit-and-miss, running skirmishes, either, but thoughtful, targeted, and detailed. In fact, Charlie Dickens exhibited such a firm grasp of the details that a few suspicious folks speculated that there must be an informant in the courthouse, an insider who was handing the *Dispatch* some confidential dope.

The editorials did not accuse Mr. DeYancy of wrongdoing. Charlie was a seasoned newsman (he'd worked on newspapers around the country) and knew better than to make unsubstantiated accusations. But he did point out that the county's roads and bridges were badly neglected. And since the county commissioners (of whom Mr. DeYancy was one) kept saying that there just wasn't enough money to do everything, he demanded that the county's financial records be opened to public examination and scrutiny. Those who read the editorials carefully came away with the idea that somebody in county government was up to something and that Charlie Dickens intended to find out who and what it was.

Then Mr. DeYancy died and any questions about his conduct as county treasurer became moot. Whatever the unknown and unknowable facts of his untimely death, Cypress County now found itself in need of a treasurer. Since the dead man had recently been elected to his fourth term and the county commissioners didn't want to spend the money to hold a new election, they decided to appoint an interim successor, someone they already knew and felt comfortable working with.

As the whole county might have guessed, the commissioners already knew and felt comfortable with Earle Scroggins, the elected probate clerk and Verna's boss, currently in his eighteenth year in office. (Men who got elected to office in Cypress County tended to stay in office as long as they remembered who had put them there. Mr. Scroggins, who had a very good memory for favors rendered, was no exception.) So nobody was surprised when Mr. Scroggins got the nod as acting treasurer to fill out Mr. DeYancy's term. People just shrugged and said, "Well, whaddya expect?"

Charlie Dickens wasn't surprised, either. But he didn't like it. He wrote an editorial charging that the commissioners were just a tad bit too comfortable—he actually dared to use the word *cozy*—with Mr. Scroggins. This was to be expected, however, since Charlie Dickens had been in the habit of criticizing the former county treasurer and everybody figured he'd probably roll up his sleeves and lay into the new one, too. That was the way newspapermen operated in the big city, and while Charlie was Darling born and Darling bred, he had worked on newspapers in Cleveland and Baltimore and New York, and that's where he'd learned those habits. That's what people said, anyway.

But most Darlingians had a few other urgent things to worry about, such as keeping their business afloat or paying the weekly bill at Hancock's Groceries. If they had been asked, they would no doubt have approved the treasurer's appointment, regardless of what Charlie Dickens wrote. Mr. Scroggins had a reputation for running a tight ship in the probate office, although the folks who worked there knew that it was really Verna's ship, not his. The county commissioners probably knew this, too, but that didn't count for much because they were eager to have Mr. Scroggins take on the treasurer's job.

And why shouldn't they be? Earle Scroggins was one of the most successful and capable businessmen in Darling, so it was easy to suppose that he would be a first-rate county treasurer as well. A stout, amiable man with a booming voice, a bald head, and a tobacco-stained white moustache that curled jauntily at either end, Mr. Scroggins could be seen smoking his cigar in the dining room at the Old Alabama Hotel or attending meetings at the Darling Savings and Trust, where he was on the board of directors. He owned a cottonseed oil mill near the river, a cotton gin on the south side of town, and a half-dozen rental properties. These enterprises demanded a great deal of his attention, however, and he rarely bothered to come to the office more than once or twice a week. But that was fine, because he could see that Verna was smart as a whip and could do the job every bit as well as he could, so there was no reason under the sun not to leave her alone and just let her get on with it—while he took all the credit, of course.

Mr. Scroggins' benign neglect of the probate clerk's office had suited Verna right down to the ground, for she preferred to set her own rules and work on her own, without interference. Of course, she always kept Mr. Scroggins pretty well up on things, saved a few papers for him to sign when he came into the office, and never let on that he was anything other than the boss. But Verna liked being in charge and she was good at it. In fact, she was so good at being in charge that folks who didn't know any better actually believed that *she* was the probate clerk.

Recently, however, even the efficient Verna had begun to feel a little bogged down with work. Mr. Scroggins' appearances in the office had not increased when he was appointed acting county treasurer, but Verna's workload certainly had, for she was now in charge of both offices. And since the county (like almost every other county in the state, and probably in the entire U.S.A.) was having trouble collecting taxes, budgets were very tight. Mr. Scroggins had already cut Coretta Cole, Verna's coworker, back to part time. Verna was doing most of Coretta's work as well as her own.

In one way, the expansion had been an easy process, since the treasurer and the probate clerk were neighbors on the north side of the second-floor hallway in the county courthouse. All they had to do to make the two offices into one was to uncover a boarded-up doorway in the wall, move a couple of desks and a filing cabinet, and presto, they were all one big happy family.

In another way, the expansion had been difficult, for the treasurer's office had responsibility for all of the county's money, which seemed to be held in a scattering of different accounts. And to make things even more confusing, Verna quickly discovered that the county's money was on deposit not just in the Darling Savings and Trust but in all three of the banks over at Monroeville, the nearest big town, which wasn't even in Cypress County. When she got things under control, Verna planned to recommend that the Monroeville bank accounts be moved back to Darling where they belonged. But she didn't think it was wise to do that until she had everything figured out and knew what was what.

Normally, of course, Verna would have turned for help to the two longtime employees in the treasurer's office, Melba Jean Manners, a rather stout, double-chinned lady in her mid-fifties, and Ruthie Brant, twenty years younger than Melba Jean and as skinny as Melba Jean was stout. But Melba Jean and Ruthie didn't seem to know very much about the way the treasurer's accounts were organized. According to them, all they did was deposit the money where Mr. DeYancy told them to put it and pay it out to whomever he told them to pay it to, recording the transactions in the big leather-bound account books that were kept on wooden shelves in the storage room. Mr. DeYancy, it seems, had been the kind of boss who liked to keep all the office business under his hat. He apparently hadn't shared it with the county commissioners, either, because when Verna inquired of them, all she got were blank stares.

As far as Verna was concerned, why Mr. DeYancy did this, whether it was because he was secretive by nature or had certain secrets he wanted to keep, didn't much matter. What mattered were the accounts. And although Melba Jean and

Ruth knew perfectly well how to do their jobs, they couldn't tell Verna a blessed thing about *why* those accounts were organized the way they were, which was what she needed to know in order to decide whether to change the process or keep on doing it the way it had been done. Since Mr. De-Yancy was dead, she couldn't ask him. And since Mr. Scroggins didn't know anything more than she did (and seemed to care a whole lot less), she couldn't ask him, either. The whole thing was, to put it simply, a tangled mess.

Verna was the soul of neatness, and this snarl of accounts had been harassing her since she had inherited it, to the point where she was having nightmares. Sometimes she dreamed that she was trying to balance a dozen different checkbooks drawn on a dozen different accounts, and every time she thought she'd just about got it all figured out, somebody came and dumped a bushel basket of tens and twenties in front of her and told her to put the money where it was supposed to go. If she didn't put it into the right accounts, she'd be fired.

Or she dreamed that she had just got all the checkbooks balanced when the banks started telephoning to say that a mysterious person dressed all in black had come in and withdrawn all the money. Every account was down to zero and all the county employees would have to go without their paychecks until she figured out where to get the money to cover the loss. If she didn't find out who had it and put it back, she'd be fired.

Poor Verna had begun to feel as if she were lost in a dark and treacherous swamp, much darker and more treacherous than Briar's Swamp, over by the river, where panthers and black bears were said to prowl amid clouds of ravenous mosquitoes. And beneath every cypress tree, there was nothing but snakes and occasional alligators and bottomless pools of black water and the smell of something rotten. The smell of trouble.

But even in her worst nightmares, Verna never dreamed that the State of Alabama would send somebody to audit the Cypress County treasurer's accounts—and not just one somebody, but two.

The first auditor had appeared on a Wednesday morning, unannounced. He flashed a wallet card with his identification and asked Verna to bring him the county books. He spent the day going over them quickly, making cryptic notes. When the clock struck five, he put his suit coat back on, tipped his bowler hat, and disappeared, muttering that somebody from the main office would be in touch if there were further questions. *Further* questions? Until the auditor appeared, Verna had not known that there were any questions at all—except for her own, of course, which were legion.

Melba Jean and Ruthie had spent the whole day nervously watching the fellow. The minute their visitor left, they collapsed into their chairs with huge sighs of relief. Verna felt like doing the very same thing, but she didn't like to appear concerned in front of the employees.

"What in the *world* do you think that man was looking for?" Melba Jean cried, all her chins rippling.

Ruthie laughed, twisting her mouth. "Maybe he thought we've been stealing money and he was trying to catch us." Her laugh was grating, like the sound that chalk makes when you squeak it on a blackboard. "Maybe he thought we'd get on an ocean liner and sail off to Paris for a long vacation. Or Rome." Her eyes glinted. "I've got me a hankerin' to see those fountains."

Verna winced. "Don't talk like that, Ruthie," she said sternly. "I am sure the man wasn't thinking anything of the sort. It's nothing but a routine audit. They do it all the time. Now that it's over, we can get back to work."

She didn't know whether the audit was routine or not. She did, however, know that Melba Jean had a tendency to gossip about office business. In Verna's opinion, this was a very dangerous thing, especially when the gossip had anything to do with money. People could get the wrong idea all too easily, and no telling where *that* would lead.

"And I don't want you two talking about this visit outside the office," she added emphatically. "There is no point in getting folks all excited when there's nothing to get excited about. This was just a routine bit of business, that's all. Happens every so often, in every county in this state. You hear?"

"Yes, ma'am," the two women chorused dutifully.

But from the glances they exchanged, Verna suspected that they had already spread the word when they went to lunch, which they always ate with a couple of women who worked in the Cypress County Title Company office across the street. The news would probably be all over Darling by the time for church on Sunday.

But if that happened, Verna didn't get wind of it. The auditor's office didn't get back in touch, either, and she was so busy doing her work that the episode slipped into the back of her mind. She was still troubled about those tangled accounts, of course, but her nervousness over the audit eventually died down.

Until, that is, the second auditor showed up, also unannounced. Where the first fellow had been polite and laconic, the second was a fussy little man barely five feet high. He had a bald head, gold-rimmed glasses, a habit of walking on the tips of his toes, and the manner of a bossy banty rooster. He arrived early one morning with a brown leather briefcase in his hand, introduced himself as Mr. Daniel Beecham, Senior State Auditor, and appropriated Mr. Scroggins' desk (which didn't much matter because Mr. Scroggins rarely used it). He hung his brown felt bowler hat on a peg, draped his suit coat over the back of Mr. Scroggins' chair, and fastened red elastic garters above his elbows, like a bank teller. Then he opened his briefcase and took out a pen, a bottle of ink, and a yellow tablet and ordered Verna to bring out the records, one large volume after another.

Mr. Beecham sat at Mr. Scroggins' desk for a full week, which of course was a week of pure hell for Verna. For the first several days, he methodically worked his way through the records of the money that the county had collected in the past four years: sales taxes, property taxes, licenses and fees, and all funds received from the state. He examined every ledger entry, dipping his pen into his ink bottle and jotting columns of figures on his tablet. He went through the records of the various checking accounts and spent a full day examining the county expenditures. Verna, whose desk was next to his, could hear the sound of the pages turning, the irritating *scritch-scratch* of his pen, and an occasional sigh, whether of weariness or impatience, she couldn't tell. It was all terribly unsettling.

Mr. Beecham was nothing if not punctual. He came in promptly at eight every morning and left with his briefcase at five every afternoon. He ate lunch at the desk, a sandwich and an apple packed for him by the cook at the Old Alabama Hotel, where he was staying. As he worked, he hummed tunelessly to himself, but he never said a word, except to ask for this or that ledger—and on the last day, to request that the office mechanical adding machine (a genuine Dalton that Verna had recently purchased for seventy-three dollars and ninety-five cents) be placed on his desk. He sometimes stopped to blow his nose into a white handkerchief, or sip coffee poured into a cup from a Thermos bottle. But otherwise, the little man did nothing but read and write for hours on end. Until the last day, that is, when he operated the Dalton nonstop, all day long, adding the columns of figures on his tablet.

Verna prided herself on being able to size people up, and

she watched Mr. Beecham's face carefully, trying to read his reactions. But she had no luck whatsoever. The little man was as stone-faced as the Sphinx. And when he left for the last time, at four fifty-nine p.m. on Friday afternoon, he said not a word of good-bye. He folded up the adding machine tape, put his tablet, pen, and ink bottle into his briefcase, put on his coat, slapped his hat on his head, and briskly left the office.

"What do you suppose will happen next?" Melba Jean asked fearfully.

"We'll all three be lynched," Ruthie said, with her grim gallows humor. "Or tarred and feathered."

"Nothing at all will happen," Verna said stoutly, summoning all her confidence. "I will see you both on Monday morning. I hope you have a very good weekend."

She had been right, at least for a short while. Things went on just as usual, with Mr. Earl Scroggins popping in only once, to pick up the quarterly treasurer's report that Verna had prepared for him to take to the county commissioners' meeting. Verna had continued as usual, too, shopping for groceries, doing her laundry, borrowing S. S. Van Dine's *The Benson Murder Case* from Miss Rogers at the library, mowing her grass, and helping the Dahlias with their new vegetable garden.

But all through the first few days after Mr. Beecham's visit, Verna held her breath, especially when Ruthie handed her the mail from the post office. She went through the stack carefully, not wanting to see an envelope from the state of Alabama but at the same time wanting to see it. The suspense was killing her.

And to make things worse, she couldn't talk to anybody about her worries. Definitely not to Melba Jean and Ruthie, for she felt she couldn't trust either of them not to spill the beans all over Darling. And not even to her best friend, Liz

Lacy. A long time ago, she had pledged to herself that she wouldn't whine about her job, no matter how bad it got. A job was a job was a *job* and you did it, come hell or high water. Complaining was a sign of weakness. Verna had never broken that rule, and she wasn't going to start now.

Anyway, as the days went by and no letter arrived, she had more or less convinced herself that things were more or less hunky-dory and she began to feel a little easier—at least as far as the audit was concerned. But she still couldn't decide how to deal with the bewildering multiplicity of bank accounts. And those awful nightmares just kept coming.

Now, Clyde lifted his head and licked Verna's chin as if to reassure her that whatever happened, she could count on him. He would always be around to take care of her and make sure that nothing bad ever happened. She was hugging him gratefully when the telephone on the wall startled her with a brassy *brriingg-brriingg-bring.* Two longs and a short. Her ring. Probably one of the Dahlias calling.

She put Clyde on the floor and went to the telephone, aware that at the very same moment, Mrs. Wilson next door on the north, Mrs. Newman next door to Mrs. Wilson, the Ferrells next door to the Newmans, and the Snows at the end of the block were all going to their telephones, too. They would cup their hands over the mouthpieces and stealthily pick up the receivers, trying to conceal the fact that they were listening in.

Which was a pretty silly thing to do, Verna thought, because everybody knew that everybody else always listened in, and monitored what they said accordingly. These days, you could get a private line, which allowed you to say anything you wanted to say without fear of people overhearing. But it was expensive. And anyway, if you weren't on the party line, you'd have to wait for news until the next time you went to the diner for lunch, or the *Dispatch* came out, or your neighbor came over to borrow an egg or a cup of sugar. Better to be on the party line and get the news straight from the horse's mouth, as it were.

Verna picked up the receiver and said hello. But it wasn't one of the Dahlias calling.

"Hello, Verna." The voice was male, and uncharacteristically hesitant. "It's Mr. Scroggins."

Verna's heart rose up in her throat, then thudded into the pit of her stomach. Mr. Scroggins had never called her at home, not once in all the years she had worked in the probate clerk's office.

"H-h-how are you, Mr. Scroggins?" she managed.

"Doin' real well," Mr. Scroggins said. "But I got some bad news for you, Verna. I'm real sorry, but I got to ask you not to come in to work on Monday morning. You jes' take the week off and stay home. A little vacation, like."

Verna gasped. "Not come in to work? But . . . but why?" She was suddenly aware of four listening ears glued to four receivers along Larkspur, between Robert E. Lee and Rosemont Street. She snapped, "All right, you all, I am asking you to get off this party line right now. You hear?"

There was one quick click, then two, then finally three.

"Anybody else?" she asked. There was silence, but of course she had no way to tell whether the fourth person was still on the line or had never been there in the first place. She turned her attention back to her caller. "All right, Mr. Scroggins. Now, why is it I'm not supposed to come to work? And who's going to manage the office if I'm not there?"

"Miz Cole is coming back full time," Mr. Scroggins said. "She can manage the place—not as good as you, but she can do it." His voice took on an edge. "And if you don't know why this is happenin', then I'm sorry for you, Verna. I never in God's green earth would've wanted anything like this, but—"

"Anything like *what*?" Verna demanded. Her knees were

shaking and it was hard to get her breath. "Why do I have to stay away from the office? Does it have anything to do with that auditor?"

"I am truly sorry but I can't tell you a thing, Verna," Mr. Scroggins said regretfully. "You are now on furlough, you might say, and I need you to give me your key to the office door. You can leave it in an envelope at the Old Alabama desk, and I'll pick it up. I'll give it back if this thing is cleared up and you can go back to work. Okay?"

*Okay? Of course it wasn't okay!* "If what thing is cleared up?" Verna asked. She could hardly grasp what he was saying. To give up her key to the office would be like giving up her right to her job. Like giving up her identity!

"Never you mind, Verna," Mr. Scroggins said, now more sternly. "Jes' you bring me your key." He paused, waiting for her reply. "Verna, you hear what I said?" Another, longer pause. "Verna? You answer me, now."

But Verna didn't answer. She hung up the receiver and collapsed into a chair.

# THREE

# Bessie and Miss Rogers

Bessie Bloodworth didn't have far to go after she left the Dahlias' clubhouse on Saturday afternoon. All she had to do was duck through the hole in the hedge and she was in the neatly kept backyard of Magnolia Manor, where she couldn't help but notice that the plants in the fourteen clay pots of thriving Confederate roses had been carefully pruned back. Miss Rogers' work, Bessie knew.

The previous spring, Miss Rogers had obtained a start from every Dahlia who had a Confederate rose in her garden—and it turned out that they all did, since everyone loved the plant, even those who didn't know that it wasn't a rose but an hibiscus. She had rooted the pencil-sized cuttings in buckets of damp sand, then moved the new plants into pots and later, moved the pots into the cellar for the winter, so they wouldn't freeze. Now, just in time for the Confederate Day celebration at the cemetery, each plant had put out an exuberant green growth. Nicely trimmed, they were ready to leave the Magnolia Manor and go to their new home at the

Darling Cemetery, where they would create a beautiful blooming hedge along the fence.

Bessie climbed up the back steps and opened the door to the screened-in back porch. The Magnolia Manor was the only home she had ever known. She had lived in the old two-story house for decades, first with her mother and father and brothers and then with her father, whom she cared for until he died. And now with the Magnolia Ladies, as they called themselves, four of them, bless 'em. Her boarders.

Of course, the house hadn't had a name back when her father (who owned and operated the town's mortuary) was still alive. But it hadn't had a mortgage, either, and after his death, it was Bessie's only real asset, except for the few dollars she got every month from Mr. Noonan, who had purchased her father's funeral parlor business.

First, she gave the house a name. Second, she got Beulah Trivette to paint a nice wooden sign for the front yard, featuring the words MAGNOLIA MANOR in fancy script, encircled by magnolia blossoms and leaves. Third, she put an ad in the Darling *Dispatch* for "older unmarried and widowed ladies of refinement and good taste, to occupy spacious bedrooms at the Magnolia Manor." She'd been afraid that if the house didn't have a name of its own, people would start calling it *Bessie Bloodworth's Home for Old Ladies* to distinguish it from Mrs. Brewster's Home for Young Ladies, over on West Plum, whose residents were so unruly that Mrs. Brewster had to set strict rules for their behavior. Bessie hoped that her residents would be dignified and refined enough not to require rules, although as time went on, she had learned that older women, even those of refinement and good taste, could be undignified every now and again.

Mrs. Brewster's wasn't the only other boardinghouse in town, of course. Mrs. Meeks rented rooms and cooked supper for single men who worked on the railroad and at Ozzie

Sherman's sawmill, and the Old Alabama Hotel offered quite nice rooms and excellent meals for travelers. But ladies were not allowed at Meeks', where the men slept two and three to a room, and people of ordinary means couldn't afford to stay at the hotel for more than a night or two. So Bessie had every reason to hope that refined widows and spinster ladies would realize that the Manor would make a lovely home.

She was right, as it turned out. Within a couple of weeks, all four of her empty bedrooms were spoken for and stayed that way. It was such a nice place to live that most of the residents remained as long as they could. But there was a waiting list, and when a vacancy did occur, Bessie scarcely had time to clean the room and wash the bedding before somebody new was moving in.

Unfortunately, Magnolia Manor was not what you'd call a money-making business, since most of Bessie's boarders were not well fixed. (If they were, they'd likely be living at the hotel or in their own houses, with colored help to cook and clean.) Mrs. Sedalius was better off than the others, for her son was a prominent doctor in Mobile. He sent his mother a monthly check for her room and board and a small allowance so she could buy things she wanted. (His checks, Bessie suspected, were guilt payments: the man rarely darkened his mother's door.) Leticia Wiggins had a widow's pension from her husband's service in the War Between the States—it wasn't much but it was regular. Miss Rogers earned a few dollars a week as the town librarian. Maxine Bechdel looked to be well off— she owned two rent houses in neighboring Monroeville—but looks were deceiving. Last month, one of her renters had paid her with a bushel of cabbages. The other had paid with a promise. Bessie and Roseanne (the colored lady who cooked and cleaned in return for room and board and spending money) had turned the cabbages into sauerkraut. There wasn't anything they could do with the promise.

Bessie would have liked to raise the cost of board and room, but if she did, some of the ladies might have to leave—and where would they go? "You can't get blood out of a turnip," she often reminded herself with a sigh. "You just have to be satisfied with the turnip." And cabbage, if that's all you had. She had read in the *Dispatch* that Senator Huey P. Long of Louisiana—a.k.a. The Kingfish—was proposing that everybody over sixty should get a government pension, the way they did in England. Bessie thought this was the best idea she had heard in a long time and had written to Senator Bankhead, one of their Alabama senators, telling him so. But she wasn't surprised when the senator didn't write back. Lots of people were afraid of The Kingfish. They said he was a dangerous demagogue who would drive the country to the brink of ruin if he got his way, and maybe they were right, Bessie didn't know. But he seemed to get a lot of things done for the little people of Louisiana. Bessie just wished he could get a few things done for the little people of Alabama, too.

But while the Magnolia Ladies didn't pay much rent, their money paid the property taxes and bought coal and electricity and food, which meant that Bessie didn't need much money. And since they couldn't pay much, the Magnolia Ladies were glad to share the work. Maxine and Leticia washed the dishes and neatened the kitchen and dining room after every meal. The sweeping and dusting was divided between Miss Rogers (downstairs) and Mrs. Sedalius (upstairs). All four helped to plant and weed and harvest the vegetable garden and tend the half-dozen Rhode Island Reds who lived in a coop beside the back fence and gave them each a fresh-laid egg for breakfast every morning. There was still a lot of cleaning and housework and maintenance left for Bessie and Roseanne. *But what of it?* she asked herself. These days, plenty of people were much worse off, and they had real jobs.

And there was the added bonus of friendship, for this

bunch of Magnolia Ladies was an exceptionally congenial one. In the evenings, Maxine and Leticia played canasta or Old Maid while Mrs. Sedalius knitted or crocheted and Miss Rogers read aloud to them. She stopped reading when it was time for their favorite programs on the radio, a fancy Crosley five-tube table model that Mrs. Sedalius' son had sent her for Christmas three years before. (He didn't bother to bring it himself, just ordered it from a catalog and had it delivered.) The ladies loved *The A&P Gypsies*, *The Firestone Hour*, and *Lum and Abner*, which starred two Arkansas hillbillies who were always being fleeced by Squire Skimp. They especially liked that one because the fictional folks who lived in Pine Ridge, Arkansas, weren't all that different from the real folks who lived in Darling, Alabama. The ladies listened and laughed and reminded themselves that people had pretty much the same problems, wherever they lived.

The Magnolia Ladies looked out for each other, too, because they were all fragile in one way or another. Leticia had fallen twice, breaking first the right wrist, then the left, and now walked with a cane. Maxine wouldn't admit it, but she was having trouble remembering names and dates. Mrs. Sedalius' eyes were going bad, which made needlework difficult, and Miss Rogers constantly fretted about her lack of money.

But they took comfort in the fact that they had one another, and they understood each other's frailties and sympathized. *Sisters* would not have been too strong a word to describe their relationship.

Unfortunately, however, their nerves had worn a little thin over the past few weeks, and the ladies were feeling tetchy. It began when a large gray tabby cat showed up on the front porch, skinny, starved, and crawling with fleas. Mrs. Sedalius happened to be sitting in the porch swing that evening, crocheting a doily. Before you could say *Bless Pat*, the enterprising cat had jumped into her lap, presenting himself for adoption. Mrs. Sedalius fell for him like a ton of bricks, according to Maxine, who had been there when it happened.

"Oh, poor, sweet kitty!" Mrs. Sedalius cried. She carried him to the kitchen, where she fed him a mashed boiled egg and bread crumbs in warm milk, then out to the woodshed, where he endured a bath. The next morning at breakfast, she announced his new name: Lucky Lindy, after her favorite flying hero.

"*Lucky* is right," Maxine muttered, stirring cream into her coffee. "That tomcat knew a good thing when he landed in it." She scowled at Mrs. Sedalius. "I hate cats. I've always hated cats. Why couldn't you get a canary?"

"I wouldn't have minded if he'd been a kitten," Leticia groused. "But this one is on his ninth life. And he's *ugly*." She nudged Maxine. "Pass the butter, Maxine."

"You'll have to keep the creature away from me," Miss Rogers said darkly. She dipped her spoon into her soft-boiled egg. "I am allergic to cat fur."

Bessie knew she should have put her foot down right then and there and told Mrs. Sedalius that Lucky Lindy had to go. But she hesitated. Mrs. Sedalius' son almost never came to visit, and the old lady had spent her days hoping for a telephone call or waiting for the mailman to bring her a letter from her "dear boy." Now, she spent her days combing and stroking Lucky Lindy and cooing over him as if he were a cute little kitten.

So Bessie waffled, thinking that the cat might be good company for the lonely old lady and help to get her mind off her neglectful son. But it wasn't long before she was sorry that she hadn't said no right off, before Mrs. Sedalius got so attached. Bessie herself wasn't particularly fond of cats, and this one—once he got his footing—was a holy terror. He—

"Oh, there you are, Miss Bloodworth," Miss Rogers said,

coming into the kitchen just as Bessie was reaching into the icebox for a cool drink. Her tone was heavy with reproof and her brows were knitted in a scowl. "I have been looking all over for you."

Miss Rogers was the only one of the Magnolia Ladies who addressed Bessie formally. Bessie had tried to coax her onto a first-name footing but had finally given up, feeling that Miss Rogers must have some sort of secret need to keep people at arms' length.

"Sorry," Bessie replied. "I was working in the Dahlias' vegetable garden." She had intended to ask Miss Rogers (also a Dahlia) if she would like to lend a hand, but the lady had been taking a nap. "Would you like some tea?" she added, taking out the frosty pitcher.

"Thank you, no." Miss Rogers said stiffly. She was clearly upset about something. "We need to have a talk. Right now. It cannot be delayed."

It was a hot Saturday afternoon and Bessie was dressed in her gardening clothes. But Miss Rogers, who was so thin she was almost gaunt, wore a dark print rayon crepe dress (nearly to her ankles) with a belt and a prissy lace-trimmed collar that buttoned up to her throat. With her round steel-rimmed glasses and her stiffly waved gray hair, and armored by her self-assured sense of the *proprieties*, she looked—and spoke—exactly like the prim and proper librarian she was.

And she was *very* prim and proper. The other Magnolia Ladies enjoyed sharing the tales of their lives and times and husbands, children, aunts, cousins, nieces, and nephews. Miss Rogers, on the other hand, kept her silence while the others chattered. Bessie knew only the dim outline of her story, but what little she knew was terribly sad. Miss Rogers had been an orphan who had never had a home of her own. She dreamed of having a small house and garden all to herself, and with this goal in mind, she had saved every penny she could lay her hands on. But then, like so many people around the country, she had yielded to the seductions of the rising stock market and had foolishly put all her savings into stocks. She had lost every cent when the market crashed on a black October Tuesday in 1929 and was left with only the pittance she earned as the town's part-time librarian. And last month, the Darling town council had begun discussing whether it could afford to keep the library open. If it closed, she would be out of a job—and completely out of money.

"A talk," Miss Rogers repeated. "Now, please."

"What about?" Bessie asked apprehensively, wondering if Miss Rogers had gotten bad news from the council. But Ophelia's husband Jed was the mayor. Surely, if the council was planning to close the library, Ophelia would have mentioned it when they were sitting around the Dahlias' kitchen table a little while ago. On the other hand, Ophelia had seemed uncharacteristically depressed today. Did she know that the library was on the chopping block, and that poor Miss Rogers was to be let go?

Miss Rogers clasped her hands together at her waist, frowned, and cleared her throat. "I wish to register a complaint, Miss Bloodworth. A very *strong* complaint." She paused for emphasis. "It's that cat, of course."

"Lucky Lindy?" Bessie put the pitcher of tea on the table, feeling a great relief. Better the cat than the closing of the library. "What's he done now?" she asked, taking four glasses out of the cupboard.

When Lucky Lindy had first arrived at Magnolia Manor, he had been crafty enough to mind his p's and q's. He had kept to Miss Sedalius' room, sleeping on her bed and eating like a horse (he had graduated from boiled eggs to leftovers from the dining table). Then, having fully recovered his strength, Lindy showed his true colors. He perfected the trick of curling himself affectionately around a person's ankles, then stretching a sneaky paw up his victim's calf and opening his claws. In the space of a few days, Lucky Lindy had shredded the stockings and bloodied the legs of all of the Magnolia Ladies, including Bessie's. (Roseanne was the only one who escaped unscathed, because she had given him a swift kick the first time he cozied up to her. "I knowed Mistah Cat gon' try somethin' mean," she declared triumphantly. "But I done got the drop on him. He ain't gonna bodder me no mo'.")

Having claimed the run of the house and yard, Lindy made it his own. He was a wildly adventuresome cat who raced up and down the stairs at all hours of the night, dragged half-dead mice and tree roaches into the house, and climbed the curtains all the way to the top. From this vantage point he would launch himself gaily into the air, alighting on all fours on the back of the sofa or a chair or even someone's head. Whoever was nearest this daredevil aviator would shriek—except for Mrs. Sedalius, who just smiled and said that Lucky Lindy was living up to his name and wasn't he *cute?*

It was this last trick that had so upset Leticia, for Lindy had leapt off the top of the living room drapery valance and landed on the lampshade next to her chair, knocking the lamp into her lap, spilling her tea, and causing her to choke on a cookie. Leticia swore that if Lindy ever again came within an inch of her, she was going to brain him with the stove poker, at which Mrs. Sedalius went into hysterics and had to be comforted with a cup of hot chocolate. This was where matters stood when Miss Rogers voiced her complaint.

"The wretched animal has torn the knitted cover off my dear little pillow," Miss Rogers said thinly. She brushed a tear from the corner of her eye. "My *grandmother's* pillow."

"Your . . . grandmother?" Bessie asked, surprised. She had been acquainted with Miss Rogers for some years but had never known that she had a grandmother—or more precisely, that Miss Rogers knew who her grandmother was. Bessie had understood that Miss Rogers' parents died when she was quite young and that she'd had no contact with her family since.

"My little pillow is the only thing I have left of my family," Miss Rogers said tearfully. "I was carrying it with me when I entered the orphanage at the age of five, and I've been told that I wouldn't let it out of my sight. It belonged to my grandmother Rose, of whom I have no memory at all. I have cherished it all these years." She gulped down a helpless sob.

Bessie stared at her. Miss Rogers was the model of stern self-control. She never allowed herself to appear irritated, never lost her temper, never cried. Verna often joked that *decorum* must be her middle name.

"I'm sorry," she began. "I had no idea that—" But she didn't get to finish her sentence.

"And now that terrible beast has destroyed it!" Miss Rogers cried raggedly. "He has torn it to shreds. This is the last straw, the very last. I'm telling you, Miss Bloodworth, you will have to make Mrs. Sedalius get rid of that cat." She pulled herself up, glaring at Bessie. "Do you hear me? Either he goes or I do!"

If this had been one of the other ladies, Bessie would have put an arm around her shoulders and soothed her. But this was Miss Rogers, who shrank away when anyone ventured to touch her, as if any show of intimacy repulsed her.

"I'm very sorry this has happened," Bessie said honestly. "The cat really is a terrible nuisance. But he means so much to Mrs. Sedalius that I've been reluctant to ask her to give him up. I'm sure we can repair whatever damage—"

"No!" Miss Rogers cried, and stamped her foot. "My dear little pillow is totally beyond repair." She gestured imperiously. "Come with me. I'll show you."

Bessie knew there was no point in arguing. She followed Miss Rogers through the dining room, up the stairs, and down the second-floor hallway, past the open doors of the three other Magnolia Ladies' rooms. While the upstairs bedrooms were the same size, Bessie always encouraged her boarders to furnish and decorate to suit themselves. All were happy to agree, so each reflected the personality of each resident.

Mrs. Sedalius had brought an antique walnut dresser and filled the top with photographs of her late husband, "her boy," and her grandchildren, along with the doilies she knitted and crocheted. Maxine had put blue wallpaper on the walls, made a ruffled blue spread for her bed, and painted her rocking chair blue. A dedicated reader and member of the Darling Literary Society, she filled several shelves with books, and books were stacked on the floor. Leticia, who didn't like to read but loved oil painting and watercolors, filled her cluttered shelves with art supplies and souvenirs from her extensive travels. Displayed on her walls were many of her artistic endeavors, as well as maps with pins stuck in to mark the places she had traveled.

Miss Rogers' room, in contrast, might have belonged to a nun. Her narrow bed was covered with a plain white chenille spread. There was a white dresser scarf on the utilitarian chest of drawers, and a plain white net curtain at the window. Three books were stacked on the shelf beside her bed: a Bible, a thick volume of Shakespeare's plays, and the library book—*The Life and Adventures of Robinson Crusoe*—that she was currently reading aloud to the ladies. There were no pictures on her walls, only one photograph on her bureau, and just one spot of color in the room: the bright red knitted pillow, about sixteen inches square, that was lying on the floor beside the bed.

Or rather, it had *once* been a red pillow. Now, the knitted cover was a gnarled, knotted mass of tangled red yarn, with loose, frayed ends spilling across the floor like a puddle of red blood. Thankfully, Bessie saw that the pillow itself, which was made of a tan-colored fabric covered with embroidery, seemed to have survived without a great deal of damage. But she felt this was little comfort to Miss Rogers.

"You see?" Miss Rogers pointed, her high, thin voice shaking. "Two days ago, that wretched cat shredded my very last pair of stockings. Today, he's destroyed my pillow. My poor pillow." She turned away, trying to conceal her tears, and Bessie's heart went out to her.

"I am really *so* sorry, Miss Rogers," she said regretfully. "I'm to blame. I should have told Mrs. Sedalius she couldn't have him, but—"

She broke off, her eye caught by the faded sepia photograph in a wood frame on the dresser. In it, a frightened-looking little girl in a starched white dress, long banana curls draped over her shoulders, clutched something large against her chest, holding it with both arms. Bessie had seen the photograph once before, when she had come into Miss Rogers' room to repair the window, and had thought then that the child was clutching a large handbag. Now, she realized that the girl must be Miss Rogers, and that it was the pillow she was hugging to her, as if it were a life preserver or something incredibly precious that she feared might be taken away.

"Is that the pillow in the photo?" she asked, before she thought. "And that's you, isn't it?" The minute the words were out of her mouth, she was sorry. Miss Rogers always made it plain that personal questions were highly offensive.

But at this moment, it didn't seem to matter. Miss Rogers reached into her sleeve for the hanky she kept tucked there. "Yes," she sniffled, and blew her nose. "The picture was taken the day I entered the orphanage in Richmond. I was five. The pillow was the only thing I had with me, the orphanage director said. No dolls, no toys, not even any clothes, except for what I had on. And my grandmother's red pillow."

Bessie took a breath and waded into new waters. "You said that your grandmother's name was Rose?" she prompted gently, thinking that if Miss Rogers could talk about the pillow even a little, she might be less likely to cry about it. "What else do you know about her?"

"Nothing at all," Miss Rogers said, and blew her nose again. "Just her first name, Rose." She paused. "No, wait, there's a little more. I recall . . . I recall my mother telling me that my grandmother drowned."

"Drowned! How horrible! Do you know any of the details?"

"None," Miss Rogers replied, shaking her head. "My mother—her name was Rose, too—said that my grandmother was a very brave woman and that she'd tell me all about it when I was old enough to understand. But then—" Her voice dropped.

Bessie took a breath and ventured a little further. "Then?" she asked softly.

Miss Rogers straightened her shoulders, as if she were facing a painful fact. "Then she and my father were divorced. They were both very young, you see, when they married. She couldn't . . . She didn't want to keep me, and he couldn't. He was in the army. So she left me in the orphanage in Richmond. I never heard from her again."

"Oh, dear," Bessie breathed. How horrible, how unimaginably horrible, to be abandoned by both your parents! She wanted to know why this had happened, but Miss Rogers' eyes were filling with tears again. So she steadied her voice and asked, in a matter-of-fact tone, "Your father's name was Rogers?"

"No." Miss Rogers went to the window and stood, looking out. Her fingers held her handkerchief, twisting it. "I've never known his name, or even who he was." Her voice dropped as if that were something that she was ashamed of. "When I was eleven, the orphanage sent me to live with Mr. and Mrs. Rogers, on a small farm in Maryland. They had no children of their own, but they had already adopted several boys to help out with the farm work. Mrs. Rogers needed a girl to help with the cooking and the housework. That's why they took me."

Bessie felt her heart turn over and she bit her lip. Her own mother had died when she was thirteen, and her father had expected her to take her mother's place in the household. But at least she had friends and a family home to ease the brutal pain of her mother's death.

"It must have been very hard for you," she said quietly, thinking that this short conversation had already shed a great deal of light on why Miss Rogers had turned from a frightened little girl with banana curls into the stiff, unyielding woman she was now. Bessie hated to admit it, but maybe she ought to be grateful to Lucky Lindy, whose nasty claws had made this intimate exchange possible.

"It was difficult to leave my friends at the orphanage," Miss Rogers said, almost as if she were talking to herself. "But I knew I couldn't stay there forever. I had to be responsible for myself. I had to earn my way in the world." She pulled in her breath. "And as it turned out, I was lucky. The Rogers were good to me, and kind. They allowed me to go to grammar school, and when I did well, they let me go to high school, too." She turned away from the window, smiling a little. "That's where I learned Latin, you know. And learned to love books. It was my dream to work in a library. My passion. And now I do." Her smile faded and her eyes became bleak. "Although perhaps not for long."

Bessie hardly knew what to say. For the first time since she had known Miss Rogers, she understood her—at least a little. If Miss Rogers could say that the people who took her were kind to her, and especially that they allowed her to get an education, she was indeed lucky. Bessie had read of instances where orphaned children were sent out to work as farmhands and mill hands and domestics and never got any sort of education.

"So you began to use their name," Bessie said at last. "Rogers."

Miss Rogers nodded. "I knew my first name—Dorothy—but there was some confusion about my surname. The documents I brought with me to the orphanage were unfortunately lost by the time Mr. and Mrs. Rogers took me. When I went to school, it was easier to use their name. And since I grew up with it, I've kept it, all these years." Her eyes went to the spill of bloodred yarn on the floor. "Like Grandmother Rose's pillow."

"Yes," Bessie said. "I see."

She did, too. As an amateur historian, she knew how important it was to be able to trace your family tree, to know where you came from and where and to whom you belonged. Poor Miss Rogers knew none of that. She had a borrowed name, a lost mother, an unknown father. No wonder she was so distressed about the damage Lucky Lindy had done. The pillow wasn't just a pillow, or even just her grandmother's pillow. It was her only link to a faraway past in which she had been loved and cared for, a time when she had been somebody's daughter, somebody's granddaughter.

Miss Rogers replaced her hanky in her sleeve, took a deep breath, and squared her shoulders. Her voice became brisk.

"Well, then. That's all there is to say, Miss Bloodworth. You have seen the damage. You must tell Mrs. Sedalius that she has to get rid of that cat. The creature simply can't be trusted."

"You're certainly right about that," Bessie said repentantly.

If she had said no to that cat in the first place, this wouldn't have happened. She bent over and picked up the pillow with its trailing strings of ripped and frayed yarn. She turned it over in her hands.

"I wonder," she said, "whether we could unravel the yarn and wash it. Then perhaps we could ask Mrs. Sedalius to knit a new cover for you, using your grandmother's yarn."

"It wouldn't be the same," Miss Rogers said, shaking her head. "That's the cover my grandmother knitted, with her very own hands."

"But it would be the same yarn," Bessie persisted gently. "And don't you think it might be better to have a repaired cover than no cover at all?"

Miss Rogers' glance went back to the shredded mass of yarn. "Do you really think it can be reknitted?" she asked doubtfully.

"I'm sure it can," Bessie said, taking charge. "But first, we'll need to finish what that awful cat started. We'll unravel the yarn and wash it. Surely we'll be able to salvage enough to knit a new cover."

Miss Rogers still looked reluctant, but she nodded. "I suppose we can try," she said slowly.

So for the next ten minutes, Bessie and Miss Rogers sat side by side on the edge of the narrow bed, Bessie unraveling the yarn onto Miss Rogers' extended hands, making a skein. The yarn, which appeared to be a two-ply handspun wool, was strong for its age, Bessie thought. It must be sixty or seventy years old, perhaps older. But it had frayed in several places (or been torn by the frenzied Lucky Lindy), and when Bessie came to a break, she twisted the ends together, splicing them. Soon, she had unraveled the last row of stitches and Miss Rogers was holding a fat red skein. Bessie pulled it off her hands and tied bits of yarn around it in several places so the skein wouldn't tangle when it was washed and hung up to dry.

While Bessie did that, Miss Rogers was turning the pillow in her hands. "There's something very curious . . ." Her voice trailed off, and she frowned, puzzled. "Whatever can it be, Miss Bloodworth?" She held out the pillow so Bessie could have a look.

Now that the red knitted cover had been removed, they could see that there was another, second cover under it. It was made of a coarse, tan-colored fabric, linen, perhaps. Both sides were covered with neat columns of colored cross-stitch embroidery in a bewildering pattern of hieroglyphics, interspersed with numerals and a few letters of the Greek alphabet. The pillow had a musty scent, as if it had been stored in a closed trunk for a very long time.

Bessie stared at it for a moment. "How mysterious," she said at last. "It looks like a secret code or something. Have you ever tried to figure it out?"

"I've never even seen it," Miss Rogers replied. "I thought . . . I assumed that there was stuffing inside the knitted cover. Or maybe a plain cotton cover, with the stuffing inside. But nothing like this." She turned it over. "What do you suppose these symbols *mean*?"

"I couldn't even begin to guess," Bessie said honestly. And then she hit on a strategy—a very clever strategy, she thought—that might keep Miss Rogers occupied while she dealt with Mrs. Sedalius and Lucky Lindy.

"I have an idea," she said. "You could copy the letters and numbers and symbols. Maybe, when we see it on paper, we'll be able to solve the mystery." She paused, thinking. "Or we could show it to somebody else. Mr. Dickens at the newspaper, for instance."

Charlie Dickens, as well as being the editor of the Darling *Dispatch*, was a veteran of the Great War, where he had served in Europe and been a captain in the army. Bessie had known his sister when they were girls, and she and Edna Fay were still good friends. Charlie was always busy reporting the news, trying to keep the antique press working, and tending to the job printing business that supplemented the slim returns from subscriptions and ad sales. She didn't think he'd be eager to try to decipher a random assortment of symbols transcribed from somebody's musty old pillow.

But he had once given an interesting talk at the Darling Literary Society on the history of codes and ciphers, which had been his specialty in the army. If anybody in town would know about such matters, he was the one. Maybe he could tell at a glance whether the symbols had any meaning. And if copying the complicated cross-stitching on her pillow would keep Miss Rogers busy and her mind off Lucky Lindy, it was certainly worth a try. In fact, that part of the strategy seemed to be working already.

"Oh, what a *good* idea," Miss Rogers exclaimed enthusiastically. "Mr. Dickens comes into the library sometimes to do research, and I know that he's interested in all manner of things. I'll start copying this immediately. Really, Miss Blood-worth, I had no idea that it might be anything other than—"

She was interrupted by a shrill shriek from two doors down the hall. Bessie jumped to her feet, startled.

And then she heard another cry. "Lindy, Lindy, you naughty, *naughty* boy! Just look what you have done to my knitting!"

With Miss Rogers at her heels, Bessie hurried down the hall to see what was wrong. She found Mrs. Sedalius standing in the middle of her room, holding a half-knitted sock in her hand. Rows of stitches had been pulled loose, and at her feet lay a tangled ball of yarn. Lucky Lindy sat on the top of her dresser, head cocked, green eyes alight with mischief.

"Oh, dear," Bessie said sympathetically. "Oh, Mrs. Seda-lius, I'm so sorry!"

"So am I." Mrs. Sedalius looked down at her sock, pressing

her lips together, shaking her head. "Bessie, Bessie," she moaned. "I have been forced to a terrible decision. I'm afraid that this will make all the ladies desperately unhappy. They will hate me for it. But I have no other choice."

Bessie pulled in her breath. "What decision?"

"I'm afraid that we'll have to find another home for dear Lucky Lindy. This is the third piece of my knitting he has ruined—two socks and a scarf." She looked mournfully at the cat. "I didn't tell anyone because I kept hoping the dear fellow would mend his ways and learn to be better behaved. But I'm afraid that he had already picked up too many bad habits before he came to live with us. He's incorrigible." Her old face crumpled. "But oh, I will miss him! It will tear out a piece of my heart to see him go."

"Oh, dear," Bessie said again. "I *am* sorry. Yes, we will all miss him. What a terrible, *terrible* shame."

She had to turn away so Mrs. Sedalius couldn't see her smile.

# FOUR

# Lizzy

Lizzy was sleeping soundly on Monday morning when she was awakened by the enthusiastic crowing of Mrs. Freeman's rooster. He lived with his harem of hens a few doors down the block and took it as his personal responsibility to wake the whole neighborhood at dawn. Lizzy tried to pull the feather pillow over her head but gave it up when Daffodil, her orange tabby, leapt up on the bed and pushed his face against hers with his rumbling purr.

"I'm up, I'm up," she grumbled. She threw back the crinkle cotton spread, slid out of bed, and went to stand, stretching and yawning, in front of the second-floor window that looked onto her backyard.

*Her* backyard. In spite of the early hour, the sight of it gave her pleasure. The weeping willow draped supple green branches over the fence, the early-morning sunlight brightened the dewy pink roses blooming against the shed, and the small kitchen garden looked green and perky after Saturday's thunder shower. The grass was especially pretty, too, because

Grady Alexander had mowed it the evening before. In partial payment, she had cooked a nice Sunday supper: fried chicken (one of Mrs. Freeman's young cockerels), peas and new potatoes, a salad of fresh lettuce and spinach, and buttermilk pie.

Lizzy wrapped her arms around herself, shivering a little as she thought of Grady. She considered him a dear friend, although her mother liked to call him her "steady beau" and Grady himself seemed to operate on the comfortable assumption that there was a wedding in their near future and a family on the not-so-distant horizon. (In fact, he had told her recently that he wanted to have at least three children, and the sooner the better, because at thirty-four, he wasn't getting any younger.) Grady had a good job as the county agricultural agent and came from a respectable family. In her mother's estimation, he was Lizzy's best chance—maybe her last chance, since she had already celebrated her thirtieth birthday—at a husband and a happy home.

But while Lizzy enjoyed being with Grady and sometimes even thought she might love him enough to marry him, a wedding in the near future was entirely out of the question. Her little house—almost a doll's house, really—wasn't big enough for two people, and she was selfish enough (that was her mother's word) not to want to give it up. What's more, she had no intention of giving up her job in Mr. Moseley's law office, or surrendering the personal independence that her weekly paycheck brought her, which was what most Darling men expected their Darling women to do when they got married. Grady wasn't *most* Darling men, of course. He said he understood how she felt about working and he'd be willing to let her continue. But she didn't like the sound of *willing to let her continue*. It ought to be her choice, not his.

And at the top of her mind was the insistent thought that this was no time to start having babies, which was another thing that Darling men expected to happen after you said *I do*. Of course, there were the usual methods that Lizzy's married friends used to avoid getting pregnant. For instance, you could try saying no until your safe period, or use Vaseline or olive oil before and douche with soap suds or vinegar or Lysol after. You could go to Doc Roberts and get a prescription for a diaphragm, which you could buy at Lima's Drugstore (if you weren't too embarrassed to purchase it under Mr. Lima's knowing gaze). Or you could try to get your husband to take precautions. But Lizzy's friends kept getting pregnant even though they said they didn't want babies, so she guessed that none of these methods were very effective.

Daffy curled himself around her ankles, purring loudly, and she reached down and picked him up. As she did, she remembered why this Monday was different, and remembering made her smile.

"This isn't your everyday Monday, Daffy," she said, rubbing her cheek against his golden fur. After a moment, she put the cat back on the bed and stripped off her filmy nightgown. "I'm in charge of the office today. And not just today, either. All this week and maybe next. It's going to be swell fun!"

She stepped into her cotton panties and put on a brassiere and slip. She was slim enough not to need a "foundation garment" or even a lighter-weight girdle, an omission that her mother—who wore a boned corset—considered disgraceful. Padding barefoot to her closet, she took out a silky rayon crepe with three-quarter sleeves and a ruffled neckline. In soft browns and orange, it was her favorite dress. She wore it when she felt like celebrating.

As Daffy watched, Lizzy sat down at her dressing table and began to brush her brown hair. "And where, you are asking, will Mr. Moseley be while *I* am in charge of the office?" Talking to a cat was one of the pleasures, she thought, of living alone. "Why isn't he sitting behind his desk, smoking his pipe and signing papers, the way he usually does?"

Without waiting for Daffy to answer her question, she picked up her brown eyebrow pencil and began to sketch out thin, stylishly peaked eyebrows. "Well, since you've asked, I'll tell you. Mr. Moseley has gone to Birmingham to meet with the Alabama Roosevelt for President club. They are planning to send a delegate to the Democratic convention next year to try and get Governor Roosevelt on the ticket. Then Mr. Moseley is driving over to Warm Springs, Georgia, where he is going to meet with the governor, who spends his vacations there. So what do you think of *that*, Daffodil? Mr. Moseley is meeting with Governor Roosevelt!"

Lizzy picked up her lipstick—a soft orangey red—and applied it deftly. She was glad that the Kewpie-doll lips of the twenties were passé and full lips, like hers, were back in fashion. That done, she added gold button earrings and turned her head this way and that, studying her reflection in the mirror. She saw a not-quite-pretty face with wide-spaced, steady gray eyes, prominent cheekbones, and a resolute chin, framed by a ripple of soft brown curls. It was the face of a woman who knew her own mind, she thought. The face of a woman who could handle just about any challenge that came her way.

She got up. "And while the cat is away, my dear, sweet Daffy, the mice—so to speak—will play. While Mr. Moseley is gone, *I* am in charge!" She bent over and swept up the cat with a fierce hug. "Isn't it wonderful, Daf? Mr. Moseley trusts me enough to ask me to manage the office while he's gone!"

And with that, she skipped down the narrow stairs and into the kitchen, where she poured out a bowl of Daffy's dry cat food and sat down to coffee and Post Toasties with fresh sliced strawberries from her own backyard. When she finished, she rinsed her dish and made her lunch: a piece of leftover fried chicken, an egg salad sandwich, and two raisin-oatmeal cookies, with two more for Verna. She and Verna planned to eat lunch together the way they always did, in Verna's office if it was raining or on the courthouse lawn if it wasn't.

The kitchen of Lizzy's bungalow was small, but there was room for a table and two red-painted chairs, a four-burner gas range, and a white GE Monitor refrigerator. The table was covered with a red-and-white-checked oilcloth. There was a red linoleum-topped counter along one wall, white-painted cupboards with china knobs, and over the sink, a wide window with ruffled dotted Swiss crisscross curtains. On the windowsill sat a red geranium in a red ceramic pot, and over the table hung a lamp with a red-fringed shade that Lizzy herself had painted with bright images of fruit and flowers. She loved her kitchen, and though it might be silly to say so, she absolutely adored her GE refrigerator. It was the one with the motor on top. It kept everything beautifully cold and even froze ice cubes! It was so wonderfully *modern* after the smelly, leaky, zinc-lined icebox in her mother's kitchen across the street.

All the rooms in Lizzy's house were small. She had bought the old place, very cheaply, from Mr. Flagg's estate two years before. She had spent several months and a fair amount of her savings having it remodeled and installing a telephone, electric wiring, plumbing, and a bathroom. She had also employed painters and paperhangers to refinish the woodwork and worn wooden floors and repaper the plastered walls to suit her taste. While all this was going on, she continued to live with her mother in the house just across the street. Until the work was finished and she was ready to move in, she kept her purchase of Mr. Flagg's house a secret—intentionally, because her mother had a habit of telling her what to do.

Mrs. Lacy, of course, was dismayed when she learned that her daughter was moving out. But that wasn't the end of it. In fact, not long after Lizzy had settled into her new home, Mrs. Lacy announced that the bank was repossessing her house, in payment of a loan she had taken out in order to speculate on the stock market. She would be moving in with her daughter.

It took a while to resolve the issue, but at the last moment, Lizzy managed to make a deal with Mr. Johnson at the Darling Savings and Trust. With money she'd been saving to buy a car, she made a down payment on her mother's house, which she now owned. She helped her mother to get a job as a milliner for Fannie Champaign (the very first job in Mrs. Lacy's life) so she could pay twenty dollars a month in rent, which Lizzy then handed over to the Savings and Trust. In ten years, if all went well, the house would be free and clear.

It wasn't a perfect arrangement, but at least it kept her mother out of her hair, most of the time. And it allowed Lizzy to keep her perfect little house to herself, which was exactly the way she wanted it. And if that was selfish—well, so be it.

Fifteen minutes later, Lizzy was walking south along Jefferson Davis Street, her brown felt swagger-brimmed hat perched at a fetching angle and her lunch in her handbag. One block later, at Franklin, she turned right and walked another block, to Robert E. Lee. Just ahead on the left was the imposing Cypress County Courthouse. Built of brick, it sat in the middle of the town square, under a stately clock tower and white-painted dome, surrounded by a few trees and neatly mowed grass. On Lizzy's right after she crossed Robert E. Lee were Musgrove's Hardware and the Darling Diner, owned and managed by her friends Myra May and Violet.

Normally, Lizzy didn't drop in at the diner in the morning, because Myra May, Violet, and their colored cook, Euphoria, were busy serving the crowd of men who regularly ate their breakfasts there. But this morning, she was in a celebratory mood—*she* was in charge of the office this week! So she opened the door and went in to get one of Euphoria's famous doughnuts. She'd take it to the office with her.

"Good morning, Liz," Myra May called from the cash

register end of the counter. Violet, carrying a tray filled with two plates of ham, eggs, and biscuits with red-eye gravy, looked up with a smile.

"Hey, Liz," she said warmly. "Nice to see you. Sit anywhere you can find a seat."

As usual, the tables were filled, but there were several empty seats at the counter, so Lizzy made her way there. The white Philco radio on the shelf behind the counter was tuned to the morning farm and market reports, and the men's voices were muted as they listened. Through the pass-through into the kitchen, Lizzy could see Euphoria, dressed in her usual white uniform, flipping pancakes and frying eggs, bacon, and ham. Myra May, wearing a white bibbed apron over her customary slacks and blouse, stepped away from the cash register and picked up a china mug.

Myra May wasn't the prettiest woman in town, not by a long shot. She had a strong face with a square jaw, a firm mouth, and deep-set eyes that seemed to look right through you. Her intense intelligence made some people squirm— especially men who weren't used to women with brains. Her friend and co-owner, Violet, on the other hand, was petite and picture-pretty, with loose brown curls, an engaging smile, and a soft heart. If you were in trouble and needed help, Violet was ready to do what she could.

Judging by looks (of course, a lot of people always do just that), Myra May and Violet might appear to be an illustration of the old adage, *opposites attract.* But whatever pulled them together, their partnership seemed to make perfect sense. As far as business was concerned, Myra May's no-nonsense, let's-get-on-with-it management skills were complemented by Violet's customer-oriented charm and friendliness. On the personal side, Violet's accepting nature allowed her to deal sympathetically with Myra May's prickly impatience and smooth out the irks and quirks in their friendship.

Violet and Myra May lived in the apartment over the diner with irresistible little Cupcake, the daughter of Violet's dead sister. Cupcake wasn't a year old yet, but she had strawberry curls and the bluest of blue eyes, and while everybody knows that there's no such thing as a perfect baby (they all cry, spit up, and dirty their diapers), Violet and Myra May were convinced that she was the nearest thing to it and counted themselves lucky to have her. Cupcake spent her days cuddled on a customer's lap or napping in a bassinet next to the door to the Darling Telephone Exchange, which was conveniently located in the back room of the diner. Conveniently, that is, because Myra May and Violet owned half of the Exchange, with Mr. Whitney Whitworth owning the other half.

The Exchange had started out with just one operator working part time. Now, almost everybody in town had a telephone and so many people made phone calls at all hours of the day and night that Myra May (who managed the switchboard) had to have an operator on duty around the clock. She was looking for somebody to replace Olive LeRoy (Maude LeRoy's youngest daughter), who was moving to Atlanta to live with her cousin and work at the telephone exchange there. Henrietta Conrad, whose mother ran the Curling Corner Beauty Salon, was trying out for the job.

Actually, Myra May had said she was glad to lose Olive, who was inclined to be talky. She needed somebody who could be trusted to keep secrets, since every telephone conversation in Darling went through the Exchange. The operators knew who'd been arrested for drunk and disorderly on Saturday night, whose aunt had her appendix out over at the hospital in Monroeville, and whose daughter had eloped with a man twice her age. They weren't supposed to listen in, of course, but everybody understood that this was pretty much unavoidable, since it was too much to ask any human being to sit in front of that switchboard for eight hours a day with her headphones on without overhearing *something*.

But Myra May held her operators to a very strict code of ethics. She told them that if she heard so much as a whisper of gossip that could have come from the switchboard, she would fire the offending person on the spot, no ifs, ands, buts, or maybes. Of course, it might be hard to tell the difference between gossip that came from the switchboard and gossip that came from somebody's party line, but Myra May was a hard woman when it came to loose lips. She didn't mind holding the threat of firing over her operators' heads.

"Coffee, Liz?" Myra May asked, picking up the mug in one hand and the pot in the other.

Lizzy considered, then shook her head. "I'll have one of Euphoria's doughnuts to take to the office, if you've got any left." She looked at the doughnut plate, covered by a clear glass dome, and saw two doughnuts, shiny with sugar glaze. They were two for a nickel. "What the heck," she said. "I'm treating myself this morning. I'll take both of them." She opened her handbag and fished out a nickel.

Myra May bagged the two doughnuts, then leaned over the counter, her face grave. "Heard anything from Verna in the past day or two?" she asked in a lower voice.

"Verna?" Lizzy took the bag. "I saw her on Saturday afternoon, when we worked at the Dahlias' garden together. Why?"

Myra May straightened, rearranging her face. "Oh, no special reason," she said, with studied casualness. "Forget I asked." She glanced at the man seated on the stool next to Lizzy's and picked up the coffeepot. "Mr. Gibbons, you 'bout ready for another cup of java?"

"No, really," Lizzy persisted, beginning to feel alarmed. "Is Verna sick or something? Has she had an accident?" She knew that Myra May was on the switchboard on Saturdays and Sundays and even some nights, until she could find a replacement for Olive. What had she heard?

"Shhh," Myra May said quickly. "Don't talk so loud, Liz."

She was looking past Lizzy with a strained expression on her face, and Lizzy turned to see Coretta Cole sitting at the nearest table, dressed in a close-fitting gray suit, white blouse with a floppy white bow, red hat, and red high heels. Her shiny black hair was as stylishly waved as if she had just stepped out of the door of Beulah's Beauty Bower, and her large, luminous eyes were carefully made up. She looked a lot like Joan Crawford, whom Lizzy had recently seen in *Our Blushing Brides*.

Lizzy had known Coretta since high school, although they had never been what you'd call close friends. In fact, Lizzy had learned through a couple of painful tattle-tale experiences that Coretta couldn't be trusted. Tell her a secret and she'd blab it all over school, exaggerating and twisting it to make you look bad and herself look good. It was like that game of telephone that people sometimes played at parties— or worse. By the time you heard your secret again, you scarcely recognized it, and you wanted to go off and hide in a corner somewhere.

Coretta had worked full time in Verna's office until the county budgets were slashed and Mr. Scroggins cut her hours in half. Verna didn't have a very high opinion of her, Lizzy knew. She complained that Coretta didn't pay careful attention when she was given instructions, so that she messed things up and somebody else (usually Verna) had to spend valuable time making them right.

And now here was Coretta, big as life and twice as natural, having breakfast with Earle Scroggins, the county probate clerk and treasurer, and Amos Tombull, the chairman of the county board of commissioners. Mr. Scroggins and Mr. Tombull (who was decked out in his summer seersucker suit, although it was only April) had their heads together, talking in low voices, while Coretta perched uneasily on the edge of her chair, sipping coffee and looking fidgety and uncomfortable, as if she herself wasn't sure what she was doing there.

And then, at that moment, Coretta turned and saw Lizzy. Her eyes, already wide, widened still further, and she squirmed uncomfortably. Yes, actually squirmed, like a catfish snagged and dangling on a fishhook, while the color rose in her cheeks. She caught Lizzy's glance, held it for a measurable moment, then turned back to her coffee and the conversation at the table.

Lizzy frowned. This was unusual, wasn't it? Why was Coretta Cole having breakfast with Amos Tombull, who pulled all the strings in county government, and Earle Scroggins, who was Verna's boss? Lizzy herself wasn't comfortable around Mr. Scroggins. He was well enough respected around town because he owned property and had the power to hire and fire, and he always managed to get himself reelected when the next election rolled around. But he wasn't much liked, except by the few who profited from his patronage. Lizzy could guess why. She had seen another side of him once in a legal dispute. Mr. Moseley called him Snake Eyes.

She turned back around. "What's going on, Myra May? Why is Coretta Cole having breakfast with Mr. Scroggins and Mr. Tombull?" She narrowed her eyes. "I'll bet you heard something on the switchboard, didn't you?"

But Myra May only pressed her lips together and shook her head. She poured coffee in Mr. Gibbons' mug and took Lizzy's nickel for the two doughnuts.

"Thanks," she said briefly, and gave Lizzy a troubled smile.

Lizzy understood that something unusual was going on, something to do with Verna. But she also knew she wasn't going to get another word out of Myra May. She would have to find out the truth from Verna herself when they had lunch together, although of course she wouldn't say that Myra May had inspired her concern. She would, however, casually mention that she'd seen Coretta Cole having breakfast with Mr. Scroggins and Mr. Tombull. Lizzy had no idea what this meant, but it certainly seemed like something Verna ought to know.

Back out on the street, thinking about what she had just seen, Lizzy headed for the office. It was still early, but there was traffic on the square, with cars and a few old trucks parked, nose to the curb, in front of the diner and Musgrove's and across the street at the courthouse. Farther down the street, tethered to the streetlight post in front of Hancock's Groceries, she saw a big brown horse. The draft animal was hitched to a wagon, and a farmer in a pair of muddy denim overalls was unloading a bushel basket of collards and a bucket of turnips. A heavyset woman in a faded cotton dress and slat bonnet clambered down from the wooden seat with a wire bucket of eggs. Yard eggs were advertised for twenty cents a dozen these days, but she would likely sell hers for eight or nine cents, which she would take in trade. Many of Hancock's customers, especially the farmers, bartered fresh-caught fish, butter and eggs, and garden truck for staples like flour, salt, coffee, and tea. Some also traded for white sugar, although at fifty-eight cents for ten pounds, sugar was almost three times as expensive as flour. Most farmers and even some townspeople used honey or molasses as sweeteners. If you knew where to look and weren't afraid of getting stung, you could raid a bee tree, and many folks made molasses from their own sorghum.

As Lizzy walked past the plate glass window of the *Dispatch* building, she could see Charlie Dickens standing at the counter, talking to Angelina Biggs, who was probably handing in the copy for the Old Alabama Hotel's menus for the upcoming week, which Charlie ran off on the old Prouty job press that filled one back corner of the print shop. Angelina managed the hotel kitchen, while her husband Artis was the hotel's general manager. Charlie didn't look up when Lizzy walked by, which was just as well, Lizzy thought. The copy for her "Garden Gate" column was due and she realized with a guilty start that she hadn't given this week's items even a moment's thought. Then she turned and climbed the stairs at the west side of the building, up to the second-floor offices of Moseley and Moseley.

Benton Moseley (the youngest and now the only surviving Moseley) had hired Lizzy a few months after her high school graduation. She had been planning to work just until she and Reggie Morris, her high school sweetheart, could get married and move into a little house of their own. But Reggie had joined the Alabama 167th and marched off to France and—like so many other American boys—hadn't marched home again.

Heartbroken, Lizzy had moved the little diamond Reggie had given her from her left hand to her right. She kept on living in her mother's house and working in Mr. Moseley's law office, which quickly became the center of her life. After all, the law office was where important things happened, where people came to get their problems solved and their mistakes fixed—or not, as the case may be. Benton Moseley was smart and progressive and (most of the time) treated Lizzy almost as an equal. For her part, Lizzy was bright and eager, a quick study, presentable behind the reception desk and pleasant on the telephone, and more talented than she knew. They got along well.

That was the good part. The other part was rather unfortunate, for Lizzy had developed a fierce adolescent crush on Mr. Moseley. She suffered the pains of unrequited love in silence, always half worried that she might slip and blurt out,

"Oh, Mr. Moseley, I *love* you!" Heartened by the goose-bump-raising thrill of a stray glance or an accidental touch of his fingers, she had even imagined that Mr. Moseley might care for her, too.

But that was silly. Romances like that happened only in the novels Lizzy liked to read. And then it all became academic, anyway, for Mr. Moseley married a beautiful blond debutant from Birmingham, who quickly became one of Darling's acknowledged social leaders. When Mr. and Mrs. Moseley hosted a dinner party or attended a function at the country club, everybody oohed and ahhed and said what a perfect couple they were.

A perfect couple, that is, until Mrs. Moseley took their two pretty little girls and went back to her parents. Lizzy couldn't decide whether to be sorry or glad about the divorce. She'd grown up with the idea that marriage was forever, and she hated the thought of Mr. Moseley being lonely and the little girls missing their father. But she had to admit that it was downright silly for people to stay in a marriage that didn't make both of them happy. And now that Mr. Moseley was single again, perhaps—

But that wasn't a thought that Lizzy allowed herself to think very often, and certainly not on this bright Monday morning, when *she* was in charge of the office. She unlocked the door and let herself in. She hung her felt hat on the peg she usually used, then with a little smile, moved it to the peg where Mr. Moseley always hung his fedora. She put her handbag and lunch into her bottom desk drawer and looked around the room, feeling quite a wonderful sense of belonging. She loved the office, the polished wooden floors and the worn but still pretty Oriental rug, the glass-fronted bookcases filled with thick leather-bound law books, the diplomas and certificates and awards of three generations of Moseleys that hung on the wood-paneled walls.

And when she went into Mr. Moseley's office to adjust the venetian blind, she stood still for a moment as she always did to admire the view of the Cypress County Courthouse across the street, where the American flag hung on one pole and the Alabama flag on the other. Lizzy's spirits always lifted at the sight, for the courthouse seemed to her to represent all that was good about the America in which she lived. It stood for law and order and justice. And not justice only for some but for all, whether you were rich or poor, male or female, a resident or just passing through—like the hungry boy who had stolen Earl Ayers' green peaches. Lizzy wasn't naive enough to think that the law was always right in every single instance. But as she had learned right here in this office, the law could be trusted to stand up for the innocent and right the wrongs done to them.

Leaving Mr. Moseley's door open, she went back to the reception room. She raised the windows to let the cool morning breeze freshen the air, then made coffee in the electric percolator, used the feather duster on the bookshelves and furniture, and ran the carpet sweeper over the rug. Usually, she checked the court calendar and Mr. Moseley's appointment book and got out the case files he would need. But Mr. Moseley wouldn't be coming in this week and she had caught up the office billing and filing on Friday. Lizzy was at loose ends.

So she poured a cup of coffee, put the bag of doughnuts on the desk, and sat down in front of her typewriter, thinking that she ought to work on her "Garden Gate" column. But she would have her coffee and doughnut first. That was when she heard the hurried footsteps coming up the wooden stairs.

Quickly, Lizzy opened the drawer and dropped the doughnut bag into it, thinking that since she had booked no appointments for Mr. Moseley this week, this must be a new client. Who else would be coming so early on a Monday morning? And if this was a new client, how would she handle the situation, now that she was in charge? If the matter could wait until Mr. Moseley got back, there would be no problem. But what if it were urgent? What if—?

But it wasn't a client. It was Verna. She was wearing her usual working outfit of dark skirt, dressy-but-practical blouse, and low heels. But she wore no makeup and her hair, usually neatly combed, was uncharacteristically disheveled. She looked distraught.

Startled, Lizzy glanced at the Seth Thomas clock on the wall. It was nearly eight thirty. Verna should be in the courthouse across the street, settling into the day's work at the county probate clerk and treasurer's office.

"Why, Verna," she said, surprised. "What are *you* doing here? Why aren't you—"

She stopped, remembering what Myra May had said (or rather, what she *hadn't* said) at the diner earlier this morning, and the strained expression on Myra May's face when she looked over Lizzy's shoulder at Verna's boss. And Coretta Cole fidgeting on the edge of her chair while Mr. Scroggins and Mr. Tombull had their heads together. Obviously, something was going on. Something serious.

"I'm here because Mr. Scroggins called me up on the phone on Saturday afternoon and told me I had to stay away from the office," Verna said tautly. "He ordered me to give him my key."

"Stay away?" Lizzy asked in dismay. Now she guessed what Myra May must have overheard when she put the call through the Exchange: Verna's boss telling her not to come to work. But she still didn't understand. "Why? Are they painting the office or something?"

It couldn't be as simple as that, though. Myra May wouldn't be worried and Verna wouldn't look so desperate over an office paint job. And there wouldn't be any nonsense about a key.

"No, they're not painting," Verna replied in a choked voice. "Mr. Scroggins told me that Coretta Cole is coming in to manage my office. Coretta Cole!" she repeated, as if she couldn't quite believe what she was saying. "Coretta doesn't know beans about anything. She always depends on me to tell her what she's supposed to do, and even then, she can't be trusted to get it right. And the other two women in the office know even less than Coretta does. When I get back—*if* I get back—there'll be chaos. Total chaos. It'll take me months to straighten things out."

"You haven't been . . ." Lizzy pulled in her breath. "You haven't been *fired*, have you?"

The way things were these days, firing was just about the worst thing she could think of. Jobs were scarce as hens' teeth, and if you'd been fired from one, it was next to impossible to get another. But if Verna had been fired, that would account for Coretta Cole, with her gray suit and red hat and Joan Crawford eyes, having breakfast with Verna's boss and a county commissioner.

But Verna was shaking her head. "Not fired—yet. Officially, I'm furloughed. But it's going to get worse, Liz. I . . . I think I'm about to be—" She stopped and took a breath, as if she had to steel herself to say the next word. "Arrested."

"Arrested!" Lizzy repeated, feeling as if the floor had just tilted under her chair. "But that can't be, Verna. What makes you think—"

"I need to talk to Mr. Moseley," Verna broke in. "This morning, Liz. Right *now*, if I can." Anxiously, she looked toward the open door to his office. "He isn't in yet? What time can I see him?"

"He's not here, Verna. He's in Birmingham, and then he's driving over to Warm Springs to meet with Governor Roosevelt. He won't be in at all this week." Lizzy shook her head, bewildered. "I don't understand. Why would anybody want to *arrest* you?"

"Not here?" Verna wailed, disconsolate. She sank into the chair on the other side of Lizzy's desk. "But I need him, Liz! I *need* Mr. Moseley."

And with that, she began to sob, which by itself was incredibly shocking, since Lizzy had never once seen her friend cry, not even when Verna sprained her ankle on the courthouse steps and had to hobble a whole block to Doc Rogers' office, leaning on Lizzy's arm. Verna was one of those stoic women who hid her feelings and kept an absolutely stiff upper lip. And now she was falling apart, right in front of Lizzy's eyes.

Lizzy stood up and took charge of the situation. "What you need more than anything else," she said firmly, "is a cup of coffee and a doughnut. And then you need to tell me all about it. *All,*" she repeated emphatically. "The truth, the whole truth, and nothing but the truth, Verna. I can't help you if I don't know every detail."

Actually, she didn't know whether she could help Verna at all. There must be something seriously wrong, if her friend was afraid of being arrested. But they had to start somewhere. And she had heard Mr. Moseley say those very same words to many clients who came to him in desperation, wanting him to fix this or that predicament they'd gotten themselves into. He always insisted on knowing every little detail about the situation, good, bad, or indifferent.

"*You?*" Verna asked in surprise, and then bit her lip. "I didn't mean—That is, I wasn't expecting . . ." She stopped, took a breath, and went on lamely, "I was hoping that Mr. Moseley would take my case, Liz. I can't ask you to listen to—"

"Oh, yes, you can," Lizzy said firmly, and put the coffee cup down in front of Verna. "If you want Mr. Moseley to take

your case, you are going to sit right there and tell me everything from A to Z, every single thing you know about this
situation. I am going to write it all down." She opened the
drawer and got out the bag of doughnuts. "When Mr. Moseley calls on the telephone, I'll relay what you've told me. He
can tell us what to do. When he gets back, he can take over."

Verna heaved an enormous sigh of relief. "That sounds
good, Liz. Actually, that sounds *swell.* I'm so grateful. I don't
know how I can thank you."

Lizzy raised her hand. "I can't promise anything, of course.
But Mr. Moseley is very good at straightening things out for
people." She paused, thinking how proud she felt when she
said that. Mr. Moseley really was a very good lawyer. "In
fact," she added reassuringly, "I've never seen him tackle a
case that turned out to be too tough to handle."

Verna's face darkened. "Have you ever seen him tackle an
embezzlement case?"

Lizzy was jolted. "Embezzlement?" She had been thinking
that Verna might be involved in a minor property dispute or
even a disagreement over an unpaid bill. But *embezzlement?*
Why, depending on the amount, that could be a felony! But
of course even if she were arrested and charged, Verna
wouldn't be convicted. Mr. Moseley would get her off,
because she was innocent. Steal money? She would never in
the world do such a thing. In fact, this whole thing was
beginning to seem like some sort of unfunny prank.

"You've got to be kidding, Verna," she said at last. "This is
a joke. Isn't it?"

"I wish it were, Liz." Verna's voice was grim. "But I'm
afraid I'm in serious trouble. Come on. Let's get started."

Still half disbelieving, Lizzy reached for her steno pad and
a pen. Ten minutes later, she had to agree. If even half of what
Verna feared was true, she was in *very* serious trouble.

# FIVE

# Myra May

Myra May got up early every morning to make the first batch of biscuits and start the grits. Mrs. Hancock, at the grocery store down the street, stocked a new-fangled quick-cooking grits for people who were in a hurry. But for pure down-home flavor, Myra May preferred the stone-ground white cornmeal she bought from a gristmill at the north end of the county. It took longer, about forty minutes, and you had to cook it just at a simmer and stir the pot every time you walked past it, or it would scorch. But whether you ate your grits plain with a chunk of butter or smothered in red-eye gravy or sliced and fried in bacon grease, or even topped with honey or molasses (which in Myra May's opinion was just plain wrong), it tasted like grits was supposed to taste. Like corn, real corn, not like library paste.

Myra May glanced into the Exchange to see Henrietta on the job, then went to turn on the lights and the Philco that sat on the shelf behind the counter. This morning, station WODX in Mobile led off with "I Got Rhythm" and "On the

Sunny Side of the Street," which made Myra jig a little as she slipped on her apron over her trousers and plaid blouse. Then she stirred up the big copper pot of grits, started the coffee, and rolled and cut out the yeast doughnuts that had been rising overnight. She remembered to light the fire under the fat kettle so Euphoria could fry up the doughnuts after they'd had another rise. Then she made three dozen biscuits (that was all that would fit into the oven at one time) and checked to see that the tables were set up and the cream pitchers and sugar bowls filled. There were lots of little details involved in putting breakfast together, and Myra May always felt best when she could stay on top of everything, even if it meant getting up very early in the morning.

About the time that the first batch of biscuits came out of the oven and the radio was playing "Them There Eyes," Euphoria arrived to take over her kitchen, where she was queen. Euphoria was famous across Cypress County for her fried chicken, meat loaf, meringue pies, and doughnuts. Without her, the diner would be in serious trouble, and she knew it. Myra May and Violet knew it, too, and made a point of never crossing Euphoria, especially when she was in a bad mood. She was likely to take off her apron, stalk out, and go on home. She tied on her capacious red and blue apron, rolled up her sleeves, and began frying doughnuts, stirring up pancake batter, and slicing ham, so everything would be ready for the early crowd. It would be all men at that hour, railroaders and sawmill hands and workers at the small Coca-Cola Bottling Plant on the south end of town, mostly single men with no woman to cook breakfast for them at home.

Violet came downstairs with Cupcake on her hip when the radio began to play Lee Morse's catchy version of "Yes, Sir, That's My Baby!" Violet was wearing a pretty blue cotton print dress, and her taffy-colored hair was smoothed back from her face and tied with a blue ribbon, with a matching ribbon in Cupcake's strawberry blond curls. She was just in time to take the second batch of biscuits out of the oven and sugar-glaze Euphoria's doughnuts, smiling so cheerfully all the while that Myra May just had to smile back at her.

Which was saying something, because before Violet came along, Myra May hadn't found much to smile about. She had even thought seriously of leaving dumpy little Darling and going off to live in a big city. She was glad now that she hadn't, for if she had gone to Mobile or Atlanta, she might have missed meeting up with Violet Sims, which would have been such a sad thing that Myra May didn't like to think about it.

Of course, it worked the other way as well, for until Violet met Myra May, she had been what her mother called *flighty*, never able to settle down to one thing in one place for any length of time. Every so often, she'd get what she called *itchy feet*, so she'd pack her suitcase and go down to the Greyhound station and buy a ticket for who knows where, just to be on the move.

But when Violet got off the bus that morning a couple of years ago, it hadn't taken her more than a few days to discover that Darling was the place she wanted to stay and that her new friend Myra May Mosswell was just as steady and solid as an anchor holding a boat in a fast-moving current. No matter how hard the current might tug or how crazily the boat might bob up and down in the water, the anchor always held. And when Violet brought her niece Cupcake home after her sister died and the baby's totally worthless drunk of a daddy tried to give the newborn away to strangers, Myra May proved to be as dependably steady and reliable for the two of them as she had been for Violet alone. So it wasn't any wonder that Violet always felt like smiling as she came downstairs in the morning, or that Myra May turned from the big copper pot of grits with a spoon in her hand and a grin on her face.

"Yes, sir, that's my baby," she sang, and waved the spoon at Cupcake and Violet. "No, sir, don't mean maybe. Yes, sir, that's my baby, *now*."

The breakfast hour was always too busy for any kind of talk except "eggs over easy" and "double up on the gravy" or "more java over here!" The railroad and sawmill workers left and the people who worked around the courthouse square began to show up—they didn't have to be on the job until nine, when the shops and offices opened. (That was when Earle Scroggins and Coretta Cole and Mr. Tombull had come in.) The table and counter traffic usually got lighter after the courthouse square gang left, and Myra May and Violet finally had time to fill their plates and coffee cups and take them to the table in the back corner beside Cupcake's bassinet, where they could relax and talk about the work that had to be done that day.

Breakfast was out of the way, but there would be another two meals to cook and serve, shopping to do, and the Exchange to keep an eye on. Myra May and Violet would be pretty busy, especially since they had cut back on the afterschool help. The breakfast traffic was still brisk but the lunch bunch had slimmed down—more folks were packing peanut butter and jelly, it seemed. And the supper business had definitely dropped off. People were holding on to their money. They just weren't eating out as much as they used to, even on Friday and Saturday nights. In the *Montgomery Advertiser*, Myra May had read that dozens of restaurants had closed their doors in New York City—this, next to a photograph of the brand-new forty-one-million-dollar Empire State Building, the tallest building in the world, which was scheduled to open in a couple of weeks. In Myra May's opinion, there wasn't any justice in the world.

This morning, Myra May sat down with her grits, eggs, and coffee, but she didn't say much. For a while, they ate in silence, Violet watching out of the corner of her eye. At last, she said, lightly, "Cat got your tongue, Myra May?"

Myra May frowned. "I'm not liking this one bit, Violet. Feels pretty serious to me, especially after I saw Earle Scroggins and Amos Tombull with their heads together this morning and Coretta Cole sitting there looking smug as a puppy with two tails."

She didn't have to say what *this* was. Violet knew. She and Myra May both worked the switchboard, and while the other operators were sternly instructed *not* to listen in, the two of them had long ago given themselves permission to break what they always thought of as the Rule, with a capital *R*. The other operators were also forbidden to talk to one another about things they heard when they were on the switchboard. But Myra May and Violet broke this rule, too—only with one another, of course, and only in private.

"Verna must be so scared," Violet said in a low voice. "I know I would be, if it was me. How's she holding up?"

"Dunno," Myra May replied glumly. "Haven't seen her all weekend. I asked Liz about her when she came in for a doughnut this morning, but she didn't seem to know a thing. Liz must've guessed that something was up, though. You should have seen the look on her face when she caught sight of Coretta Cole, having breakfast with those two bigwigs. Between them, they pull every string that ever gets pulled in Cypress County."

"I thought Coretta was a friend of Verna's," Violet said.

"Obviously not." Myra May's mouth tightened. "You don't treat a friend like dirt, the way Coretta is treating Verna. But five will get you ten that she won't be in Verna's job for long. She is totally disorganized. She'll make a mess of that office in nothing flat." Myra May had met Coretta when they both volunteered to run the Children's Day program at the park for the Darling Ladies Club. Myra May had ended up doing most of Coretta's work.

"She's probably thrilled to be working full time again," Violet said softly. "I heard from Mrs. Musgrove at the hardware store that Coretta's husband got laid off out at the Coca-Cola bottling plant. The Coles have two kids in high school. I'm sure they're hard up for money."

"You're too softhearted, Violet. Everybody's hard up for money. And it's no excuse for being underhanded. Why, Verna taught Coretta all she knows about that office. And now Coretta is taking Verna's job!"

This wasn't a wild guess. Myra May and Violet had pieced together what they knew about the situation from several overheard phone conversations, going back to the previous Thursday.

It had started with a call from the state auditor to Mr. Tombull, chairman of the board of county commissioners, at Tombull's Real Estate, out at the end of Dauphin. Violet had to stay on the line at the beginning of the call because Mr. Tombull couldn't be found right away. She needed to be sure he was available, so that she could connect the two parties. When he finally came on the line, slightly winded, the auditor announced right off the bat that there was a fifteen-thousand-dollar discrepancy in the county treasurer's accounts. This announcement was so shocking that Violet didn't stop listening, the way she was supposed to. Unashamedly, she eavesdropped on the rest of the conversation.

The auditor said he had sent Mr. Tombull a report of the missing funds, which had been turned over to Cypress County by the state of Alabama from the gasoline tax, to be used for road and bridge upkeep. The letter accompanying the report said that the county should begin its own investigation immediately.

"When a situation like this happens," the auditor said, "we usually leave it up to the county to decide how it should be handled—that is, whether or not to bring in the local law enforcement. But we do expect that it will be dealt with expeditiously and the culprit brought to justice as soon as possible." He had paused, cleared his throat, then added in an even sterner voice, "It goes without saying, Mr. Tombull, that there will be a full restitution of funds. This is the gasoline tax fund." From the tone of his voice, it sounded as if the money were sacred.

"Oh, of course," Mr. Tombull had replied, obviously caught off guard by this unexpected turn of events but attempting to cling to his dignity and authority. "We'll get the person who did this. And oh, yes, sir. Full restitution. Of course, of course."

Myra May was as astonished as Violet when she learned this news. Luckily, she was on the switchboard when the next call went through, no more than an hour later, from Mr. Tombull to Earle Scroggins. Mr. Tombull was as irate as a mule with a mouthful of bumblebees.

"How'd you let this happen, Earle?" he demanded. "We figgered you knowed what you was doin' with those dang accounts. First I've heard about this-here audit, too. Whyn't you tell me 'bout it when it happened, 'stead of lettin' me hear it from the state auditor?"

But that was as much as Myra May got to hear at that moment, because Nona Jean Jamison wanted to talk long distance to Chicago, which meant that Myra May had to route the call through Montgomery, Nashville, Memphis, and then to Chicago, which took four or five minutes.

By the time she got back to Mr. Tombull and Mr. Scroggins, Mr. Scroggins was saying, touchily, "I said I'd handle it, Amos, and I will. O' course, I cain't rightly guarantee anything about the money. Restitution, I mean. But I'll do the best I can to get to the bottom of this and see it's made right, far as I'm able. You can count on that."

"You better, Earle," Mr. Tombull growled. "You hear me?

You jes' better do that." He paused. "The other commissioners are gonna need to know about this. And what about the law? I'm thinkin' we oughta get Sheriff Burns in on it from the start. That way, there ain't no question."

There was a long silence. "Well," Mr. Scroggins said, "how 'bout you let me see what I can do first, Amos? We can always bring the sheriff in later, if'n it turns out we need the law." He gave a meaningful cough. "Best thing 'ud be to handle it without the newspaper gettin' wind of it, wouldn't you say? Long as we can, anyway. Charlie has got a dickens of a nose for news, if you get my drift."

Mr. Scroggins laughed as though that were funny, but Myra May noticed that Mr. Tombull didn't laugh at all. Instead, he said, "I'm also thinkin' you oughta mend a fence or two with Charlie Dickens, Earle. He's not like his daddy. He's a sharp son of a gun and he wants to run that paper like it was the *Baltimore Sun*." His voice hardened. "There's ways to make him back off. If you get my drift."

And then on Saturday, Mr. Scroggins made two calls, the first one to Verna (which Violet overheard), telling her not to come in to work on Monday and to turn over her key. And the second one to Coretta Cole (which Myra May overheard), telling her that he wanted her to come back full time and manage the office. He said that he was putting Verna "on furlough" while they straightened out a few things.

"I'm gettin' the locks changed on the office door, too," he added. "I'm gonna give you a new key, Coretta. I want you to be the first one there every mornin' to unlock and let the other girls in, and the last one to leave every night. And if you can find out which one of 'em has been talkin' outta turn to Charlie Dickens over at the *Dispatch*, I'd be glad if you'd tell me. That may have gone down all right with DeYancy, but I won't tolerate it. You got that?"

Coretta hadn't bothered to ask the whys and wherefores.

She wasn't the kind who did. The less she knew, the better she liked it—which is how Myra May saw it, anyway.

And by that time, Myra May and Violet had put two and two together and had come to the logical conclusion: there was fifteen thousand dollars missing from the county treasury and their friend Verna Tidwell was under suspicion.

"Do you think Verna will actually be . . ." Violet hesitated, looked over her shoulder as if to make sure that nobody else could hear her, and mouthed the word *arrested*.

"It didn't sound like Earle Scroggins was terribly anxious to get the sheriff in on this." Frowning, Myra May forked a bit of sausage, ran it through the soft yolk of her fried egg, and dredged it in grits. "I wonder why. You'd think he'd go straight to the law with his suspicions and let the sheriff investigate, wouldn't you?"

"Well, yes." Violet frowned. "And how can he be so sure that Verna is involved? Does he have some kind of evidence against her?"

"He doesn't have any kind of evidence," Myra May replied indignantly. "For one thing, Mr. Tombull couldn't have the report from the auditor's office yet. It was just mailed on Friday." She put down her fork. "Anyway, you know there can't be evidence against Verna, Violet. She's as honest as the day is long. She'd never take anything that didn't belong to her. Not one red cent."

"I agree." Violet pushed her plate away. "But *somebody* took that money, if the state auditor is right and it's truly missing. And surely he wouldn't make a mistake of that size." Cupcake was fussing in her bassinet and she got up and went to pick up the baby.

"Fifteen thousand dollars," Myra May said in a hushed voice. "Almost more than I can imagine."

"Me, too." Violet sat back down with Cupcake on her lap and picked up a spoon. The baby smiled and waved her fists, anticipating breakfast. "But as I say, Myra May, somebody took that money. And since the auditor figured out that it was missing, there must be some evidence of some sort." She splashed a little cream onto the grits, stirred it in, and spooned up a bit for Cupcake, who smacked her lips and cooed, then leaned forward for more.

"I suppose." Myra May pulled her brows together. "So maybe there's evidence. But it can't point to Verna, because she didn't have anything to do with it. And if Mr. Scroggins thinks she does, he's crazy as a bedbug."

Violet looked up. "Unless," she said quietly, "somebody *made* it point to Verna."

Myra May stared at her. "You don't think—"

"I'm afraid I do," Violet said. "In which case, it might be a good idea to let Verna know what we know. It sounds like the deck might be stacked against her. And somebody's dealing off the bottom."

Myra May considered this for a moment. "How about if I talk this over with Liz first," she offered. "Liz has a good head on her shoulders, and she works in a law office. She might be able to—" She didn't get to finish her sentence.

"Miz Mosswell," Euphoria called from the kitchen. "I got the grocery list ready. Somebody gonna go shoppin' this mornin', or do I gotta cook what's on hand?"

Myra May picked up her plate and silver and stood up. "I'll go, Euphoria. What do we need?"

Euphoria cackled. "Jes' 'bout everything. List as long as my arm."

Myra May sighed. "Well, let me see how much cash we have in the register."

"Long as we can git chickens, eggs, and ham, we'll be all right," Euphoria replied. "Them green beans is comin' on in the garden out there, and we'll have okra and black-eyed peas right soon."

"Well, that's good," Myra May replied absently. She was already thinking about talking to Liz and wondering how much she could tell her without breaking the Rule. "I guess we can feed folks out of the garden."

At the table, holding the baby in her lap, Violet pressed her lips together. She wasn't thinking of the Rule. She was thinking of that fifteen thousand dollars that was missing from the county treasury and imagining all the ways they could use that money, if they had it.

# SIX

# Bessie

At Bessie Bloodworth's suggestion, Miss Rogers had worked over the weekend to copy onto paper the mysterious symbols and letters that were cross-stitched on her grandmother's pillow. She had done the work with painstaking care, making sure to get every little line and dot just right. In the process, she had gained a new respect for her grandmother's cross-stitching skills, which were truly quite fine. In fact, some of the stitched symbols were so minuscule that Miss Rogers had to use a magnifying glass to make them out. Perhaps even more importantly, she had learned her grandmother's initials. On one side of the pillow, in tiny letters, she had found the word *Rose* and a date, *July 16, 1861,* embroidered in the tiniest of stitches.

"Eighteen sixty-one!" Miss Rogers exclaimed, as she reported this discovery to Bessie as the two of them were collecting the bedsheets for Monday's laundry. (Each Magnolia Lady stripped her own bed and piled the sheets in the hallway.) "Eighteen sixty-one was just thirteen years before I was born. The first year of the War Between the States." She pulled her brows together. "And to think that I owe this interesting bit of information to the claws of that wretched cat. Is it actually true that he's going to a new home?"

"I sincerely hope so." Bessie picked up a pillowcase. "I telephoned Ophelia last night, after Lucky Lindy did himself in by unraveling Mrs. Sedalius' knitting. It turns out that Lucy Murphy has been looking for a barn cat to keep the mice down, so Ophelia volunteered to take Lindy out to the Murphys' place this afternoon. Lucy and Ophelia married cousins, you know." She paused. "Ophelia also thought she might know where to find a kitten, too—to replace the cat. I hope you won't object."

Miss Rogers sighed. "Cat fur is my bête noire. But a kitten is certainly preferable to that scruffy fellow who likes to leap off the draperies and onto our laps. Still, I have to be grateful that he unraveled the cover of my pillow. I might never have discovered that it concealed something important."

Bessie dumped Maxine's sheets into the basket. "I've got to go shopping this morning. Would you like to come along? We could take your transcription to the *Dispatch* office and show it to Mr. Dickens. He might be able to tell us something about it."

Miss Rogers hesitated. "I hope you don't think . . . That is, I've been reconsidering the plan we talked about and . . ." Her voice trailed off and she started again, tentatively. "While I'm acquainted with Mr. Dickens as a library patron, I'm not entirely comfortable around the man. He makes me feel . . ." She stopped, coloring. "You're going to think I'm very silly."

"No, not at all," Bessie said. She straightened up and looked at Miss Rogers. "I've been acquainted with Charlie Dickens for a good many years. He's a very bright man, but he's . . . well, he's skeptical, and critical. And he lived in many different places before he came back here." Charlie may have grown up in Darling, but his years of travel and his life in big cities had given him a different perspective on small-town life. Most Darlingians no longer saw him as a local boy.

"Precisely," Miss Rogers said in a grateful tone. "Thank you, Miss Bloodworth. Mr. Dickens can be extremely critical at times. And there is something quite ironic about that eyebrow of his. When he lifts it, it's as if he's secretly laughing at something you've said. I would be glad to have his opinion about the symbols on the pillow. But I would prefer not to hear him say that it's just some sort of female foolishness." She sighed. "Which I now suspect that it is."

"You do?" Bessie asked sympathetically. "Why?"

"As I copied things down, I tried to figure out for myself what they might mean. I confess that I found myself at a total loss. I have enjoyed words and language all my life, and thought I might find some meaning in it—if it was a code, that is. But the more I looked at it, the more it looked like so much gibberish. I thought perhaps I might mail Mr. Dickens a copy, with a letter explaining where I found it. He could telephone me with his opinion, or write it down and mail it back." She shook her head dispiritedly. "But I don't want to go to a lot of trouble just to have him tell me that it's all just nonsense and that I'm an old fool for taking it seriously."

Bessie understood Miss Rogers' reluctance, but she hated to see her drop the project so quickly. And besides, now that she'd had time to think about it, she herself was intrigued by the symbols and numbers. Were they just so much gibberish? Or was there a hidden meaning, perhaps a clue to the story behind the pillow? As an historian of sorts, Bessie couldn't help wanting to know more.

She picked up the laundry basket. "Tell you what, Miss Rogers. I have to go to Hancock's for groceries after Roseanne and I finish with these sheets. The *Dispatch* office is right next door. I could take your copy and leave it. If Mr. Dickens is interested, he can reply either by telephone or by mail." She paused. "Would you like me to do that?"

Miss Rogers looked doubtful. "You're sure? You aren't afraid the man will raise that ironical eyebrow at you?" She laughed, but only a little.

Bessie smiled, thinking that Miss Rogers was beginning to seem like a real person, now that she had revealed a few chinks in her armor of prim self-assurance. "He might. But if he does, I'll simply raise my eyebrow right back." She leaned forward and lowered her voice. "His younger sister Edna Fay and I were best friends when we were girls. I know a secret about Mr. Dickens."

This was true, although the secret was only mildly embarrassing or perhaps even endearing, depending on your point of view. It definitely wasn't scandalous and it had happened a very long while ago. It was a high school romance, documented in a couple of passionate love letters that a young Charlie Dickens, smitten, had written to Angelina Dupree, who was now married to Artis Biggs, the manager of the Old Alabama Hotel. Angelina had returned the letters, and Bessie and Edna Fay had found them when they were snooping in Charlie's room after he went off to his first year at Alabama Polytechnic. Faces burning, hearts pounding, the girls had read them, giggling hysterically the whole while, of course. To this day, Bessie remembered those letters, in which a passionate young man had poured out the dearest hopes and dreams of his heart, and very poetically, too. She occasionally thought about them when she saw Charlie or Angelina around town, and wondered whether they remembered them as well as she did.

That was the thing about living in a small town, where people sometimes knew too much about one another, or knew secret things or things that had been hidden so long they were almost forgotten. The past was always intruding on the present, even when you least expected it. You never knew when some little something—the smell of a flower or the sound of a voice—was going to pull you back into what once was. Sometimes, it was hard to tell just where the past ended and the present began, and some people seemed mostly to dwell in the past. History was Bessie's hobby, so she knew this very well.

"Well, then." Miss Rogers straightened her shoulders. "If you're willing to brave the lion in his den for me, I'm sure I'd be grateful. Thank you, Miss Bloodworth." And she actually put out her hand.

Bessie took it and held it for a moment. Miss Rogers' fingers were sticklike, almost all bone, and rather chilly.

"You're welcome," she said, feeling moved by what felt like an offer of friendship. "And I really wish you'd call me Bessie. After all, we've been living together for several years, and both of us are Dahlias. Shouldn't we be on a first-name basis?"

Miss Rogers withdrew her hand.

Bessie had been born and raised in Darling and couldn't imagine a different life for herself, although she sometimes envied people like Charlie Dickens, who had been to New York and Paris and Cleveland and Baltimore and who knows where else. But if you had lived in a big city for a while, you would surely have seen how dirty and ugly and unfeeling it was, with nobody but strangers wherever you looked. When you got to Darling, you'd notice the difference. You'd be grateful.

And there was plenty to be grateful for, in Bessie's opinion. For one thing, the town looked pretty much as it always had, and if you weren't aware of the current sorry state of national affairs, you couldn't tell it by looking around Darling. It was a lovely place, with huge magnolia trees along the streets and flowers in the yards and friendly people and a fascinating history. Mobile was seventy miles to the south, a half-day drive, more if the roads were bad and you had to get a farmer and his horse to pull you out of a mud hole. Montgomery, the state capital, was a hundred miles north, too far to drive unless you absolutely had to and were a glutton for punishment. If you didn't want to drive, of course, you could take the train both ways. The Louisville & Nashville Railroad went north and south out of Monroeville, twenty miles to the east, and there was a local spur that went to Monroeville. Get on the train in Darling first thing in the morning, get off in Mobile before lunch or in Montgomery by early afternoon.

The site for the town was picked out in 1823 by Joseph P. Darling. He had come all the way from Virginia in a wagon pulled by a team of oxen, with his wife, five children, two slaves, a pair of milk cows, and a horse. He intended to keep on going as far as the great Mississippi River, where he planned to start a cotton plantation and make a lot of money, now that Mr. Jefferson had bought and paid for the Louisiana Purchase.

But Mrs. Darling had other ideas, as the story had been told to Bessie by one of their descendants. The Darling party camped for the night beside Pine Mill Creek. When Mrs. Darling got up the next morning, the rain had put the camp-fire out, the wood was soaked, and breakfast was cold corn pone and last night's cold coffee. For Mrs. Darling, who was tired to death of traveling, that was the last straw.

"Mr. Darling, I am not ridin' another mile in that blessed wagon," she said. "If you want your meals an' your washin' done reg'lar, this is where you'll find it—soon as you put a roof over my head. Until then, I ain't gettin' back in that wagon for love nor money. You kin put that in your pipe an' smoke it."

Confronted with this ultimatum (and without his coffee), Mr. Darling took a long look around. He noticed the rich soil, the Alabama River flowing quietly not far away, the fast-moving creek where they were camped, and the fish in the creek and the wild game in the woods. He took into account the abundant timber—loblolly and longleaf pines on the gently rolling hills, with tulip trees and sweet gum in the bottoms, as well as pecan and sycamore and magnolia and sassafras. He also took into account the fact that he liked clean britches and his three squares a day. Altogether, he felt compelled to reply, "Well, if you insist, Mrs. Darling. You can take your bonnet off and get out your washboard. We're stayin'."

And stay they did. Mr. Darling cut enough loblollies to build a cabin for the family, another for the slaves, and a barn for the animals. More Darlings trickled out from Virginia, and before long, the Darling clan had built a general store, a sawmill, a gristmill, a school, and a church. More folks came, of different religious persuasions, so they needed more churches. And the more people came, the more money they brought with them and earned when they got there, so they definitely needed more stores where they could spend it. It wasn't long before Darling became a county seat and got dirt sidewalks and a brick courthouse with a bell tower and a county government and a county sheriff. It was on its way to being a real town.

Darling wasn't an isolated, out-of-the-way town, either, the way some little towns were, stuck way out in the elbow-bend back of nowhere. Steamboats chugged up and down the Alabama River, picking up cotton and delivering supplies at plantation landings, which made it easy to go south to Mobile or north to Montgomery, if somebody wanted to. And not long after the War, the owners of the sawmill, the hotel, and the bank scraped the money together to build a railroad spur that connected Darling to the Louisville & Nashville Railroad just outside Monroeville, which meant that everybody could go pretty much anywhere they wanted, even when the roads were bad (which they were, most of the time) or the river was flooded (which it was, every spring).

But mostly, people who were born in Darling were content

to stay right there, since it was a very nice town. Some, of course, went off for the sake of adventure or because they had to, like the boys in gray who marched off to the tune of "Dixie" and the boys in khaki who marched off to "The Stars and Stripes Forever." Some of them didn't come home again because they couldn't, and a few decided to go and live where they could get a better job and make more money. But in general, the men who left came back as soon as they could and married their hometown sweethearts and lived happily ever after, right there in Darling.

But not Charlie Dickens, who (as Bessie knew) had gone off to Alabama Polytechnic Institute in Auburn after high school and then to New York to the journalism school at Columbia University and after that to a reporting job on the Cleveland *Plain Dealer*. And after the army and France, it was back to the States, moving from place to place. Finally, he got to Baltimore, where he landed a good job as a reporter on the city desk at the *Sun*, until a new editor took over and the two of them discovered that they didn't see eye to eye about a great many important things, mainly having to do with Charlie's passion for investigative journalism. He had written a couple of in-depth features about police corruption in the city and raised some hackles in the police department and the mayor's office. And that was the end of his reporting career at the *Sun*.

About that same time, Doc Roberts diagnosed Charlie's father—the owner and editor of the Darling *Dispatch*—with lung cancer, and Charlie came home to help out. Then Mr. Dickens died, and there was the newspaper with no editor and there was Charlie, a newsman with nowhere in particular to go. It seemed like the natural thing for him to settle down to his father's job. Or try to, since he didn't have any experience in managing a rural newspaper with a small subscription list, not much advertising, and a faltering job printing business on the side.

He didn't have a sweetheart to come home to, either, since Angelina Dupree had married Artis Biggs just five months after Charlie went away to college, which was probably what turned him sour on love. (The fact that Angelina and Artis' first boy arrived on the scene seven months to the day after the wedding might have had something to do with it, too. Or maybe it was because Charlie suspected that Angelina fell for Artis because he drove the first Buick in town, while Charlie was saving his money for college.) But that had been a long time ago, and Edna Fay said Charlie didn't harbor hard feelings.

Charlie himself had never married. He often said he'd seen too many bad marriages to be anything but skeptical about the possibility of marital happiness. And that he had seen too much of the world out there to be anything but skeptical about the possibility of anybody living happily ever after in Darling, which (he said) was nothing more than a two-bit Southern town that figured it was worth twenty-five dollars. And even when he became the editor of the *Dispatch*, which you would think would be a kind of rah-rah cheerleading job, he didn't try to hide that opinion.

Bessie knew all this because of being best friends with Charlie's kid sister. Edna Fay was married to Doc Roberts and kept busy managing his office, but she and Bessie still got together as often as they could. When they did, Bessie always asked about her brother and Edna Fay was always glad to give her an earful of the inside story, which is how Bessie had managed to keep track of Charlie's whereabouts and what fors through the years.

But not because she especially cared, of course. Like Charlie, Bessie had been sour on love, too, for her heart had been broken forever when her fiancé, Harold Hamer, skipped town on the very day they were planning to buy their wedding rings. At least, that's what Bessie thought, until just six months ago, when she was going through a box of old papers from her father's funeral parlor business, which she had sold to Lionel Noonan. That's when she figured out what had happened to Harold, and why. It took her a while to get over the shock, but knowing the truth made her feel better. She could finally stop grieving over the past and get on with the present.

Bessie was reflecting on all this as she walked toward the square that morning, having hung the sheets on the backyard clothesline and left Roseanne to finish the rest of the laundry. Her first stop was at Lima's Drugstore, on the southwest corner of the square, where she bought a box of Wildroot Wave Set for Leticia Wiggins, a tube of Dr. West's toothpaste for Mrs. Sedalius, and some Blue Jay corn plasters for herself. Then she took a shortcut across the courthouse lawn to the grocery store, where she handed her weekly shopping list to Mrs. Hancock.

Bessie always took care with her list, including the prices and totaling them up at the bottom so she'd be sure to stay within the week's grocery allowance. Today, she was getting two pounds of spare ribs (twenty-five cents), two pounds of Eight O'Clock coffee (forty-five cents), self-rising Split Silk flour (twenty-four-pound bag for sixty-five cents), ten pounds of red potatoes (fifty cents), four pounds of prunes (twenty-five cents), a one-pound box of Blue Grass macaroni (five cents), a three-pound bag of grits (ten cents), and two boxes of Octagon soap powder (twenty-five cents).

She was standing at the counter when she smelled something tangy and turned to see a box of oranges, sitting on top of a barrel of cabbages. The hand-lettered sign said that they were nineteen cents a dozen, a bit pricey, but they did smell good. The Magnolia Ladies loved nothing better than fresh-squeezed orange juice for breakfast, and she could dry the peels for flavoring.

"I'll take a dozen of those oranges, too," she said impulsively, and Mrs. Hancock nodded approvingly.

"Good you got 'em now," she said, putting them into a paper bag. "That's such a nice price, they'll all be gone in another hour or two."

Bessie didn't think it was a nice price. She'd bought oranges last month at fifteen cents a dozen. But it didn't pay to argue with Mrs. Hancock, who owned the only grocery store in town. Before the Crash, there'd been talk about A&P building a self-service market on the other side of the square, where Sevier's Stationery had burned down a few years ago.

But Bessie thought it was just talk, with the economy so shaky. At least she hoped so. If A&P opened a store here, that would likely be the end of Hancock's. But A&P wouldn't give credit—you'd have to pay every time you went shopping. They wouldn't deliver, either. Mrs. Hancock would jot down each amount and the total ($2.69) in her black book, and then put Bessie's purchases in a cardboard box for Old Zeke to deliver to Magnolia Manor. Bessie or Roseanne would come in and pay the bill, in cash, at the end of the month. Some folks couldn't pay everything they owed every month, and Mrs. Hancock would give them a hard look and sometimes a little lecture. But she'd carry them until they got back on their feet—or as long as she could, anyway. And in the meantime, she'd take on trade anything they could give her, from chickens and eggs to woodstove lengths.

Bessie left the groceries to be delivered, went back out onto Franklin Street, and walked one door to the east, to the *Dispatch* office, to leave Miss Rogers' paper with Charlie Dickens. She was just about to enter when, to her surprise, the door was flung violently open and Angelina Dupree Biggs rushed out. Her face was flushed, her eyes were wide, and her yellow straw hat was crooked. She ran straight into Bessie, bumping her so hard that she almost knocked her over.

Back in high school, Angelina had been a slightly plump but very pretty girl, blond and blue-eyed, with bee-stung lips and a figure that was nicely rounded in all the right places. She had a perky personality that (along with her physical attributes) made her the most popular girl in school. All the boys were crazy about her, so when Bessie read Charlie's torrid love letters, they hadn't come as a big surprise. Edna Fay had made fun of her brother's extravagant language and Bessie had joined in. But she had been unaccountably affected by the depth and sincerity of Charlie's passion and wished with all her heart that Harold Hamer, her sweetheart, would write letters like that to her. Harold couldn't, because he was basically your boy next door. Charlie could, because he had always had a way with words, even when he was still a skinny, all-elbows boy with brown hair that stuck up no matter how much Brilliantine he put on it.

But Angelina had never been what you'd call skinny, even in high school. For the past several years, she had run the kitchen at the Old Alabama Hotel, where her husband Artis was the manager. It was her duty to sample the pies and cakes and fried chicken and potato salad the cook produced, and as a result, she had gained quite a few extra pounds, many of them settling comfortably around her hips and bottom.

So when she flung open the door and ran into Bessie, the impact nearly knocked Bessie off her feet. Bessie gave an involuntary "oomph!" and grabbed at the door to keep from being bowled over.

"So sorry," Angelina gasped. She seized her hat with both hands and jammed it on her head. "I didn't see you, Bessie. Door didn't hurt you, did it?"

"I'm all right," Bessie said, and sucked in a deep breath. With it, she got an overwhelming whiff of Emeraude perfume. Angelina must have soaked herself with the stuff. "Are you okay?"

Angelina nodded, but Bessie thought she was fighting back tears, which was odd, because over the years, Angelina had settled into an almost stolid placidity. Bessie, who had worked with her on several Ladies Club committees, had never once seen her upset.

"You're sure?" Bessie persisted. "You're not hurt, are you?"

"Yes," Angelina gulped. "I mean, no. Sorry, Bessie—I gotta go." And she blundered off down the street, nearly running into Myra May Mosswell, who was just coming out of the diner, carrying her shopping basket and heading up the street toward Hancock's.

"Wonder what got into Miz Biggs," Myra May said, when she was within speaking distance of Bessie. She glanced back, following Angelina's progress across the street. "That lady really oughta look where she's going. Heavy as she is, she's kind of like a battering ram when she gets up a head of steam."

"No idea what could have set her off that way," Bessie said. "How are you, Myra May?"

"I've been better," Myra May said grimly. "Have you seen Verna this morning?"

"No, I haven't." Bessie frowned. "Why? Is something the matter?"

Myra May looked as if she might be about to speak, then changed her mind. She shook her head mutely. "On my way to the grocery," she muttered. "See you later, Bessie."

Myra May's evasiveness made Bessie curious, but she was still wondering why Angelina had come shooting out of the *Dispatch* office like a pebble out of a peashooter. Did it have something to do with Charlie Dickens? Surely not—their relationship was ancient history. Wasn't it?

She opened the door and went inside. The newspaper occupied one large room (partitioned into several spaces) on the building's street level beneath the second-floor law office where Liz Lacy worked. The front door opened with the chirpy *ding-ding* of a bell, and the visitor stepped up to a wooden counter a few paces inside, which was always stacked with the latest edition of the *Dispatch*. It was an eight-page weekly, four pages of ready print (world news, photos, comics, and women's items printed by a shop in Mobile and shipped to Darling by Greyhound bus) and four pages of home print. Behind the counter was the editor's desk and, behind that, a row of tall wooden bookshelves filled with bound volumes of newspapers formed a partition that blocked off the composing room, where the Linotype, type cases, makeup tables, and job press were located. Along the back wall sat the formidable-looking newspaper press surrounded by stacks of newsprint and buckets of ink. Charlie ran the press on Thursday nights, so he could get the *Dispatch* into the mail on Friday. When it was operating, it rattled every window in the old building and the windows of Hancock's Groceries on one side and the Darling Diner on the other.

Just behind the customer counter, under a hanging lamp, stood the editor's desk, with a black Remington typewriter, a dictionary, and a stack of wooden letter trays. That's where Charlie Dickens was seated in a wooden desk chair, hunched over his typewriter and pecking furiously with two fingers, slamming the carriage hard when he came to the end of a line. An empty bottle of Hires Root Beer sat on the corner of his desk, next to an overflowing ashtray. The place smelled of cigarettes and ink. And of Angelina's perfume.

Charlie looked up and saw Bessie and smiled, a little crookedly. He rolled his chair back, pushed himself out of it, and came to the counter. He was wearing his usual green eye-shade, and the sleeves of his white shirt were rolled up, his tie loosened. He was a large man, several years older than Bessie, and his hair was thinning on top. His penetrating gaze didn't quite match the soft plumpness of his face.

"Bessie Bloodworth," he said, in his rumbling voice.

"Don't see you in here much these days. How ya doin' this mornin'?"

Bessie knew that Charlie Dickens had been to college and journalism school and spoke French and German as well as English. But she had heard him say that folks were always a little easier with him if he "talked down-home." She thought he was probably right.

"I'm doing right well, thank you, Charlie," Bessie said. She wanted to ask why Angelina Dupree Biggs had flown out of the *Dispatch* so fast that she barreled over anybody in her path, but she resisted the temptation, in part because of the downturn of Charlie's mouth. His eyes were dark and he looked troubled. Whatever had propelled Angelina out the door obviously hadn't made Charlie very happy, either.

So she settled for, "How's Edna Fay? I saw in last week's paper that she went down to Mobile for a week to visit your aunt."

"She did," Charlie said, "but she's back now. I'll tell her you asked." He became businesslike. "Somethin' I can do for you, Miss Bessie?" He reached for the pad on which he took down job printing orders or advertisements that people wanted to place in the paper. "You wantin' to run another ad for your boardin'house, I reckon."

He was obviously not interested in small talk, and Bessie had the feeling that this might not be a very good moment to ask him a favor. But she opened her purse and took out the folded paper Miss Rogers had given her.

"No, not an ad," she said. "All my ladies are settled in for the duration, looks like."

Charlie nodded at the paper. "Then you got a story for me, I reckon. From the garden club, maybe?"

His eyebrow was quirked and his tone was mildly sarcastic, in that way of his that irritated some and intimidated others. Charlie made it no secret that he didn't think highly of women who spent their time going to meetings of garden clubs, bridge clubs, needlework clubs, or other ladies' groups. Bessie wasn't clear whether he disapproved of women who held a job or ran a boardinghouse, but she thought he probably did.

"No, it's not a garden club story," she replied briskly. "Sorry to disappoint you." She smiled at him as if to say, *There, was that ironic enough for you?* She unfolded the paper, cleared her throat, and began.

"A friend of mine"—she and Miss Rogers had agreed that she wouldn't use any names—"discovered some odd symbols and numbers cross-stitched on a very old pillow that once belonged to her grandmother. They seemed very curious to us, and we thought . . . that is, we wondered . . ."

She took a breath, fumbling for words. Under Charlie's half-amused, skeptical gaze, this suddenly seemed like a very foolish errand, and she wished she hadn't volunteered. But now that she had started, there was nothing to do but stumble on.

"It . . . it occurred to us . . . that is, to me, that it might be . . ."

"Yes?" Charlie drawled, half teasing. "Might be what? Come on, out with it."

She took another breath. "Well, a cipher or something like that. You know, a secret code. I remembered that *wonderful* talk you gave at the Literary Society last year. I thought you might be interested in having a look."

She bit her tongue. Emphasizing *wonderful* might have been a little bit too much, but she thought she should compliment him. His paper had been genuinely interesting.

Charlie all but rolled his eyes. "What in the world gave you the idea that somebody's grandmother's old needlework might be a secret code?" he asked with a disparaging chuckle. "Seems far-fetched to me. Why would a grandmother want to stitch out a cipher?"

When the question was put that way, Bessie didn't have a good answer. In fact, she had no answer at all. She couldn't very well tell Charlie that the idea had come into her mind when she was trying to distract Miss Rogers from being angry and upset about the destruction of her pillow's knitted cover. So she said the only thing she could think of.

"Well, I once heard that certain quilt patterns were used as secret codes to tell slaves where to go on the Underground Railway." This was true. She had read a magazine article about an old Negro woman who claimed that blocks like Wagon Wheel and Log Cabin and Crossroads, together with fabric colors and certain embroideries, held clues that helped escaped slaves find their way to freedom in the North. Some folks didn't believe her, but the story had sounded plausible to Bessie.

"Never heard that tale," Charlie said skeptically, but he looked halfway interested. "You actually think it might be true?"

"I don't know," Bessie admitted. "But I suppose it could be, the same way that ships used to use flags for signals before the wireless was invented. Different colored flags meant different things, and flags aren't anything but pieces of fabric sewn together, like quilts." She looked at him. "Isn't that so?"

"Well, yes," Charlie said, grudgingly. "Hadn't thought of it that way, but I suppose that's what they are. There are flags that represent each letter of the alphabet. In the Battle of Jutland, during the Great War, the Royal Navy sent over two hundred fifty flag signals. And flags are still used at sea, because some ships aren't yet equipped with a wireless."

Bessie remembered that he had included this information in his talk and was a little encouraged. She nodded and plowed on.

"And I read once that Mary, Queen of Scots, had a secret language that she used to send messages to her friends. That was after Queen Elizabeth shut the poor thing up in prison and wouldn't let her talk to anybody for fear they'd be hatching up a plot. I don't know that she embroidered her messages on hankies, but I'm sure she *could* have. Her jailors might suspect if they saw pieces of paper going back and forth, but they probably wouldn't look twice at a lady's silk hanky or an embroidered scarf. Don't you think?"

Bessie stopped. She was afraid that she was babbling, but Charlie's eyes were narrowed and he looked thoughtful. "Never heard that story, either," he said, "but I suppose it's possible."

"Well, then," Bessie asked reasonably, "why not a pillow?"

With a sigh, Charlie reached for the paper she was holding. "Okay. Let me have a look at these 'symbols' of yours." He squinted down at Miss Rogers' copy for a minute, then went to his desk, picked up a pair of metal-rimmed glasses, and hooked them over his ears. He came back to the counter and studied the paper a moment longer as Bessie held her breath. There were no sounds other than the hollow *tick-tock* of the old wooden clock on the wall.

At last he put the paper down on the counter, his forehead wrinkled. "Where'd you say you got this?"

Bessie let out her breath and repeated what she'd already told him. "My friend has a pillow that she inherited from her grandmother. It has these symbols embroidered on it, on both sides. She copied all of them."

"How old is your friend?" He frowned. "Not being nosy, just trying to get some kind of historical fix on this stuff, whatever it is."

"To tell the truth, I don't know how old she is, exactly. But her age doesn't matter. Her grandmother's initials and the date are right there." She pointed to the very bottom of the page.

"Yes, I saw them." Charlie bent closer, peering at the paper. "Rose," he read aloud. "July 21, 1861." He looked up, frowning a little. "What did you say your friend's name is? Or, more to the point, what was her grandmother's name?"

"My friend was an orphan," Bessie replied. "Her papers were lost at the orphanage and she never knew her family name. All she knew was that her grandmother's name was Rose. The pillow belonged to her—to her grandmother, I mean."

To Bessie, who loved to spend time digging into Darling's history and researching genealogies, not knowing the family name seemed like a very great tragedy, akin to waking up in an utterly strange place and not being able to remember where you were or how in the world you got there. She herself had uncovered some truly horrifying secrets about her own family, and particularly about her father, but she still cherished his name, because it connected her with a family past. She couldn't imagine how Miss Rogers could have endured it all those years, not knowing who her people were.

"The pillow was the only thing she had that belonged to her family," she added. "It had a cover on it, a knitted cover, which had never been removed—until Saturday, that is. The cover was pulled off, unraveled, actually, by accident. My friend had never seen those symbols before."

"Anything else?" Charlie prodded.

Bessie thought. "Well, her mother's name was Rose, too," she said slowly. "My friend remembers her mother telling her that her grandmother was a very brave woman. She drowned, apparently."

"She drowned?" Charlie repeated. He pursed his lips and pushed them in and out, frowning as if he were trying to grasp an elusive memory.

"That's what my friend remembers." She looked back at the paper lying on the counter. "Do you think those symbols mean anything?" She almost hated to ask the next question, because she was afraid he would laugh at her. "Do you think they might really be some sort of secret code?"

"I doubt it," he said. But he didn't laugh. "They are certainly curious, I'll say that much." He straightened up. "You're not in a tearing hurry for an answer, are you?"

"A hurry?" she answered with a chuckle. "That pillow has been lying around for nearly seventy years. I doubt if a few more days is going to make any difference in the scheme of things."

He nodded. "Well, then, if you'll leave this with me, I'll do a little research on it and see what I can find out." He lifted his hand in a warning gesture. "Don't get your hopes up, Bessie."

"I won't," Bessie said. She smiled. "Thank you, Charlie. I was afraid . . . I was afraid you'd think I'm being pretty silly about this."

"Oh, I do," Charlie said with a shrug that was meant to look careless. "But I get pretty silly sometimes, too—when it comes to things I'm interested in." He paused for a moment, shifting his weight uncomfortably. "I guess you saw Angelina Biggs rushing out of here as you came in."

"I did," Bessie said. She smiled wryly. "She nearly bowled me over, in fact."

He paused again, as if he were fishing for words. This hesitation was so totally unlike Charlie Dickens that Bessie was surprised. Finally, he said something entirely unexpected, in a voice that was almost tentative. "Afraid she was a little upset. But I want you to know I had nothing to do with it, Bessie."

*Nothing to do with it?* Why should Charlie think that *she* would think he had something to do with Angelina's hasty, blundering exit?

But there wasn't a tactful way to ask this nosy question. And anyway, Charlie was turning back to his desk, obviously putting an end to the conversation. Over his shoulder, he added, "I'll give you a call if I learn anything about this so-called secret code of yours."

"Thanks," Bessie said, still puzzling over what he'd said about Angelina Biggs and slightly offended at his patronizing reference to that *so-called secret code of yours*. She pushed open the door and left, going kitty-corner across the square to Mann's Mercantile. Roseanne's old straw broom was in tatters, and she needed a new one. Miss Rogers wanted some black darning cotton for her stockings, and Bessie was looking to buy three yards of bleached cotton to make dish towels for the kitchen.

If Bessie had stepped out of the *Dispatch* office just a minute or two earlier, she would have seen Myra May heading back from the grocery store, her shopping finished for the morning. But Myra May didn't go back to the diner, at least, not right then. Instead, she turned at the corner of the *Dispatch* building and went quickly up the stairs to the second-floor law office. Bessie wouldn't have wondered at this, for Liz Lacy and Myra May Mosswell were good friends. She would have thought that Myra May was just dropping in to trade a little gossip and maybe have a cup of coffee before she went back to work.

But truth be told, Myra May had a much more serious errand. She had decided that she needed to tell Liz what she and Violet had learned when they broke the Rule. She wanted to get Liz's advice about what to do.

# SEVEN

# Lizzy, Verna, and Myra May

It had taken Lizzy quite a while to reach Mr. Moseley in Birmingham, where he was closeted in a morning meeting of the Alabama Roosevelt for President club, but their conversation took only a few minutes. She hung up the receiver and put the black candlestick telephone back on her desk, then turned to Verna, who was leaning forward eagerly in her chair.

"Well," Verna demanded. "What did he say? Is he going to take my case? What am I supposed to do?"

Lizzy took a breath, knowing that Verna would not be happy to hear the message. "Mr. Moseley says he's terribly sorry but there's nothing he can do unless you're actually arrested." She hurried on. "He understands how you feel about taking some sort of action immediately, but he says that isn't a good idea. For one thing, you don't even know what's really going on. It's probably just a mistake. He says you should go home and wait to see what happens."

"Go home and wait?" Verna cried desperately. "No, Liz! I can't!"

"But you *have* to, Verna." It took an effort, but Liz made her voice firm. "You may be jumping at shadows, you know. This problem, whatever it is, could get sorted out in a couple of hours and you'll be back at work." She took a breath. "Of course, if you should get arrested—although we hope it won't happen—Mr. Moseley says you need to call me right away and I'll come and post bail. That way you won't have to spend the night in jail."

Lizzy occasionally made arrangements on behalf of one or another of Mr. Moseley's clients with Shorty Boykin, Darling's only bail bondsman, who had a storefront office next door to the jail. It was painful to think of doing it for one of her friends, but she certainly knew the procedure.

Verna pushed herself out of her chair and began to pace back and forth in front of Lizzy's desk, her shoulders bent, her hands clasped behind her back.

"I can't just go home and wait for the sheriff to show up, Liz. I've got to find out what's going on. This is either a huge mistake or . . ." Her voice dropped. "Or somehow, for some reason, somebody's trying to frame me. For something. For embezzlement."

"*Frame* you?" Lizzy asked doubtfully, thinking that Verna had probably been reading too many of those murder mysteries she liked so much. Lizzy knew what *frame* meant, because she'd heard the word in *The Last Warning*, starring Laura La Plante, which she and Grady had seen at the Palace a couple of weeks before. But who in the world would want to frame Verna? And why?

"Yes. Frame me. Make me look guilty of something." Verna threw out her hands. "It's the only explanation I can come up with. Nothing else makes sense. That's why I've got to find out what's going on. I need to know what really happened to that money. And the sooner the better."

"But how is that possible?" Liz asked reasonably. "Unless you want to go directly to Mr. Scroggins and ask him to—"

"Ask Earle Scroggins?" Verna interrupted her with a harsh, impatient laugh. "He won't tell me anything." She reached the edge of the carpet and turned. "I'll just have to conduct my own investigation, Liz. I've known ever since I took over the treasurer's office that there was something goofy with the bank accounts, I just couldn't put my finger on exactly what it was. But now I will, I swear it." Her voice hardened and her eyes were flashing fire. "If money is missing from the county treasury, I'll find out where it went and who took it—or die trying."

Lizzy shivered, not liking the sound of those last three words. "But Mr. Scroggins told you to turn in your key. How could you manage to get into the office to—"

Verna barked another harsh laugh. "You don't think I gave that man my *only* key, do you? I'm not that dumb, Liz. I had two duplicate keys made at the hardware store a long time ago, just in case I lost one." She sat back down in her chair, looking pleased with herself. "What's more, I also have a key to the courthouse. I can get into that building any time I want to."

"Oh," Liz said. That kind of precaution was exactly like Verna, who liked to have everything under control. But still— "You'll have to do it at night, won't you? How long is it going to take?"

"Of course I'll have to do it at night," Verna said shortly. "And it's not going to take that long, either. I watched that man—that auditor—when he was going through those books. He had a face that was carved out of stone and I couldn't tell a blessed thing by his expression. But I know which records he spent the most time working on, and I made it a point to glance over his shoulder whenever he seemed to linger over certain pages. I noted them down, so I have a pretty good idea of where to look."

Lizzy frowned, thinking what Mr. Moseley would say if he thought his client (assuming that Verna actually became his client) intended to trespass on county property, especially when she might be facing a charge of embezzling county funds. Hoping to dissuade her, she said, "But isn't it awfully risky, Verna? If you're caught, people will think you were there to try to cover something up. It will look just terrible. And if somebody's trying to frame you, won't they be expecting you to do something just like this?"

Verna was irritatingly sure of herself. "I won't be caught, Liz. I'll come in after dark and leave before dawn, and I'll work in the room where we keep the records. It doesn't have any windows. Nobody will know I'm there. And when I'm through, I'll have a suspect list. I might even be able to tell you who dunnit."

Lizzy wished that Verna hadn't read quite so many crime stories, but now she was curious. "A suspect list? Who do you think might be on it?"

Verna looked thoughtful. "Mr. DeYancy set up those multiple accounts. And he never let Melba Jean or Ruthie know why or what was going on. At least, that's what they *said.*"

"But Mr. DeYancy is dead," Lizzy objected.

"Suddenly and unexpectedly dead," Verna pointed out in a meaningful tone.

Lizzy frowned. "You're suggesting that Mr. DeYancy's dying had something to do with—"

"I'm not suggesting anything," Verna said flatly. "Just thinking about a list of possible suspects. Mr. Scroggins would have to be on it, of course. And anybody who's had access to those account books over the past year or so. Including Melba Jean and Ruthie. One or the other of them might just be playing dumb. Or maybe even both of them. They might know a lot more about those accounts than they're letting on. In fact, I have the idea that Ruthie—"

She stopped, hearing footsteps on the stairs, and her eyes widened. "Quick!" she hissed. "It might be the sheriff. Or

Mr. Scroggins! I don't want anybody to find me. Where can I hide?"

Liz didn't stop to ask why Verna thought the sheriff or Mr. Scroggins would be looking for her in Mr. Moseley's law office. "In the broom closet," she said quickly, and pointed.

In a flash, Verna jumped out of her chair, disappeared into the closet, and pulled the door shut behind her.

But it wasn't the sheriff or Mr. Scroggins. Myra May Mosswell stepped through the door, carrying a basket full of groceries.

"Well, hello again." Lizzy was relieved to see her friend, but a little surprised. Myra May was always so busy at the diner in the mornings—she almost never took the time to drop in. And they had spoken just a little earlier. "Nice to see you, Myra May. Sit down and have a cup of coffee with me, won't you?"

At that moment, she saw Verna's coffee cup and her untouched doughnut. Hoping that Myra May hadn't noticed, she quickly gathered them off the desk.

Myra May put her basket down beside the door and took the chair Verna had just vacated, not appearing to realize that the seat was still warm or that a cup of coffee and a doughnut had just disappeared from Lizzy's desk. Her face was troubled and she leaned forward, her voice urgent.

"No coffee, thanks. I really need to talk to you about Verna, Liz. I'm afraid she's in serious trouble."

Lizzy wasn't terribly surprised that Myra had some information, given what she had witnessed at the diner that morning, but she wasn't sure how to respond. "What kind of trouble?" she asked, uncomfortably aware that Verna could hear every word.

"Money trouble. Thousands and thousands of dollars worth of trouble."

"Thousands?" Lizzy croaked, shocked. From what Verna

had told her, she was aware that some amount seemed to be missing from the county treasury. But she had no idea how much. *Thousands?* That was real money. All of a sudden, Verna's plight became more real, and much more frightening.

Myra May was nodding. "Violet and I . . . well, we overheard several telephone conversations over the weekend." She held up her hand. "I know, I know. We're not supposed to listen in, and mostly we don't. But once Violet heard how much money was involved and connected it with Verna's office, we felt we had to. Now, I'm not sure what to do, whether I should tell Verna or—"

"Of course you should tell me," Verna said indignantly, pushing the closet door open and stepping out. "I need to know, Myra May. I have a *right* to know!"

Myra May jerked around. "You were hiding, Verna!" she said in an accusing tone. "You were listening. You were eavesdropping!"

"Pot calling the kettle black," Verna muttered darkly.

"Verna came here because she wanted to get Mr. Moseley's advice about something that's been bothering her," Lizzy explained in a soothing tone. "When she heard you coming up the stairs, she thought you might be somebody she didn't want to see."

"Then she went into the closet so she could eavesdrop," Myra May said reproachfully.

"Not exactly," Verna replied. She pulled another chair forward and sat down. "But now that I've heard it, I want to know everything you know, Myra May. And I want to know *now.* So spill those beans."

Myra May became sympathetic. "I'm sure you do, Verna, and I don't blame you one bit. If I were in your shoes, I'd want to know it, too. The trouble is, I don't know what you can *do* about it."

"Well, we won't know what we can or can't do until you

tell us what you know," Lizzy pointed out, trying not to sound impatient. "Come on, Myra May. Now's the time. Tell."

And for the next few minutes, Myra May told, while Verna listened in growing disbelief and Lizzy shook her head, clucking her tongue softly.

"Fifteen thousand," Verna said numbly. "I knew things were a mess in the treasurer's office, but I had no idea the mess was that *big*." She swallowed. "Fifteen thousand?" she repeated. "And they're talking about restitution? That's crazy, Myra May! I see the account books every week. The county doesn't have that kind of money. It's barely got enough to make the payroll."

"By restitution," Lizzy said gently, "they probably meant that the thief—whoever it is—will have to give it back."

"And you said that Amos Tombull wanted to get the sheriff to investigate—" Verna began.

"But Earle Scroggins didn't," Myra May broke in. "Which I couldn't figure out." She frowned. "You'd think Mr. Scroggins would want to get to the bottom of it right away, wouldn't you? Maybe he doesn't trust Sheriff Burns to handle the investigation."

"I wouldn't blame him." Lizzy giggled. "Mr. Moseley always says that Sheriff Burns couldn't investigate his way out of a paper bag." She paused, pursing her lips. "Or maybe Mr. Scroggins just doesn't want to look bad. Maybe he thinks he can figure out what happened and take care of it himself without anybody else finding out."

"I think you've put your finger on it, Liz," Verna said grimly. "Remember, he didn't want Charlie Dickens getting wind of it. If people read in the newspaper that fifteen thousand dollars is missing from the treasurer's office, they might blame Mr. Scroggins and refuse to reelect him. And the thing that man wants most in life is to win every election right up to the moment he keels over *dead*." She smacked her fist against the arm of her chair. "Now I have fifteen thousand reasons to get started on my investigation—tonight!"

Myra May gave her a quizzical glance. "Investigation?"

Verna pulled herself up importantly. "I have a copy of the key to the office, Myra May. Tonight, after it gets dark, I'm going to have a look at those account books myself. I made notes while the auditor was doing his work. I'm sure I can figure out where that money went. And you mentioned that the state auditor is sending a report to the office. Maybe I can get a look at that. I might even be able to copy the pertinent information from it."

"Uh-oh," Myra May said softly, ducking her head.

Verna and Liz traded uneasy glances. "Uh-oh?" they asked in unison.

"Yeah." Myra May sighed. "There's one thing I forgot to tell you. When Mr. Scroggins called Coretta Cole to ask her to come in and manage the office while you are taking a furlough, he said he was getting the locks changed. He would be giving her a new key."

"Getting the locks changed!" Verna wailed. "Oh, no! I can't *believe* it! That means I can't get into the office! I won't be able to get a look at the books!"

Lizzy couldn't help breathing a sigh of relief. But she only said, "Oh, that's too bad, Verna."

But Verna wasn't giving up so easily. After a moment, she said, "Both Melba Jean and Ruthie owe me. Maybe I can get one of them to loan me her key so I can copy it."

Myra May shook her head. "That won't work, either, I'm afraid. Mr. Scroggins told Coretta that she's supposed to unlock the office in the morning and lock it up in the evening. He doesn't trust either of the women who work there. He says one of them has been carrying tales to the newspaper." She wrinkled her nose. "*Girls*, he called them," she said disgustedly. "I hate it when men call grown women *girls*."

"Carrying tales to the newspaper?" Lizzy asked. She considered. "I've always wondered how Charlie Dickens managed to find out so much about what was going on in the county treasurer's office. It does seem that he'd have to have an inside source."

Verna bit her lip. "Well, I know I can't get the new key from Coretta. If I even so much as hinted at it, she'd run straight to Mr. Scroggins and tell him. You can't trust that woman any further than you can throw her."

"I have to agree, Verna," Lizzy said ruefully. "Coretta definitely isn't the most reliable person in the world. In my experience, she can't keep a secret for more than about thirty seconds." She qualified her statement. "At least, that's the way she behaved when we were in school together. But that's been a few years ago. Maybe she's changed."

"I don't know about keeping a secret," Myra May replied, looking serious. "But if I were Mr. Scroggins, I wouldn't depend on her to run my office. I don't understand why he's willing to put so much trust in her." She paused, lifting her shoulders and letting them fall. "Well, I guess I've told you everything that Violet and I were able to learn. The question is, what's next?"

There was a silence. Verna looked down at her hands and twisted them in her lap. "I was banking on being able to get into the office and start my own investigation. But now that's impossible." She sighed heavily. "To tell the truth, I don't . . . well, I don't know what to do next."

It was unusual, Lizzy thought, for her friend to say anything like *I don't know*. Verna always had the answer to everything. But what *could* they do?

Myra May had mentioned that the auditor was mailing a report from the state office. "It's too bad we can't get our hands on that auditor's report," she mused. "It might have something we could go on. A hint as to where the money went, for instance. Maybe we could ask Melba Jean or Ruthie to see if they could get it for us?"

"Maybe," Myra May agreed. "As long as they don't tell Mr. Scroggins."

Verna shook her head. "They wouldn't do it," she said gloomily. "They'd be too afraid of getting fired. Anyway, I wouldn't trust them to keep their lips buttoned. Both of them talk too much."

Lizzy picked up a pencil and began to doodle on her desk blotter. What would Mr. Moseley do if he were here right now? She drew a question mark, then drew a circle around it. If Verna were his client, how would he advise her?

Verna straightened her shoulders. "Well, I'll tell you one thing I am *not* going to do," she said determinedly. "I am *not* going home and wait for somebody to knock on my door and accuse me of taking fifteen thousand dollars."

"You mean, you're going to *hide out?*" Myra May asked, puzzled. "But where?"

"I don't have any idea." Verna's shoulders slumped again. "To tell the truth, Myra May, I am totally frazzled. I haven't had any sleep for two nights, worrying about this. I had a plan—a really swell plan for conducting my own investigation—but now I can't get into the office. I don't know what's next."

Lizzy had to admit that she had no idea what Mr. Moseley would advise Verna. But all of a sudden, she knew what *she* should do. She put the pencil down and stood up behind her desk, taking charge of the situation.

"Myra May," she said, "I'm afraid that you and Violet already know way too much about this situation. Too much for your own good, I mean. We don't want anybody else getting into trouble over this. So it's better if you don't know where Verna is going or what she's going to do. That way, if anybody comes around asking where she is, you can tell them you have no idea."

"Wait a minute," Verna put in. "Where am I going? What am I going to do?"

"Good-bye, Myra May," Lizzy said with great firmness. "Thank you for coming to tell us what you know." When Myra May just sat there, looking puzzled, she added sweetly, "It's really time for you to go now, don't you think? You must have a *lot* of work to do this morning."

"Oh, sure," Verna said, suddenly understanding. "Yes, thank you, Myra May. We don't want to keep you any longer. But you will keep us posted, won't you? If you happen to hear anything else, I mean."

Myra May got the hint. Smiling, she stood and pushed her chair back. "Yeah. You're right. I've got to get Euphoria's groceries back to the diner, and then I'm headed over to the Beauty Bower to get a shampoo and a haircut." She bent over and gave Verna a quick kiss on the cheek, then lifted her hand to Lizzy. "Hope it all turns out okay. You two be good now, you hear?"

"We hear," Lizzy said, and grinned. "We'll try."

"No, we won't," Verna put in, and managed a small smile.

A moment later, Myra May could be heard clattering down the stairs. "Well?" Verna asked, as the footsteps faded away. "You obviously have something in mind, Liz. What is it?"

"Hang on." Lizzy was reaching for the telephone. "I've got a couple of calls to make. Then we can figure out what to do."

A few moments later, both conversations concluded, Lizzy put down the telephone and turned back to Verna.

"How would you like to spend a few days in the country?" she asked.

# EIGHT

# Ophelia

When Angelina Biggs telephoned that Monday morning and asked if she could stop in for a few minutes, Ophelia Snow was glad to say yes. Angelina was a dozen years older, so they hadn't been friends in school. But they liked each other, and since Darling was a small town and both were heavily involved in community affairs, they bumped into one another quite often, although never quite as violently as Angelina had bumped into Bessie earlier that morning.

Over the years, Ophelia and Angelina had come to share several common interests. They were good cooks, and they both liked to sew. Ophelia's layer cakes always took the blue ribbon at the Cypress County Fair, and Angelina made up the menus and supervised the kitchen at the Old Alabama Hotel, where her husband was the manager. Angelina had taught Ophelia her three personal secrets for 100 percent successful meringues. ("Let the egg whites warm up to room temperature after you've separated them from the yolks—and be sure there's not a speck of yolk in the whites. When you've beat up a good, strong froth, add a quarter teaspoon of cream of tartar to stabilize it, then add the sugar a tablespoon at a time, not too fast or it'll get syrupy.") Ophelia, an expert seamstress, had shown Angelina how to make her own dress patterns using newspapers for the pattern paper. This was a good thing, for Angelina was large, with big hips and a heavy bust, and Ophelia had noted lately that she was getting even larger. Ready-made dresses didn't fit her, not even the *stout ladies* sizes in the Sears catalogs.

There were other connections. Both Jed Snow and Artis Biggs were on the Darling town council. Jed was in his second term as mayor, and Artis had been mayor previously and would likely get elected mayor again, when Jed's term ran out. The men were good friends, so the two families got together every so often for Sunday dinner or a picnic at the park. And just last year, Ophelia and Jed had thrown an anniversary party when Angelina and Artis celebrated their thirtieth anniversary.

After Ophelia hung up the phone, she went to the kitchen and put on another pot of coffee, then got out the last two of the freshly baked sticky buns they'd had for breakfast—Angelina had a sweet tooth—and put them on a plate. It was wash day and Florabelle, the colored help, was working in the washhouse in the backyard, so Ophelia and Angelina could have a good, quiet talk.

Carrying the coffeepot, cups, and sticky buns on a tray, Ophelia paused in the parlor door. It was a pretty room with crisscross curtains of ivory French marquisette, a piano (Ophelia's daughter Sarah was taking lessons), and a cozy pairing of davenport and chair upholstered in a rich Jacquard velour, with taupe and rose-print cushions. Ophelia was very proud of these two pieces of furniture. She had bought them, and a stylish walnut coffee table, on the easy time-payment plan from the Fall and Winter 1929 Sears catalog, where they were pictured in full color on page 926. Actually, it was the color that had seduced her—that, and the first sentence in the catalog description. *Tastes trained to discriminate will quickly recognize the superlative quality, which gives this splendid set distinction.* Ophelia felt that *tastes trained to discriminate* exactly described her.

But even though Jed had agreed that their splendid new furniture truly did have distinction, Ophelia was painfully aware that the purchase had *not* been a good idea. For one thing, she had lied to Jed about how much it had cost and how much she'd have to pay every month. The davenport had been nearly seventy dollars, the chair thirty, and the coffee table eight, plus an additional eleven dollars in "time payment terms." Ophelia had put twelve fifty down and promised to pay ten dollars a month for eighteen months.

Ten dollars a month! It hadn't seemed like much at the time, but now her insides shriveled with cold fear whenever Ophelia thought of the debt she'd incurred. Jed gave her an allowance and pretty much left the running of the house to her and—like most men—had no idea of the prices of furniture and rugs and curtains. When he'd asked how much the furniture cost, she'd been afraid to tell him the whole truth, especially when she figured out that she'd be paying eighty-five dollars more than the price of the furniture for the privilege of making those eighteen monthly payments! So she had cut the price in half when she told him. He'd thought *that* was too much. Ophelia knew he'd be furious if he ever learned how much she was really paying.

The furniture had arrived six months ago, and she was already two months behind in her payments. No matter how many corners she tried to cut in her household budget, there just wasn't enough money to go around. She had gotten to the point where the only other way she could think of to make those awful monthly payments was to let Florabelle go.

But that was almost unthinkable. Florabelle kept the house spotless and did the laundry and the heavy work and had raised both of Ophelia's children from the time they were born. And anyway, Florabelle needed the money. Her husband was out of work and she was trying to keep her girls in school.

But yesterday, in one of Ophelia's despairing moments, another possibility had occurred to her. It said in the time-payment contract that if she didn't send the money, Sears would come and repossess the furniture, as long as it was in good condition. (They didn't say what would happen if it wasn't.) Well, she thought, maybe that was the smart thing to do. Stop making the payments altogether, and eventually Sears would wise up and come and get the furniture. Since the family hardly spent any time at all in the parlor, everything looked like new, so there was no question about Sears taking it back. Or maybe they would have second thoughts about sending a truck all the way from Mobile just to pick up three measly pieces of used furniture. Maybe they would forget about the payments and decide to just let her keep everything.

Yesterday, she had pushed this idea to the back of her mind, but now here it was again, presenting itself as an option that would not only relieve her of a mountain of worry but allow her to face her husband with a clear conscience. Now, as she looked around the room, Ophelia decided that—once the Sears suite was gone—she could salvage the wicker settee that was in Mother Snow's attic and make new cushions for it, and repaint the old rocking chair out in the shed. She hated the thought, since regardless of its cost and all the problems it posed, the living room furniture was beautiful, much nicer than that of any of her friends (except for Mrs. George E. Pickett Johnson, whose husband owned the Darling Savings and Trust Bank, and Mildred Kilgore, who was married to the owner of Kilgore Motors and lived near the ninth green of the Cypress County Club golf course). Since Jed was the mayor of Darling and owned the only feed store in town, Ophelia had felt that, by rights, she ought to have a very nice parlor where she could entertain her friends.

She sighed. But if they couldn't afford it, well, they couldn't, that was all. Yes, letting Sears take the furniture back was the right thing to do. And as she set the tray down on the dear little walnut coffee table and moved around the room, straightening things and flicking off a few specks of dust, she felt a sense of relief at having come up with a solution she could live with. Some of her natural buoyant optimism began to return. Now, all she had to do was keep the furniture clean until Sears came to get it. Of course, she'd have to come up with some sort of explanation for Jed—and her friends, too, who would wonder what had happened. But she'd worry about that later. She was sure she could think of something. And anyway, Jed was so distracted these days, he might not even notice the furniture was gone.

By the time Angelina Biggs knocked at the door, everything was ready. But when Ophelia opened the door to greet her guest, she was appalled. Angelina's usually well-kept blond hair was disheveled, her face was mottled with ugly red blotches, and she was fighting back tears. She was wearing a bright green rayon dress that seemed to magnify her considerable size, and she must have doused herself in a quart of Emeraude. The scent enveloped her in a cloying cloud.

"Why, what's wrong, Angelina?" Ophelia cried, and pulled her into the house. "Come in, dear, and tell me all about it!" She put an arm around the woman's heaving shoulders and led her into the parlor. "Sit down and have a cup of coffee and a sticky bun. That'll make you feel better."

Angelina gulped, sat, sipped, and nibbled, and in a few moments, was sufficiently restored so that she could talk.

"I'm sorry, Ophelia," she choked out. "I really shouldn't . . . It's too much to expect you to—"

"Yes, you really should," Ophelia broke in, bracing herself against a wave of Emeraude. "And, no, it isn't too much. Please tell me what's wrong. All of it. The whole thing."

They were sitting side by side on the davenport now, and she patted Angelina's arm, sympathetic, but by now deeply curious. Was there some sort of health problem? A family difficulty? Problems at the hotel? Money? Likely money. It seemed that everybody had money troubles these days.

"Well, if you insist." Angelina put down her cup and reached into her handbag for a cigarette. "It's Artis, Ophelia. He—" Her face twisted. "He's having an affair."

Ophelia stared at her, taken completely aback. An affair? Artis Biggs? Of course, he was very good-looking—one of the best-looking men in Darling, with a ready smile and dark hair graying at the temples. He was trim, too, unlike Angelina, who had let herself gain far too much weight. To give her credit, though, Angelina was trying to lose. She had recently confided to Ophelia that she was taking Dr. Baxter's diet pills, a much-touted way to trim off the pounds. She had read about the pills in one of the beauty magazines she subscribed to. She had started smoking, as well—a surefire aid for weight loss, according to the cigarette advertisements. Lucky Strike, for instance. "Reach for a Lucky instead of a sweet."

As Ophelia got up to fetch an ashtray, she remembered hearing that Angelina and Artis had married young, when Angelina was right out of high school. She had been Darling's Cotton Queen in her senior year and everybody thought she was the most beautiful thing on God's green earth. While an engagement had not been formally announced, it was considered a sure thing that she would marry Charlie Dickens as soon as he finished up at Alabama Polytechnic and had the money to support a wife. But then Angelina had been smitten with Artis and married him and started having babies right away. And Charlie had finished at Poly and gone off to New York and then to the army.

And Artis must be—why, he must be fifty now, if he was a day, Ophelia thought, with some consternation. A *fifty-year-old* man, having an affair? She'd never heard of such a thing. And with whom? Who was the lady? How were they managing to carry it off? Darling was such a small town—weren't they afraid of getting caught?

But Ophelia had more tact (and better sense) than to ask these nosy questions. Instead, she said, "Are you *sure*, Angelina? Are you very sure?"

It was a question that came straight from the heart, because she herself, just last year, had suspected Jed of having an affair with his cousin Ralph's wife, Lucy. As it turned out, there had been nothing to the story that had gone around town, spread by that awful Mrs. Adcock, their busybody neighbor. Ophelia had been sorry ever since for failing to trust her husband, and sorry that she had thought badly of Lucy, who was really a very sweet young woman. Thank heavens she had held her tongue until she learned the truth. She had never had to confess her foolishness to Jed, and she and Lucy had become the best of friends. But she still cringed when she thought of the terrible pain she would have inflicted if she had made those groundless accusations.

Angelina had no such qualms, apparently. "Oh, I'm sure, all right," she said bitterly, blowing out a puff of blue cigarette smoke. "They've tried to keep it secret, but they can't fool me." She lowered her voice and bent toward Ophelia. "I've seen the evidence with my own eyes, Ophelia. With my very own eyes."

"The . . . evidence?" Ophelia faltered, drawing back a little. Something about Angelina's tone frightened her. It sounded sly, almost as if she were taking a kind of perverse pleasure in what she had learned.

Angelina looked straight at her. "The sheets," she whispered hoarsely.

Ophelia's hand flew to her mouth. "Oh, dear," she whispered. "Oh, gracious me!" She could feel her cheeks coloring. "I didn't think . . . I mean, I can't imagine—"

"I know," Angelina said with a kind of grim satisfaction. "I couldn't imagine it either, Ophelia. But then I found out. They're using different rooms every time they meet. Their little love nests." Her voice became acid. "They get together at least once a week, although I've never been quite quick enough to catch them at it."

"Do you know who she is?" Ophelia asked, then turned away, adding plaintively, "No, don't tell me, Angelina. Please. I don't want to know. Really."

It was true. She didn't want to know. In fact, Ophelia (who always tried to look on the bright side of things, no matter how much effort it took) did not want to hear another word of this dirty, sordid tale. She would never be able to look Artis Biggs in the face without imagining him cheating on his wife of thirty-something years. And what would she say to Jed the next time he suggested that they invite Artis and Angelina over for Sunday dinner? *I'm sorry, dear, but I refuse to have that awful man in my house. He has been fooling around with another woman. He has committed the sin of—*

Ophelia shuddered. She couldn't bring herself to even think the word. It was just too horrible.

Angelina tapped her cigarette on the ashtray. "I would be glad to tell you who she is, Ophelia," she said regretfully, "but I just don't know. I've only seen him, not her. Creeping out of the room, I mean. Out of the room and down the back stairs." There was, Ophelia thought, an odd glint in Angelina's eyes. "I hid in the second-floor alcove and watched.

Hoped I'd see her, but no such luck." She snorted. "Only saw him, the *sneak*."

"You . . . spied?" Ophelia asked weakly. In the most dreadful depths of her suspicions of Jed, she had never seriously considered spying on him. She wouldn't have *dared*. It would have been horribly embarrassing if she had actually caught him.

"Of course I've spied," Angelina said reasonably, smoke curling out of her nostrils. "How else am I going to catch them?" Without pausing for breath, she said, "But there's more, Ophelia. The real reason I'm so upset right now is that Charlie Dickens tried to kiss me!"

"Kiss you?"

Ophelia's mouth dropped open. If she had been surprised to learn about Artis' marital transgressions, she was utterly astounded by this revelation. She knew Charlie Dickens. He covered most of the town's political and social events for the *Dispatch* and was always lurking unobtrusively with his notebook and pencil. In all situations, Charlie was unfailingly a gentleman. He might be a little cynical and condescending sometimes—he was a worldly man who had traveled a lot and saw things from a big-city point of view—and he and Jed definitely didn't see eye to eye on politics. But she couldn't imagine him attempting to kiss Angelina Biggs. In fact, she had a hard time imagining that he would find her at all attractive, given her . . . well, her increasing size.

Angelina's eyes narrowed. "You find that surprising?" Her voice was thin. "I suppose you didn't know that we were sweethearts back in high school. Did you?"

"Well, yes," Ophelia said. "Yes, of course." Everyone knew that.

"Then why are you surprised? He was madly in love with me. I suppose he still is, poor man, even though I went and married Artis instead of him. But that's no way to treat a lady. Kissing her. Attempting to *paw* her."

She popped the last bite of sticky bun into her mouth while Ophelia tried to think of something else to say. But before she could, Angelina went on, speaking with her mouth full.

"I see that you haven't eaten that second bun, Ophelia. They're awfully good. Mind if I have yours? And I think I'll just help myself to another cup of coffee. Pardon my fingers."

Without waiting for Ophelia to say yea or nay, Angelina put down her cigarette and plopped the bun on her plate. Then she picked up her cup, leaned over, and reached for the coffeepot on the tray.

What happened next would live in Ophelia's memory like a horrible nightmare. For years afterward, she would replay the whole awful scene in her mind, over and over, as if it were a loop of movie film endlessly repeating itself, every lurid detail seared into her mind like a hot brand, clear and unforgettable.

Angelina leaning forward, picking up the coffeepot with her right hand and pouring coffee into the cup she held with her left hand. Angelina splashing hot coffee onto her pale, plump wrist and her bright green rayon dress, her pretty mouth forming a perfectly round O of shock and surprise. Angelina *dropping* the full cup of coffee, right onto the taupe-colored seat cushion of Ophelia's beautiful Jacquard velour davenport.

It was a half hour later. Angelina had gone, still bleating her apologies for the large, dark stain she had left on Ophelia's beautiful new sofa. Ophelia had scurried to fetch towels to sop up the coffee, but she might as well have saved her efforts, for the thirsty velour soaked up the hot liquid like a sponge and the stain spread and spread and kept on spreading, until the entire taupe-colored cushion was the color of coffee. All she could do was stare at it in horror, fighting the hot, despairing tears. Sears wouldn't take the furniture back, because it wasn't in good condition. It was as plain as the nose on your face— even plainer—that the davenport was ruined. And the coffee table, too, for while they were trying to clean up the coffee, Angelina's cigarette had fallen out of the ashtray and burned an ugly scar into the beautiful walnut top.

Ophelia spent the next little while alternately scrubbing the cushion and the burn stain (which certainly didn't serve any good purpose and probably only made things worse) and sobbing (which didn't help anything, either). But her tears did bring her to a couple of important conclusions. She was going to have to tell Jed the truth. And she was going to have to get a job. Of course, everybody said how hard it was to find work these days, but she could type sixty words a minute without any mistakes and spell *very* well, and while her high-school shorthand was pretty rusty, she was sure with a little practice she could take dictation. Surely there was someplace in town, the bank maybe, or one of the offices in the court-house, that could use a good typist. Unfortunately, she'd never had a job because she and Jed got married right out of high school. Did you really *have* to have references? How did you go about finding a job if you'd never had one before?

She was still kneeling on the floor with a rag in her hand, puzzling over these questions, when the telephone on the hallway table rang—a long, imperative ring, just one, and then one again, because the Snows had a private telephone line. In her budgetary desperation, Ophelia had proposed that they go back to the party line (which would save a whole dollar every month), but Jed refused. As the mayor, he often talked about town business on the phone and didn't want anybody listening in.

Swiping her nose with the back of her hand, Ophelia picked up the receiver. Liz Lacy was on the other end, and she had a very odd request.

"I've just talked to Lucy Murphy," she said. "She's agreed to put Verna up in her spare room for a few days. I wonder if you'd be willing to drive Verna and her dog out there. This morning, if you can manage it."

"Verna?" Ophelia asked, frowning. "Why in the world would she want to stay out at Lucy's?"

Lucy (who was also a Dahlia) lived four miles outside of town. She had finally prevailed on her husband Ralph (Jed's cousin) to get electricity and the telephone installed in their house out there. She was still working on Ralph to put in an electric water pump and a toilet.

"And what about Verna's job?" she went on. "How will she get to work every day? It's pretty far to walk, and Lucy doesn't have a car. Why—"

"I'm sorry, Ophelia," Liz cut in firmly, "but I can't answer your questions—at least, not now. All I can tell you is that it is really, *really* important for Verna to go out of town for a few days. Not too far out of town, though. Lucy's place is just right, especially with Ralph gone this week." Lucy's husband worked on the railroad and was away a lot of the time. His absence was one of the things that had given rise to the gossip about Jed and Lucy. "It's also important that nobody know about this," Liz added, "so I have to ask you to keep it under your hat. Will you drive her out there?"

Ophelia was taken aback by the request, but both Liz and Verna were very good friends—and Dahlias, to boot. "Yes, of course I will," she replied.

"Oh, thank you! Verna's going home right now to pack a few things. If you can pick her and Clyde up at her house in fifteen minutes, that would be swell." Liz's voice became urgent. "And please, Ophelia. Don't tell a soul about this, even Jed." She paused, as if she were thinking. "Especially not Jed."

"I won't." But as she hung up, Ophelia was frowning. Especially not Jed? What was going on? What was it all about?

She turned just then, catching sight of the coffee-colored cushion, and her stomach turned over. Whatever Verna's trouble was, it paled in comparison to her own. Somehow or another, she was going to have to find a job so she could pay for the furniture. And she was going to have to do it right away. Today, if possible. Tomorrow at the latest.

But where? And *how*?

# NINE

# Beulah

As the bell over the door tinkled, Beulah Trivette looked up from the head of dark hair she was cutting. This head happened to belong to Alice Ann Walker, cashier at the Darling Savings and Trust, who took an early lunch hour once a month and came over for a quick trim. Beulah smiled at Myra May, who had just opened the back door and come into the Beauty Bower.

"Good mornin', hon," she chirped. "How's every little thing at the diner? You doin' okay?"

"It's getting hot out there," Myra May said, loosening the collar of her plaid blouse. "And it's only April. Hello, Beulah, Alice Ann. I know I'm a little early, but I just finished grocery shopping and thought I'd come on."

"Mornin', Myra May," Alice Ann said. "It's not just hot, but humid, too. I can sure tell it in my hair. It's so fine, when the weather's soggy, all the spring come out of the curl. I go out to work in the garden and come back looking like something the cat dragged in." Alice Ann was a Dahlia, like

Beulah and Myra May. Mostly, she grew vegetables to feed the Walker family, but she also had quite a few roses, pass-along plants she had collected from the Dahlias' plant swaps.

"It's fine, all right." Beulah, a buxom blonde with a pretty face and a sweet smile, regarded Alice Ann's hair with a critical look. "I could try to sell you some of that expensive curling lotion I've got over there on the shelf, but—"

"Sorry, Beulah," Alice Ann interrupted with a sigh. "I'm doin' real good to afford to get my hair cut once a month. I couldn't buy any of that expensive stuff, even if it made me look like Greta Garbo."

"Gif me a vhisky," Myra May said, in a husky imitation of Garbo's voice. "Ginger ale on the side, and don't be stingy, baby."

It was the famous first line of Garbo's most recent movie, *Anna Christie*, with Charles Bickford. Mr. Greer, who owned the Palace Theater, had made a special effort to get the movie, which was a talkie. The whole town had turned out for the grand occasion. Darling was still buzzing about it, and everybody was trying to find an excuse to use Garbo's line.

"You sound just like Garbo, Myra May." Beulah laughed, a generous, full-throated laugh that made people naturally smile when they heard it. "And you hold your horses, Alice Ann. What I was about to tell you was that you can make your own settin' lotion that's near 'bout as good and a durn sight cheaper than that expensive stuff in the fancy bottle. All you do is stir up a teaspoonful of honey in a half cup of warm water and add a tablespoon of lemon juice and maybe a drop or two of your favorite perfume. You can spray it on or just dab it on your pin curls when you set your hair at night. Works real fine."

"Oh, that's swell, Beulah," Alice Ann said eagerly. "Honey is one thing I got plenty of these days. Arnold keeps two hives out behind the barn. We don't hardly have to buy sugar. And we're thinkin' we might could have some honey to sell come fall." Alice Ann's husband had lost his leg in a railroad accident. The railroad said it was his fault (which it wasn't) and wouldn't pay him any money—wouldn't even help with the doctor bills. He whittled wooden whirligigs and other garden art objects to bring in some extra cash.

"Honey and lemon juice," Myra May said thoughtfully. "Sounds like something Violet would like to know about." She looked around. "Bettina's not here today?" Bettina was Beulah's helper.

"She had to run to the Mercantile to pick up some material for the new smocks she's sewin' up for us," Beulah said, turning back to Alice Ann's hair. "She'll be back in a jiffy to shampoo you. Or if she isn't, I'll do you myself when I'm done cuttin' Alice Ann. Sit down and have a cup of coffee while you're waitin', sweetie. Oh, and Miz Adcock brought some cupcakes. She was Bettina's nine thirty, so there's still plenty left."

Beulah liked it when her clients (she never thought of them as customers) brought something for their friends to nibble on while she and Bettina made them beautiful. She herself always provided a pot of coffee, and in the summer, there was iced tea in the icebox. It made the day seem more like a pleasant tea party with friends than a long day of standing on her feet behind the hair-cutting chair or bent over the shampoo sink.

Beulah's Beauty Bower, on Dauphin Street, was one of the two places where every Darling woman went to get beautiful. The other was Conrad's Curling Corner, on the north side of town. The Dahlias always preferred the Bower, of course, because it was owned and managed by one of their own, and because everybody agreed that Beulah beat Julia Conrad hands down when it came to style and creativity. Beulah was a serious artist of hair.

Beulah had been raised by her single mother on the wrong side of the railroad spur that connected Darling to the Louisville & Nashville Railroad, just outside of Monroeville. Her innate talent for hair made itself known as early as high school, where she was the first to bob hers, creating a fad for bobbed hair that swept like a spring tornado through the school and caused all the Darling mothers to pull theirs out in sheer agony at the sight of all those bobs.

On the day after graduation, fired with an artist's ambition, Beulah filled a brown cardboard suitcase with all the clothes she had, climbed on the Greyhound bus, and rode to Montgomery to pursue her dream. She got a job as a waitress to make ends meet and signed up for the full course at the Montgomery College of Cosmetology, where she learned all she needed to know "to make the ordinary woman pretty and the pretty woman beautiful," as the college proclaimed in its advertisements. Beulah wielded a mean marcel iron, made pin curls and finger waves with an astonishing flair, and finished first in a final exam that covered everything from the basics of beauty to the safe use of toxic chemicals.

Beulah graduated at the top of her class and earned the MCC's first-class certificate of achievement. Flushed with success, she got back on the Greyhound and rode home to Darling, determined to introduce all the women in town to the fine art of beauty, whatever their ages and social station and whether they knew they needed it or not.

Beulah was petite, pretty, blond, and significantly endowed, and many Darling young men (especially the bunch that hung out at the Watering Hole on Saturday nights) were wild to sample her considerable charms. But Beulah possessed an admirable brain and a generous helping of self-discipline as well as beauty and ambition. Instead of letting herself go gaga over one of the town rakes and rascals, she married Hank Trivette, the son of the pastor of the Four

Corners Methodist Church, a sedate young fellow who came from the *right* side of the spur tracks. Hank loved Beulah not only for her outstanding physical attributes, but for her unaffected compassion and her generous good humor. Beulah (who had a practical soul hidden beneath those other endowments) loved Hank for his good common sense, his respectability, and his handy way with tools. He was marrying beauty and sweet spirit. She was marrying up.

Beulah and Hank had two children, Hank Jr. and Spoonie. After Hank was born, they bought a nice frame house on the best end of Dauphin Street, big enough for their growing family and for Beulah's business. Hank enclosed the screened porch across the back for the beauty shop, repaired the back steps so the ladies wouldn't turn an ankle, wired the place for electricity, and installed shampoo sinks and hair-cutting chairs and big wall mirrors. Beulah (who was as talented with a paintbrush as she was with a pair of scissors and a comb) wallpapered the walls of the Bower with her favorite fat pink roses, painted the wainscoting pink, and hung her Montgomery College of Cosmetology certificate of achievement beside the door, where everybody could see it when they came in. Then she painted the words *Beulah's Beauty Bower* on a white wooden sign and decorated it with painted flowers. Hank hung the sign out front, where anyone walking or driving down Dauphin Street would be sure to see it. She was open for business.

The Bower was so attractive and Beulah was such a skilled beautician that every single customer walked out the door feeling much more beautiful than when she walked in. So she naturally made a second appointment and then a third and told all her friends that the Bower was the very best beauty parlor in town. A few months later, business was so good that Beulah hired Bettina Higgens, not the prettiest flower in the garden (as Bettina herself put it) but a willing worker who quickly came to share Beulah's commitment to beautifying Darling, one lovely lady at a time.

But of course, people didn't come to the Bower just to get pretty. They came to talk about what was on their mind, to brag about a new grandchild or to complain about a new daughter-in-law, and to discuss what was going on with their neighbors. It was right up there with the party line as the best way to get an earful of the latest Darling news.

As Myra May poured herself a cup of coffee and sat down to wait for Bettina, Beulah said to Alice Ann, "Alice Ann, honey, you got something on your mind? You're awfully quiet this morning. Everything all right out at your house? Arnold ain't sick again, is he?"

It was a kind and caring question, not asked out of nosiness or prying. Beulah's heart was as large and soft as her other endowments and she was truly concerned about her clients' welfare—and her own, as well, but in a roundabout way. In her philosophy, beauty really was more than skin deep, and if something nasty and ugly was nagging at you, eating away at your insides like a mean old weevil munching the insides of a cotton boll, you could never be truly beautiful. Your beautician would fail. And Beulah hated to fail.

Alice Ann sighed. "No, Arnold isn't sick, and, yes, everything's all right at home, more or less." She lifted her head and said, to both of them, "Is something going on with Verna Tidwell? I'm worried about her."

"Verna?" Beulah asked, surprised. "I don't believe I've heard a thing about her recently." She *click-clack*ed her scissors. "In fact, I haven't seen her outside of our Dahlia meetings in a while. Seems like she's been working long hours over at the courthouse." She leaned forward, lifted her comb and scissors, and snipped a lock over Alice Ann's right ear. "Her job has just about doubled, you know. Mr. Scroggins is now the county treasurer, as well as probate clerk."

"I know," Alice Ann said seriously. "When Mr. DeYancy was treasurer, he put some of the county's money in our bank. I've seen the accounts—several of them, actually. But not *all* the money," she added. "One of the tellers told me that a lot of it's over in Monroeville, in a couple of the banks over there. I've never figured that out. Seems to me it all ought to be in one place so people could keep better track of it."

Myra May had been silent for a moment, listening to this. Now, she took a sip of coffee. "So how come you're worried about Verna, Alice Ann?"

Her tone was casual, but Beulah picked up on something— some sort of tension or apprehension, something—beneath it. She glanced quickly over her shoulder at Myra May, who always knew what was going on in Darling. She worked the switchboard and waited tables and the counter at the diner, which gave her the chance to hear all kinds of things. What she missed, her friend Violet was bound to pick up.

Myra May returned Beulah's inquisitive glance, her expression carefully blank. Not even her eyebrow twitched.

Now Beulah was sure of it. Something was going on. "Yes, Alice Ann," she said, echoing Myra May's question. "How come you're worried about Verna?"

Alice Ann met Beulah's eyes in the mirror. She hesitated, frowning, and Beulah knew that she was debating whether and how much she could tell without breaking one of the bank's standard rules. "Well, because of something that happened on Friday. Of course, I'm not supposed to talk about what goes on at the bank, and I'm definitely not supposed to criticize. But . . ."

She took a breath and her voice became indignant. "But if I were Verna, I'd want to know what they did. And speaking personally, I don't think it's right for somebody at the bank, even if he is the president, to go poking around in people's bank accounts. That's private."

Beulah knew that Alice Ann was talking out of her own bitter personal experience. Not long ago, she had been suspected—wrongly, of course—of taking money from the bank. She must be remembering what had happened and how it felt.

"If this has got something to do with our Verna, we should hear it," Beulah said decidedly. "She's a Dahlia." She bent over and whispered into Alice Ann's ear. "When we're talkin' about another Dahlia and wantin' to help her, it ain't gossip, and that's the good Lord's truth." Beulah never encouraged talk that was mean and hurtful. But when one of her friends was in trouble, she definitely wanted to know.

Myra May obviously felt the same way. "Please, Alice Ann," she said quietly. "If Verna has a problem, we might be able to help."

"Well, maybe just this once," Alice Ann said, pretending reluctance, and Beulah stepped back, suppressing a smile. Alice Ann had been primed to tell and hoping that somebody would give her a little nudge. "It's got to do with some money that turned up in Verna's savings account not long ago. I don't feel right telling you how much, but it was a tidy little sum. I know because I'm the one that wrote in the numbers." Her laugh was brittle. "And I don't mind telling you that I'd be tickled pink if somebody put that amount of money into my bank account. I'd pay off all our bills and get Arnold fitted for an artificial leg at the hospital down in Mobile. Oh, and a roof on the house. And a new water well. I'd still have plenty left over, too."

"Well, hooray for Verna," Beulah said enthusiastically, and flicked the comb down the back of Alice Ann's head, looking for ends she needed to snip off. She was thinking that Verna's financial windfall, whatever its source, must have been fairly substantial. It cost a bundle to dig a well and put on a roof—not to mention buy a new leg. "So she's got some extra cash. Doesn't sound like much of a problem to me."

Myra May put down her coffee cup, got up from her chair, and came to stand behind Beulah, where she could see Alice Ann's face in the mirror. Beulah felt her tautness, as if Myra May were a wound-up watch spring about to let loose and let fly.

"Yes," Myra May said, trying to sound casual. "What's the problem, Alice Ann?"

Alice Ann fidgeted under her pink cover-up cape. "Well, the problem is that Mr. Scroggins—Verna's boss—came in on Friday and asked to see Mr. Johnson. They went into Mr. Johnson's office and closed the door. A little while later, Mr. Johnson came out and asked me to get out the records of Verna's account. He looked them over and made some notes and took them back to his office, where Mr. Scroggins was waiting. I'm sure Mr. Johnson must have showed him the notes."

Beulah was incensed. "What a lot of nerve!" she exclaimed hotly. "Bank accounts are supposed to be private! I don't want Mr. Johnson makin' notes about how much money I've got in the bank and givin' the information to other folks. If he can do it to Verna, he can do it to anybody. To me or—" Indignantly, she pointed her rattail comb at Myra May. "Or you, Myra May. Or Violet or Liz or anybody! What gives that jerk—pardon my French—the right to go pokin' around in people's personal business?"

"That bothered me, too, Beulah," Alice Ann confessed. "All weekend long, I kept thinking how wrong it was, what Mr. Johnson had done. Mr. Scroggins, too. I kept wondering whether I should phone up Verna and let her know about it. But Arnold, he didn't think I should rock the boat. If Mr. Johnson found out, I could lose my job." She bit her lip. "But after what happened this morning, I am really sorry I didn't."

"Why?" Myra May's voice was still casual, but Beulah heard that note of deep unease. "I mean, what happened this morning to make you sorry, Alice Ann?"

Alice Ann gulped. "What happened was that Mr. Scroggins showed up again, just before I came over here." She looked up and her eyes met Beulah's and Myra May's in the mirror. "And this time, he had the sheriff with him. They both went into Mr. Johnson's office."

"The sheriff!" Beulah and Myra May exclaimed in alarmed unison.

Alice Ann nodded. "And then Mr. Johnson came out and got the book with Verna's account in it. This time, he didn't bother taking any notes. He just carried that book back into the office with him. A little while later, maybe ten or fifteen minutes, Mr. Scroggins and Sheriff Burns left. That's all I know." She took a deep breath. "Oh, I do wish I hadn't listened to Arnold! If I had given Verna a word of warning, she might . . . Well, maybe she could figure out what to do. And whatever they're thinking about her and that money, I know they must be wrong."

"Oh, dear goodness," Beulah said, truly distressed. "I wonder what in this blessed world is goin' on. What do you suppose, Myra May? What can it mean?"

But Myra May was striding toward the door. Over her shoulder, she said, "Beulah, I'll have to reschedule my appointment. Maybe tomorrow—I'll phone you up. Okay? Oh, and tell Bettina I'm sorry I missed her, will you?"

"Sure thing," Beulah said, but Myra May was already flying out the door and down the back steps, the screen door banging shut behind her.

"My goodness," Alice Ann said weakly, and didn't say another word until Beulah brushed the hair from the back of her neck and whipped the cape off her. Then she took two quarters out of her purse and handed them to Beulah.

"Thank you, Beulah," she said. And then, "I wish . . . I just wish—" She looked away. She didn't finish her sentence.

"I know," Beulah said sympathetically. "But you did the

best you knew how, Alice Ann. And thank you for telling us about Verna's situation. I know it wasn't easy. But us Dahlias have to stand together. We're all we've got."

Mutely, Alice Ann threw her arms around Beulah and they gave each other a long, hard hug.

A little while later, Beulah was sweeping Alice Ann's hair off the floor. Bettina, a tall, gangly young woman in a red print dress, had come in with three yards of pretty rose pink print cotton from the Mercantile and was happily chattering about the smocks she was going to make. But Beulah was only half listening. She was thinking about what Alice Ann had told them and wondering what Myra May knew about the situation. She obviously knew *something*. What was it?

Bettina looked up at the clock. "Eleven," she said, folding the cotton and putting it back into the bag. "I wonder where Miz Biggs is. She's almost never late." Angelina Biggs had a standing appointment for a shampoo and set on Mondays at eleven.

As if on cue, the bell tinkled, the door opened, and Mrs. Biggs burst in. Her hat was askew, there was a fresh coffee stain on the skirt of her green rayon dress, and her face was red and blotchy, as if she'd been hurrying—not a good idea in this heat, especially when you were as oversized as Mrs. Biggs, who found it hard to fit comfortably into the chair at the shampoo sink without parts of her hanging out.

Beulah was almost never judgmental when it came to beauty or the lack of it. She was confident that every woman had in her what it took to be truly beautiful. All a woman had to do was get shined up—with a little expert help, of course. But Beulah had seen photographs of Mrs. Biggs when she was young and gorgeous, with a full head of luxuriant blond hair and a curvaceous shape. She couldn't help thinking that under all that regrettable stoutness was a perfect figure, just dying to come out and be admired by all. In fact, she had heard that Mrs. Biggs was trying to reduce by taking some of Dr. W. W. Baxter's famous patent-medicine diet pills—the extra-strong ones. Beulah sincerely hoped that the pills would turn the trick. But from what she had seen on Mrs. Biggs' plate at the last church social (the Biggses were members of Hank's father's congregation), it wasn't likely. The lady had tucked into several helpings of Granny Mitchell's potato salad, four pieces of Jed Snow's mother's fried chicken, three big spoonfuls of Mrs. Vaughn's green beans and fatback, and two generous slices of Doris Wedford's pecan pie, topped with Aunt Hetty Little's pecan praline ice cream. Beulah had the feeling that even Dr. Baxter's diet pills—extra-strong or not—were no match for Mrs. Biggs' very healthy appetite.

But she betrayed none of this when she said cheerfully, "Good mornin', Miz Biggs. And how are you on this beautiful Monday mornin'?"

"Oh, Beulah," Mrs. Biggs said, and gulped back a sob. "I tell you, I am so discombobulated, I just about don't know whether I'm up or down or inside out!"

"Bettina," Beulah said, divining that Mrs. Biggs had something on her mind, "why don't you go in the back room and fold the towels while I do Miz Biggs?" Bettina, understanding the situation, picked up a basket of towels and vanished.

Beulah went to the shampoo sink. "Miz Biggs, you just come over here and sit yourself down in this chair and put your feet up on this stool. A nice shampoo with plenty of hot water is always balm to the soul."

A few minutes later, Mrs. Biggs, draped in a pink cover-up cape, was lying in the chair, face up. Her eyes were closed, her toes were turned up, and her head was in the shampoo sink. Beulah was beginning the second lather, humming happily to herself. Next to cutting hair, she loved to wash it, pushing her fingertips firmly into the scalp, scrubbing and massaging and rinsing and scrubbing and rinsing again. For her, it was joy, pure joy, and she prided herself that her clients loved it, too. They always smiled blissfully and, when she was finished, told her that she was the best shampoo artist they had ever met, which for Beulah was every bit as good as the money she got paid for a job well done.

Mrs. Biggs, however, wasn't smiling, blissfully or otherwise, and the frown furrows between her eyes were deep as ruts on a muddy road. Beulah didn't like the look of that. Frown furrows on a lady's face were a sign that something unhappy was going on inside the lady's head and heart— something that might keep her from becoming as beautiful as possible.

As the shampoo bubbles frothed like meringue through her fingers, Beulah used her standard question to get Mrs. Biggs' mind off whatever was making her unhappy. "How's every little thing over at your place? Mr. Biggs doin' okay, is he?"

Mrs. Biggs opened her eyes, then closed them again. "Everything is just hateful, Beulah." Her voice became bitter. "Mr. Biggs is havin' himself an affair. He won't sleep with me, but he'll sleep with *her*."

Beulah's jaw dropped. Clients sometimes said unexpected things, especially when they were flat on their backs with their eyes shut and their heads in the shampoo sink, which tended to reduce their inhibitions and divorce them from their everyday realities. But in all the years she had been asking her *how's every little thing* question, nobody had ever answered it quite that way. She was awfully glad she had sent Bettina to the back room to fold the towels and that there was nobody else in the shop to hear what she'd just heard.

Especially because she didn't believe it. Artis Biggs had finished sowing his crop of wild oats before he got to be twenty-one. Now fifty-something, he was a man of upstanding reputation, a deacon in the Four Corners congregation, a former mayor, and the manager of Darling's best hotel. If this story got out, and whether there was anything to it or not, the scandal was going to rock Darling to its very foundations—not to mention what it would do to Four Corners. Hank's father, the Reverend Dr. Trivette, would be shattered. He put his faith in all his deacons.

What's more, Beulah felt strongly that Mrs. Biggs shouldn't go around saying such things, right or wrong or somewhere in the middle. What went on between a woman and a man in their bedroom should be held sacred and not told to anybody, not even to the woman's beautician in the privacy of the shampoo sink at the Beauty Bower. And if Mrs. Biggs was telling this story here, she could be telling it anywhere. Everywhere, for that matter, and to everyone. To Mrs. Hancock at the grocery, or over at Mann's Mercantile, or (heaven help her) to Mrs. Adcock, Darling's most notorious gossip.

"I am downright sorry to hear that," Beulah managed. "I hope it turns out for the best." She changed the subject hurriedly, saying the first thing she could think of. "Bettina just got back from the Mercantile a bit ago. You should see what she bought—three yards of the prettiest pink cotton you'd ever hope to see. She's going to make new smocks for us, with *The Beauty Bower* embroidered across the front in old-timey letters. When we get through with your shampoo, I'll have her show it to you."

But Mrs. Biggs was not to be distracted by pink smocks or old-timey letters. "He'll regret this," she cried fiercely, her eyes squeezed shut now, her pudgy fingers clutching the arms of the shampoo chair like swollen claws. "Soon as I catch them. They'll *both* regret it!"

Beulah pulled in her breath, feeling unsure and helpless in

the face of such wrath. "Well," she ventured, "maybe it's not what you think. Appearances can be deceiving sometimes. People don't always—"

"Not *this* time!" Mrs. Biggs cried, smacking the flats of her palms on the arms of the chair. "I have seen him with my very own eyes, Beulah, coming out of those rooms. They do it on the second floor, you know. Every chance they get. Every morning."

"Oh," said Beulah, and began to hurry with the rinse. Maybe a little splash of cold water would cool Mrs. Biggs down and make her think twice about what she was saying. But the lady was so heated that even a little rivulet of cold water dripped on her forehead didn't dampen her fires.

"Oh, yes," Mrs. Biggs said fiercely, clenching her fists. "Oh, yes, Beulah, oh, yes, yes, yes. The awful truth is that men are lecherous and treacherous by their very natures. Their *natures*, mind you, deep down in the depths of their souls! And not just Mr. Biggs, either. Why, do you know, when I went into the *Dispatch* office this morning to leave an advertisement for the hotel menu, Mr. Dickens tried to kiss me!"

"*Kiss* you?"

Hastily, Beulah squeezed the water out of Mrs. Biggs' hair. She was seized by an unaccountable and nearly irresistible urge to giggle. Charlie Dickens was a confirmed bachelor who never displayed any interest in women—although Beulah had heard that he might have his eye on Fannie Champaign, who owned the hat shop on the square. And of course, she knew that Mr. Dickens and Mrs. Biggs had been high school sweethearts. But that was decades (and eighty or ninety pounds) ago.

"Yes, kiss me!" Mrs. Biggs kicked her heels against the stool. "Why, the man was so passionate, he nearly knocked me off my feet. I swear, Beulah, it was all I could do to escape from the place with my virtue intact. As soon as I am pinned up and dried and combed out, I am going straight to the sheriff and swear out a warrant against Mr. Dickens for assault with attempt to molest. I'm sure Bessie Bloodworth will testify to what happened. I bumped into her as I was running away from him this morning. She saw how terribly upset I was."

"Oh, dear," Beulah said faintly, looking down at the sink. The drain was clogged with a large clump of Mrs. Biggs' hair and the water wouldn't go down. She turned off the faucet.

"Oh, dear is right!" Mrs. Biggs was shrill. "And then I am going back to the hotel and wait for that husband of mine to go prancing up to that second floor. I am going to catch him in the act. In the very *act*, you just wait and see if I don't."

But Beulah wasn't listening. She was staring in horror at the clogged drain, at the hank of wet hair she was holding in her hand, and at the large and clearly visible bare spot on Mrs. Biggs' shiny pink scalp.

Mrs. Biggs stopped talking. Her eyes flew open and she caught sight of the horrified look on Beulah's face. "What's wrong?" she asked.

Beulah was so dismayed that she almost couldn't answer. But true beauty could never be served by a lie. She took a deep breath and uttered the terrible truth.

"It's your hair, Miz Biggs. It's falling out!"

Mrs. Biggs screamed and struggled to sit up. "My *hair*? My *hair* is falling out? What have you done, Beulah Trivette? What have you done to my beautiful *hair*?"

"I . . . I just shampooed it the way I always do," Beulah said in a small voice, knowing that a beautician worth her Montgomery College of Cosmetology certificate of achievement should never find herself in such a terrible position. "Honest, Miz Biggs, all I did was—"

Wet hair dripping, Mrs. Biggs boosted herself out of the

shampoo chair and ran to the mirror to examine the bare spot on the side of her head. "Just look at what you've done!" she shrieked wildly. "Just look!"

"But I didn't do *anything*," Beulah protested. "I only washed your hair the way I always do and—"

"I will sue you!" Mrs. Biggs cried. She ripped off her cover-up cape, threw it on the floor, and stamped on it. "I will tell everybody in town that you've ruined my hair! I will destroy you. You will never have another customer!"

Beulah looked down at the hair in her hand, remembering something she had learned in cosmetology school. A suspicion began to form. "Miz Biggs," she said, "those diet pills you're taking. What did you say they've got in them?"

"My diet pills are none of your beeswax!" Mrs. Biggs cried hysterically, searching around for her handbag. "And don't you try to change the subject, Beulah Trivette. I am going to sue you, do you hear? I'll take you for every penny you've got!"

Beulah carefully laid the hair aside and took a deep breath, thinking that Mrs. Biggs' response was totally out of proportion. Put it together with the story about her husband fooling around and Mr. Dickens trying to kiss her, and it was beginning to sound as if the poor woman had finally and totally lost all her marbles.

Was it the Change, which had driven Beulah's great-aunt Clarice to pick up a butcher knife and attempt to amputate an important feature of great-uncle Abner's anatomy?

Or was it an inherited malady? (Beulah had heard that Mrs. Biggs' mother, Lucretia Dupree, had once spent six months in the State Hospital for the Insane.)

Or was it—

Beulah straightened her shoulders. Whatever it was, she had no doubt that Mrs. Biggs, who was well liked and well connected, could do a great deal of damage to her and to the business of beauty to which she had devoted her life.

"Please sit down, Miz Biggs," she said as soothingly as she could. "Let's just get you pinned and dried and try to figure out what's goin' on here. I'm sure I can style your hair so nobody will ever know—"

"So nobody will see that you've made my *hair* fall out?" Mrs. Biggs cried. She picked up a magazine and threw it violently against the mirror. "So nobody will notice that you've *ruined* me *forever*?"

"But I didn't," Beulah insisted, trying to be reasonable. "I just shampooed you, the way I always do. Please, let's just—"

"Let's just *nothing*." Mrs. Biggs located her handbag and snatched it up. "I am leaving! And don't you try to stop me, Beulah Trivette. I am going to hire myself a *lawyer*!"

And with that, she flung open the door and stormed out of the Bower, her hair limp and dripping wet over her shoulders.

Bettina came running into the room. "Oh, my goodness, what *happened*?" she asked anxiously. "Where is Miz Biggs going? Is everything all right, Beulah?"

"No," Beulah said miserably. "Everything is all *wrong*, Bettina." And then it all hit her like the ceiling caving in on her head and she began to cry.

Bettina put an arm around her and sat her down in the shampoo chair that Mrs. Biggs had so recently vacated. "There, now, you just rest yourself for a minute and cry, honey. A cry will do you a world of good. You just have a good one while I fix us some nice cold lemonade."

Bettina was right. Twenty minutes later, after a nice long cry and a cold glass of lemonade, Beulah had a plan. She left Bettina in charge of the Bower and set off to Lima's Drugstore, on the southwest corner of the courthouse square. There, she went to the pharmacy counter at the back of the store and asked Mr. Lima if he had any of Dr. W. W. Baxter's diet pills in stock. He took a slender cardboard package off the shelf and handed it to her. Peering at the contents, which were printed in the tiniest of letters, she saw that the pills contained strychnine, arsenic, caffeine, and pokeberries.

*Arsenic!* Her suspicion was confirmed. Back at the Montgomery College of Beauty, she had learned that arsenic—even fairly low dosages, over an extended period of time—could make your hair fall out. Strychnine poisoning, she had read somewhere, could result in extreme agitation, anxiety, and delusions.

Well, that's exactly how Angelina Biggs had behaved: agitated, anxious, and delusional. The pills were supposed to be safe, of course, and there was such a thing as the Pure Food and Drug Act, which was meant to keep manufacturers on the straight and narrow. But the government couldn't be everywhere at once, even if it had the best intentions in the world, which it probably didn't. And mistakes could easily be made in the manufacturing process. For instance, what if somebody dumped too much arsenic into a batch of pills, or too much strychnine, or both? And what if Mrs. Biggs took twice as many as she was supposed to? Or three times as many?

She glanced at Mr. Lima, a tall, thin man in his early fifties, dressed in a long white coat. He was standing behind the counter, recording a prescription in a ledger. She waited a moment, then cleared her throat. At last he raised his head, looking at her over the tops of his gold-rimmed glasses.

"Were you wantin' to purchase those diet pills, Miz Trivette?"

"No," she said, and put the package down. "But I'm worried about someone who has purchased them, Mr. Lima. I'm afraid she may be taking too many, and the pills are seriously affecting her health."

Mr. Lima pulled his brows together. "Who's that you're talkin' about?" he demanded brusquely. "Directions are printed right there on the package—one a day, ever' mornin'. And I tell all my customers not to take too many. Arsenic and strychnine—" He shrugged his thin shoulders. "Well, you gotta be careful, is all. That's exactly what I tell anybody who buys these things. Follow the directions and be careful." A frown. "Who'd you say it was?"

"It's Miz Angelina Biggs," Beulah said, and looked Mr. Lima square in the eye. She added, "Reason I'm worried, Mr. Lima, is her hair's fallin' out. I saw it when I shampooed her over at the Beauty Bower, not a half hour ago. And she's tellin' some pretty wild stories about a couple of our menfolks here in town. To tell the truth, she sounds like she's ravin'."

With a sigh, Mr. Lima went back to his ledger, running his finger down the page. "Well, it says here that Miz Biggs bought three packages two weeks ago today." His finger tapped the column. "Three packages, twenty-four pills in each package. I s'pose if you can get a look at those packages, you can count what's left and tell how many she's taken. That way, you'd know for sure."

Beulah frowned, trying to imagine asking the anxious, agitated, and delusional Mrs. Biggs if she could count her diet pills. "And just how do you suggest that I do that?" she asked.

Mr. Lima stretched his thin lips in a bleak and unhelpful smile. "That, Miz Trivette, is your problem, not mine."

# TEN

# Lizzy

Lizzy prided herself on her ability to manage Mr. Moseley's office, but that Monday, things happened that seriously challenged her organizational and management skills. It was one of those days when if it wasn't one thing, it was another.

For instance, Lizzy was just getting a good start on her "Garden Gate" column (she had written the first two items) when Ophelia dropped in. She came to say that she had delivered Verna and Clyde to the Murphy place and they were comfortably installed in Lucy's front bedroom. But Ophelia stayed a little longer and then stayed some more, and then finally came out with what was obviously bothering her. She had to find a job.

"A job?" Lizzy had repeated, surprised. "But—"

"Please don't ask why," Ophelia said miserably. "I just *have* to get work. I can type sixty words a minute without any mistakes, and I can spell, and I can take shorthand. Well, I can with a little practice," she amended. "I had shorthand, back in high school, and I still have my Gregg book and some old steno pads." She looked around. "I was wondering . . . that is, do you think Mr. Moseley could use another assistant?"

Lizzy thought about her workload, the firm's bank account, and said, regretfully, "I really don't think so, Ophelia. I can ask Mr. Moseley, but even if we needed the help, which we don't, we couldn't afford it."

Ophelia sighed. "Well, I had to start somewhere. You were the first person I thought of. Can you come up with any other possibilities?"

Lizzy frowned. "Jobs are pretty scarce just now. I guess if I were you, I'd look in the *Dispatch* want ads. Or maybe I'd run a work-wanted ad myself."

Ophelia brightened. "That's a swell idea, Liz. I think I'll go downstairs and talk to Mr. Dickens about running an ad. I wouldn't have to put my name in it, would I?"

"I don't think so. Maybe something like *Excellent typist looking for work. Sixty words per minute, no mistakes, also short-hand.* Something like that."

"I'll do it," Ophelia said decidedly. "That's a lot better than hoofing it from one business to the other, looking for work. That's so depressing."

Lizzy nodded, although she wasn't sure that a newspaper ad, all by itself, would get Ophelia a job. She'd probably end up hoofing it—and even then, finding something would be a matter of luck, one of those right-place-at-the-right-time things. "I hope you get what you're looking for," she said.

"Thanks." Ophelia paused, looking a little guilty. "Oh, by the way—if you see Jed, please don't mention this." She turned down her mouth. "I . . . I haven't told him yet. I don't know how he's going to take it."

*Uh-oh,* Lizzy thought. It sounded as if Ophelia was in some kind of trouble. But she didn't like to pry into her friends' business, so she just nodded.

After Ophelia left, Lizzy settled down to work again. But she managed to write only two more items for her column when Old Zeke, the colored man who delivered grocery orders for Mrs. Hancock and did odd jobs around the neighborhood, showed up to report that Sheriff Burns had come knocking on Verna's front door—with a warrant.

As Lizzy pieced the story together later, it had happened this way. Just before Ophelia arrived to drive her out to Lucy's place, Verna got one of her bright ideas. She went next door and told Mrs. Wilson that she planned to visit a friend in Nashville for a few days and would appreciate it if Mrs. Wilson would keep an eye on things at her place. If anybody happened to come looking for her, Mrs. Wilson should tell them she had gone to Nashville and then telephone Miss Lacy in Mr. Moseley's office and let her know who was asking, so Miss Lacy could relay the message. (Verna later told Lizzy that she had stumbled on this idea, a classic strategy of misdirection, in one of the true-crime magazines she was always reading.)

Mrs. Wilson was happy to help out in this way, for Verna had been ready to lend a hand in Mr. Wilson's last illness and Mrs. Wilson (who was eighty-five and not as spry as she used to be) was grateful to have a neighbor who didn't mind picking up one or two things at the Mercantile or getting one of Doc Roberts' prescriptions filled at Lima's Drugs on the way home from work.

Anyway, Mrs. Wilson didn't have much else to do. She spent her days rocking on her front porch, crocheting granny squares for afghans for the missionary box at the church and keeping an eye on the neighborhood in general. She certainly didn't mind watching Verna's front door and letting Verna's visitors know that she was out of town. Nothing very exciting had happened on the block since the month before, when Mr. Renfro's second cousin (the Renfros lived across the street) had parked his old Buick out front and neglected to put on the hand brake. Mrs. Wilson had seen the car start to roll down the hill and shouted out a warning, but it was too late. With Mr. Renfro and his cousin in hot pursuit, the Buick had rolled merrily all the way down Larkspur to Rosemont. There, it smashed into a light pole and caved in the radiator, which had spouted like Old Faithful out in Yellowstone Park.

Mrs. Wilson knew it wasn't funny, especially because when the light pole went down all the lights in the neighborhood went out. But she had to laugh because the chase reminded her so much of the Keystone Kops. Mr. Renfro looked a lot like Fatty Arbuckle, who had starred in Mr. Wilson's favorite Keystone Kops movie, *The Gangsters.* When the Palace showed a Kops flick, Mr. Wilson, God rest his soul, had always been the first one in line, no matter how many times he had already seen the movie. He was heartbroken when Fatty got in trouble over that girl in San Francisco back in 1921 and got tried for manslaughter, not once but three times before a jury finally saw the light and acquitted him.

And when Sheriff Burns parked his Model A at the curb, marched up the front porch steps, and banged on Verna's door, Mrs. Wilson had another laugh. Roy Burns (whom Mrs. Wilson had known ever since he was a little kid with a runny nose who went around with his pet chicken under his arm) had grown up to be another Fatty Arbuckle lookalike. She was still chuckling about that when she called out, "If you're lookin' for Miz Tidwell, Sheriff, she's gone off to visit a friend in Nashville. She left just a little bit ago. Won't be back for a few days."

"Now ain't that a coincidence." The sheriff scowled, took off his hat, and scratched his head. "I'm lookin' to have a little talk with her and she runs off to Nashville." He pushed out his pudgy lips and squinted at her. "Wouldn't happen to know the name of her friend, would you, Miz Wilson?"

"She didn't say," Mrs. Wilson replied, suddenly and uncomfortably aware that Roy Burns might not have come calling to ask Verna to contribute to the county employees' welfare fund. She sat back in her rocking chair and picked up her current granny square and her crochet hook. "Is it impo'tant, Sheriff?"

"I reckon it is," the sheriff said with heavy irony, "or I wouldn't have this here warrant in my pocket, would I? And I wouldn't be wastin' my time bangin' on this here door, neither."

A warrant? "Well, now, I don't reckon you would," Mrs. Wilson replied thoughtfully. "You have a good day, Sheriff."

"I'll do that," the sheriff said. "You happen to hear from Miz Tidwell, you tell her that I was here. And that I'm lookin' to talk to her jes' as soon as she gets back." He stomped to his Model A and drove off, trailing a cloud of dust.

Mrs. Wilson put down her crocheting and puckered her forehead in a frown. Verna had told her to telephone Miss Lacy in Mr. Moseley's office if anybody came calling. But Mrs. Wilson was thinking that she was on a party line and maybe Verna wouldn't want everybody in town to know that the sheriff had dropped by to see her with a warrant in his pocket, which they certainly would, if the Newmans or the Ferrells or the Snows happened to pick up the receiver.

Mrs. Wilson was still considering the possible ins and outs of this when she looked up and saw Old Zeke trudging slowly down Larkspur, pulling a rusty red wagon with wooden slat sides. The wagon was empty. She had seen him earlier, when the wagon was full of groceries and he was on his way to make deliveries. He was likely on his way back to Hancock's for another load.

"How are you today, Mr. Zeke?" she called out pleasantly.

Old Zeke wore bib overalls and a sweat-stained brown felt hat mashed down on his grizzled head. He'd been a middleweight before the Great War, traveling around the Southern circuit, fighting any fool who would climb into the ring with him. Now, he was bent and frail, his nose misshapen, his face as leathery as a piece of old cowhide hanging on the side of a barn. He lifted his head and shaded his eyes, as if the bright sunshine was too much for him.

"T's right po'ly," he replied in his cracked voice, "but I sho' do thank'ee for askin', Miz Wilson."

Mrs. Wilson understood. Old Zeke was known to indulge in the local moonshine and was a frequent overnight guest at the county jail on the second floor of Snow's Farm Supply. He always felt poorly after a riotous weekend.

She pushed herself out of her rocking chair. "Would you mind doing a little something for me? I need to send a note to Mr. Moseley's office." The office was next door to the grocery store, so it wouldn't be out of his way. "I don't happen to have any spare change right now, but I'd be glad to give you some cookies. Would that be all right?"

"Cookies." Old Zeke grinned toothlessly. "Cookies is allus good. Ol' Zeke likes cookies."

And that's why, ten minutes later, Old Zeke, hat in hand, was standing like a battered Western Union delivery boy beside Lizzy's desk and Lizzy was opening an envelope with her name written on the outside. She took out a note, seeing that it came from Verna's next-door neighbor.

"Thank you for bringing this, Zeke," she said, and reached into the drawer where she kept the office petty cash. She took out a dime and gave it to him. He pocketed it eagerly and looked around.

"You got 'ny jobs Old Zeke might could do?" he asked hopefully. "Sweepin'? Fixin'? Totin'?"

"Not here in the office," Lizzy replied. "But could you mow the front yard at the Dahlias clubhouse? It's looking a little shaggy." The Dahlias managed the garden, but Zeke kept the grass looking nice.

He brightened. "Sho' thing, Miz Lacy." He put his hat on his head and saluted. "I'll do it this evenin'."

When Lizzy read the note, she was glad that Mrs. Wilson had had the presence of mind to write down what she had seen, rather than go to the telephone. It would not have been a good idea to let everyone in Verna's neighborhood know that the sheriff was knocking at her door. She frowned apprehensively. He'd said he had a warrant. Was it a search warrant, or a warrant for her arrest? Either way, he had to have some sort of probable cause before the judge would sign off on it. Probable cause—what was it?

But while she was worrying about this, the telephone rang with an urgent question from one of Mr. Moseley's clients that required fifteen minutes of research before she could call him back with the answer. Then Judge McHenry's clerk called to say that the judge had mislaid a document in one of Mr. Moseley's court cases and hoped that Miss Lacy could replace it. She located a copy, locked the office, and ran across the street to the courthouse, where she left the document with the clerk and then came back, to another ringing phone.

This time it was Mr. Moseley, asking her to take dictation over the telephone, then type the letter, sign it for him, and make sure it went out in today's mail. Thinking of Verna and the warrant, she wanted to ask Mr. Moseley about probable cause, but he was in a hurry, so she skipped it. Anyway, he wouldn't be happy to hear that Verna had refused to follow his advice to stay home and wait for the sheriff. He would be especially unhappy to learn that Lizzy had aided and abetted her decision. It was probably better not to open the subject.

Lizzy had finished typing the letter and was getting ready to take it to the post office when she heard footsteps coming up the stairs and Myra May pushed the door open. She was panting.

"I thought you went over to Beulah's to get beautiful," Lizzy said. She didn't say so, but Myra May's hair looked no different than it had earlier that morning. What's more, there were deep puckers of worry in her forehead.

"I did," Myra May answered breathlessly. "But while I was waiting for Bettina to come and shampoo me, I heard something you ought to know about. And Verna, too, wherever she is. Thought I'd better come straight on over here and tell you."

Quickly and succinctly, Myra May reported what Alice Ann Walker had said about Mr. Scroggins, Mr. Johnson, and the sheriff, all showing a great interest in Verna's bank account.

"Alice Ann wouldn't tell us how much got deposited into Verna's account," she concluded. "But she did say it was a tidy sum. Said it would be enough to get Arnold a new leg and a roof on the house and a new water well, plus paying off her bills, so it sounds like it must be in the thousands of dollars." She frowned apprehensively. "Did Verna ever happen to mention how she managed to get her hands on that much money?"

Taken aback by this new information, Lizzy shook her head. "You know how closemouthed Verna is. She almost never discusses her personal money affairs with me—or anybody else."

But money was so hard to come by these days, and Verna's only income, so far as Lizzy knew, was her job, which certainly wouldn't pay enough to put a new roof on the Walkers' house or buy Arnold a new leg. So where *did* that deposit come from?

She paused, thinking that since Myra May had brought this piece of news, she ought to tell her what she had just

learned from Mrs. Wilson. "That money in Verna's account—
it must be the reason for the sheriff coming to her house a
little while ago," she said. "He had a warrant. I don't know
whether it was a search warrant or an arrest warrant."

"A *warrant*?" Myra May asked, lifting both eyebrows. "My
gosh, Liz. How'd you find that out?"

"From Mrs. Wilson, Verna's next-door neighbor. Verna
told her that she was going to Nashville."

"Did she?" Myra May asked. "Go to Nashville, I mean."

Lizzy only shrugged.

"Ah, I see." Myra May chuckled, then turned serious. "The
sheriff." She pressed her lips together, shaking her head.
"Sounds to me like Scroggins and the sheriff think Verna had
something to do with that missing money, Liz."

"Sounds that way to me, too," Lizzy said grimly. She narrowed her eyes. "I wonder what Mr. Moseley will say when he
finds out that Mr. Johnson let Mr. Scroggins have a look at
Verna's bank account. I'm not sure, but I think they should
have told the sheriff he had to get a warrant to do that." She
thought of something and brightened. "If I'm right, and if
the case comes to trial, Mr. Moseley might be able to get it
thrown out."

"Oh, really?" Myra May asked. "How?"

"Tainted evidence. When the police don't do things the
way they're supposed to be done, Mr. Moseley objects. If the
judge agrees, he refuses to allow the evidence to be entered in
the case."

Myra May gave her an admiring look. "You tell Mr. Moseley that he definitely ought to object to Mr. Johnson and Mr.
Scroggins snooping in Verna's bank account. They've got no
business doing that." She paused curiously. "Are you going to
tell Verna about this?"

"Yes, but I can't leave the office until quitting time and I
don't want to use the telephone. Lucy's on a party line. I

promised Bessie I'd come to her card party tonight, but I guess I'll have to cancel. I'll ask Grady if I can borrow his car and drive out to the Murphys'." Lizzy clapped her hand over her mouth. "Oh, *blast*," she said disgustedly. "Now I've gone and let the cat out of the bag."

"You can trust me," Myra May replied in a comforting tone. "I won't tell a soul. And I'm glad she didn't go all the way to Nashville." She tilted her head. "Would you like to borrow Big Bertha instead, Liz? I'm taking a shift on the switchboard tonight, or I'd offer to drive you. But I'd be glad to lend you the car, if you like."

Lizzy considered. Big Bertha was Myra May's old Chevy touring car, and probably a good alternative. If she asked Grady to lend her his car, he would volunteer to drive, and she didn't think it was a good idea to share any of this with him. Grady was a dear and she loved him, but he could be a stickler when it came to rules. He might not understand about Verna hiding from the sheriff when there was a warrant out on her. And now that she had spilled the beans, she might as well take up Myra May on her offer.

"Thanks," Lizzy said gratefully. "I'd love to borrow Big Bertha. That's really good of you, Myra May."

Downstairs, the old job press in the *Dispatch* office started up. It wasn't as loud as the newspaper press, but it made quite a racket.

Myra May raised her voice. "Good, hell. You know me, Liz. *Curious* is my middle name. When you bring Bertha home, come in for a cup of coffee." She gave Lizzy a wicked grin. "Maybe I can get you to tell me how much Verna really has in that bank account—and where she got it."

"Well, I don't know about that," Lizzy said with a chuckle, picking up the letter she had to mail and pushing back her chair. "I'll walk with you. I'm headed for the post office."

# ELEVEN

# Charlie Dickens

Downstairs, in the *Dispatch* office, Charlie Dickens finished repairing the ink roller on the old Prouty job press, a real antique he had inherited with the business, and began printing the menus for the Old Alabama Hotel. While he worked, he was puzzling over what had happened that morning during that surprising and painful encounter with Angelina Dupree Biggs, his high school sweetheart.

Angelina was water under a very old bridge, very long ago, and their flaming, furtive passion—now as cold and unappetizing as last night's okra gumbo, and difficult, embarrassing even, to remember—was a thing of a long-dead past. Angelina had decided not to wait for Charlie to finish college and get a job that would support her in the style to which her mother thought she should become accustomed. She had opted instead to become Angelina Biggs, and Charlie's love for her (if that's what it was, or something else) had died a sudden and chilly death.

This had happened so long ago that Charlie had all but

forgotten it, except to be glad, now and again, that Artis Biggs and his Buick had come along when they did. Not being married to Angelina, he had been able to cut his ties to Darling. Not being married to anybody, he had been able to travel and work and play whenever and wherever and as much or as little as he pleased, having to consider only his own wants and whims. And as a bachelor, he had no wife to nag him about his drinking. He bore no ill will toward Angelina for jilting him, quite the contrary. He was glad that she had married a man who gave her children and treated her right. It had all worked out, the way things usually do if you let them alone for long enough.

At least, that's what Charlie had thought until this morning, when Angelina (now almost twice the size she had been when he could scoop his arm around her tiny waist and twirl her around the dance floor) had come into the *Dispatch* office. She was there to turn in the copy for the next week's menus for the Old Alabama Hotel, the way she usually did. Angelina was always a little diffident on these occasions, as if she might be remembering what had once been between them and wondering if Charlie remembered it, too, which he did, sometimes, in the way of a man who remembers a dream of something beautiful glimpsed long ago.

But this morning, Angelina had done something totally unexpected. Instead of staying on the customer's side of the wooden counter that divided the public area from the working area, she had come around behind it, and before he realized what was happening, she had accosted him. Yes, *accosted* him—there was no other word for it. She had flung her plump arms around his neck and pressed the soft, heaving pillows of her bosom against him in a way that inspired not passion but panic in Charlie's breast. The room was brightly lit and the two of them were standing in full view of the sidewalk. What if somebody walked past the plate-glass window and looked in?

"Stop it, Angelina," he commanded hoarsely. "You gone crazy or something? Just quit! You hear me? Quit!" He grabbed her arms and pushed them down to her sides, freeing himself from her grip.

"Of course I'm crazy, Charlie," Angelina had cried ecstatically, throwing her head back and looking up at him with half-closed eyes like someone drugged. The heavy fragrance of her perfume enveloped him in a cloud and he almost gagged. "I am crazy for you, just like I've always been. And I've seen the hunger in your eyes. I know you're crazy for me, too!"

"Hunger?" Charlie was nonplussed. "Angelina, if I have ever once given you even the smallest reason to think I was hungry for you, I honestly and sincerely apologize. I never intended any such thing. Quite the contrary, I—" He stopped. If he said what he was thinking—that she was nothing like the slim perfection he had once known, that he did not find her appetizing in any sense of the word—she would be devastated.

"Don't try to deny it, my darling," she begged, reaching for him again. She was panting heavily, her red lips parted. "I know I hurt you when I married Artis. I was such a fool. My mistake has cost us so many years. But we're grown-ups now. We can be honest with each other about the way we feel. We *have* to be honest! We have to own up to our love! We're hungry for each other!" And she pulled down his head to hers and kissed him, full and hard on the lips.

That did it. That was the last straw. Charlie wrenched himself out of her passionate grip, turned her around, and marched her to the other side of the counter.

"Go home, Angelina," he said firmly, pushing her in the direction of the door. "Go back to the hotel. Go back to Artis. He's your husband, for God's sake. And you have *children*. Think of your children!"

"My husband!" she cried feverishly, stamping her foot. "That lecherous old goat? That . . . that *philanderer?* Artis is having an affair. He and his mistress meet every day on the second floor of the hotel."

Charlie pulled himself up straight. So that was what this was all about. Angelina must have figured she'd get even by having a tit-for-tat affair with an old high school flame. But Charlie wasn't stupid enough to let himself get snared in that kind of trap. And in Angelina's current frame of mind, he knew there wasn't any point in trying to reason with her. He had to be cruel to be kind.

"I don't care if Artis is having himself *two* affairs," he said coldly. "I don't care if he's having a dozen. That's got nothing to do with me. Now, you just scoot yourself out of here, Angelina, and go on back to Artis. We'll forget that this ever happened." He grasped her arm and gave her a little shove.

Her pudgy face crumpled. "Oh!" she wailed. "Oh, oh, Charlie Dickens, shame on you! I never thought I'd see the day when you—*you* of all people!—would reject me. You loved me once." She held out her hands beseechingly. "I know you still love me!"

It was clear that he would have to take drastic action. "Out!" he roared. "You git yourself out of here before I lose my temper!" Hastily, he retreated behind the counter, feeling that he had to put a solid barrier between himself and this crazy woman.

Angelina stared at him for a moment, her eyes brimming with tears, then turned and flung open the door. And that was the end of it—or rather, it should have been, if Charlie could have pushed it out of his mind as easily as he had pushed Angelina out of the office.

And it wasn't as if he didn't have other things to think about—to worry about, actually.

The evening before, Zipper Haydon, who had operated the

aged Linotype for the past two decades, had told Charlie he was quitting. He'd be glad to hang around and teach his replacement to operate the machine, but he'd come to the end of the line. It wasn't unexpected, of course. Zipper was seventy-five and had a hard time getting around, with one crippled foot and an arthritic right elbow that gave him a lot of pain when he went to pull the casting lever on the old machine.

But predictable or not, losing Zipper was still a blow. Zipper had come to work at the *Dispatch* when Charlie's father was the owner and editor, and he was a mainstay of the business. He might be worn out and subject to breakdowns, like the old Prouty job press, but he always kept on plugging. Even with so many people looking for work, Charlie knew he'd never be able to find a skilled Linotype operator for the fifteen dollars a week he paid Zipper.

The machine wasn't difficult to learn and Zipper had offered to teach him, but Charlie knew that wasn't the answer. He was in way over his head already, what with the job printing business he was still learning and that old Babcock flatbed cylinder press that broke down every few weeks. He'd been trained as a reporter, for Pete's sake, not as a publisher, pressman, press repairman, job printer, advertising salesman, and subscription manager. There was no way he was going to add Linotype operator to his already long list of responsibilities. But finding somebody in Darling who could type and correct copy when necessary, who could learn the Linotype and come to work on time and do it all for less than fifteen dollars a week—that wasn't going to be easy.

Charlie was fretting about this and worrying about what he was going to do when Zipper's two-week notice period was over and he was without a Linotype operator, when the bell over the door tinkled and Ophelia Snow walked in. She was wearing a practical-looking white V-necked blouse and dark skirt, and her brown hair was drawn back away from her face.

"Good mornin', Miz Snow," Charlie said, switching off the job press and going to the counter. "What can I do for you today? Want some printin' for the feed store, maybe?" In addition to being the mayor of Darling, Ophelia's husband Jed owned Snow's Farm Supply a block west on Franklin. Jed sometimes sent his wife with orders for printed signs, posters, and the like. Charlie was always glad to get the work. The job printing didn't bring in much and he hated to run the noisy old Prouty, but it was extra income and he needed it.

"Well, no," Mrs. Snow said hesitantly. Her forehead was furrowed and her brown eyes were troubled. "Not today, anyway. I'd like to place an ad. A classified ad."

"Good enough." Charlie took out the ad form he had printed up. "Classified is two cents a word if you want to run it just once. You get a discount for multiples. What category? Help Wanted? Is it for the feed store?"

"No, not for the feed store," Mrs. Snow said quickly. She thought a moment. "Work Wanted, I guess. Or Job Wanted."

"That would be Situation Wanted," Charlie said, and picked up his pencil. "Okay. You give it to me and I'll write it down."

Mrs. Snow bit her lip. "Well, I guess maybe, *Fast typist, takes shorthand, seeks full-time work. Phone 1422.*"

Charlie wrote this down, then frowned. "We don't usually put a telephone number in for something like this. Crank calls, you know."

"Well, then, how—"

"I'll put in a box number and *Care of* Dispatch. The replies will come here. And you don't get charged for those words." He looked back at the ad. "Most people would also put in something like *experienced, will provide references*," he said. "Want to include that?"

"I'm . . . not experienced," Mrs. Snow confessed, "except as a housewife and mother." She brushed a strand of flyaway brown hair out of her face. "And I don't have references—at least, from an employer. But I'm very anxious to work," she added quickly. "Maybe we could say that? Something like *eager and willing*? No," she corrected herself. "Don't put in the *and*. It's another two cents."

Charlie looked at her, surprised. "This is for *you*? You're looking for work?"

Mrs. Snow pulled herself up. "Yes. Yes, it's for me. But I wish . . ." She bit her lip again. "I haven't told my husband yet. So I would appreciate it if you didn't mention it until I've had a chance to talk to him." She took a breath. "Tonight. I'll tell him tonight." She said it as if she were steeling herself to something very difficult.

Charlie put his pencil down, an idea beginning to form. "You say you're a fast typist," he said, peering at her. She had always struck him as a competent woman, although there was an air of uncertainty about her. Lack of confidence, he thought. "How fast?"

"Sixty words a minute, when I was in high school," Mrs. Snow replied proudly. "And no errors. Of course, that was a while ago and I'm a little out of practice. But I'm sure I'll pick it up again." She smiled engagingly. "Typing is like riding a bicycle. Once you've learned, you don't forget."

No errors. Accuracy was more important than speed, for what he had in mind. In fact, speed was out of the question on that machine. It was one letter at a time. "And you've never worked before?"

She frowned. "I work all the time. I've worked for years. But not for money." She sighed. "I'm sure that's a strike against me."

"Tell you what, Miz Snow," he said, coming to a sudden decision. "I've got a position here at the *Dispatch* that you might be able to fill. You'd have to show you could do it, though."

"A job . . . here?" she gasped incredulously. "As . . . as a *reporter?*"

*Well, now that you mention it,* Charlie thought. But he said, "No, as a Linotype operator. Mr. Haydon—you probably know him—has to quit, for health reasons. He'll be here in the morning. Maybe you could come in and take a little aptitude test on the machine."

The Linotype machine was thought to be too hard for women to operate, but Charlie had known a couple of female Linotype operators in other small newspapers. If Ophelia Snow could type and had enough strength to operate the levers, she'd do okay. She'd need help in handling the type cases—lead was heavy. But he had to give Zipper a hand, so there'd be no difference there. If she could do the work . . .

"What time tomorrow?" she asked eagerly.

"Eight in the morning," he replied.

"I'll be here." She smiled, her eyes lightening. "I can't thank you enough for giving me the opportunity—"

"Wait," he said. "Don't you want to know how much it pays? It's not very much. Only ten dollars a week to start. You'd have to come in on Tuesday, Wednesday, and Thursday, all day. If it works out, we can discuss a raise."

"Ten dollars!" she said excitedly. *"Ten dollars!* Oh, my goodness! Oh, my gracious sakes alive, that would be *wonderful*, Mr. Dickens. Just wonderful!" She straightened her shoulders and tried to put on a businesslike expression, obviously making a special effort to contain her delight. "I'll see you first thing tomorrow."

Charlie shook his head as she almost danced out the door.

# TWELVE

# Lizzy and Coretta Cole

Lizzy hadn't been back from the post office for very long when she heard footsteps—heavy, lumbering footsteps, this time—coming up the stairs. The office door flew open and Mrs. Angelina Biggs burst through. Although the sun was shining brightly, her hair was dripping wet and her eyes were wild and crazy.

"I want to see Mr. Moseley!" she cried, arms flailing. "I'm going to hire him to sue Beulah Trivette and Charlie Dickens and Artis Biggs! I'm suing all three of them for every penny they've got!" She whirled around like a dervish. "Where is Mr. Moseley? When can I see him? Where? When? Where?"

"I'm sorry, but he's not here," Lizzy said, blinking at this unusual behavior. People sometimes were a little frantic when they came to consult Mr. Moseley, but she had never seen anything like this. "Please sit down, Mrs. Biggs, so I can take your information. When Mr. Moseley gets back, he'll call you to schedule a consultation and—"

"I am *not* sitting down!" Angelina Biggs cried, whirling

faster, her arms out, her green dress ballooning out around her pudgy knees. Her ample chins rippled and the flesh under her arms swung like loose sleeves. "No, no, no! If I sit down, the rest of my hair will fall out."

"I beg your pardon?" Lizzy stared at the whirling woman.

"My hair," Mrs. Biggs cried. "I have to keep moving or my hair will fall out." She made a three-hundred-sixty-degree turn. "That's why I am going to sue Beulah Trivette. It's all on account of her. She's ruined my beautiful hair."

Lizzy didn't scare easily, but the skin on the back of her neck was prickling. Something was very wrong here, and a lawsuit wasn't going to solve the problem. But what should she do? What would Mr. Moseley do if he were here?

While Mrs. Biggs lumbered around the reception area like a half-crazed circus elephant, knocking over chairs and small tables, Lizzy picked up the phone. Violet Sims, who was working the switchboard, came on the line and she said, very low, "Violet, this is Lizzy Lacy. Listen, I need you to call Artis Biggs at the hotel and tell him to get over to Mr. Moseley's office as fast as he can. His wife is here, and she's—well, I can't tell whether she's drunk or having some sort of . . . um, seizure, I guess you'd say."

Her eyes widened as Mrs. Biggs blundered into an end table and toppled a lamp, smashing the paper shade. "Tell him to hurry," she added urgently. "And maybe he could ask Mr. Dickens downstairs in the *Dispatch* office to give him a hand. I think it's going to take two strong men to handle her."

Lizzy put down the phone. "May I fix you a cup of coffee?" she asked pleasantly, as Mrs. Biggs whirled against the magazine rack, splintering it.

"No, no, no!" Mrs. Biggs cried. "Mr. Moseley! I want Mr. Moseley!"

It seemed like an eternity, but it was only a few moments later when Artis Biggs raced up the stairs, with Charlie

Dickens on his heels. At the sight of her husband, Mrs. Biggs began to shriek like a banshee.

"I'm suing you," she shrilled, waving her arms wildly. "You better not lay your filthy hands on me! You lecherous old coot! You reprobate! I'll see you in court!" She whirled on Charlie. "You, too, Charlie Dickens! I'm suing you, too, for assault with attempt to molest."

Mr. Biggs sighed heavily. "Thank you for calling me, Miss Lacy," he said with a grim look. "Mr. Dickens and I will take it from here." He glanced around the office, seeing the smashed lampshade and the splintered magazine rack. "I'll be glad to pay for any damage she's caused. Just send me a bill."

"I'll ask Mr. Moseley, but I don't think that will be necessary," Lizzy said. "I just hope Mrs. Biggs will be all right."

"So do I," Mr. Biggs muttered, as he tried to hang on to a flailing arm. "I just wish I knew what ails her. She's been like this for a couple of days now. It's like she's goin' crazy. She's drivin' *me* crazy, anyway." He put his arm around his wife's ample waist. "Come on, now, sweetheart. Settle down. Settle down, and we'll get you home to bed."

"Bed!" Mrs. Biggs shrieked. "Don't you talk to me about bed, you philanderer! You Don Juan, you!" She turned on Charlie Dickens. "And you, you . . . you Casanova!"

It required the combined efforts of both men to wrestle Mrs. Biggs down the stairs and get her headed back toward the hotel, lurching along between them like a drunk on the way home after a thirsty night on the town. Lizzy watched from the office window, shaking her head at the sight, which would have been funny if it hadn't been so sad. Mrs. Biggs had always seemed like a quiet, thoughtful person. What in the world was making her act this way?

She was about to turn away from the window when she saw Beulah Trivette hurrying across the courthouse square

toward the trio. The group paused while Mrs. Biggs struggled against the men's restraint and Mr. Biggs listened, at
first impatiently and then with growing seriousness, to what
Beulah had to say. Then Beulah joined them and the quartet
hustled toward the hotel as Lizzy puzzled over what it all
meant. She'd have to ask Beulah for an explanation, first
chance she got.

The rest of the day went by in the same first-one-thing-
then-another manner, although without any more exciting
whirling dervish episodes. By the time the old-fashioned
grandfather clock had struck five, Lizzy was more than ready
for the long work day to end. She had hoped to get a free hour
to finish her "Garden Gate" column, but that hadn't happened. So she walked hurriedly past the window of the *Dispatch* office, not wanting to catch Charlie Dickens' glance. If
she'd looked in, she might have seen Charlie bent over a
library book instead of his typewriter, turning the pages with
a rapt attention.

When Lizzy got home, she went straight to her bedroom,
where she kicked off her shoes, unfastened her garter belt,
and peeled off her stockings. As she did nearly every day after
work, she washed them in the bathroom sink with a sprinkle
of Ivory soap flakes. These were rayon service-weight stockings, reasonably sheer, and at fifty cents a pair at the
Mercantile—forty-eight cents postage paid from the Sears
catalog—you learned to take care of them. For another dollar,
you could buy chiffon-weight silk stockings with the new
slenderizing French heels. But Lizzy had only one pair of
those, which she saved for very special occasions, like the
monthly dances at the country club. Rayon was plenty good
enough for the office—but then, it had to be, didn't it? And
anyway, she was lucky to have what she had. Some women
couldn't even afford rayon.

Stockings washed and dripping over the towel bar, Lizzy

stepped into the blue cotton wrap dress with the white pique V-necked collar that she liked to wear around the house and padded barefoot into the kitchen. There, she poured a glass of lemonade from the pitcher in the refrigerator and took it into the grassy backyard, where Daffy was having his afternoon nap under a rosebush. He opened one eye, saw Lizzy, and closed his eye again.

When she'd first moved into her house, Grady had built a wooden garden swing, painted it white, and hung it from the limb of the live oak. Lizzy had made a seat cushion and covered it with orange and blue oilcloth. That's where she sat now. She sipped her cold drink, pushed herself back and forth with one bare foot, and thought over all the things that had happened that day, especially Myra May's report of Alice Ann Walker's story about what happened at the bank and the sheriff's subsequent appearance—with a warrant—at Verna's house. Obviously, Verna was on Roy Burns' wanted list. There was apparently enough money in her bank account to make her a suspect in the fifteen-thousand-dollar theft from the county treasury. Lizzy knew that Verna would never have stolen anything from the county treasury—but where had she gotten that money? Could she explain *that* to Roy Burns' satisfaction?

Lizzy frowned and sipped her lemonade. She was wishing she had been able to talk to Mr. Moseley about this and wondering if she had done all she could when she heard a woman's husky voice, a bit tentative, calling from the side-yard gate.

"Yoo-hoo, Liz. Liz Lacy. Do you, um, have a minute to talk?"

Lizzy stood up from the swing. "Hi. But who—"

Then she caught sight of her visitor, standing beside the gate. It was Coretta Cole, still wearing the same gray suit and red hat and heels that she'd had on that morning, when Lizzy had seen her having breakfast with Mr. Scroggins and Mr. Tombull.

"Coretta!" Lizzy exclaimed in great surprise. "What are you doing here?" And then, realizing that she sounded less than gracious, she added, "Push up the latch and come on in."

Coretta did as she was told, walking across the grass on her toes so that her stylish three-inch heels wouldn't sink into the earth. She was glancing around in a covetous way.

"Gee, Liz, this is a swell little place you've got here. Very pretty. All yours?"

"If you mean, do I live here alone," Lizzy replied, guardedly, "the answer is yes." It had been her experience that the less you told Coretta, the better.

Coretta's giggle was mischievous. "Well, darn. I thought maybe you and Grady Alexander were—"

"No," Lizzy said firmly. "We are *not*, and don't you go telling people that we are. That just wouldn't be true." She paused as Coretta, uninvited, sank down in the swing. Then, remembering her manners, she added, "There's cold lemonade in the refrigerator. Would you like some?"

Coretta shook her head. She had a sharp chin and chiseled cheeks, and her dark eyebrows were tweezed thin and arched over her Joan Crawford eyes.

"Thanks," she said. "It's sweet of you, Liz, but I can't stay too long. My hubby promised to cook supper for us tonight, since it's my first day back at work full time. He's expecting me to come straight home." She paused. "You know that Ted got laid off out at the Coca-Cola bottling plant, I reckon. He's been out of work for a couple of months."

"Yes, I heard," Lizzy said. "I'm sorry, Coretta." It was a true statement. You had to feel sorry for anybody who was out of work. In times like this, once somebody got laid off, it was nearly impossible to get another job, unless they wanted to leave Darling and try their luck in Memphis or Mobile or New Orleans.

"Thanks. I don't mind telling you that Ted and I were

looking at the bare bottom of the barrel when Mr. Scroggins called and told me I could come back to work full time. We're so hard up, we haven't been able to get the car fixed for months and months." Coretta glanced at Lizzy's bare feet, then down at her own high heels. "Do you mind?" she asked plaintively, batting her mascaraed eyelashes.

Without waiting for an answer, she bent over and pulled her shoes off, wiggling her toes in their silk stockings. "It's the first time I've worn them to stand up in all day," she said with a sigh, "and my feet are killing me."

"No, of course I don't mind." Lizzy sat down on the other end of the swing, noticing Coretta's silk stockings with a covetous feeling and wondering how somebody who couldn't afford car repair could buy silk stockings and new shoes. And that great-looking gray suit, too. She had seen it on the manikin in the window at Mann's for seven fifty, just a couple of weeks before.

Coretta took off her red felt hat and put it on the swing between them, patting her dark hair back into its sculptured waves. "To tell you the truth, Liz, I could hardly believe it when Mr. Scroggins called. Seemed like something I was dreaming, I'd been wanting it so bad. And Ted—well, you should have seen him. He was so relieved, he cried." The words were tumbling out fast, as if they'd been stoppered up in a bottle and she was finally letting them out. "It's not like I'm getting paid a fortune, you know. But we've got two boys, and we were hoping they could go to college. College is probably out the window now, but that doesn't mean we have to stop dreaming. Me getting a regular paycheck again—well, it maybe means the oldest can go to Poly when he graduates high school."

Lizzy listened, wishing that Coretta would get to the point. Why was she here? What did she want? She felt a bubble of hot resentment rise up inside her at the thought that this was the woman who had taken her best friend's job. Had she come here to brag about it? To rub it in? Or was she trying to say that circumstances had forced her to do it and she was sorry?

"Look, Coretta," she said, when the cascade of words slowed down. "I don't mean to be rude, but if you're in a big hurry to get home and eat supper with Ted and the boys, maybe you'd better tell me why you're here."

Coretta turned her head away. She didn't speak for a moment, then, instead of answering directly, she said, in a low voice, "I saw you this morning, in the diner. Sitting at the counter. Watching me."

"I wasn't *watching*, exactly," Lizzy replied evenly. It sounded like Coretta was accusing her. "But I will admit to wondering why you were having breakfast with the county treasurer and the chairman of the county board of commissioners." She frowned. "Doesn't that strike you as a fair question?"

"It was just supposed to be Mr. Scroggins," Coretta said, her voice defensive. "He was going to tell me some things I needed to know about the office. Mr. Tombull happened to come in to get his breakfast, so Mr. Scroggins didn't have any choice but to invite him to sit down with us. It definitely wasn't my idea. And Mr. Scroggins never did get around to telling me what I was supposed to know, so I've been flying blind all day. The other two women in the office—well, they don't know beans about anything. You ask one of them a question and she just stares at you with a blank face. I mean, I know they probably don't like me very much, given the situation, but that's not my fault." She stuck out her lower lip. "Between them and my shoes killing me, it's been just awful, all day long."

"Wasn't such a good day for me, either," Lizzy remarked, thinking about Verna and Alice Ann Walker and the sheriff and Mrs. Biggs.

Coretta rushed on, gathering steam. "Anyway, I wanted to talk to Verna, so I was planning to go over to her house after work. I didn't want to because I knew it would be awkward, but I thought I'd better do it anyway. Then I got the word that she had gone to Nashville." She gave Lizzy a sideways glance. "So I decided to come over here and talk to you. I said to myself, Liz Lacy is Verna Tidwell's best friend. They're thick as thieves. Liz will know what's what. And why."

Lizzy was surprised. "Who told you about Verna going to Nashville?"

"The sheriff came into the office this afternoon. I heard him and Mr. Scroggins talking about it. But then I—" She stopped as though she might be going to say something else and decided not to. She took a breath and began again.

"Look here, Liz. I reckon I should start from the beginning. When Mr. Scroggins called to tell me I could start working full time again, he said it was because Verna is in some kind of trouble. Money trouble. He said he had to put new locks on the office doors to keep her from using her key to get in." She raised an inquiring eyebrow. "Do you know about this?"

"I know that it happened," Lizzy said cautiously, not wanting to give too much away. "But I have no idea why."

"It's got to do with the state audit. And the report." Coretta was perspiring. She opened her leather handbag, took out a hanky, and delicately patted her forehead and cheeks. "Verna tell you about that?"

Lizzy hesitated. "Um, she told me that a couple of auditors came into the office a while ago. She didn't mention a report." That was true. It was Myra May who had told her—and Verna—about the report.

"Well, the report came in today's mail." She paused, her face becoming serious. "And all I've got to say is, it's a good thing Verna is in Nashville." She looked over her shoulder as if she was afraid that somebody might be lurking on the other side of the privet hedge. "And for pity's sake, don't tell anybody—especially Mr. Scroggins—that I've been here and talked to you. I am taking a big chance, Liz. A lollapalooza of a chance. I could lose my job—or worse."

Lizzy narrowed her eyes. "Are you trying to scare me, Coretta? What do you mean, *or worse?*" She was thinking that Coretta hadn't changed much since high school after all. She had always loved to dramatize herself.

"I'm not trying to scare you, honest I'm not." Coretta sounded earnest. "I just want to be clear. This isn't a little Sunday School party. It's serious business." She rolled her eyes. "To tell the truth, I wish I'd told Mr. Scroggins to go jump in the river when he told me come back to work—and if I'd've known then what I know now, maybe I would've. But I need the dough real bad. And I can't back out now. I've got to do things the way Mr. Scroggins and Mr. Tombull want me to or they might think I had something to do with it."

That was the last straw. Lizzy stood up and put her hands on her hips. "Coretta Cole, you are talking like a character in a Hollywood movie. You can stop beating around the bush and come straight out with what you know, or you can march out of that gate and straight on home. What's it going to be?"

Coretta squared her shoulders defiantly and Lizzy thought for a minute that she was going to get up and leave. Then she slumped. "Sorry," she muttered. "Okay, here's what I know, so far, anyway. There's fifteen thousand dollars missing from the county treasury."

"Fifteen thousand!" Lizzy pretended astonishment.

Coretta held up her hand and hurried on. "The county commissioners are putting the thumbscrews on Mr. Scroggins to find out where that money went. They're telling him he's got to get it back fast, too—he's the treasurer now, so it's his responsibility. Mr. Scroggins has convinced himself that Verna took it. He talked Mr. Johnson at the bank into letting him have a peek at Verna's savings account, which he says has ten thousand dollars in it. He told Sheriff Burns to go to Judge McHenry and get a warrant. Verna is going to be arrested as soon as the sheriff locates her. He says once he's got her in custody, she'll have a chance to explain herself."

Lizzy chewed on her lower lip. Ten thousand dollars was a fortune! Where on God's sweet green earth had Verna gotten that much money? She had no income other than her job and no property other than her house, and she'd used her husband's life insurance to pay off the mortgage. Her family had been dirt poor, and none of them were left. Why, if she didn't know Verna as well as she did, she herself might suspect that—

She shook her head. No, of course not. That was out of the question. Verna wouldn't. She simply wouldn't. Not under any circumstance.

Lizzy took a breath. "I guess I don't understand why you're telling me all this," she said quietly. "Or why you care, Coretta. From what I've heard, there's no love lost between you and Verna. I'd think you'd be just as happy if she got into some serious trouble. So why are you—"

"No love lost is right," Coretta broke in, her sharp face hardening. "And I'll be the first to say that, in the normal way of things, I'd be just as glad to see Verna Tidwell taken down a peg or two. She is one smart cookie, but she is the very worst supervisor I have ever worked for." The words were coming out fast now, as if Coretta had been thinking about this for a while. "She acts like you already know what you're supposed to be doing, and when she wants something done, she tells you really fast. She doesn't give you time to ask questions, and then she gets mad when you don't get it right the first time. She hates mistakes, and once you've made one, she figures you'll make more, which of course you do."

Lizzy winced. Coretta's description might be a little harsh, but it was accurate enough. Verna had high expectations of herself and everybody else, and she didn't tolerate mistakes. She was not the world's best teacher, especially if you were a slow learner.

Coretta wasn't finished. "But when it comes to money, I've got to say this for Verna. She is totally and completely honest. She is so honest, it would make you sick. And as for keeping track, she cannot rest until she knows where every single penny is and what it's doing there. The county's bank accounts were a total mess when Verna inherited them, and trying to figure out what's what has literally given her nightmares." She paused for emphasis. "Somebody must have taken that fifteen thousand dollars, Liz, since it's gone. Or at least, that's what the auditor says, and his report shows it, I guess. But I just can't believe it was *Verna* who took it."

"I see," Lizzy said, and waited.

"And there's something else." Coretta's eyes narrowed. "If Verna is made to look like the guilty party, the guilty party will get away with murder."

"Murder?" Lizzy asked, startled. She immediately thought of the inexplicable death of Mr. DeYancy, the former treasurer, who had died (or so the coroner said) of alcohol poisoning. *"Murder?"*

"In a manner of speaking, that is," Coretta said hastily. "What somebody is getting away with is fifteen thousand dollars of the taxpayers' money, which is a huge amount of money. If we don't do something about it, Verna will get the blame and somebody else will get a potful of money." She leaned forward. "I for one don't think it's fair. It's just plain wrong for them to do Verna like that. And I think I know what can be done about it."

Lizzy frowned, not quite believing what she was hearing.

"Let me get this straight. You're saying that you've come up with a way to help Verna out of the jam she's in?"

"That's right," Coretta said, lifting her chin. "But I can't do it by myself. I'm going to need help."

Lizzy sat back, thinking. She wanted to believe that Coretta was being sincere. But everything she knew about this woman told her that Coretta couldn't be trusted. Tell her a secret and she would exaggerate and twist it to serve her own purposes, and then she'd blab it all over the place. Agree to do something with her, and she'd change her mind halfway through and quit. She sneaked a sideways glance at Coretta. True, all that had been quite a few years ago, when they were in school together. Coretta was older now and more mature. Maybe she meant what she said. Maybe she had changed.

Or maybe not. She might be the same old Coretta. And if she ran true to form, she would finagle it so that she'd end up looking like a hero and Verna would be in even deeper trouble.

Lizzy sat back and folded her arms. "Just what is it that you think you can do?" she asked warily. She would go along with this scheme just far enough to find out what Coretta had in mind.

"I can go undercover in the office," Coretta said, and batted her Joan Crawford eyes.

"Undercover?" Incredulous, Lizzy fought the urge to giggle.

"Exactly," Coretta replied earnestly. "I can be a *spy*. But as I said, I'm going to need help. This isn't an operation I can carry out by myself."

Now, Lizzy did laugh, skeptically. "That's rich, Coretta. Really rich. Just who do you think you're going to spy on? Those two women in the office? And how is that going to help Verna?"

If Coretta was offended by Liz's skepticism, she didn't let on. "I don't know enough to figure out what's going on all by myself. But Verna does." She leaned forward, her dark eyes glittering. "I have access to the account books, and I have a key to the office. I can smuggle the books out to Verna, wherever she is. Or I can smuggle Verna into the office, if she'd rather me do that. I'm thinking that if she uses the auditor's report as a guide, she'll be able to figure out what happened to that money. At least, she might come up with a pretty good idea." She patted the handbag she had put between them on the swing. "In fact, I've brought the report with me. I think she needs to see it."

Lizzy was taken aback. Smuggling Verna into the office was very close to Verna's original scheme for conducting her own investigation, when she thought she still had a key that worked. Maybe what Coretta was suggesting was doable. On the other hand, maybe it was a put-up job, some kind of trick.

"The report," she said. "May I see it?"

"Why?" Coretta asked uneasily.

"Because I want to make sure it's the real thing," Lizzy said.

"Well, I guess it's okay," Coretta said, and reluctantly pulled a large envelope out of her handbag.

Lizzy opened it and scanned the three sheets of paper. As far as she could tell, the report was genuine. It had what appeared to be the seal of the state auditor's office at the top of the first page and a signature and another seal at the bottom of the third.

She handed it back with a frown. "I don't understand, Coretta. Why would you even think of doing such a dangerous thing? Why would you *risk* it? If Mr. Scroggins found out what you were doing, he'd fire you so fast it'd make your head spin. And then both you *and* Verna would be out of a job. If Verna winds up in jail, you might be in there with her."

"Why would I do such a dangerous thing?" Coretta repeated, with the air of someone who has thought all this out. "Because I don't like what's happening here, Liz. This whole situation stinks to high heaven. It's corruption, that's what it is, and Verna is getting blamed for it. Like I said, I am not a big fan of hers, but what's happening is just plain wrong."

"Yes, but the risk—"

Coretta lifted her chin. "Some things are worth taking a risk for, Liz. I do have my principles, you know."

"I didn't say you didn't," Lizzy said, although that was exactly what she was thinking. Coretta had never struck her as the type to take a risk on principle.

"You didn't have to," Coretta replied regretfully. "I can tell." She became very serious. "Anyway, I don't believe Verna took that money. But like I said, I'm going to need help to prove it." She gave Lizzy a straight, hard look. "Actually, Liz, I'm going to need *Verna's* help. Before I can do anything, I need to sit down and talk to her, so we can make a plan."

"Talk to . . . Verna?" Coretta sounded convincing, but all their past history rose up in Lizzy's mind like a dark shadow. Maybe she was working for Mr. Scroggins—or for the sheriff. Or both. Maybe this was a ploy, a trick to find out where Verna was, so the sheriff could come and arrest her.

"Yes, talk to her," Coretta insisted. "I need to sit down with her and map out a strategy. Like right away." Her voice became emphatic. "Like tonight."

"Tonight?" Lizzy asked. "But Verna has taken the train to Nashville. You can't—"

"Uh-uh," Coretta interrupted, shaking her head definitively. "I know for a fact that she didn't take that train to Nashville."

Lizzy shifted uneasily in the swing. This wasn't going the way she wanted it to. "I don't understand. What makes you think she hasn't—"

"Because," Coretta broke in, "I telephoned Mr. Gilmer, over at the depot, and asked him if Verna Tidwell was on the noon spur train to Monroeville. That's the train she'd take if she was going to Nashville. But she didn't. Mr. Gilmer says he hasn't seen her." Coretta gave Lizzy a penetrating look. "Of course, if it occurred to me to check out her story, Liz, it could occur to the sheriff as well."

That was true, Lizzy thought, with a cold feeling in her stomach. Maybe Sheriff Burns had already talked to Mr. Gilmer. But she tried to parry.

"Well, then, maybe she got a ride to Monroeville with Mr. Clinton. She does that sometimes, when she goes shopping. She could have caught the train at the L and N depot."

Mr. Clinton drove an old red Ford two-seater back and forth between Darling and Monroeville, twenty miles away. Two trips in the morning, two trips in the afternoon. He charged fifteen cents for a one-way trip, a quarter if you wanted to go both ways. It might be a little crowded, since Mr. Clinton was known to put as many as four riders in the backseat, along with all their packages. Sometimes people had to sit on other people's laps.

"Uh-uh." Coretta shook her head. "On my way here, I happened to see Mr. Clinton letting people out at the diner. He said he definitely didn't give Verna a ride today. So if she didn't take the spur train and she didn't ride with Mr. Clinton, she's still here. In Darling, I mean. Hiding out." Her voice tightened. "And *you* know where she is."

Lizzy stared at her, torn between two perplexing possibilities. It was possible, just possible, that Coretta really wanted to help Verna find out what was going on and that she was willing to take a big risk to find out who had taken that money. On the other hand, she could just as easily be working for Mr. Scroggins, and she wanted to learn Verna's whereabouts so she could turn her in to the sheriff. She had said she needed money—maybe she had been promised a reward. Or maybe she figured that she could put Verna out of the way permanently, and she would get Verna's job. Which was it? Was Coretta telling the truth, or was she lying?

Coretta stood up. "Look, Liz, all I want to do is to help Verna out of this tight spot. Honest to God, I truly do. But to do that, I have to talk to her. I want to show her the auditor's report—that's why I smuggled it out of the office." Her voice became more demanding. "Are you going to help or not?"

Lizzy sat limp for a moment, not knowing how to respond. She had always had a way with words. But for once in her life, she didn't know what to say.

# THIRTEEN

# Charlie

When Lizzy walked past the *Dispatch* office on her way home from work, Charlie Dickens didn't look up and wave at her for the simple reason that he had his nose in a book—a library book. Or to be more precise, a *scrapbook*, one that he had borrowed from the library.

Charlie had not been thrilled that morning when Bessie Bloodworth had handed him that transcription of the indecipherable symbols and numbers some little old lady had embroidered on a pillow, wondering whether it might be some sort of "secret code." In fact, at first, he had thought the whole thing was pretty silly. He had even teased her a little about it, but she hadn't been offended. And when she smiled, he'd noticed the laugh wrinkles crinkling around her mouth. It occurred to him that Bessie Bloodworth was an attractive lady—for her age, of course. She had gone to school with his sister Edna Fay, he remembered, which made her just three or four years younger than himself. While Charlie preferred his women even younger (around the age of Fannie Champaign, for instance) he had to admit that Bessie had taken a lot better care of herself than had Angelina Biggs. At the thought of Angelina Biggs, he had shuddered and made himself stop thinking of women. Women could get a man in trouble.

After Bessie left, Charlie had given her paper another skeptical look. Secret code? He seriously doubted it. He'd had considerable experience working with codes and ciphers when he was in France during the Great War. And when the fighting was over and he'd been sent back to Washington, he'd been interested enough to do some historical research on the topic. In his experience, people just didn't go around embroidering secret codes on pillows. As for the symbols and numbers on that piece of paper, well, yes, he supposed they might look to the untrained eye like some sort of cipher. But more likely, it was only some sort of silly female exercise. Some Southern lady showing off her fancy needlework skills. A strange sort of sampler, nothing more.

But then Charlie had seen the name and the date—*Rose, July 21, 1861*—and something, some fragment of memory long buried under the detritus of facts that filled his mind, had begun to stir, like a seed swelling and growing and reaching toward the light.

*July 21, 1861.* The day every schoolboy in the South was taught to hold dear. The day of the First Manassas (the Battle of Bull Run as the Union called it), the first battle of the War Between the States and perhaps the Confederacy's most glorious day.

The battle was fought between General P. G. T. Beauregard's unseasoned Southern army and the equally untested Northern troops commanded by General Irvin McDowell. The two forces met at Manassas Junction, just twenty-five miles to the west of Washington, near a stream called Bull Run, which eventually flowed into the Potomac. Since it was Sunday and Manassas was so close to the city, throngs of

Union supporters had made a grand holiday of it, driving across Aqueduct Bridge in their elegant black carriages, laden with picnic baskets and bottles of fine wine and silver flasks filled with bourbon. They were all there, the cream of Washington society, senators, cabinet members, and their gaily garbed ladies, out to enjoy the spectacle of a splendid Union victory, the first and last battle of what they confidently predicted would be a very short war. Hawkers and peddlers lined the road, selling everything from sandwiches to spyglasses and battle maps and clever canes that unfolded into a seat. A correspondent from the *Times* of London was there to report on the battle. And so was Mathew Brady, already famous for his photographs of illustrious people. Determined to be the first man in history to photograph a battlefield, he had loaded a wagon with his large camera and plate holder, put on his straw hat and saber, and joined the crowd heading for Manassas Junction.

Early word filtering back from the battlefield gave General McDowell's federal troops the victory, but the truth was something very different and entirely unexpected. By evening, it was clear that the South had triumphed. Back in Washington, Secretary of War Seward reported to President Lincoln that he had received a telegram saying that McDowell was in full retreat and pleading for General Scott to rally his troops and save Washington from the attack that was sure to follow. There was nothing between the victorious Rebels and the defenseless capital but crowds of wounded and disorganized stragglers, jostling for road room with a stampede of panic-stricken fleeing spectators—including a frightened Mathew Brady, who had narrowly escaped capture. The battle had been a rout, a clear, decisive Confederate victory that had left the North defeated and demoralized and the South in jubilant celebration.

A Confederate victory. Charlie frowned and scratched his

head. But there was more. Some recollection was tugging at him, had been tugging at him ever since he had seen that name and the date. A memory of an unusual circumstance of that battle and the name Rose—and particularly about a secret code. What was it? *What?*

But while Charlie was deeply and fervently interested in many things—contemporary politics, and the disastrous state of the economy, and the crying need for a stronger and more progressive hand at the helm than Hoover's—Civil War history had been of only passing interest, back when he was a schoolboy and still felt a patriotic stirring for the Confederacy. So he put Bessie Bloodworth's paper aside and went back to his typewriter, pausing only occasionally to attempt (unsuccessfully) to remember what it was about the First Manassas that he might once have known but by now had almost completely forgotten. Almost, but not quite.

An avid reader, Charlie Dickens possessed an extensive personal library of books he had collected over the years. In his opinion, books were the most important pieces of furniture—furniture of the mind—that a man could own. His bookshelves included several books on codes and ciphers, but he knew there was nothing in them that would help him decode (if there was any message to decode, which was still doubtful) the symbols on the paper Bessie Bloodworth had given him. And he possessed not a single book on the Confederate victory at Bull Run.

But the Darling library might. Like most small-town libraries, its holdings consisted mostly of fiction and some fairly recent nonfiction. But it had been given several collections of antique books by people who had inherited them and didn't want to keep the musty old things, which of course nobody in his right mind would want to actually sit down and read. Charlie thought he might be able to locate something that would help him remember what he had forgotten about somebody named Rose and a secret code and the First Manassas. The library would be open from two to five that afternoon. He would drop in and see what he could find.

And having settled the matter for the time being, Charlie went back to his two-finger attack on his old black Royal. But not for long. He had just started work on a story about the Darling town council when he was interrupted first by Ophelia Snow, looking for a job, and then by Artis Biggs, needing help with his wife, who (it turned out) had popped her cork in Mr. Moseley's law office and was threatening to sue both of them, Artis for divorce and Charlie for sexual assault. And on the way back to the hotel with Angelina, who was dragging her feet and shrieking like a crazy woman, Beulah Trivette had come along with her story about the diet pills. At first it had seemed pretty far-fetched, but by the time Beulah had finished telling them about what was in the pills and about Angelina's hair falling out, both he and Artis were convinced, especially since they could see a big bald spot on the side of Angelina's head.

After Charlie left Artis to put his crazy wife to bed, he strode back across the street with a lighter step and relief in his heart. Angelina wasn't going crazy after all, and she wasn't really in love with him. And Artis (or so he claimed, and Charlie believed him) wasn't carrying on an affair on the second floor of the hotel. He was merely checking the rooms to see what kind of job the maids were doing.

Charlie sat down at his typewriter again and knocked out the lead for the town council story. He was leaning back, scratching around in his brain for the first sentence of the second paragraph, when the alley door opened and Ruthie Brant slipped in. She glanced over her shoulder to make sure she hadn't been observed and closed the door behind her. If anybody did happen to see her and wondered why an employee from the county treasurer's office was going into the

*Dispatch* through the back door, Ruthie would explain that she was dropping off a story about the latest bridge club meeting and thought it was quicker to come down the alley instead of along the street. Ruthie Brant was not by any stretch the best-looking girl in Darling, but she could make up a tale faster than green grass goes through a goose.

However, it was not what Ruthie Brant did or didn't look like that interested Charlie and brought him to immediate attention whenever she came sneaking in through that back door. It was what Ruthie Brant *knew*, and the tales she had told him over the past months were never made up. They were the good Lord's honest truth.

In fact, it was Ruthie Brant's covert operation as an informant that had provided the foundation for the scathing editorials about the county treasurer's office that appeared in the *Dispatch* and gave the county officials, especially Mr. Amos Tombull, such heartburn. The editorials had been laced with enough facts to startle a few Darling folks and raise a few Darling eyebrows. And—more to the point—they had frightened Mr. Jasper DeYancy into believing that the editor of the *Dispatch* knew a lot more than he was saying and was prepared to tell the whole story when the time was ripe.

For while he had not one stick of proof to buttress his conclusion, Charlie had convinced himself that Mr. DeYancy's death was a suicide disguised as an accident, cleverly designed to allow the Widow DeYancy to collect her husband's considerable life insurance. (In Charlie's opinion, "accidentally" drowning yourself in a gallon of chain lightning was a good deal more pleasant and a great deal less messy than "accidentally" blowing off your head when you were cleaning your gun, which was the way other Southern gentlemen had elected to leave this life.)

And while Charlie regretted Mr. DeYancy's untimely end, he did not feel guilty about it or even one whit responsible, for when a man sets out to deceive the public that elected him to office, he deserves whatever tree limbs or boulders might fall on his head or whatever newspaper editorials might appear in his path. He ought to be man enough to stand up and take it, instead of looking for the exit.

And further*more*, even though Jasper DeYancy was dead and unavailable for comment and his deceptions (if any) could not be proved, Charlie's suspicions about the operation of the county treasurer's office had lingered on like a bad smell out behind the barn—had been heightened, even, with the appointment of Earle Scroggins to the post.

Now, seeing Ruthie (whom he thought of as a kind of secret agent, *his* secret agent), Charlie felt an anticipatory tingle in his typing fingers and his nose for news began to twitch, the way it used to when he was doing a piece of investigative reporting for the *Baltimore Sun* or the Cleveland *Plain Dealer*—back in the days when he was a real reporter on a real news beat.

Reaching for his pack of Lucky Strikes, he said, "Well, hullo there, Ruthie. Got somethin' new for the readers of the *Dispatch*?"

"Have I ever," Ruthie replied, with a lopsided grin that brightened her sallow face and gave her the look of a sly puppy that has just polished off the beefsteak her master left too close to the edge of the table. "Have I *ever*, Mr. Dickens. The state auditor's report came today. You are goin' to like this. It's a bombshell."

*State auditor's report!* Ruthie had kept Charlie informed about the two visits from the auditor's office, so the report itself wasn't much of a surprise. But if it was indeed the bombshell that Ruthie thought it was, this might be news he could use. He shook out two Luckys and offered Ruthie one and a click of his cigarette lighter.

"That's good, Ruthie," he said, hooking the toe of his shoe

around the rung of a straight chair and pulling it toward his desk. "That is *real* good. Now, you just sit yourself right down in that chair and tell me all about it. From the top. With facts, of course. I need the *facts*." He said this emphatically, because while Ruthie could string together an intriguing narrative, she often needed to be prodded for the facts.

"I'm supposed to be taking a break from the office, so I don't have a lot of time," Ruthie said, leaning back in her chair, stretching out her rayon-stockinged legs, and pulling on her cigarette. "This'll have to be quick."

"The quicker the better," Charlie said, thinking about the empty inches in the right-hand column above the fold on page one. He twirled the Royal's platen to roll the narrow, column-width roll of newsprint he was typing on to a clear spot, and hunched over the machine. "Okay, Ruthie, my girl," he said around his cigarette. "Shoot."

Ruthie shot. And it was a doozey.

The trouble was, Ruthie's bombshell was all story. And while the story was full of intriguing surprises and fascinating speculations, it suffered from a distinct shortage of facts.

And for the life of him, Charlie couldn't think of a way to confirm what Ruthie was telling him.


A half hour later, still thinking about the bombshell Ruthie Brant had dropped in his lap, Charlie put his Panama hat on his head, shrugged into his suit jacket, and locked up the *Dispatch* office. Then he headed over to the Darling library, which was located on the west side of the courthouse square, at the back of Fannie Champaign's milliner's shop, Champaign's Darling Chapeaux. The little library had its own separate entrance, so that patrons did not have to go through the millinery shop, a fact for which Charlie was grateful. He was in no mood to see Fannie Champaign today, or any other day, for that matter.

Not that Fannie had ever actually said no when he asked her to go to a movie or out to dinner. She just hadn't said anything, which in Charlie's mind—well, in anybody's mind—was as good as a no. He had met plenty of stubborn women in his time, but Fannie was the stubbornest by far, with an independent streak a mile wide and two miles deep. He had come to the conclusion that he wasn't going to get anywhere with her, and he knew it.

So he walked quickly around the building to the back, to the door with the painted sign announcing that he had arrived at the Darling Library (QUIET PLEASE). He opened the door and went in.

The library's small front room contained the librarian's desk, a rack of narrow wooden drawers that held index cards with the titles and call numbers of every book, and a small table and chair where you could sit and read in front of the window. The desk was occupied by Miss Dorothy Rogers, who was about as stiff an old spinster as Charlie had ever encountered. He'd had one or two run-ins with her about overdue books. The last time, he'd had to pay a sixty-cent fine, which (in his opinion) was more than the book—*The Economic Consequences of the Peace* by John Maynard Keynes—was worth. It had been a good book, but *sixty cents?* He felt sure that Keynes would agree with him.

Miss Rogers looked up. "Oh, Mr. Dickens," she said, in a sprightlier tone than he had expected. "How nice to see you. What may we help you with today?" She wore, Charlie thought, an oddly hopeful expression and he wondered briefly, with more than a touch of condescension, what she was hoping for.

Hoping to keep her job, he thought then, and his condescension disappeared with a jolt. Miss Rogers struck him as the kind of woman who lived for her part-time job at the little library. But he knew from his attendance at the town council meetings that there wasn't likely to be a library much longer. City revenues were down all over Alabama, and the libraries were among the first victims to fall to the budget-cutting ax. It was a damned shame, but that's how things were these days. Unless some sugar daddy came along and bailed them out, Miss Rogers and the library were about to come to the end of the road, at least until the economy turned around. And Charlie hadn't seen any sugar daddies loitering around outside.

"Thanks," Charlie said in reply to her question. "I'm not looking for anything special." He didn't want to be bothered by a fidgety old lady fussing around, trying to show him this or that just to prove that she was earning her pittance of a salary. "I'll just browse through the books, if that's okay."

She nodded, trying not to look disappointed, and Charlie went into the other, larger room, where floor-to-ceiling bookshelves covered all four walls, with two rows of back-to-back waist-high shelves down the middle. Until last year, the council had always set aside a few dollars for new book purchases. That wasn't happening this year, but the Ladies Club and the Dahlias' garden club had got together and raised some money with an auction and variety show. (Charlie didn't have much use for ladies' clubs, but occasionally they did something he approved of. Raising money for library books was one of them.)

Miss Rogers had put the money to good use. She had bought *The Sound and the Fury* by William Faulkner (which Charlie had tried to read but got exasperated after the first dozen pages and gave it up); *A Farewell to Arms* by Ernest Hemingway (an easier novel that Charlie had checked out more than once); and *Look Homeward Angel* by Thomas Wolfe, who wrote in something called a stream-of-consciousness style that made Charlie dizzy. If you had a story to tell, just by golly tell the damn thing, he thought, with the impatience of the born newspaperman, and stop meandering around. The other books Miss Rogers had bought were more to Charlie's liking—a mystery by a novice writer named Ellery Queen, *The Maltese Falcon* by Dashiell Hammett, and a new S. S. Van Dine. It appeared that Miss Rogers was as fond of a good mystery as any of the Darlingians who frequented the little library.

But it wasn't the newer titles that interested Charlie, not today, anyway. Several years before, Miss Rogers had reshelved all the books according to the Dewey Decimal System. The history books were all in the nine hundreds, so that's where he started browsing. There were titles on Roman history, British history, and American history. And, yes, as he had expected, there was nearly a full shelf of Civil War history, including a leather-bound copy of a book called *My Imprisonment and the First Year of Abolition Rule at Washington* by R. O'Neale Greenhow, published in London in 1863; a collection of newspaper clippings pasted into a flimsy scrapbook; and a history of Civil War battles written by an obscure Confederate officer. He carried all three books to the desk, expecting that Miss Rogers would object to his taking the scrapbook, which looked as if it might disintegrate when the pages were turned.

But she only gave his gatherings a puzzled look, cautioned him to be *very* careful not to lose any pages of the scrapbook, and wrote his name and the due date on the white cards in the front of the books, then filed them in the tin box on the corner of her desk.

"Two weeks," she said, handing them back to him and adding, with an enigmatic significance, "I hope you'll find what you're looking for, Mr. Dickens."

Charlie was still trying to figure out what that was supposed to mean as he walked around the building and nearly stumbled over Miss Fannie Champaign, who was kneeling in the path, tending a flower bed. She was wearing a pale green straw garden hat decorated with green silk roses. Beside her was a basket half filled with weeds.

She straightened up and looked at him, and he was struck once again by how pretty she was. Not beautiful, no, not that, but pretty in a comfortable sort of way, with the look of a woman who was at home with who she was and how she had got there. Miss Champaign had come to Darling some two or three years before. Many Darlingians had been deeply curious about her, especially since she was a single woman with no visible means of support and no friends and relations to welcome her to town. People were too polite to ask, but the questions were on everyone's mind, for she was something of a mystery. Where did she get her money? Why had she come to Darling? Charlie had heard that she had been engaged once, when she was much younger, and that her work as a milliner often took her to Mobile and beyond, where she sold her hats to wealthy customers in fancy shops. More than that, he didn't know, although of course he was as curious as anybody else.

But then she had opened her hat shop and the Darling ladies fell in love with her romantic creations—floppy-brimmed hats with meringue puffs of ribbon-laced tulle and gardens of silk blossoms. Miss Champaign's hats were very like those worn by Southern ladies before the War Between the States and very *unlike* the smart, sleek, head-hugging felt cloches that were all the rage just now, and everybody loved them—even the Darling men, who (truth be told) didn't like those snug felt helmets much, anyway. Charlie agreed. A lady's hat should make her look like a lady, not like a German artillery officer.

He managed to stop before he actually stepped on her.

"Good afternoon, Miss Champaign," he said, and removed his Panama hat.

She looked back down and pulled a handful of weeds. "Good afternoon, Mr. Dickens," she said. And that was all.

He took three careful steps around her, then paused, wondering if, after all, it might be worth trying again. Probably not. And if she said no again, it would be the last time. The very last time.

He cleared his throat. "I was thinking of having dinner at the hotel this evening," he said, although he hadn't been thinking anything of the sort. "Perhaps you might join me?"

She pulled another batch of weeds. The sunlight glinted on her russet hair. "No, thank you," she said, and he thought he heard a hint of something like regret in her voice. Just a hint, but enough (despite his resolution) to embolden him.

"Tomorrow, then," he said, and thought about the Old Alabama's menus, which were the same for every week. "Tuesday night is chicken night, as I remember. Baked with dressing."

"I don't believe so, Mr. Dickens, but thank you for the invitation."

"You're welcome," Charlie said with resignation, and put his hat back on his head. He paused, and then said outright what was in his mind. "Miss Champaign, is there a ghost of a chance you will ever say yes to me—about anything?"

She seemed startled by that but paused to consider for a moment, still holding her handful of weeds. "I don't know that I can answer that, Mr. Dickens. I suppose it would all depend."

He leaned forward, watching her. "Depend on what?"

"I have no idea," she said, and tossed the weeds into her basket.

With a sigh, Charlie walked back to the newspaper office, where he sat down at his desk and began to turn the pages in the old scrapbook, which proved to be clippings from the Richmond, Virginia, *Daily Dispatch* of the early-to-mid-1860s. At the time, Richmond was the capital of the Confederacy, of course. That's what he was doing when Lizzy walked past the window without seeing him, on her way home from work.

Back in the library, Miss Rogers took out the cards she had just filed and studied them. When Bessie Bloodworth had returned from the *Dispatch* office that morning, she had reported that Mr. Dickens seemed to have some interest in the transcription of the symbols and numbers and had promised to look into the matter. When he had come into the library a little while before, Miss Rogers had felt a bright flare of hope, thinking that perhaps he had come to pursue his research into the secret code, if that's what it was. Miss Bloodworth said that she hadn't mentioned her name to him, so Mr. Dickens could have absolutely no idea that she was the owner of the embroidered pillow.

She put the three cards on the desk and studied them. She knew the books he had taken, of course. She was intimately acquainted with all the books in her little library and felt toward them as she would have felt toward her children, if she'd had any. She had cataloged each one of them, dusted them daily, and had read a great many (even those that she felt were undeserving, for she hated for any book to feel neglected).

She could tell you where the books had come from, too, for she included that information on their cards. *My Imprisonment* and the scrapbook of clippings had been the gift of a lady from Richmond, Virginia, who had lived out her last years with her Darling daughter. The history of Civil War battles was written by a Confederate captain named Adam Warren and had come from the collection of the founder of the

Darling Academy, a nephew of the author. None of the three books, as far as Miss Rogers could see, had anything remotely to do with the transcription of symbols on her grandmother's pillow. Mr. Dickens must have been exploring some other research topic when he borrowed them.

With a feeling of deep disappointment, she put the three white cards back in the tin box and closed the lid, sighing heavily as she put the box in the drawer. It was time to resign herself to the bitter truth. The mystery of her grandmother's embroidered pillow—what it meant and why it was made—would never be solved.

# FOURTEEN

# Lizzy, Verna, and Coretta

Myra May's large green 1920 Chevrolet touring car, aka Big Bertha, was parked in the ramshackle garage behind the diner. With twenty-five thousand miles under her wheels, Bertha was on her fifth set of tires and her second carburetor and she had a bad case of the rattles. But her green canvas top was still in one piece, the red painted spokes in her wheels were still bright, and she could purr like a kitten when she was feeling good. Lizzy had borrowed the car before, so she felt comfortable driving it. And the way things turned out, she was glad that she hadn't asked Grady if she could take his Ford. She ended up making two trips out to the Murphy place that evening, one by herself and the other with Coretta Cole. And then there was that midnight adventure at the courthouse. Grady would never have understood.

Lizzy made the first trip right after Coretta left her house. She ate a quick sandwich, then hurried to the diner, got Bertha's key from Myra May, and drove the four miles out to the

Murphys' place to discuss Coretta's offer with Verna. As she had expected, it was a hard sell.

At first, Verna refused to even consider talking to Coretta. But at last she threw up her hands and said, "Well, it's for damn sure that we're not going to get anywhere the way things stand. I'm stuck out here, without a key to the office and no access to any of the records. So I guess I'm willing to listen to what Coretta has to say, if you think I should. But I don't want her to know where I am—just in case she's a double agent."

"A double agent?" Lizzy asked, mystified.

"A spy who says she's working for one side but is secretly working for the other," Verna said. She grinned. "Really, Liz, you should broaden your horizons. Try *The Thirty-Nine Steps*. It's a great spy novel."

"But how are you going to talk to Coretta if you don't want her to know where you are?" Lizzy asked reasonably. "You can't talk on the phone, it's a party line. And if I bring her out here—well, she'll know where you are."

Verna waved her hand airily. "I'm sure you'll come up with something, Liz. Use your imagination. I'll talk to her. But it's my way or no way."

It took some thinking, but Lizzy had come up with a solution. By eight fifteen, when the sun had set and the April night had fallen like a dark, sweet-smelling cloak over the streets and houses of Darling, it was time to get started.

Big Bertha made such a clattering racket that Coretta Cole heard the car coming a block away and didn't wait for Lizzy to squeeze the *ooga-ooga* horn when she pulled up in front of the house. Wearing a dark brown sweater over a print dress, her handbag on her arm, Coretta hurried down her front steps and climbed into the front seat beside Lizzy.

"Here I am," she announced, adding expectantly, "Where are we going?"

"You have the auditor's report with you?" Lizzy countered. "Verna asked me to be sure."

"It's right here." Coretta reached into her bag and produced the envelope. Lizzy took Myra May's flashlight out from under her seat, checked to see if all three pages were there, then handed it back.

"Good enough," she said. "Now, hold still." She whipped out a large red-and-blue-striped bandana. "I'm going to tie this over your eyes."

"A blindfold?" Coretta squawked, holding up her hands. "I don't want to wear that thing! It's ridiculous!"

"You don't have any choice, Coretta," Lizzy said firmly. "You are wearing this, or you're going right back into your house and I'm heading home. Which is just fine with me. It's been a long day. I'd just as soon have the evening to myself."

"You don't want me to know where Verna is staying," Coretta accused, pouting. "You don't trust me to keep it secret."

"How did you guess?" Lizzy asked grimly. "Now, turn around."

Awkwardly, still protesting, Coretta turned in the seat. Lizzy folded the bandana over Coretta's eyes and knotted it securely in the back.

"At least it's dark and none of the neighbors can see me," Coretta grumbled, scrunching down in the seat. "I must look like an idiot."

"You look like somebody who's about to embark on a dangerous spy mission," Lizzy said with a laugh. Then she put Big Bertha into gear and they chugged off down the street.

The Murphy place was about four miles outside of town, heading south. Earlier, Lizzy had taken the quickest way, straight out Jericho Road. But that wasn't the route she took now. She drove out to the north side of town, weaving from one street to another, until she got to Sherman's sawmill. The freshly sawn pine boards had a distinctive odor, and somebody was running the sawmill, getting out a big order of sawn boards. If Coretta had a lick of sense, she would recognize the smell and the sound and think that they were heading for a destination north of town.

They weren't. Lizzy circled around and drove back into Darling, making a right turn onto Franklin, past the courthouse, then turning left on Rosemont. By that time, she figured that Coretta must be thoroughly confused, so she took the next right and headed south on Briarwood Road, past the Dance Barn, until she got to Jericho Road. When they reached the Murphys' place, Lizzy brought Bertha to a stop and turned off the motor. She climbed out and opened the passenger door.

"Can I take this off now?" Coretta asked plaintively, reaching for the blindfold.

"Nope," Lizzy said, and escorted Coretta up the dirt path to the porch. The old frame house was unpainted and needed some repairs, but after Lucy joined the Dahlias, each member of the club had given her several plants and volunteered to help fix up the yard, badly neglected since the death of Ralph Murphy's first wife. The weeds had been replaced by a row of rosebushes in front of the porch, some azaleas, and even a few camellias. They had planted gladiolas along the fence and fancy-leaved caladiums and gloriosa lilies under the big trees. Out back, Lucy planted a large vegetable garden, and behind that, she and Ralph had put in an orchard of young green peach trees. Lucy hoped to make a little extra money by selling peaches at the market.

When Lucy answered Lizzy's knock at the door, Lizzy held her finger to her lips. Lucy stepped back with a conspiratorial nod, a scruffy gray tabby cat winding himself around her ankles. Lizzy was sure that Coretta had never met Lucy and wouldn't recognize her voice, but there was no point in taking that risk. She led the blindfolded woman inside.

In the front bedroom, Verna was sitting cross-legged on the bed, reading a book. She looked up. "Well, Coretta," she said pleasantly. "Did you and Lizzy have a nice ride out here?"

"It was a long way," Coretta said in a complaining tone. "This place must be ten or twelve miles out in the country." She reached for the blindfold again. "Can I take this off now?"

"Uh-uh," Lizzy said. "We'll just leave it on. You don't need to see Verna to talk to her." She steered Coretta to a rocking chair near the bed, then opened Coretta's handbag and took out the manila envelope. "Here, Verna. Take a look at this. Coretta says it's the auditor's report."

Verna spread the pages out on the quilt and spent several long moments looking at them.

"Mmm," she said, half under her breath. "Fifteen thousand in the red. My, my." She looked again at the figures, turned a page, and then another. "I think I'm seeing a pattern," she said after a little while. "And it's giving me an idea of where else I might look  if I can sit down for an hour or two with a couple of the office ledgers." She glanced at Coretta, who was sitting stiffly in the rocking chair, her lower lip pushed out like a pouty child. "Liz told me your idea, Coretta. But are you really sure you want to get involved in this? It could be risky."

"I don't mind taking a few risks," Coretta said, almost defiantly. "I just don't think it's right that the blame is being pinned on you."

There was a jagged edge to Verna's laugh. "I guess it's dangerous to have money in the bank." She looked at Lizzy. "Want to know where I got the ten thousand dollars that's in my account at the Savings and Trust, Liz?"

"If you want to tell," Lizzy replied quietly, knowing that Verna always kept her private business to herself.

"My aunt Mildred died and left a piece of property to me—an orange grove in Florida. That was six or seven years ago, after the Florida real estate bubble burst. Back then, you couldn't unload Florida property if you paid somebody to take it off your hands. As far as I knew, it wasn't worth a plugged nickel." She tilted her head. "But to my surprise, a buyer came along a few months ago and offered me ten thousand dollars. I sold the orange grove and put the money in the bank."

"Ah," Lizzy said, and smiled. "I'm sure you can prove that to the sheriff, when he asks. And to Mr. Scroggins. So maybe we don't need to worry about you getting arrested. We can all go home and—"

"Proving it might be a little difficult," Verna broke in. Her face was dark. "The deed was lost years ago, and I had to get Aunt Mildred's lawyer to research the title before the sale went through. I don't have all the paperwork yet. Anyway, even if I could prove it, they would suspect me as long as they feel like it." Her voice was determined. "I have to find out what happened to that missing money."

"But maybe you don't have to do that now," Lizzy said. "Tonight, I mean."

"You're wrong, Liz." Verna shook her head emphatically. "I didn't take that money. But somebody needs a fall guy, and I'm convenient. Until the real thief is found, I'll always be a suspect in some people's minds. And in the meantime, I'm out of a job—and my bank account is likely to be frozen." She turned to Coretta. "Coretta, I'm sorry to disappoint you, but we don't really need a spy. What we need is for you to go to Musgroves and get a copy of that new key. Then—"

"Actually, I did that already," Coretta said, sounding smug.

"You did?" Verna asked, surprised. "Why?"

Below the bandana, Coretta's mouth turned down. "Well, to be honest, I've been known to lose a key every now and then. So I thought it would be a good idea to have a spare. I don't intend to let Mr. Scroggins know I copied it. But I don't mind telling you, Verna. In fact, I don't mind showing you." She groped around blindly. "Where's my handbag, Liz?"

Lizzy handed her the bag and Coretta felt inside. Finding a key, she held it up. "This is what you're asking for?"

"You bet!" Verna jumped off the bed and snatched the key. She sat back again, the bedsprings creaking. "Liz, on second thought, let's take that blindfold off. It must be uncomfortable for Coretta."

"Oh, but I don't think—" Lizzy began. She still wasn't convinced that Coretta was on the level. But Verna gave her a meaningful look and she got the point. It was impossible to judge Coretta's sincerity when her eyes were covered and they couldn't see the expression on her face. She got up to do as Verna asked.

"Oh, thank you!" Coretta exclaimed, as Lizzy untied the knot and pulled the bandana off. She looked around, blinking against the light and rubbing her eyes with the back of her hand, smearing her mascara. "Whew! What a relief. That feels so much better."

Verna leaned forward. "I want to thank you for the key, Coretta. It's going to come in handy."

"Oh, but I didn't mean for you to *have* it," Coretta protested, frowning. "I just meant to show it to you." She held out her hand. "I'll need to have it back. Mr. Scroggins made it very clear that I'm not supposed to—"

"No to that, Coretta." Verna waved off her gesture and put the key under the pillow. "I'm keeping it. And this way, you see, you don't have to be involved at all. I can go to the office at night by myself and—"

"But I *want* to be involved!" Coretta's tone was earnest. "And I can help, too. You may want different ledgers. I know where they are and I can get them for you. I'll save you time. I'll be useful. You'll see, Verna. I'll be a *big* help."

Lizzy felt a shiver of apprehension and her suspicions—which had never been entirely eased—ratcheted up another notch. Coretta certainly sounded sincere, but why was she so anxious to get involved in something that didn't concern her? What if she really *was* a double agent? What if she was helping the sheriff or Mr. Scroggins set a trap?

Verna was silent for a moment, considering. Then she spoke. "Since you feel that way about it, Coretta, let's do it tonight."

"Tonight?" Coretta asked uncertainly.

"Verna," Lizzy said, "I really don't think—"

"Tonight." Verna sat forward on the edge of the bed, her eyes intent. "Let's get it over with—the sooner the better, don't you think?"

"But I wasn't expecting—That is, I didn't plan to—" Coretta swallowed and looked away. "Actually, I promised Ted I wouldn't be out late this evening. So if you don't mind, I'd prefer to put it off. How about tomorrow night? That would really be better for me. Much, much better. I—" She stopped, looking from one of them to the other.

Lizzy thought there was a cornered look in her eyes, and with good reason. If Coretta was on the up-and-up, it shouldn't matter to her when they did it. If she was a double agent (to use Verna's term), she would want time to set the trap—that is, to notify whoever she was working for. Since they couldn't be sure of Coretta's loyalty, they ought not to give her that chance.

"I agree with Verna," Lizzy said emphatically. "There's no time like the present, you know. Better that we do it tonight, while everybody's thinking that Verna has gone to Nashville." Unless, of course, it was too late, and Coretta had already passed the word that Verna was still in Darling. She glanced at Coretta, but there wasn't a flicker of expression on her pretty face. It betrayed nothing.

But Verna was shaking her head. "I would prefer to do this alone. The job isn't likely to take all night, but it's certainly going to take several hours. You could find it hard to explain that at home."

"Well, if you think it really *has* to be tonight," Coretta said slowly, "I'm afraid that leaves me out." She turned to Lizzy. "I told Ted that you and I were going to a girls-only card party out in the country and that I'd be home in a couple of hours. I never dreamed that there might be—" She pulled down her mouth. "I guess I just didn't think ahead, that's all."

Lizzy thought that Coretta looked genuinely disappointed. She couldn't decide whether it was because the other woman had truly wanted to be a part of this adventure, or because she had been told to go along with the plan and report back to . . . well, to whoever.

Verna pushed her lips in and out, thinking. "I guess that settles it," she said finally. She looked at Lizzy. "But it would be good to have a lookout. Liz, would you be willing to wait downstairs and let me know if anybody happens along? Of course, nobody has a reason to come to the courthouse late at night, but you never know."

"Sure," Lizzy said. "I can do that." She wasn't eager to spend a couple of hours hanging around the main floor of the dark courthouse, but she felt she needed to stand by Verna. And she did wonder whether it was smart to talk about their plans in front of Coretta, just in case she—well, just in case.

"Okay, then," Verna said. "Tonight's the night." She grinned mischievously. "This way, it'll be over and done with before I lose my nerve." Her grin faded and she shot a surreptitious glance at Coretta. "At least, I hope it will," she added, half under her breath.

When they headed back to Darling a little while later, Coretta was sitting next to Lizzy in the front seat of Myra

May's touring car, and Verna was riding in the back. But because Lizzy still felt she couldn't trust Coretta, she had blindfolded her again. There was still a problem—a big problem—and Lizzy hadn't quite figured out how to deal with it.

If Coretta was on their side, she would go home and go to bed and not say a word to anybody—well, except for maybe Ted. But if she was working for somebody else, the minute she got home, she'd be on the phone to whoever it was, telling them that if they hurried, they would catch Verna in the act of burgling the county treasurer's office.

There had to be a way of keeping her from doing that. But how? They couldn't put a gag in her mouth and hold her captive until Verna was finished going through the accounts.

Could they?

# FIFTEEN

# Charlie and the Dahlias

About the time Lizzy was making her early-evening trip out to the Murphy place to talk to Verna about seeing Coretta, Charlie Dickens was eating supper at the diner. As usual, he was perched on the stool at the far end of the counter, where he was least likely to be disturbed by people who wanted to bend his editorial ear about this pet peeve or that pet project. He was digging into a plate of Euphoria's fried liver and onions, with generous sides of boiled green beans with fatback and onions, potato salad, and sliced fresh tomatoes, on special for thirty cents.

Charlie ate as he usually did, listening to the news on the Philco behind the counter while he read an article in the *Atlanta Constitution* about the likelihood of Governor Franklin Roosevelt's nomination at the 1932 Democratic convention in Chicago. Although the convention was more than a year away, the *Constitution* was already optimistic. "As far as the South goes," Senator William J. Harris of Georgia was quoted as saying jubilantly, "it's all Roosevelt."

Of course, that wasn't exactly true, for right here in Darling, as Charlie was well aware, there were plenty of folks who felt that Roosevelt was dangerously liberal, maybe even socialist in his views. They saw the governor as old money from the northeast, a patrician snob who seemed to be possessed by the rash idea that he could hand out twenty million taxpayers' dollars to the unemployed. Why, just look what he had done with that relief system of his in New York State, not to mention the old-age pension and unemployment insurance he was pushing through his state legislature. Hand a man like Roosevelt the power of the presidency, and there was no telling what he might do. The conservative Democrats were laying odds on John Nance Garner, Speaker of the House. Garner was a Southerner, a Texan, a regular guy whom Southern folks could count on to see things their way.

Anyway, Charlie knew that even if every Southern delegation went for FDR, they couldn't carry the convention. Under party rules, the winning candidate had to muster a two-thirds majority, and there were other strong candidates. One of Roosevelt's opponents was former governor of New York Al Smith, who was backed by newspaper magnate William Randolph Hearst. Smith, a Catholic and a Progressive, was hampered by his landslide loss to Herbert Hoover in 1928. But Hearst was using his publications to spread the rumor that Roosevelt—who had contracted polio some years back— couldn't stand the strain of the presidency. *Time* magazine had just joined the Hearst-sponsored *Stop Roosevelt* chorus, repeating the rumor that while FDR might be mentally fit for the job, he was "utterly unfit physically"—this, despite the fact that a panel of noted physicians had just examined him and found that he had the "necessary health and powers of endurance" to carry out presidential duties. Mrs. Roosevelt was reported to have quipped that "if infantile paralysis didn't kill him, the presidency won't."

Charlie folded his newspaper and laid it aside. Roosevelt's candidacy wasn't the only thing he had on his mind tonight, not by a long shot. He was still juggling the bombshell that Ruthie Brant had dropped on him that afternoon—a big fat bombshell that any investigative reporter would love to explode like a giant firecracker all over page one. But like the other offerings Ruthie had brought him, this one was long on narrative and light on the facts. He was still trying to figure out how he could confirm it—especially the part about the auditor's report.

Of course, it would be best if he could see it for himself and dope out what it meant. But how was he going to get his hands on the damn thing? One thing for sure, Earle Scroggins wasn't going to hand it over. Not if it said what Ruthie Brant claimed it said. Fifteen thousand dollars missing from the county treasury? Scroggins and the commissioners would keep that under their hats as long as they could—as long as the *Dispatch* let them, that is. Charlie was well aware of his responsibility as a guardian of the people's interest in their government, even when the people themselves weren't very interested in their interest.

Charlie had something else on his mind as well—the information he had uncovered at the library about that "secret code" Bessie Bloodworth had given him. After looking over the scrapbook and reading parts of the book he had borrowed, he had decided to have another talk with Bessie and ask her if he could get a look at that pillow. Since there was nothing he could do tonight about that explosive inside dope Ruthie Brant had slipped him, he'd walk over to the Magnolia Manor as soon as he polished off a slice of Euphoria's chocolate pie.

Charlie's trip to the Darling library and the couple of hours he had spent with the fragile old scrapbook and the history of Civil War battles had given him the information he needed to fill in the gaps in his spotty schoolboy memory of the facts of the First Manassas. As he leafed through the yellowed pages, reading contemporary accounts from the *Richmond Daily Dispatch* and battle reports compiled by a Confederate army captain, he had begun to formulate an exciting and (he thought) entirely plausible theory about the identity of the person who had stitched those unusual symbols and numbers on the pillow. And when he read the first few pages of *My Imprisonment*, he was even more convinced that he was right. Charlie now wanted to see that pillow for himself. He had an idea about it that he felt he just had to test out.

So when he finished his pie, he left coins on the counter and stopped at the hotel to buy a seven-cent cigar. He ran into Artis Biggs and inquired after his wife, learning that Doc Roberts had confiscated Dr. Baxter's diet pills and was treating Mrs. Biggs for nervous prostration.

"Good news," Charlie said, adding fervently, "I hope she has a full recovery." He meant it. As far as he was concerned, anything that kept Angelina from throwing her arms around him again was good news.

Leaving the hotel, he went down the block and—yielding to an impulsive temptation—stopped in Pete's Pool Parlor, where he shot a few balls with Freddie Mann and Len Wheeler, who ran the repair shop at Kilgore Motors. Freddie, as usual, had a flask in his back pocket and didn't mind sharing it around. He got it from his second cousin, Mickey LeDoux, who managed a big moonshine operation over by the river. Everybody in town (including the sheriff) knew that Mickey's finest could be bought off the shelf behind the horse harness and saddles in the back room at Mann's Mercantile. But nobody would ever spill the beans to the occasional revenuer who dared to show his face around town. Mickey LeDoux's corn whiskey was Darling's best-kept secret.


While Charlie was shooting pool and taking a nip from Freddie's flask as it went around the table, Bessie and Miss Rogers were setting things up for the Dahlias' usual Monday-night card party. People took turns hosting the party. It was open to all the members, but it was a rare evening when everybody could make it.

Miss Rogers didn't usually play cards, although she allowed herself an occasional game of Rook, which was what they were playing tonight. So Miss Rogers would be there, and Bessie, of course, and Beulah Trivette and Fannie Champaign, who was joining them for the first time. Verna and Liz almost always came, but Liz had called to say that Verna had gone out of town to visit a friend and that something urgent had come up and she—Liz—wouldn't be able to make it. Lucy Murphy had company (she didn't say who), and Ophelia had to go to a dramatic recital at the Darling school, where her daughter was giving a dramatic recitation of "Annabelle Lee" by Edgar Allan Poe. Alice Ann Walker and Earlynne Biddle had a quilting club meeting. Myra May Mosswell was on the switchboard. Aunt Hetty Little wouldn't come unless they played poker, Mildred Kilgore wouldn't come when they played Rook, and Voleen Johnson never came under any circumstance.

So there would be just the four of them. And since the Magnolia Ladies had traipsed off en masse to play bingo at the Odd Fellows Hall on Franklin Street, Bessie set up the card table in front of the big window in the parlor, saying a fervent thanks to the blessed fate that had exiled Lucky Lindy from their midst. Ophelia had taken the cat out to Lucy Murphy's place. He would never again launch himself from the top of the curtains into some unsuspecting lady's lap.

While Bessie fetched the chairs from the dining room, Miss Rogers put out the evening's refreshments on the cherry sideboard, on top of a white cloth embroidered with roses. There was a delicate china platter filled with a selection of Roseanne's cookies and a large pressed glass pitcher of lemonade with a pretty garnish of fresh mint from the garden.

Bessie had just set out the fourth chair when she looked out the window and saw Beulah and Fannie walking together up the path to the front porch. When she opened the front door, they were chattering excitedly about what had happened to Angelina Dupree Biggs that day.

"Can you *feature* that?" Beulah was saying to Fannie. "In fact, I wouldn't have believed it if I hadn't held her wet hair in my very own two hands."

"What's happened to Angelina Biggs?" Bessie asked curiously, remembering her odd encounter with the woman in front of the *Dispatch* office. "I ran into her this morning, and she seemed . . . well, strange. Very odd."

"She's been poisoned!" Fannie Champaign exclaimed, taking off her hat and putting it on the hallway table. This one was yellow straw with a wide, floppy brim and a fine yellow feather band. Fannie owned Darling's only hat shop and liked to wear her hats as an advertisement. If you admired the one she had on at the moment, she'd be glad to tell you how much it cost and encourage you to try it on in front of the nearest mirror. If you liked it, she'd sell it to you right off her head, with a nice little discount because it was "gently worn."

"Poisoned!" Bessie exclaimed, taken aback by this news.

"Beulah will tell you all about it," Fannie added, snatching a glance at herself in the mirror and patting her hair. "She's the one who figured out what was wrong with the poor thing. Mrs. Biggs, I mean." She shook her head at Beulah.

"Beulah, I am just amazed at the way you put those clues together. I swear, honey, you are the sleuth-in-chief, just like Miss Marple. You know what Miss Christie says. Miss Marple 'always knew every single thing that happened and drew the worst inferences.'" She laughed, a sweet, tinkling little laugh.

A few weeks earlier, Fannie had given a talk at the Darling Literary Society on *The Murder at the Vicarage*, Agatha Christie's new mystery, and had quoted a number of lines she liked. She had also read aloud bits of the *New York Times* review of the book. The reviewer had been patronizing in an unmistakably male sort of way, feeling that Miss Christie was far from "being at her best" in the book. "The local sisterhood of spinsters is introduced with much gossip and click-clack," he had written. "A bit of this goes a long way and the average reader is apt to grow weary of it all, particularly of the amiable Miss Marple, who is sleuth-in-chief of the affair." The members of the Literary Society (fully half of them were Dahlias) had giggled at the phrase *local sisterhood of spinsters.* That was exactly how they liked to describe themselves, although not all of them were spinsters.

"There's something wrong with Mrs. Biggs?" Miss Rogers asked, coming into the parlor with another plate of cookies. "I hope it's not too serious. She is one of the library's most supportive patrons." She paused, and her tone became slightly disapproving. "She rather enjoys romantic novels. *The Sheik* seems to be her current favorite. In fact, I believe that the book is a day or two overdue. I shall have to telephone her."

Bessie refrained from rolling her eyes. She had started to read the novel, which was still wildly popular, even though it had been out for over ten years. But she stopped when she got to the part where the hero, Sheik Ahmed Ben Hassan, had dragged the heroine, Lady Diana, into his tent and cruelly ravished her while she screamed and resisted. Bessie knew she was old-fashioned, but she didn't feel that the hero of a book ought to behave in such a violently lecherous fashion, even if he was a lord of the desert. In the movie based on the book, Rudolph Valentino (Sheik Ahmed) had taken pity on Agnes Ayers (Lady Diana) and had been a great deal more romantic—it was Hollywood, after all. But the scenes were still shocking enough that the film had been banned in Kansas City. Bessie found it interesting that Angelina Dupree Biggs was a fan of the book.

"The poor dear is losing her hair," Fannie explained. She rolled her eyes. "Isn't that just too hideous for words?" She paused, reflecting. "Actually, I have a draped satin toque— teal blue—that would be appropriate for such a situation." She looked at Beulah. "Do you think it would be too forward of me to offer to loan it to her until her hair starts coming back in? Assuming it does, that is," she added thoughtfully. "It might not."

"I think you should definitely offer," Beulah said, although the thought of Angelina Biggs in a teal blue satin toque made her lips twitch. It was something that Lady Diana would have worn, however, so maybe Angelina would accept. "Fannie, that is very gracious of you."

"Mrs. Biggs is losing her *hair*?" Miss Rogers asked in horror. She put the plate down with a little thud and her hand flew to her own hair, as if to assure herself that it was where it belonged.

"I knew something was wrong the moment I saw her this morning," Bessie said somberly, remembering how Angelina had blundered out of the *Dispatch* office—and how Charlie Dickens had disclaimed any responsibility. "But *poisoned*? Somebody has poisoned Angelina Dupree Biggs? Who in the world would do such a thing?"

"She was doing it to herself," Beulah said. "Can you *imagine*?"

Fannie saw the sideboard and clasped her hands. "Oh, just look at those charming refreshments! Miss Rogers, they *do* look delectable! You are such a *dear.*" She started forward as if to help herself, but Miss Rogers stepped in front of her.

"We usually wait until after we've finished a round, Miss Champaign," she said primly.

"Oh, sorry," Fannie replied, disappointed, and turned away.

"That's all right," Miss Rogers said in a comforting tone. "You're new. We understand."

"What was she doing to herself?" Bessie asked.

"Taking Dr. Baxter's diet pills," Beulah explained, seating herself at the card table. "Fannie, honey, you're going to be my partner, so you sit opposite."

*"Diet pills?"* Bessie asked incredulously, taking the chair to Beulah's right. Miss Rogers sat opposite her, straightening the white lace cuffs on her mauve dress. "How could a little thing like diet pills poison anybody?"

"Because they have arsenic in them," Beulah said.

"Arsenic!" Bessie and Miss Rogers exclaimed in one voice.

"Yes, arsenic—would you believe?" Beulah replied, fanning herself with her hand. "And who knows how much. I mean, I doubt that anybody's watching when the pills are being made. They could make a mistake with their measurements and quantities and the like and nobody would be the wiser." Without a pause, she added, "Miss Rogers, dear, those cookies look utterly *divine.* You're sure you won't relent and let us have just one before we start?"

"I think we can wait until we've Rooked," Miss Rogers said as Bessie reached for the box of cards in the middle of the table.

"There was strychnine in them, too," Fannie put in. "In the pills, I mean. And pokeberries. And goodness only knows what else." She made a face. "I'm sure there are rules about such things, but the government can't peek into every box."

"Pokeberries and strychnine may be bad, but it was probably the arsenic that made her lose her hair," Beulah said. "I was giving her a shampoo and it started coming out by the handfuls. By the *handfuls*, I mean. I've read about arsenic making your hair fall out, but this is the first time I've seen it." She sighed heavily. "That was when she threatened to sue me," she added. "When her hair came out in my hands."

"Dear me," Miss Rogers said, pursing her lips and looking distressed. "Oh, *dear*, dear me." Miss Rogers disliked litigation of any sort, feeling that people ought to solve their differences outside of the courtroom if at all possible.

"But there's more," Fannie said, clasping her hands under her chin and leaning forward eagerly. "Tell them, Beulah."

"I'm not sure I should," Beulah said in a hesitant tone. "It's sort of private. I mean, it's really not a pretty thing to talk about."

"Nothing is private in this town," Bessie replied matter-of-factly. She opened the box of Rook cards and began to take out the twos, threes, and fours. "Pretty or not pretty, we're all going to hear it sooner or later. Sooner, probably. Word has a way of getting around, you know."

"I can't argue with that." Beulah sighed. "Well, if you really want to know, she was threatening to sue her husband for carrying on an affair in the second-floor bedrooms at the hotel. And Mr. Dickens for trying to kiss her this morning. *Assault with the attempt to molest* was the way she put it."

"Molest!" Bessie exclaimed, nearly dropping the cards. "I don't believe it! Charlie Dickens would never in the world do something like that!" *But Sheik Ahmed Ben Hassan certainly would,* she thought grimly. Was that where Angelina had gotten the idea? From that dreadful romance novel?

"It had to have been her imagination," Fannie put in, and

lowered her eyes. "Mr. Dickens is a complete gentleman. A gentleman through and through."

Bessie frowned. She wondered how Fannie Champaign knew what kind of a gentleman Charlie Dickens was, but she didn't want to ask.

Beulah nodded, agreeing with Fannie. "Her husband swears he's never had an affair with anybody, and I believe him—if only because I am positive that I would have heard about it if he had. You'd be amazed what women say when their heads are in the shampoo sink. I hear about every affair in town, uncensored."

Miss Rogers tsk-tsked with her tongue.

Beulah gave Miss Rogers an understanding smile. "I know—it's just awful, isn't it? Anyway, it's my opinion that the pills were driving her crazy. Either they weren't made right or she was taking too many of them." She paused. "I talked to Mr. Lima at the drugstore this afternoon, and he told me that she bought three packages two weeks ago today. There are twenty-four pills in each package, so when Mr. Biggs counts them, he can tell how many she's taken."

"Maybe it was the pokeberries that gave her hallucinations about Mr. Dickens," Fannie said thoughtfully.

"Or maybe it was Sheik Ahmed," Bessie said. The others gave her a blank look and she added, "She's been reading the book, hasn't she? Maybe she started imagining that she was Lady Diana, and Mr. Dickens was the sheik and he intended to ravish her."

"I suppose it's possible," Fannie said doubtfully.

"Books are powerful things," Miss Rogers said in a cautioning tone. "I often think that it takes a person of high moral standards to resist the ideas that are found in some books."

Beulah's sigh was full of compassion. "It's such a pity. All she wanted to do was lose that weight and get beautiful again. You've got to give her credit for that. Beauty is every woman's birthright."

"It's a good lesson for all of us," Miss Rogers said decidedly. "If someone needs to lose weight, they shouldn't take pills. And certain books should be read with caution, so as not to inflame the imagination."

"I'll say amen to that," Bessie said, and picked up the cards. Since she was the hostess, she was the dealer for the first round, so she shuffled and cut the deck, then dealt the cards one at a time, dealing a five-card nest of rook in the middle of the table. She was dealing the last card when there was a knock on the door.

"Drat," she muttered, and got up. "Don't anybody move. I'll make short work of whoever it is."

It was Charlie Dickens, standing at the door with his Panama hat in one hand and an unlit cigar in the other. "I wanted to talk to you about that pillow, Miss Bloodworth," he said. "I have an idea that I'd like to test out, but I—" He looked over her shoulder and saw the group in the parlor. "Oh, sorry," he muttered. "Didn't realize you had company. I'll come back another time." He turned to go.

"Oh, it's just the Dahlias," Bessie said. "It's our Monday-night card party." Still holding the doorknob, she considered. "Are you saying that you think there's something . . . well, interesting about that paper I gave you? Do you think it might really be a . . . a secret code?"

"I do," Charlie Dickens said. "And I have an idea about who your friend's grandmother might be. I was hoping to see the pillow. It might give me something more to go on."

"Oh, really?" Bessie exclaimed with mounting excitement. "Then why don't you come in and meet my friend. I'm sure the rest of us won't mind delaying our game while you and Miss Rogers sort things out."

"Miss Rogers?" Charlie Dickens asked, surprised. "You

don't mean . . . It's Miss Rogers' grandmother who made the pillow?"

Bessie sniffed, thinking that she smelled a whiff of whiskey on Charlie's breath. But she only said, "Indeed. And I'm sure that she will be delighted to let you see the pillow. She has it upstairs in her room." She hesitated, adding apologetically, "But I'm afraid I'll have to ask you to leave your cigar outside. I hope you don't mind. The Magnolia Ladies are not very fond of cigars."

"Sure thing," Charlie Dickens said. He laid his unlit cigar on the porch railing and followed Bessie inside.

And Bessie had been right. Miss Rogers (who turned petal pink when Mr. Dickens came in and Bessie explained why he was there) was thrilled to acknowledge that she was the owner of the pillow and then to scurry upstairs to her bedroom and bring it down. She also brought the twisted, gnarled hank of red wool yarn that Lucky Lindy had unraveled with his sharp claws and put it on the card table where everyone could see it.

"A cat did *that*?" Fannie Champaign exclaimed incredulously. When Mr. Dickens came in, Fannie had slid him a glance that Bessie couldn't read, which had made her even more curious about the two of them—although why it mattered to her, she could not have said. Charlie Dickens was only the brother of an old friend. She had no interest in him at all.

Bessie cleared her throat. "Lucky Lindy was a cat of many talents," she put in. "One of our Magnolia Ladies was quite fond of him—until he unraveled one too many of her knitting projects."

"He was a dreadful nuisance," Miss Rogers said emphatically, "but I must confess that I am grateful to him for pulling that knitted cover apart. I had no idea that my pillow was embroidered with all these signs and symbols." She held it up for everyone to see. "On both sides, too."

She handed the pillow to Charlie Dickens, who took it over to the bridge lamp for a careful examination.

"But where did the pillow come from?" Beulah wanted to know, so of course Miss Rogers had to tell everyone the whole story, while Charlie Dickens continued to turn the pillow in his hand, studying it minutely as he listened to the tale.

"Such a lovely story, Miss Rogers!" Fannie exclaimed. "To think that you have something that your grandmother made with her very own hands. I wish I had some reminders of my family." She put her head to one side, adding, "Although perhaps I don't. We weren't a very happy family, come to think of it. I don't think I'd care to be reminded."

Beulah smiled. "A family treasure, Miss Rogers. What you have is a wonderful family treasure."

"It's more than that," Charlie Dickens remarked. "Much more." They all turned to look at him as he came to the table. "What you have, Miss Rogers, may be a *national* treasure. Or perhaps I should say, rather, a Confederate treasure. Something that all true daughters and sons of the South would be proud to call their own. Congratulations." He bowed with a gallant flourish, and Bessie got another whiff. He had definitely been drinking. Nobody else seemed to notice it, though.

"Con . . . gratulations?" Miss Rogers asked hesitantly, flushing. "But I don't understand. It's just a . . . it's just a pillow, that's all. A pillow with strange symbols all over it."

Bessie leaned forward urgently. "The symbols," she said. "What do they mean, Mr. Dickens?"

Instead of answering, Charlie Dickens asked, "Does anyone have a pair of sharp-pointed scissors?"

Bessie got up and went across the room to the table next to her chair and fetched the scissors from her sewing basket. "Will these do?" she asked, handing them to him.

"Perfect," Charlie replied. To Miss Rogers, he said, "With

your permission, I would like to open a seam along one side of your pillow. I will try very hard not to damage the material. May I?"

Miss Rogers hesitated as if she might say no, then drew a breath. "Of course, if you feel it's necessary," she said, and then added, impetuously, "Oh, but do be careful, Mr. Dickens. It's an antique. That pillow is as old as I am."

"That can't be so very old," Charlie Dickens said in an unusually chivalrous tone, and began snipping at the seam on the left side of the pillow. The thread was thin but the stitches, which had obviously been put in by an expert seamstress, were firm. The snipping took several moments.

The Dahlias, their Rook game forgotten, watched Mr. Dickens intently. "What is he trying to do?" Beulah whispered, and Bessie said, "Just wait, dear, you'll see."

When he was finished, Charlie Dickens opened the seam with his fingers and began fishing around inside the pillow, gently and carefully. And then he found something. As the Dahlias watched, holding their collective breaths, he drew out several folded papers.

"Why, what on earth!" Miss Rogers exclaimed in great surprise. "I've had that pillow since I was a child and I had no idea there was anything in it—except for the stuffing, of course. What *is* it, Mr. Dickens? What have you found?"

Charlie Dickens had unfolded one of the papers and was scanning it quickly, his expression changing from curiosity to amazement and then to exultation.

"I was right!" he exclaimed. "I knew it—I was right!" He tossed the paper down in front of Miss Rogers. "Take a gander at that, Miss Rogers. Just take a gander at *that*!"

Miss Rogers gave it a fearful glance, as if it held some bad news, but she didn't touch it. Instead, she looked up and asked, in a strained, breathless voice, "What's all this about, Mr. Dickens? Please explain." She took out a white lace-edged hanky and touched her lips. "Does it . . . does it have to do with my grandmother?"

"I do believe it does." Charlie Dickens drew himself up and looked around the table. "Has anyone here ever heard of the Confederate Rose?"

There was a babble of voices, all speaking eagerly and at once.

"The Confederate rose?" Bessie asked, puzzled. "Why, certainly. We know that flower. But I don't know what that has to do with—"

At the same time, Beulah said, "I have one growing beside my back fence. It's just gorgeous. But what—"

And Fannie said, "The Confederate rose is a favorite of mine, as well. However, I don't quite see—"

Miss Rogers raised her hand and the others stopped speaking, in deference.

"The Confederate rose? We're all familiar with it, Mr. Dickens—a beautiful shrub, with blossoms that are white when they first open. Then they turn pink, then red, and then a deep, bloodred. Confederate ladies planted it in honor of their brave fallen soldiers, who shed their blood for the Cause. But it isn't a rose at all, you know," she added in a reproving tone. "It's an hibiscus, and we should pay it the honor of using its real name. *Hibiscus mutabilis.*"

"And that's not all," Bessie put in. "Tell him, Miss Rogers. Tell him about your project."

Miss Rogers smiled proudly. "Of course. I am happy to tell you, Mr. Dickens, that our Darling Dahlias have propagated and raised fourteen new *Hibiscus mutabilii*, one for each Dahlia. We intend to plant them in the cemetery before Confederate Day, so everyone can see them when they come for the celebration. We'll be glad to give you all the details, if you'd like to print a story in the paper."

But while everyone was speaking, Charlie Dickens had

been shaking his head and frowning, trying to get a word in edgewise. When Miss Rogers finally finished, he spoke up.

"I am sure your flowers will be very beautiful, but that's not what I am talking about." He picked up the paper that lay on the table in front of Miss Rogers. "This is a letter from the woman that people in the South, in Richmond, particularly, called the Confederate Rose—Rose Greenhow. She spied for the Confederacy during the first months of the War Between the States, until President Lincoln had her locked up."

"The Confederate Rose, a spy?" the Dahlias exclaimed, their voices rising in a babble of astonishment. "A *spy*!"

"A spy," Charlie Dickens confirmed. "A very valuable spy who was responsible for the South's success at the First Manassas."

"Manassas!" An awed murmur went around the table. "Manassas!" As daughters of the Confederacy, each of the Dahlias understood the sacred significance of what the North called the Battle of Bull Run, the South's first and most memorable victory.

"Yes, Manassas," Charlie Dickens repeated. He unfolded the other papers he held in his hand. "These are letters to President Jefferson Davis and General P. G. T. Beauregard and to Rose Greenhow's daughter. And these"—he held up several pages covered with indecipherable symbols and letters—"appear to be coded materials, perhaps copies of reports she managed to smuggle to Confederate officials during the months that she was imprisoned."

"Astonishing," Bessie exclaimed.

"Incredible," Fannie said, and Beulah murmured, "Imagine that. A woman spy!"

"But . . . but what does it all *mean*, Mr. Dickens?" Miss Rogers whispered, fanning herself with her white hanky.

"It means," Charlie Dickens replied, "that your grandmother, Rose Greenhow, made this pillow and used it as a hiding place to conceal some of her Confederate correspondence. And unless I miss my guess, the symbols embroidered on the cover are a key to her cipher—the one she used to encode her messages, that is. I haven't had time yet to work it all out, but that's my initial impression."

"You're saying that my grandmother was a Confederate *spy?*" Miss Rogers asked uncertainly. Her cheeks were flushed and her eyes were wide.

"That's exactly what I'm saying," said Charlie Dickens, drawing a chair up to the table and sitting down. "I've been doing some reading this afternoon, and I've learned quite a lot. Let me tell you about her."

Bessie pushed back her chair and stood up. "If we're going to do that," she said decidedly, "we are must have refreshments. I'll bring them over to the table and we'll eat while we listen." And to Miss Rogers, she said sternly, "And I don't want to hear a word of objection, Miss Rogers. Not a single word."

# SIXTEEN

# The Confederate Rose:
# "A Dangerous Character"

This is the story that Charlie Dickens told the Dahlias that evening about Miss Rogers' grandmother, Rose O'Neale Greenhow. He acknowledged that he had read hastily and that there were many gaps yet to fill in. But he would do his best to learn more details, and he promised that when he had collected all the facts—or as many as he was able to get—he would write up a more complete account for the newspaper. For now, he read part of the story from notes he had taken during his afternoon's research.

Rose O'Neale was born in Port Tobacco, Maryland, in 1813 or 1814. Her father owned a small plantation and grew tobacco and wheat until he was murdered by his slaves, leaving his wife with four daughters, five hundred sixty acres, and very little money. Rose, the youngest, was intelligent, pretty, and quick to learn. When she became a teenager, she was sent with her sister to Washington, D.C., to live with her aunt, Maria Hill. Mrs. Hill and her husband ran a fashionable boardinghouse in the Old Capitol building, where

Supreme Court justices, congressmen, and senators lodged while the Court or Congress was in session. The Hills were Southerners and their boardinghouse (which had been the home of Congress for eleven years after the British burned the capitol in 1814) was especially popular with Southern politicians.

Young Rose blossomed in this highly politicized social milieu, where everyone (especially the men) thought her beautiful. And she was. She had a pale olive complexion, shiny black hair parted down the middle and pulled back from her oval face, and an hourglass figure. Bright, well-read, and a lively, opinionated conversationalist, she loved the intrigues and conspiracies of Washington politics and learned to navigate them very well. She was mentored by Dolley Madison, the widow of the former president, considered the queen of Washington society. Mrs. Madison took an interest in the young girl, whose coquettish, flirtatious manner earned her the nickname Wild Rose. She was said to be bold, brave, and brazen, ready for any adventure, the more exciting the better.

In 1835, Rose married Dr. Robert Greenhow, an urbane Virginian who worked in the State Department and pursued an avocation as an historian. They bought a house on K Street, across from the home of former president John Quincy Adams. Through her husband, Rose gained a wider knowledge of the inner workings of the government and a greater acquaintance with government officials, for the Greenhows entertained often. Rose bore her husband eight children. The last, a girl born in 1853 and named for her mother, was called Little Rose. Robert Greenhow died the following year. At forty, Rose was a grieving but strikingly handsome widow, widely recognized as a lady of influence—and still as bold and brazen as the Wild Rose of her youth.

Over the years, Rose had strengthened her social and

political contacts with the South. Her sympathy for state's rights, her conviction that slavery was constitutionally protected and morally sound, and her belief in the right to secession continued to grow after her husband's death. She was strongly influenced by her friendship with John C. Calhoun and particularly with James Buchanan, whom she advised to run for president in 1856 and with whom she corresponded and met frequently during his presidency. When Lincoln was elected in 1860 and talk about secession turned into calls for action, a Southern colonel named Thomas Jordan asked Rose to organize her friends and Confederate sympathizers into a ring of spies. Colonel Jordan gave her a cipher and asked her to encrypt all her messages to him. She spent many hours practicing with the cipher, until she could use it quickly and accurately.

Hostilities began in April 1861 when the South attacked Fort Sumter and Lincoln called up troops, intending to quickly put down the Southern rebellion. The two sides were at war, and Rose was listening to a variety of informants. Some shared military secrets straight from the War Department, while others simply reported what they saw and heard around the city, where the Union troops were gathering, arms and munitions were being stored, and blockade plans were being discussed.

In July, Rose learned that the Union army was preparing to attack General Beauregard's headquarters a few miles outside of Washington, near a small river called Bull Run. She sent two secret messages via courier alerting Beauregard to the plan and giving him enough time to summon General Joseph E. Johnston, who brought his army by train from the Shenandoah Valley. Joining forces, the two Southern armies surprised the Yankees with the ferocity of their defense, and the forces of the North were utterly routed. It was the first battle—and the first victory—of the war. When it was over,

Confederate President Jefferson Davis was happy to give Mrs. Greenhow the credit for the South's success. "She is," he said, "our Confederate Rose."

From April through July, Rose continued to use her cipher to send coded messages about the activities of General McClellan and General McDowell, reporting the number of troops, their movements, and their artillery. She sewed these notes into various pieces of clothing that she gave to her female couriers. Women crossing the lines were rarely searched, so it's likely that a fair amount of information was conveyed.

But suspicions were raised in Lincoln's War Office when it became known that Rose was entertaining far into the night. Her guests included several important federal officials, notably Henry Wilson of Massachusetts, the powerful chairman of the Committee on Military Affairs. Pillow talk, exclaimed the War Office, and called in Allan Pinkerton, who was directing counterintelligence operations in Washington.

"Mrs. Greenhow must be attended to," the assistant secretary of war told Pinkerton. "She is becoming a dangerous character." Pinkerton began to watch Rose's house, taking note of the comings and goings of her many male visitors, and on August 23, he placed her under house arrest. Upon searching her home for further evidence, he found thirteen love letters from Senator Wilson, as well as maps of Washington fortifications and notes on military movements. But while he was convinced that she was communicating in code, he was unable to find the key to her cipher.

Rose was confined to her home for five months. During this time, she took every opportunity to send the Confederacy as much information as she could gather. Finally, in January 1862, with her eight-year-old Little Rose, she was sent to Old Capitol Prison—ironically, the very same building that had once been her aunt's fashionable boardinghouse. She was held there until May, when she and her daughter were released and deported to Richmond, Virginia, the capital of the Confederacy.

In Richmond, the Confederate Rose was hailed as a heroine and feted throughout the city. But Jefferson Davis had need of her diplomatic skills and soon dispatched her to Europe. For the next two years, she traveled through France, attempting to enlist the aid of European countries on behalf of the South. In France, she was received by Napoleon III. In Britain, she had an audience with Queen Victoria and wrote a memoir titled *My Imprisonment and the First Year of Abolition Rule at Washington*. Meanwhile, she found a Parisian school for Little Rose, the Convent du Sacré Coeur, where she felt that the girl would gain a good education.

In September 1864, Rose left Europe to return to the Confederate States, carrying official dispatches and two thousand dollars in gold earned from the sale of her memoir and intended for a Southern relief fund. She sailed on the *Condor*, a British blockade runner that ran aground near Wilmington, North Carolina. Rose fled the grounded ship by lifeboat for the nearby shore. But the skiff capsized, and Rose, weighted down by the gold she carried, was drowned.

As the word spread, the Confederate Rose was mourned across the South. When her body was recovered, she was given a state burial in Wilmington, where her coffin rested on a bier covered with a Confederate flag and every civic leader praised her heroism and patriotic devotion. The Wilmington *Sentinel* had the last word:

> At the last day, when the martyrs who have with their blood sealed their devotions to liberty shall stand together, firm witnesses that truth is stronger than death, foremost among the shining throng, coequal with the Rolands and Joan d'Arcs of history, will appear the Confederate heroine, Rose A. Greenhow.

# SEVENTEEN

# Charlie

When Charlie finished, he leaned back and glanced around the table, satisfied that he had told the story well. The Dahlias, who had been listening to him with rapt attention, let out their collective breath in one long, tremulous sigh of mingled amazement, regret, and bone-deep satisfaction. Bessie Bloodworth was blinking as if someone had just turned on the lights after a movie show. Fannie Champaign was gazing at Charlie with an unreadable expression on her face. Miss Rogers was weeping into her white lace-edged hanky, and Beulah Trivette was leaning toward her, patting her arm gently and murmuring, "There, there. You just have a good cry, Miss Rogers. We feel for you, we purely do."

All four women, as Charlie could see, were deeply affected by the story of the Confederate Rose. He, on the other hand, was much more interested in investigating the puzzle of the cipher than in the emotional theater of Rose Greenhow's melodramatic life, which read like a Hollywood movie script.

In fact, he had to suppress a sardonic smile when he considered the *Sentinel*'s praise of Rose Greenhow as a martyr who had been devoted to liberty. The woman had done all she could on behalf of slavery, and the "liberty" the *Sentinel* praised was the freedom to own slaves. But Charlie wasn't going to call attention to this significant irony, and if the Dahlias noticed, they didn't speak of it. They had been utterly captivated by the story.

"I . . . I don't know how to thank you, Mr. Dickens," Miss Rogers finally managed through her tears. She gulped back a sob. "It's . . . it's just so overwhelming. I have spent my whole life not knowing who my family was, and now I discover that my grandmother was a legendary Confederate heroine and my mother was educated in France and—"

"Your mother?" Fannie asked in a wondering voice.

"Your mother was Little Rose, wasn't she?" Bessie said, remembering that Miss Rogers had told her that her mother's name was the same as her grandmother's.

"Yes," Miss Rogers said. "Yes! My mother told me that my grandmother was a very brave woman, and that she died by drowning. And now I know that it happened when she was in the service of our dear Confederacy!" She looked up at Charlie Dickens. "It's so hard to believe, but that . . . that book you borrowed this afternoon—*My Imprisonment*." Her tone was tremulous. "It was written by my grandmother, wasn't it?"

"It was," Charlie replied, thinking that it had been quite a remarkable coincidence to discover Rose Greenhow's book in the little Darling library. He would have to find out how it got there. "I'll return it to the library tomorrow, Miss Rogers, so you can read it for yourself. You'll probably want to try to do more work on your family tree to confirm the little I've been able to dig up so far, and of course to learn more. Rose Greenhow was apparently survived by several children and—"

"So I may have cousins!" Miss Rogers exclaimed, clapping her hands excitedly. "I may have whole *families* of cousins, all over the country, and perhaps even living aunts and uncles! Oh, Mr. Dickens, how can I thank you? How can I *ever* thank you for all your wonderful investigative work!"

Charlie grinned at Bessie. "You should thank Miss Bloodworth," he said, "for bringing me the cipher and suggesting that it was a secret code." He paused. "I wonder—would you mind if I borrow the documents that I took out of the pillow? I'd like to send copies to a friend who teaches at the University of North Carolina. He might be able to shed more light on them. And perhaps he knows of other materials that are available. Of course I'll be very careful with them."

"Please take them," Miss Rogers said, and blew her nose. "I'll appreciate anything else you can find out about my . . . my grandmother." She gave a dainty little hiccup. "My grandmother, the Confederate Rose."

"The Confederate Rose, our heroine," Fannie murmured, her eyes on Charlie.

A ripple of laughter ran around the table and everyone seemed to relax.

"I've never known anybody whose grandmother was a spy," Beulah said enviously, shaking her head. "Just think of all the good she did for our boys at Bull Run! Oh, Miss Rogers, you must be very proud."

"I'd love to know more about her," Fannie said. "And to think that she and your mother were sent to prison together!" She lifted her eyes, sighing. "Such a *romantic* story. The Confederate Rose."

Her glance shifted to Charlie, and he thought, with some surprise, that it was an appreciative glance. He wondered whether he had inadvertently stumbled across the key to

Fannie Champaign's heart—and having done so, whether he truly wanted to open it.

Bessie Bloodworth was looking straight at Miss Rogers, one eyebrow cocked. "This will give us a whole new perspective on you, Dorothy." Charlie caught the slight emphasis on *Dorothy* and wondered at it.

Miss Rogers looked straight back. "I should certainly hope so, *Bessie*." Another emphasis. Then she smiled. "Isn't it lovely that we have already agreed to plant all those Confederate roses in the cemetery for Confederate Day?" She pulled in her breath and said tentatively, "Perhaps . . . perhaps we could mention Rose Greenhow at our ceremony?"

"I think we can do better than that," Bessie replied. "I think the Confederate Rose ought to be the main feature of our program. Liz is organizing the event. I'll talk to her and see what we can work out."

Charlie pushed his chair back. "Well, ladies, I've interrupted your card game quite long enough." He tucked Miss Rogers' papers into the pocket of his jacket. "Thank you for letting me have a look at your pillow, Miss Rogers. I'd like to come back with my camera and photograph it—perhaps tomorrow, if that would suit you. As I said, I do believe you have a national treasure."

"Yes, by all means, Mr. Dickens." Miss Rogers touched the pillow with one finger. "A national treasure." Her voice was soft, as if she were savoring the words. "A secret code, embroidered by my grandmother—my grandmother, the Confederate *spy*."

Bessie Bloodworth stood. "Mr. Dickens," she said firmly, "we have been remiss. We've been eating and drinking in front of you, while you told us this marvelous story. Now it's your turn. You are not leaving here until you've had some refreshment. I'll fix you a plate."

Miss Rogers got up, too. "And I'll get another pitcher of lemonade, Bessie."

It was nine thirty by the time Charlie retrieved his unlit cigar from the porch railing, stuck it into his mouth, and walked out onto Camellia Street. The night was pitch-black and there was a distant growl of thunder, with lightning flaring to the west. He could smell the rain coming, the warm, restless scent of damp earth and wet trees, mixed with the sultry fragrance of magnolias and the lighter perfume of honeysuckle and sweet peas and roses that tumbled over the fences along the street.

He picked up his pace. Maybe he should have taken the umbrella that Bessie Bloodworth had offered him. But if he hurried, he could make it home—he rented two large upstairs rooms from Mrs. Beedle, a block north of the courthouse square—before the rain arrived.

The brick sidewalk along Camellia Street was narrow and uneven and there were no streetlights. Seven or eight years ago, in the mid-1920s, Ozzie Sherman had installed a big Delco diesel generator to power his sawmill north of town. Ozzie was a first-class entrepreneur, and before long, he had formed the Sherman Electric Company and talked the Darling town council into a contract to run electricity through the town and install streetlights around the square.

A year or two later, when things were still booming, the council had bought Sherman Electric from Ozzie and added two new Delcos, expanding the electrical system across town. They had made a deal with the county, as well, to run electricity all the way out to the Cypress County Fairgrounds— an important deal, for electricity at the fairgrounds would make it possible to book big events that wanted to operate after dark.

But the money hadn't held out. After the market crashed and the economic downturn began, the town and the county had run out of cash. Everything had stalled, the county's road and bridge projects, Darling's plans, everything. There wouldn't be any civic improvements in Cypress County for a long time to come, as Charlie had pointed out in his various editorials.

But a streetlight on Camellia would have been an unwelcome intrusion, Charlie thought. The dark was soft and warm and the occasional golden glow from a parlor window spilled out onto the sidewalk, offering enough light so that strollers could avoid the worst of the uneven surface. A few people sat in their porch swings and gliders, listening to radios perched on the sills of open parlor windows, the tips of cigarettes glowing in the dark. Somebody played a guitar, singing along softly.

Charlie strode down the street, swinging his arms, feeling good. It wasn't every day that he could help a sweet little lady librarian get acquainted with her grandmother or get his hands on a cipher that had been squirreled away, likely, since the first year or two of the Civil War. His interest in this matter wasn't entirely philanthropic, however. It was nice to be able to help Miss Rogers, yes. It was even nicer to discover the key to a cipher that had apparently eluded Civil War espionage buffs for decades—and embroidered on a pillow, no less. *So like a woman,* he thought ironically. Put it on a pillow, right out in plain sight—although this pillow, he gathered, had been hiding under a knitted cover for some seven decades.

He reached Robert E. Lee, crossed the street, and headed north toward the courthouse square, patting the bulk of the papers in his jacket pocket. He would telephone his friend, Professor Litton, first thing in the morning. It would really be swell if Litton could help him find out more about the Confederate Rose. It would make a great story for the newspaper. He composed the first sentence in his head. *Miss Dorothy Rogers, Darling's beloved librarian, recently learned that she is the granddaughter of Rose Greenhow, the notorious Confederate spy.*

*Beloved?* Probably not, but it sounded good. And definitely not *notorious*, even though that was accurate. *Celebrated* was better. *Rose Greenhow, the celebrated Confederate spy, who saved the day at First Manassas and got the Boys in Gray off to a triumphant start.*

Charlie made a sour face. *Got them off to a triumphant start on the long road to inevitable defeat* was more like it, but he wouldn't write that, either. Write that, even though it was true, and half his subscribers would cancel. The other half would organize a tar-and-feathers party.

But there was something else he could do. He could telephone his friend Horton Lomax, who was an expert in old ciphers and the editor of the *Codes and Ciphers Journal*. In fact, it would be a good idea to stake his claim to the Rose Greenhow cipher key right away—offer to write a paper for Horton's journal, for instance. And if the pages he had discovered hidden in that pillow yielded what he guessed they would— well, they just might translate into a treasure that would bring in some serious moola. Museums didn't have much dough these days, but lots of rich people still had money. Some wealthy collector of Confederate memorabilia might want this stuff—including the embroidered pillow—for his collection.

But it wasn't his treasure, Charlie reminded himself. It was Miss Rogers' treasure, and if it helped her weather the storm that was likely to blow her over when the library closed (because he was sure it would), well, that would be a good thing. As he strolled along, he whistled quietly, feeling unusually pleased with himself. For Charlie Dickens did not make a general habit of doing good for other people. In fact, he rather cultivated the guise of a hard-nosed, cynical newspaperman whose main concern was looking out for Number One. But he had been moved by Miss Rogers' delight tonight, and the thought of having helped her discover her relationship to the Confederate Rose, who was brave and loyal, if a bit overly dramatic about it—well, it made him feel good, that was all.

And feeling good by doing good translated, surprisingly, into a bouncy step and a jaunty swing to his shoulders as he walked along the quiet street of this small town where he had grown up, in a nice house on the best street. Darling definitely wasn't Paris or London or Berlin, where Charlie had enjoyed a riotous good living, lavishly laced with good wine, beautiful women, and boisterous song. But then he'd got the boot in Baltimore and he was still trying to figure out what the hell he was going to do when his dad took sick and died, which had hit him harder than he'd expected. He hadn't been home for years—you'd've thought losing the old man would have been easier to deal with.

So he'd been pretty much at a low point when his dad died and he had to take over the *Dispatch*—not just the newspaper, but the print shop as well. And now here he was stuck with the damn thing. There wasn't a ghost of a chance of selling out, not in this economic climate, and he was too stubborn to walk away from something he'd put his time and effort into, even if it had been a mistake.

So Darling was home now, like it or not. And since that was how it was, well, it wasn't a bad thing to lend a hand where he could now and then, especially if there might be a little something in it for him.

He reached the corner of Robert E. Lee and Dauphin, at the southeast corner of the square, by the Old Alabama Hotel. He stopped for a moment, glancing up at the clock on the courthouse bell tower. Nine forty-five, not that late, and still no rain. Instead of going back to his flat, he could drop in at Pete's and play another game of pool. Or he could walk over to the *Dispatch* office and catch up on the work he'd set aside in favor of those Civil War books he'd got from the library. He decided on the office. Since he was a kid, he'd always been a night owl. He'd liked working after hours, when everybody else had gone home to bed and the bright lights were a barricade against the dark outside the window, which he always knew was there, even when he couldn't see it. Working nights, a guy didn't get interrupted. A guy could think long thoughts, put some meat on the bones of his prose. Could have a drink or two, some smokes—writing went better with booze and a cigarette. What's more, there was an umbrella in the office. If it was raining when he finally left, he'd go home dry.

He picked up his pace, passing the courthouse. On the right, on the other side of the street, was Kilgore Motors, the local Dodge dealership. The lights were off and the place was dark, but Charlie knew what was in the showroom. He'd had a look the previous week, a long look, since looking didn't cost a red cent. Didn't cost anything to sit under the wheel and dream, either. And there'd been plenty to dream about. The latest DH Six four-door sedan, two-tone mint green and teal blue, with black fenders and running boards, enough shiny chrome to break your heart, an ebony-paneled dashboard, and wire wheels with adjustable spokes and nonskid balloon tires. Roger Kilgore claimed it would do ninety on a good straightaway, and Charlie didn't doubt it. All for only $865—although there weren't many people in Darling who had that kind of money to blow on an auto. Mr. Johnson at the Darling Savings and Trust, maybe. Or one of the bootleggers, who wanted a car that would pull away fast and hold its own in a hot chase. Charlie certainly didn't have it—his pockets were empty. The *Dispatch* might turn a profit some-day, but not yet.

Past Kilgore's was Mann's Mercantile, and kitty-cornered, Musgrove's Hardware. There were no lights in any of the businesses—except upstairs over the diner, where Myra May and her friend Violet lived with Violet's little girl. And while he couldn't see the back of the diner from here, he knew there was a light in the office of the telephone exchange, where somebody was on round-the-clock duty at the switchboard.

It had just started to rain when Charlie crossed the street to the *Dispatch* office, unlocked the door, and went in, flick-ing on the light switch, inhaling (as he always did) the sharp scent of printer's ink, paper, and cigarette smoke. He sur-veyed the room: the old black Babcock cylinder press, a four-pager, against the back wall; the prewar Linotype machine that only Zipper Haydon knew how to operate, with the Miles proof press on the table beside it; the old Prouty job press; the sturdy marble-topped tables where the pages were made up; the printers' cabinets; the stacks of paper, press ready; and his battered desk with its tower of overflowing wooden in-boxes.

More overflow than Charlie liked to see, really, especially when he had just three days to get this week's paper out and Zipper coming in tomorrow to start setting columns. He turned on the green-shaded lamp on the corner of his desk, sat down, and opened the bottom right-hand drawer of his desk, taking out a full bottle of Mickey LeDoux's corn whiskey—white dog, some of the locals called it, or tiger spit, or chain lightning—and a glass. He poured and downed it, neat and fast. It wasn't sipping whiskey. It was gettin'-drunk whiskey, not the kind you were inclined to savor at the back of your throat.

He wiped a hand across his mouth. Thus fortified, he was ready to pick up where he had left off on the editorial for

Friday's paper. He would a whole lot rather be working on Ruthie Brant's story, but he hadn't yet figured out a way to verify the auditor's report of the missing money. So he was writing about the state of the cotton market, the drought, and the job market. He planned to end his editorial with Herbert Hoover's pie-in-the-sky presidential promise to put two and a half million people back to work. The unemployment rate was now fifteen percent and still rising. *Where were those two and a half million jobs?* he would ask. *Still buried under Hoover's hopeful imagination,* he'd answer. There was no way to conjure them up unless the federal government put some muscle and money behind the effort. But Hoover wanted to depend on private business to come up with the jobs, and look where that was getting them. Nowhere, that's where. Private business would do what was good for its investors, that was the bottom line. And right now, jobs for the jobless wasn't good for investors.

He lit another Lucky Strike, flexed his fingers, and attacked his typewriter.

# EIGHTEEN

# Lizzy, Verna, and Myra May

Lizzy, with a blindfolded Coretta in the front beside her and Verna in the rear seat, drove Big Bertha back to Darling, taking another circuitous route. Coretta had given Verna what she needed—the copy of the state auditor's report and a key to the office—and Verna seemed confident that she knew what to look for. But Lizzy still wasn't sure that Coretta could be trusted.

If Coretta was on their side, there was no problem, and she and Verna could go to the courthouse and do what had to be done. But if Coretta was what Verna called a double agent, she would telephone whoever she was working for as soon as she got home and tell them that she had given Verna the key to the county treasurer's office. Somebody would call the sheriff and Verna would be a dead duck.

Lizzy had considered (not very seriously) the idea of holding on to Coretta while Verna did her work. But to do that, they would probably have to tie and gag her, which seemed pretty extreme, not to mention illegal. As she drove, Lizzy wracked her brain, trying to come up with another strategy. And then finally, just as they got back to town, she thought of something that might work. About six or eight blocks from Coretta's house, she brought Big Bertha to a stop.

"End of the line," she said, and turned off the ignition.

Verna leaned forward. "Why are we stopping here?" she asked.

Lizzy mouthed, *Just wait,* and Verna, frowning, sat back. Lizzy leaned over and untied Coretta's bandana. "There you are," she said soothingly. "I'll bet that feels better, doesn't it, Coretta?"

Coretta didn't answer. Rubbing her eyes, she looked around, spotting the sign that pointed to the Cypress Country Club. "Hey, wait," she said accusingly. "I thought you were taking me home. But we're all the way out by the country club. You don't expect me to *walk*, do you? It's acting like it's going to rain."

"Afraid so," Lizzy said. She reached across Coretta and opened the passenger door. "Verna and I have an errand to do before we go to the office, so we're letting you out here. You're only about six blocks from home. If you hurry, you'll get there before it starts to rain."

"Eight blocks is more like it," Coretta grumbled, getting out of the car. "Happy hunting, Verna," she snapped, and slammed the door hard to show that she was peeved at the idea of having to walk.

Verna got into the front seat and they drove off. "What was that all about?" she asked curiously. "Why didn't we just drop her off at her house? It'll take her another fifteen minutes to get home, if she walks fast."

"Because I'm afraid she can't be trusted," Lizzy said, and explained her plan.

"Ah," Verna said, understanding. "Liz, that is very, very

clever." She grinned. "We'll make an espionage agent of you yet."

Lizzy parked Bertha in her garage and she and Verna went through the diner's back door. The diner was closed and Myra May was at the switchboard. She took off her headset and turned around.

"Hey, Liz," she said. "Hi, Verna."

"Thanks for letting us use your car," Lizzy said. "She got us there and back without any problems. And no flat tire," she added. The last time she'd borrowed Bertha, she'd had a flat.

"I hope everything works out," Myra May replied. She raised an eyebrow at Verna. "Aren't you supposed to be in Nashville, visiting a friend?" she asked slyly.

"It was a short trip," Verna replied with a chuckle. "I came straight back."

"We have another favor to ask, Myra May," Lizzy said. "Coretta Cole is on her way home right now. When she gets there, she may try to make a telephone call to . . ." She frowned. "Well, we're not exactly sure. Maybe Mr. Scroggins or Mr. Tombull—or maybe somebody else. If she does this, she'll want to tell the person she's calling that Verna has the key to the treasurer's office and will be there tonight. We hope you will . . . that is, we wonder if you could . . ." She took a breath. "Well, keep that call from going through."

"In other words," Myra May said quietly, "you want me to pull the plug."

"Something like that," Lizzy said in an apologetic tone, and Verna added, "Look, Myra May, we're trying to figure out who took that money from the county treasury. I have a copy of the auditor's report. It looks to me like there are several good clues in it, for somebody who knows how to follow them. If I can get just a few hours with the account ledgers and some other records in the office, I think I can track down the thief. But if—"

"But if Coretta makes that call, Verna could end up in jail," Lizzy finished the sentence.

"And whoever she warns," Verna continued, "may have a chance to destroy the evidence so *nobody* can follow the clues."

"I see," Myra May said. "So all I have to do is—" The switchboard buzzed and she turned around. "That's her now," she said.

"So she didn't go home and go straight to bed!" Lizzy exclaimed. "Which means—" She stopped. No, it didn't necessarily mean that. Maybe Coretta was calling her mother, or her sister, or a friend. Maybe her phone call had nothing to do with what had happened tonight.

"We won't know what it means until we find out who she's calling," Verna said urgently. "Myra May, could you—"

But Myra May had already put on her headset and turned back to the switchboard. "Number please," she said crisply, and paused. Then she turned back to Verna and Lizzy, putting her hand over her microphone. "She's calling Mr. Scroggins."

Lizzy pulled in her breath. Beside her, Verna stiffened. "I knew it," she muttered. "What a *crook*!"

Myra May turned back to the switchboard. "I'm sorry," she said sweetly, "but that number is busy. Please try your call again later." She broke the connection without waiting for a reply.

"Perfect!" Lizzy breathed out. "Now she'll just keep trying, over and over again. Thank you, Myra May. Thank you!"

"So," Verna said grimly. "That was Coretta's plan all along. She'd give me the key, and then Scroggins would close in on me. Or he'd send the sheriff. It was a setup. A trap that I was supposed to step into." She looked at Lizzy. "And you turned the trap around, to catch *her.* Thanks, Liz."

Myra May took off her headset again. "You don't think Coretta will go to Mr. Scroggins' house, since she can't telephone him?"

"He lives five miles out in the country," Lizzy said. "I know for a fact that the Coles' car has been out of commission for several months, and it's too late to borrow a car from the neighbors. At least, I hope it is," she added, under her breath. She had thought of this, and decided that—short of kidnapping Coretta and physically detaining her—there wasn't anything they could do to stop her. If she desperately wanted to get in touch with somebody, she would. They'd just have to take their chances.

Verna nudged Lizzy. "We'd better get going, Liz. I'd like to get in and out of that office as fast as possible."

"Is there anything else I can do?" Myra May asked. "Besides making sure that Coretta doesn't connect with Mr. Scroggins tonight, that is."

Lizzy chuckled. "Well, you might monitor calls to the sheriff's office and pull the plug if the caller wants to report a break-in at the courthouse. It would be really good if we could keep Verna out of jail until she figures out who dunnit."

"Jail?" Myra May shifted uncomfortably. "I hope it doesn't come to that. You two be careful over there. You hear?"

"We hear," Lizzy and Verna said in unison.

# NINETEEN

# Charlie, Lizzy, and Verna

Several glasses of Mickey's tiger spit and half a pack of Luckys later, Charlie Dickens looked up at the old octagon Regulator clock on the wall and saw to his surprise that it was half past twelve. He remembered being vaguely aware, some while ago, that the courthouse clock was striking midnight, and he realized that his eyes felt grainy, his shoulders were stiff, and he'd had too much to drink. Time to head for bed. He could finish what he was doing—typing (and editing as he typed) Doris Trask's messily handwritten piece about the Darling Mothers Club raffle—in the morning. Trivial stuff, in his opinion, not worth the ink and paper it took to print it. What he really needed, what would put the *Dispatch* on the map, so to speak, was a good story, a bombshell story like the one Ruthie Brant had brought him that afternoon, which he couldn't publish because he didn't yet have the facts.

Charlie finished the sentence and stopped typing, leaving the paper—a narrow three-foot-long role of newsprint a little wider than column width, which made it easier to write and edit a story to the right length—in the Royal. He put the whiskey bottle, half empty now, back in the bottom drawer of his desk, picked up his hat, and went to the door. The rain had stopped—no need of the umbrella after all—and the quarter moon shone silvery through a gauzy veil of clouds. The air had been rinsed cool and clean by the rain, and he filled his lungs with it. Good. The air tasted good. A dozen deep breaths of that good clean stuff and he'd be sober, more or less. He turned off the lights and locked the door.

It was very quiet out on the street. The clouds that raced across the moon cast fleeting shadows under the chinaberry trees on the courthouse lawn and splashed silver shimmers of moonshine on the puddles in the street, while the darkened windows of the stores and shops around the square caught the fleeting glimmers and flickered them back.

But the buildings on the square were not completely dark. For as Charlie looked up at the courthouse, directly opposite the *Dispatch* office, he caught a glimpse of a dim electric light in one of the second-floor offices, the county treasurer's office, he thought it was. As he watched, a shadowy shape, a woman's shape, he thought, moved past the window. A moment later, the light went out and the window was dark—but not quite, for another light had gone on, in an inner room. And then that light disappeared, fast, as if a door had shut.

Charlie hesitated, took another step, thinking that bed was what he really wanted and perhaps a nightcap from the bottle he kept stashed under the loose floorboard in his closet, where Mrs. Beedle wouldn't find it when she cleaned. But then he stopped, frowning. It was after midnight and the offices in the courthouse were supposed to be locked up tight. The only person who ever worked late over there was Verna Tidwell, who had a habit of staying after hours and coming in on weekends, especially since Earle Scroggins had taken over

DeYancy's job and put her in charge of the treasurer's accounts.

But Verna Tidwell wasn't working late tonight. In fact, Verna Tidwell wasn't working in the treasurer's office at all now, according to Ruthie Brant, who had dropped that information along with the bombshell about the state auditor's report into Charlie's lap that afternoon. Verna Tidwell had been furloughed. At least that was the story. *Canned* was more like it, Ruthie had said. And Earle Scroggins had changed the locks, so Verna no longer had a key. What's more, the sheriff had tried to serve a warrant on her, but she had fled to Nashville to avoid being arrested.

Charlie stood for a moment on the sidewalk, swaying just a little, his head cocked, looking up at the black window. It had been a long day. He was ready to head for bed, which now seemed to beckon with an almost seductive charm. The only thing better would be a woman in it.

But somebody was in the treasurer's office, somebody who didn't want anybody to know that she (Charlie was sure that the figure had been a woman) was there. He knew it wasn't Ruthie Brant. Ruthie liked to snoop but she was bone lazy. Once the workday was over, she was on her way home as fast as her feet could carry her. The other employee, Melba Jean Manners, was a stolid, silent woman who had about as much initiative as a snail, as far as Charlie could tell. It wouldn't be her skulking around up there after hours.

But Coretta Cole—now, Coretta was another matter, and Charlie raised his eyebrows, considering the possibilities. Ruthie had said that Coretta Cole had taken over for Verna. Charlie didn't know Coretta Cole. Maybe she was like Verna, somebody who doted on work, or was so anxious to do a good job that she was willing to come in after hours, even stay all night if she had to.

And then he thought of something. That story Ruthie had

given him. He knew a few things and suspected more, but that was mostly what he had—suspicions. Maybe Coretta Cole would help him out, especially if he caught her by surprise and asked her a few probing questions. Ask in the right way, and she might even let him see that state auditor's report. And that was what made up Charlie's mind—the idea of catching Coretta Cole by surprise, at a moment when he might be able to provoke her into telling him what he wanted to know.

Now, if Charlie had been completely, 100 percent sober, he probably wouldn't have thought this was such a good idea. For one thing, the woman behind that window blind might not be Coretta Cole. For another, maybe Coretta Cole (if that's who it was) would tell him to go to hell and how to get there, too. Or, if he surprised her and she panicked, she might just bash him over the head with whatever weapon came to hand—and call the sheriff, to boot.

But while Charlie was sober enough to navigate, his judgment was what you might call *slightly impaired*. So, fueled by his whiskey-soaked idea of persuading Coretta Cole to substantiate Ruthie Brant's claim, he headed across the street toward the side door of the courthouse, thinking that it was a good thing that he'd held on to that courthouse key.

The previous year, Amos Tombull, the chairman of the county board of commissioners, had asked Charlie to do some historical research for a tourist pamphlet on the old gristmill out on Pine Mill Creek. Before they had run out of money and abandoned the project, Charlie had been given a key to the records vault in the basement, where he had spent several tedious hours looking for details about the mill, which was almost as old as Darling itself. The vault was like a dungeon, musty and foul-smelling, and the records were powdered with decades of dust and mold. Conveniently, the same key opened the building's north-side door, and Charlie had kept it. No newspaperman ever returns a borrowed key, of course, because he never knows when it might come in handy. Like tonight.

So Charlie tried to put the key into the lock and turn it. When it wouldn't work, he realized that he was putting it in upside down and corrected the problem. The door, unlocked, gave easily, with only the slightest creak and he stepped inside. At that moment, he thought he heard the dull sound of another door thudding, somewhere upstairs, and furtive footsteps.

Charlie frowned again, his newspaperman's nose twitching. The treasurer's office occasionally kept sums of money overnight, if a cash tax payment came in after the bank closed, for instance. It would be easy for somebody, an employee, maybe, to come in and take the money. It was risky, but if that person knew what she was doing and took a moment to doctor the records, she could probably get away with it.

He pursed his lips. He was standing in a long, narrow corridor that ran the length of the building. There were stairs at either end, up to the second floor and down to the basement— not that Charlie could see them, for the place was black as the inside of a tomb and the air was thick and stale, like the air in a closed vault. It settled over his head and shoulders like a heavy caul, making it hard to breathe.

Charlie wouldn't have admitted it, of course, but there was something more than a little frightening about this dark. It probably had to do with the history of the old courthouse, which had been built back in 1897. The following year, it had been the scene of a dreadful double murder, two women shot to death at the stroke of noon in the courtroom that occupied the center part of the building. The killer had run up the stairs to the bell tower and jumped off, killing himself.

Not the end of the story, of course. The ghosts of the

murdered women were said to be pursued through the halls of the building, even during the daylight hours, by the ghost of their murderer. Every year, several people—even people who hadn't heard about the killings—claimed to have seen them on the stairs or in a hallway. Then, in 1907, on the tenth anniversary of the murders, at the stroke of noon, a violent tornado had reached down out of the sky and ripped off the bell tower. The tornado's timing was just too coincidental for some folks. The following Sunday, the minister at the Baptist church said it was the good Lord's retribution for the horrible double murder and suicide. Whatever you thought of this explanation, the ghosts of the two women continued to reappear from time to time after the tower was rebuilt, but the ghost of their killer had disappeared. It was never seen again.

Charlie himself had never encountered the ghosts, of course, not even when he went down to the archives vault to look for the information on the gristmill for the commissioners' pamphlet. He didn't believe in ghosts—in fact, Charlie had long ago decided that he didn't believe in anything he couldn't see, touch, smell, or hear. But just the same, the dark felt thick and heavy with a sinister presence, and his fingers were trembling slightly when he put out his hand to feel along the wall for the light switch that he knew was to the right of the door.

But suddenly, somewhere in the dark, he heard the scurry of light footsteps, a scuffling sound, and a whisper, a woman's urgent whisper. "No, don't come down! Somebody's here."

Charlie froze. But this was no ghost, and he recognized the voice.

"Liz Lacy," he said, his voice sounding unnaturally loud in the silence. "What the devil are you doing here, at this hour? Who's with you? Who's that upstairs?"

The sound of footsteps, coming down the stairs. "Charlie? Charlie Dickens, is that you?"

"Yeah," Charlie said. "It's me." A flashlight shone suddenly in his face. "Put that thing down," he said, adding, "Please," as an afterthought. Liz Lacy turned the light away and set it upright on a stair. Its dim glow provided enough light so that he could see her, standing now in the hallway. "What are you doing here?" he repeated.

Liz took a breath. "I could ask you the same question," she answered, raising her voice and glancing over her shoulder, up the stairs. She was clearly stalling for time. "What are you looking for? Why are you here?"

"Just doing my job," Charlie replied. "I was working late, across the street. I saw a light upstairs, in the treasurer's office. I came to investigate." He grinned amiably. "That's what a newspaperman does, you know. He investigates. That's how he gets his stories."

"Well, you can stop investigating," Liz said irritably. "It's only Verna Tidwell. She works here. She . . . she forgot something in her office and came back to get it. I'm waiting for her." She raised her voice a notch, cautiously. "Verna, it's okay. It's just Charlie Dickens."

"Forgot something?" Charlie chuckled sardonically. "*Forgot* something? Forgot she'd been furloughed, did she? Forgot that she was supposed to be in Nashville?" He paused and hardened his voice. "Where'd she get the key, Liz? I heard that Earle Scroggins changed the locks so she couldn't get in."

"Charlie Dickens?" another voice asked, and Verna Tidwell came down the stairs, pausing on the last tread. "What are you doing here at this hour of the night?"

"That question has already gone the rounds a time or two," Charlie said with a chuckle. He leaned one shoulder against the wall. The alcohol that had fogged his brain had evaporated and in his now-sober state, it occurred to him that Verna Tidwell might be a lot more willing to talk than Coretta Cole would have been. And if she'd had the time to go through the records upstairs and find whatever she was looking for, she might know a great deal.

"I suppose you were looking for that state auditor's report," he hazarded.

In the silence, Charlie heard Liz pull in her breath. Then Verna said, low and steadily, "Who told you about that?" When he didn't immediately answer, she raised her voice. "Who *told* you?"

"Oh, word gets around," Charlie said carelessly, now very sure. Grinning, he pushed himself away from the wall. "Hey, how would you two ladies like to come over to the *Dispatch* office for a drink and a little conversation? I think we might be able to do some business. What do you say?"

"I really don't think we—" Liz began, but Verna stopped her.

"Just what kind of business did you have in mind?" she asked warily.

"You might call it a little trade," Charlie replied. "I mean, look at it this way, Verna. I'm sure you don't want Earle Scroggins and the county commissioners to know that you've been working late tonight—*after* you were furloughed and locked out of the office. And when you're supposed to be in Nashville, where the sheriff can't get at you." He raised his hand against the flurry of her protests. "I have some questions I want answered, for a story I'm working on."

Nobody spoke for the space of several breaths. "A little trade," Verna Tidwell said at last. "Your silence for my answers."

"That's blackmail, Charlie," Liz said in a reproving tone. "I thought you were above that."

"Blackmail?" Charlie raised both hands. "Whoa, now, Liz. Watch who you're callin' a blackmailer. Me, I prefer to think of it as a trade. I've got something you want, you've got something I want."

"You're writing a story," Verna said speculatively. "Is it anything like those earlier editorials you wrote about Mr. DeYancy and the county treasurer's office?"

"Something like that," Charlie answered evasively. "All I need are a few confirmations and a fact or two. So . . ." He shrugged. "How about it?"

Lizzy looked at Verna. "I guess it's your call," she said.

"I'm willing to discuss it," Verna replied guardedly. "But I won't make any promises about confirmations. Or facts." She glanced at Lizzy. "It might be better if we used Mr. Moseley's office, though. It's less . . . well, public than the newspaper. Somebody might see me and wonder why I'm not in Nashville. Is that okay, Liz?"

"That's fine with me," Lizzy said. "I'll make us some coffee."

"Coffee sounds swell." Charlie opened the door, then stepped aside. "Ladies first."

# TWENTY

# Lizzy, Verna, and Charlie

Lizzy plugged in the electric percolator and began making a pot of coffee while Verna and Charlie Dickens sat down on either side of the table in Mr. Moseley's conference room. Lizzy was glad that Verna had suggested coming to the office, where they couldn't be seen from the street. And Charlie definitely didn't need another drink. What he needed was coffee, and plenty of it. She could use some, too. It had been a long day, and from the way things looked, it wasn't over yet.

Verna must have decided to share at least some of what she knew. As Lizzy came into the conference room and set the mugs on the table, she was saying, "In addition to identifying how much is missing, the auditor's report pinpoints which bank accounts the money came from. Two of them, actually, both in Monroeville, at different banks."

"Different banks? Monroeville?" Charlie reached for the coffee. "That's a little unusual, isn't it? I would've thought that the Cypress County accounts—if there had to be more than one—would be right here in Darling. Monroeville is in Monroe County."

"Unusual, you bet," Verna said emphatically. "The county's accounts—six of them—are held in three different banks in Monroeville, and in the Darling Savings and Trust. If you ask me, I think it was set up that way so the money could be moved around without leaving a clear trail. Just in case somebody asked—although apparently nobody did, until the audit."

"Ah, the old short con." He put his mug down, grinning bleakly. "You never know which cup hides the pea—or even if there is a pea. And usually there isn't. Usually, it's been palmed by the operator. And you're out whatever money you put down. Tough tiddy."

"Yeah." Verna put her elbows on the table and cupped her hands around the mug. "The con. Here's how it went, at least as far as I've been able to dope out. On July thirtieth last year, the State of Alabama sent Cypress County a check for fifteen thousand dollars from the state's gasoline tax account. The money was earmarked for road improvements, bridge repair, and so forth."

"Like the bridge on Pine Mill Creek," Lizzy guessed, "where Bunny Scott was killed. It was washed out over a year ago, and hasn't been fixed yet." She'd heard a lot of grumbling about that bridge, because people had to make a ten-mile detour to avoid the washout.

"Exactly," Verna said. "And there are several other projects that have come to a standstill—such as extending electricity out to the county fairgrounds—because the money meant for them was diverted to the road fund instead, to cover emergencies. Only there hasn't been enough to go around, so even the emergencies don't get covered."

Charlie downed another gulp of coffee. "The gasoline tax money came from the state and went . . . where?" His voice was sounding steadier, Lizzy thought.

Verna met Charlie's eyes with a straight, hard gaze. "What I'm telling you is off the record for now, Charlie. I've got to decide what to do with the information—that is, who should take it from here. The sheriff or—" She shook her head, frowning. "There's a warrant out for my arrest. I'm not sure who I can trust."

"You don't see a notebook in my hand, do you?" Charlie countered.

"No, but I want to hear you say it," Verna said firmly. "Just three little words. Off the record. I don't want to read about this in Friday's paper." She gave him a crooked grin. "The Friday after, maybe, but not just yet. And not with my name on it. You got that?"

Charlie looked disgruntled. "Okay. Off the record," he growled. "For now. But when I do the story, I've got to be able to nail it down with some sort of attribution. I can't just say *anonymous*."

"You could say *sources in the county courthouse*," Lizzy suggested helpfully. "Knowledgeable sources, maybe. Informed sources."

"I'd rather have a name," Charlie said.

"You're not going to get it," Verna replied. "I have to live in this town. And I'd like to hang on to my job."

Charlie sighed. "You're a hard lady. Well, go on. What's the bottom line? Where did that money go? Off the record," he added. "Damn it."

"The bottom line," Verna said steadily, "is that the state's fifteen-thousand-dollar gas-tax payment went to settle a mortgage on Jasper DeYancy's Sour Creek Plantation."

Charlie's eyes widened and he put his mug down with a thump. "You're pulling my leg."

Taken aback, Lizzy stared at Verna. The Sour Creek Plantation was one of the oldest and most revered of all the plantations on the Alabama River. Over past decades, going back to the time of Jasper DeYancy's father and grandfather, it had been known for its prodigious production of cotton, peaches, and peanuts. But the drought and boll weevils had been hard on the DeYancys, as on all the farmers around Darling, and many of the fields lay flat and fallow, baking under a hot, dry sun, while the price of cotton went down, down, down.

But the Big House remained as lovely and graceful as ever, rising out of the river-borne mists like a romantic vision of the antebellum South. It was painted white as whipped cream, with green shutters and a gabled portico with fluted white pillars, and surrounded by sweeps of green lawn, a gorgeous garden of azaleas, roses, and ancient trees draped with silvery Spanish moss. Lizzy had never been inside the Big House, but the DeYancys entertained frequently, and she had heard tales of crystal chandeliers and Oriental rugs and cases full of leather-bound books and engraved family silver and oil portraits of the DeYancy women framed in gold. The family fortunes were thought to be framed in gold, too.

"Nope, not pulling your leg," Verna said flatly. "The abstract on the DeYancy place is in the probate clerk's office, from the earliest land grant claim down to the present. I checked it tonight, after I tracked down the information from the bank accounts."

*Ah,* Lizzy thought—*of course.* Of all people in Darling, Verna Tidwell was the one person who would know how and where to lay her hands on this kind of information. She had worked in the probate office for years and years. If you asked her where to find the abstract of any piece of property in the county, she'd be able to tell you. A look at the abstract would reveal any and all financial transactions recorded against the property, such as deeds, wills, probate records, court litigations, tradesmen's liens, and tax sales. And—yes—mortgages.

"In the records for 1924," Verna went on, "I found the original entry for the mortgage on the Sour Creek Plantation.

It was held by the Merchants Bank down in Mobile, for fifteen thousand dollars, due January 12, 1930. It wasn't paid, though, not even the interest. And in June of last year—June 1930—the bank began foreclosure proceedings."

"Uh-oh," Charlie said softly.

"Yes," Verna said. "But on August tenth, the full amount of the mortgage was repaid. Fifteen thousand dollars. There's no record of exactly how it was paid, but I was able to backtrack through the Monroeville bank accounts. I found three checks, one for six thousand five hundred dollars, another for four thousand five hundred dollars, a third for four thousand dollars, written on separate county accounts. The checks were dated August fourth, fifth, and sixth."

"Written to whom?" Charlie asked sharply. "To the bank?"

Verna laughed dryly. "He wasn't quite that barefaced about it, but almost. The checks were written to Mrs. De-Yancy's father. Howard Carruthers. For 'road materials.'"

Charlie whistled low, half under his breath.

Lizzy sat back in her chair. Mrs. DeYancy's father owned a gravel pit on the far southern border of the county. "Gosh." She whooshed out her breath. "Fifteen thousand dollars is a *whole lot* of gravel."

"You said it, Liz," Verna replied. "And the amount—a total of fifteen thousand—and dates are just too coincidental."

"Wait a minute," Lizzy objected. "If the checks were in payment for road materials, even if those were bogus charges, the money wouldn't have shown up as missing in the audit. Right? So how—"

Verna nodded approvingly. "You're right, Liz. But for some reason—carelessness, maybe, or an effort to conceal what was being done—the payments weren't recorded in the proper accounts. That's why the state auditor didn't spot them. If they'd been properly recorded, I doubt if the theft would ever have been discovered."

"And the gravel?" Charlie asked, and answered his own question. "It was probably never ordered. And never delivered."

Verna made a face at Charlie. "You interrupted before I could search for the two Carruthers' invoices. But I agree. The delivery probably never existed."

Charlie was eager now. "And I'm willing to bet that the bank records will show that the fifteen thousand that went to the Mobile bank to pay off the DeYancy mortgage came out of the Carruthers' account," he said excitedly. He paused, shaking his head. "Corruption and outright thievery," he muttered. "I wonder if that's why DeYancy killed himself. He figured that if he was out of the picture, there would never be any investigation. The plantation would be safe and his insurance would bring a nice little bundle that would take care of his wife for life."

"Killed himself!" Verna asked, both eyebrows going up.

"But I thought it was alcohol poisoning," Lizzy protested. "An accident. That's what everybody said." She pointed at Charlie. "That's what *you* said. In the newspaper."

"I had to say it. I didn't have any evidence to the contrary. And it was alcohol poisoning, all right," Charlie said grimly. "But whether it was accidental or intentional, we'll probably never know. Or if it was intentional, whether it was DeYancy's intention or somebody else's."

Lizzy gasped. "You mean, you think he might have been . . . *murdered?*"

"Alcohol is a pretty convenient weapon, Liz," Charlie said, very seriously. "It doesn't leave any fingerprints or ballistic traces. Drink enough, or drink the wrong stuff, and you're dead. Happens all the time, especially since everybody and his cousin cooks his own mash. Quantity, not quality, is what they're after." He reached for the coffeepot and filled his mug, then leaned back. "So, Verna, what are you going to do with this information?"

Verna sat still for a moment, her fingers laced around her mug. Finally, she pushed it away. "Charlie, you've been watching the county commissioners more closely than I have. Do you have any reason to suspect that Amos Tombull might be in on this theft?"

Charlie considered, then shook his head. "I don't think so, Verna. Of course, the Tombulls and the DeYancys move in the same social circle, and the two men probably did their fair share of hunting and fishing together. But Tombull has always seemed on the up-and-up to me. The only thing I've ever been able to fault him for was being too cozy with Earle Scroggins."

Lizzy leaned forward. "Verna, do you think Mr. Scroggins knew? About that mortgage payment, I mean."

"I don't know," Verna replied, and her face darkened. "But there was that nasty trick that Scroggins pulled at the bank."

"What nasty trick?" Charlie wanted to know.

"Verna sold a piece of property she had inherited," Lizzy explained, "and deposited the money in her account at the Darling Savings and Trust."

"Ten thousand dollars," Verna said, and Charlie raised his eyebrows. "Florida property," she added. "It was a surprise to me, too."

"Anyway," Lizzy went on, "Mr. Scroggins went to Mr. Johnson and asked him to take a look at Verna's account. They saw the money from the property sale and decided it must have come from the county treasury. It wasn't fifteen thousand, but I guess they figured she spent the rest."

Charlie frowned. "That's pretty slick, Liz. How the devil did you find out about it?"

"Oh, we Dahlias have our ways," Lizzy said with a chuckle.

"Anyway, that's how the sheriff got involved. On Mr. Scroggins' say-so, with Mr. Johnson's connivance."

"A warrantless, illegal search of the bank records," Charlie said, shaking his head. "Pretty dumb, if you ask me." He grinned at Lizzy. "Your boss will have a lot of fun with that one."

"Scroggins was anxious to push the whole thing off onto me," Verna said. "I'd say that he's definitely involved in trying to stage a quick cover-up. But I don't have any way of knowing how much he knew about DeYancy, Carruthers, and that fifteen thousand. He might have been in on it from the very beginning. Or he might not have known anything until that audit report came through—and then he started trying to protect DeYancy's reputation."

"Or his own skin," Lizzy said. "He might've been afraid that he'd get blamed. And that the voters would remember, come the next election."

"Back to my question, Verna," Charlie said. "What are you going to do with this?"

She paused. "I'm taking a chance, but I think I should have a talk with Amos Tombull. If the county commissioners conducted their own official investigation and if they did it right, with a little nudge in the right direction, they'd pretty quickly figure out what happened. The mortgage and the payoff are both recorded in the property abstract. All they have to do is look for the checks to Carruthers and move forward from there." She paused. "Anyway, that's what the state wants the commissioners to do. Investigate. I think they might be afraid to try to cover things up, with the state auditor looking over their shoulders."

Lizzy put down her coffee cup. "I agree, Verna. I think that's exactly what you should do. Talk to Mr. Tombull. First thing tomorrow morning."

Charlie looked up at the clock on the wall. "It's already tomorrow morning." He grinned. "And don't forget. The minute you're in the clear, Verna, I get the story."

Verna gave him a tight smile. "That's right, Charlie. You get the story."

# TWENTY-ONE

# Monday, April 27, 1931

Confederate Day, an Alabama state holiday, was celebrated on the fourth Monday of April. It marked the surrender of Confederate General Joseph E. Johnston to Union General William Tecumseh Sherman, on April 26, 1865, after the last major Confederate offensive of the War near Durham, North Carolina.

Confederate Day was always an important day in Darling. Last year, there had been four Confederate veterans to be honored—white-haired, bearded old men who got their gray uniforms out of the camphor chest and proudly donned them for the parade around the courthouse square, down Robert E. Lee, and out Schoolhouse Road to the Darling Cemetery. Last year, they'd ridden in two cars, but old Abner Prince hadn't made it through the winter, and the three who were left would be riding in Andy Stanton's open-topped 1928 Franklin touring car, with Rebel flags fluttering fore and aft and Andy at the wheel, decked out in his summer whites, with a

Rebel flag stuck in the band of his white straw hat and a big cigar stuck in his mouth.

The ceremony took place at the cemetery, where the town's Stars and Stripes were run down for the day and the Confederate flag run up beside the stage that had been built for the occasion. The Reverend Carl Mason of the First Baptist Church gave the invocation, Mayor Jed Snow gave the welcome, and the speeches flowed like good corn whiskey.

And at the very end, there was a special tribute. Lizzy Lacy, dressed in her prettiest spring dress and wearing a new pink straw hat with pink and green velvet ribbons, reminded folks that they should be sure to notice the row of Confederate roses along the fence at the front of the cemetery.

"The planting of the Confederate roses was a project of the Darling Dahlias Garden Club," Lizzy said, "led by Miss Dorothy Rogers, whom all of you know as our town librarian. Miss Rogers, will you please stand so we can thank you for helping to make our cemetery the most beautiful in Cypress County?"

And Miss Rogers, blushing as pink as a peony, stood up and received the audience's appreciative applause. When the clapping had died down, she said, in her prim, precise voice, "I'd like everyone to know that the Confederate rose isn't a rose at all. It is actually an hibiscus. *Hibiscus mutabilis* is its real name." As everyone chuckled, she sat down again, smiling and obviously glad to have set the record straight.

"And there's another Confederate Rose to be honored today," Lizzy went on. "Miss Rogers recently learned that she is the granddaughter of Rose Greenhow, whom many have called the Confederate Rose. Mrs. Greenhow served as a Confederate spy in Washington, D.C., during the first year of the War Between the States. In 1862, she was imprisoned by President Abraham Lincoln." (At the mention of Lincoln's

266 *Susan Wittig Albert*

name, a low, hissing exhalation of breath swept through the audience.) "After her release, she was sent to Europe by President Jefferson Davis"—someone in the back row cheered—"as an ambassador for the Confederacy. Upon her return, she was shipwrecked and drowned, weighed down by the gold she was bringing for the Confederate treasury." (Someone cried, "Oh, dear!" and quite a few people clapped.)

"Over the years," Lizzie said, "Miss Rogers kept a piece of her grandmother's needlework. It was recently discovered that this needlework provides a key to some of the puzzles of Mrs. Greenhow's espionage. To tell this part of the story, I'll call on Mr. Charles Dickens, editor and publisher of the Darling *Dispatch*."

At that point, Charlie got up and told about the secret code that Mrs. Greenhow used to send messages to General P. G. T. Beauregard, and about the key to the code that was embroidered on the outside of the small pillow that Miss Rogers had kept ever since she was a little girl. Hidden in the pillow were several important documents. He had been in touch with two experts who had verified this surprising discovery. They would be using the information it provided to uncover more of the mysteries surrounding the work of Mrs. Greenhow, who had contributed so much to the Confederate cause.

When Charlie sat down, Lizzy presented Miss Rogers, who by this time was utterly engulfed in tears, with a certificate (printed in fancy letters on Charlie's job press) that honored the Confederate Rose. Then, as she did each and every year without fail, Mrs. Eiglehorn recited all five stanzas of Henry Timrod's poem, "Ode," ("Sleep sweetly in your humble graves, Sleep, martyrs of a fallen cause . . ."), which was first recited on the occasion of decorating the graves of the Confederate dead at Magnolia Cemetery in Charleston, South

Carolina, in 1867. After that, Eva Pearl Hennepin, accompanied by Josiah, led everyone in a rousing rendition of "Dixie":

> *I wish I was in the land of cotton,*
> *Old times they are not forgotten;*
> *Look away! Look away! Look away! Dixie Land.*
> *In Dixie Land where I was born in,*
> *Early on one frosty mornin',*
> *Look away! Look away! Look away! Dixie Land*

And then, to the very same tune and at the very top of their lungs, everyone sang "The Confederate States of America War Song," which they all knew by heart:

> *Southern men the thunders mutter!*
> *Northern flags in South winds flutter!*
> *To arms! To arms! To arms, in Dixie!*
> *Send them back your fierce defiance!*
> *Stamp upon the cursed alliance!*
> *To arms! To arms! To arms, in Dixie!*

After all four verses of that rousing battle hymn, the crowd quieted and George Timson played "Taps" on his bugle and the Confederate flag was lowered to half-staff, where it would fly for the rest of the day. Reverend Trivette gave the benediction (he was much too long-winded, as usual), and the beautiful ceremony was over.

The members of the Daughters of the Confederacy went through the cemetery, placing beautiful wreaths of spring flowers on the graves of Darling's Confederate dead. While they were doing that, everyone else took their picnic baskets and jugs of tea and lemonade and adjourned to the neighboring picnic ground for a huge potluck and musical jamboree, featuring all the local fiddlers and guitar players and accordion players playing old-time music.

The Dahlias, with their families, had commandeered several picnic tables in the shade of a pair of large sycamore trees. They spread tablecloths on the tables and put out platters heaped high with fried chicken and barbecued spareribs, covered with tea towels to keep away the flies. With the platters, there were big earthenware crocks filled with green beans cooked with fatback, creamy potato salad, Mildred Kilgore's coleslaw with pecans, and Aunt Hetty Little's stewed okra with bacon, tomatoes, and corn. There were dozens of deviled eggs and pints of pickles and gallons of iced tea and lemonade, and far more chocolate cakes and sweet potato pies than everybody could eat, along with Mildred Kilgore's homemade strawberry ice cream, made with fresh berries in the Kilgores' hand-crank ice cream maker. It was a picnic potluck to remember, especially because Miss Rogers couldn't help bursting into tears every time she looked at the certificate honoring the Confederate Rose.

After the meal was over and the leftover food (there wasn't much) put back in the picnic baskets, the men went to play horseshoes and talk politics while the women sat at the tables, chatting and listening to the music and watching the boys playing baseball in a nearby field while the girls played jacks and jumped rope.

Lizzy and Verna had just sat down together when they were joined by Myra May and Violet, who was carrying Cupcake on her hip. Cupcake and Violet wore matching yellow ribbons in their hair.

"Well, hey, Verna," Myra May said, "I heard from Buddy Norris yesterday that there is no longer a warrant out for your arrest. Congratulations." Buddy Norris was Sheriff Roy Burns' deputy. He was sweet on Violet, so he hung around the diner whenever he wasn't riding around on his Indian Ace motorcycle, keeping the peace. The sheriff liked to brag that Buddy was the only mounted deputy in all of Alabama.

"Word travels fast," Verna said. "But, yes, Buddy got it right. The warrant's been canceled."

Violet perched Cupcake on her knee, fluffed up the baby's strawberry curls, and retied her yellow ribbon. "Just out of curiosity, Verna," she said, "how did you manage that?"

"It wasn't easy," Verna replied in a mysterious tone.

"She discussed the whole thing with Mr. Tombull," Lizzy said. "It didn't take much to convince him that Earle Scroggins had trumped up the 'evidence' against her. Scroggins wanted to shovel the problem under the rug so he wouldn't look bad to the voters, so he jumped at the first explanation, which was *definitely* not the right one. What's more, the way he went about it meant that his so-called 'evidence' would never have been admissible in court." At least, that's what Mr. Moseley had said when Lizzy told him about it by telephone. (Actually, what he said would have earned the ire of old Judge Parker, who never allowed swearwords in his courtroom.)

"That's right," Verna confirmed. "After Mr. Tombull thought about it, he said he'd have Scroggins cancel the warrant." She grinned. "Scroggins wasn't very happy about that, but he did it."

Myra May propped her elbows on the table and leaned forward. "This is not to be repeated," she said in a low voice, "but I hear that the commissioners are going to tell Mr. Scroggins that he has to step down as acting treasurer. He'll keep his job as probate clerk, because that's an elected office. But he's finished as treasurer."

Lizzy and Verna exchanged startled glances. "You're kidding," Verna said incredulously. "Where'd you hear that?"

"Just never you mind," Myra May said loftily, and Violet busied herself playing pat-a-cake with Cupcake. Lizzy knew that it had been overheard on the switchboard.

"Well, I guess I'm not surprised," Verna said after a moment. "I had to tell Mr. Tombull the whole thing, which included that business with Coretta Cole. It was obvious that Scroggins was using her to set a trap for me. I don't blame Coretta—her family needed money and she did what she had to in order to get it. And she signaled her ulterior motive strongly enough to raise our suspicions—Liz's and mine, I mean."

"That's true," Lizzy said. "The way Coretta acted, neither of us felt we were able to trust her. The more I've thought about it, the more I think it was deliberate. She was letting us see that she couldn't be straight with us."

Verna nodded, agreeing. "Anyway, Scroggins was way out of line, doing what he did at the bank, *and* with Coretta. If he got away with pushing the blame onto me, there was no telling what else he might try the next time he had a chance. Mr. Tombull is a straight shooter. I guess he figured that now was a good time to clean house in the treasurer's office, since he had the auditor's report in his hands." She grinned. "And especially after Charlie Dickens interviewed him for that article he's planning. I think Mr. Tombull saw the writing on the wall, so to speak."

"I suppose the next question is who the county commissioners are going to appoint to fill the treasurer's job," Lizzy said. "If Scroggins is out, who's in? One of the commissioners, maybe?"

"Uh-uh." Myra May shook her head, her eyes alight. "Guess again." Violet giggled.

"You *know*?" Verna asked in surprise, looking from Myra May to Violet.

Lizzy elbowed her. "There's precious little these gals don't know," she said. "Even when a meeting is held behind closed doors, they're bound to get wind of it, sooner or later."

"Well, *who*, then?" Verna demanded.

Myra May and Violet looked at one another. Violet raised her eyebrows. Myra May nodded. Then they both leaned forward and said, together and in a loud whisper, "Verna Tidwell!"

Lizzy gasped. "Verna?"

"Me?" Verna exclaimed, rolling her eyes. "That's ridiculous. That bunch of old rascals would never in the world appoint a *woman* as county treasurer—not even on an acting basis."

"Maybe they've decided to appoint somebody who knows what she's doing," Violet suggested. "After all, you were the only one who knew how to track down that missing money. Scroggins didn't even know where to begin."

"Right," Myra May said. "So appointing you would seem to be a smart move, wouldn't you say?"

"Maybe." Verna's tone was acid. "But nobody ever accused the Cypress County commissioners of being smart. Mostly, they just do as little as possible and hope for the best. They wouldn't appoint me—they know I would actually do the job."

"Well, no skin off our nose if you don't believe us," Myra May replied with a shrug. "You'll hear about it soon enough. The commissioners are meeting tomorrow night. If I were you, Verna, I'd expect a telephone call and an invitation to the meeting. You should go."

"And be prepared to act surprised when they announce their decision," Violet put in. "You don't want them to know that you were tipped off ahead of time."

Lizzy looked from Myra May to Violet. "You're really serious about this, aren't you? You're not making it up?"

"Of course we're not making it up," Violet said, and smiled at Verna. "Congratulations, Verna. We're all very proud of you. Why, I'll bet that you're the only female county treasurer in the whole state of Alabama."

"I never count my chickens before they're hatched," Verna muttered. "I'll believe this when it happens. *If* it happens."

"When what happens?" Ophelia asked, coming to the table with a pitcher of lemonade.

"Nothing," Verna said hastily, and held up her glass. "Are you offering refills on that lemonade?"

"Gif me a vhisky," Myra May said huskily. "Ginger ale on the side, and don't be stingy, baby."

"Congratulations on your new job, Opie," Lizzy said warmly, as Ophelia filled the glasses. "Charlie Dickens says you're a whiz on that Linotype machine."

"New job?" Bessie slid onto the seat next to Lizzy. "Ophelia has a job?"

"At the *Dispatch*," Ophelia said proudly. "Mr. Haydon is teaching me the Linotype machine. And Mr. Dickens says that if things work out, maybe I can take a crack at being advertising manager. He hates to sell ads," she went on in a confiding tone. "But the newspaper needs more income. And I know all the store owners, so I don't think I'd have any problem talking to them about taking out ads in the paper."

Myra May gave her a sharp look. "If I'd known you were looking for a *job*, Ophelia, I would have asked if you wanted to work on the switchboard. I've had it up to here"—she put her hand to her forehead, above her eyebrows—"with sweet young things. I need someone mature."

"Well, I'm mature, but I couldn't," Ophelia said apologetically, pushing her hair back behind her ear. "Jed wouldn't want me to work nights or weekends. Mr. Dickens told me I could set my own hours at the *Dispatch*. Of course, it doesn't pay much," she added. "But it pays enough."

Lizzy looked curiously at Ophelia. Enough for what? she wanted to ask, but she didn't. Ophelia probably had a special project in mind. Maybe some more new furniture for her house, like that pretty living room suite she'd bought from

Sears a while back. Lizzy admired that little walnut coffee table.

"I always heard that the Linotype was too big a machine for a woman," Violet said, frowning. "Isn't it hard to operate?"

"Not in the slightest," Ophelia replied. "I think men just say that because they're afraid that women will take their jobs." She tilted her head to one side. "You have to have patience, yes, and it helps if you already know how to type. And I can't lift a full case of type—not yet, anyway." She lifted her arm and flexed her bicep. "But that may change. And I'm here to tell you that anybody who can operate a sewing machine and run up a dress pattern can certainly learn the Linotype."

"That's wonderful, Ophelia," Bessie said. "Now, when I read the newspaper, I'll know that you were the one who put all those words on paper." She paused, looking around the table, as if to make sure that she had everyone's attention. "Speaking of jobs, have you heard about Miss Rogers?"

"Uh-oh," Verna said ominously. "Has the town council closed the library?"

"It doesn't have to," Ophelia put in. "Not for a while. That's what Jed says, anyway. Somewhere, the council has found some money to keep it open." She paused, frowning. "He didn't tell me any of the details. I guess it's not definite yet."

Bessie dropped her voice. "The money your husband was talking about," she said quietly, "is coming from the sale of Miss Rogers' family heirlooms—the pillow and the documents that were hidden inside it."

"She's *sold* them?" Lizzy cried, alarmed. "Oh, no! They were really important to her!"

Bessie held up her hand. "It's okay, truly, Liz. Now that she knows who her family was, she feels a lot less anxious about hanging on to a piece of the past. She decided to put the pillow and the documents to good use, so she sold them to a collector in Wilmington. He apparently has a few other things, including an autographed copy of Rose Greenhow's memoir. He plans to donate everything to a local museum, where people can see them and understand what a courageous woman Miss Rogers' grandmother was."

Myra May clapped her hands. "Good for Miss Rogers," she said. "I knew she had it in her—she just had to find it, that's all." On Violet's lap, Cupcake clapped her hands and crowed happily, and they all laughed.

"And here's the best part," Bessie said. "Once the items are installed in the museum, she'll be invited to Wilmington to see them. Isn't that wonderful?"

"It really is," Violet agreed. "Miss Rogers will love it." She shook her head. "But I don't see how any of that is going to help the library."

"The money isn't coming to Miss Rogers," Bessie explained. "She's giving it to the town council, with the stipulation that they use it to keep the library open—and let her use some of it for more books."

"What a wonderful idea!" Lizzy exclaimed.

"More books," Verna said. "I'm for that."

"You bet," Myra May replied emphatically.

"Let's drink to Miss Rogers," Ophelia said, lifting her lemonade glass.

"And to the Confederate Rose," Bessie said.

"To the Confederate Rose," they all said, in unison.

# Historical Note
## Rose Greenhow, Civil War Spy

The characters who appear in *The Darling Dahlias and the Confederate Rose* are entirely fictional—that is, except for the Confederate Rose herself: Rose O'Neal (sometimes spelled O'Neale) Greenhow, who was born in 1813 or 1814 and died by drowning on October 1, 1864. I have taken the story of her life, as it is related by Charlie Dickens in Chapter Sixteen, from a variety of sources, including *Wild Rose*, the excellent biography by Ann Blackman that appeared in 2005. If you'd like to learn more about Rose Greenhow, look for Blackman's book.

Historians have debated the value of Rose's spy craft and the importance of her espionage. Her coded dispatches were not the only secret information that General Beauregard received about the movement of Northern troops before the First Battle of Bull Run (as it was called by the North), but it is clear that the Confederate command placed a great deal of confidence in the intelligence she provided, which she obtained by listening to and asking questions of the government officials and military officers she entertained in her Washington home, on West Sixteenth Street, within sight of the White House.

Using a simple substitution cipher created by Colonel Thomas Jordan (whom espionage novelists would call her "spymaster"), Greenhow encrypted messages and concealed them in the clothing and other objects that her female friends wore or carried as they traveled from Washington to Manassas and Richmond. According to Blackman, Rose's encrypted reports were "generally accurate and contained useful notes about the numbers and movements of Union forces around Washington." Coded replies and requests for further information were carried back to Rose by Confederate couriers, usually Southern sympathizers, civilians who made their homes in Washington and were allowed to travel freely. This back-and-forth went on for months throughout 1861. Finally, the assistant secretary of war assigned Allan Pinkerton to establish a twenty-four-hour watch over her home, and, in early 1862, to place her under house arrest. When that did not stop her activities, she was imprisoned in the Old Capitol building, where she was held until her release and deportation to the South.

Rose bore eight children, including Little Rose, who had only one daughter, and it appears that there are no living Greenhow descendants. Miss Rogers' relationship to Rose and Little Rose is entirely fictional, as is the embroidered pillow and the documents hidden within it. But such a thing is possible, don't you think? And it makes a good story.

Rose Greenhow could not change the outcome of the War Between the States. But she did what she could to serve the Confederacy. And in the end, she died for it.

## ROSE GREENHOW'S CIPHER

*Credit: This cipher was redrawn by Peggy Turchette from the version reprinted on p. 176 in Fred Wrixon's book,* Codes, Ciphers, Secrets, and Cryptic Communication, *Black Dog & Leventhal, 1998. The original is held by the North Carolina Office of Archives and History, Raleigh, North Carolina.*

# Recipes

*If there were no other reason to live in the South,*
*Southern cookin' would be enough.*
— MICHAEL ANDREW GRISSOM,
*SOUTHERN BY THE GRACE OF GOD*

I have chosen recipes for this book that not only illustrate the wide range of foods that appeared on Southern tables during the early 1930s, but also have some historical interest, in terms of ingredients and preparation.

## *Dr. Carver's Peanut Cookies #3*

*George Washington Carver was the most famous African American scientist and teacher of his era. He spent most of his professional life as a faculty member at Tuskegee Institute and was widely respected for his assistance to small farmers in improving their farming methods and his research into new uses for peanuts, sweet potatoes, pecans, and other Southern crops. He included recipes in his agricultural bulletins in order to demonstrate a variety of uses for the crops. This popular recipe is from* How to Grow the Peanut and 105 Ways of Preparing it for Human Consumption, *Tuskegee Institute Press, Bulletin Number 31, June 1925.*

⅓ cup butter
2 eggs, well beaten
½ cup sugar
½ cup flour
½ teaspoon baking powder
½ cup finely chopped peanuts
1 teaspoon lemon juice
¾ cup milk

Cream butter and add sugar and eggs. Sift the flour and baking powder together. Combine the butter and flour mixtures. Then add the milk, nuts, and lemon juice. Mix well and then drop mixture from a spoon to an unbuttered baking sheet. Sprinkle with additional chopped nuts and bake in a slow oven (about 300 degrees). Makes about 2 dozen cookies.

## *Lizzy Lacy's Buttermilk Pie*

*This old-fashioned, easy-to-put-together pie is a longtime favorite in Southern families, for many had their own milk cow. But before refrigeration was developed, milk soured quickly in the warm climate of the South, so the cream was churned into butter, which could be preserved almost indefinitely in brine. Buttermilk, the liquid that remained in the churn after the butter formed, was mildly tart and very refreshing. Cultured buttermilk, the product that you see in the dairy case at your local supermarket, is lightly fermented, pasteurized skim milk. It is not nearly as rich as the buttermilk our great-grandmothers used, but it is still an*

*effective ingredient. If you don't have buttermilk, you can cre-*
*ate an acceptable substitute by adding 1 tablespoon of lemon*
*juice or white vinegar to 1 cup of fat-free, skim, or whole*
*milk.*

½ cup butter, room temperature
2 cups sugar
3 eggs
2 rounded tablespoons flour
1 cup buttermilk
Dash of nutmeg
1 teaspoon vanilla
Zest (grated rind) of two lemons
Unbaked 9-inch pie shell

Cream butter and sugar. Mix eggs and flour and beat into the
butter/sugar mixture. Stir in buttermilk, nutmeg, vanilla,
and lemon zest (if you have it). Pour into the pie shell and
bake at 350 degrees for 45 minutes. The top should be lightly
browned and the center should jiggle. Don't overbake—the
pie will set as it cools.

## *The Darling Diner Grits*

*In the South, breakfast without grits isn't breakfast. Grits (or*
*hominy grits) were adapted from a cooked mush of softened*
*maize eaten by Native Americans. It was likely introduced to*
*the colonists at Jamestown around 1607 by the Algonquin*
*Indians, who called it* rockahominy, *meaning hulled corn.*
*The word grits comes from the Old English* grytt *(bran) or*
greot *(ground) and is usually treated as a singular noun. The*
*colonists made grits by soaking corn in lye made from wood ash*

*until the hulls floated off. It was then pounded and dried. Modern grits (also called* hominy, *derived from* rockahominy) *is made without lye. Most Southerners prefer stone-ground grits to instant or quick-cook grits because the germ is still intact and it simply tastes better. Grits may be served with sausage or ham, with bacon and eggs, baked with cheese, or sliced cold and fried in bacon grease (my mother's favorite way of serving it).*

**1 cup stone-ground grits**
**Water for rinsing**
**4 cups water**
**½ teaspoon salt**
**2 tablespoons unsalted butter, divided into 4**

To rinse, pour the grits into a large bowl and cover with cold water. Skim off the bits of floating chaff, stir, and skim again. Drain in a sieve. Bring 4 cups of water to a boil in a large pan. Add salt and gradually stir in the grits. Reduce heat and simmer, stirring often, until the grits are thick and creamy, about 40 minutes. Pour into four bowls and stir in butter.

## *Euphoria's Southern Fried Doughnuts*

*Since Euphoria bakes a great many meringue pies, the diner's kitchen is equipped with an electric beater, which also makes short work of mixing up a batch of doughnuts. (In their 1929 catalog, Sears and Roebuck sold a stand model, manufactured by Arctic, for nine dollars and ninety-five cents.) This recipe makes about a dozen doughnuts, a sweet alternative to biscuits for a Southern breakfast. Other traditional recipes include sweet potato doughnuts, mashed potato doughnuts, and* calas, *New Orleans doughnuts (rather like fritters) made from cooked rice, eggs, flour, and sugar.*

2 tablespoons lukewarm water
1 teaspoon sugar
1 (¼-ounce) package active dry yeast (2 ¼ teaspoons)
3 ¼ cups flour
1 cup milk
½ stick (4 tablespoons) unsalted butter
2 large eggs
2 tablespoons sugar
1 ½ teaspoons salt
½ teaspoon cinnamon
5 to 6 cups vegetable oil (for frying)

To proof yeast (that is, to make sure that it's fresh and active), place warm water in shallow bowl. Stir in sugar until dissolved. Sprinkle yeast across the solution and stir until dissolved. Let stand for 5 to 7 minutes. Fresh yeast will bubble. If it doesn't, toss it out and try again with fresh yeast.

Combine flour, milk, butter, eggs, sugar, salt, and cinnamon in large mixer bowl and add yeast mixture. Mix at low speed until a soft dough forms, then increase to high and beat for 3 minutes. Scrape dough from sides of bowl and brush lightly with oil. Cover with a damp towel and let rise in a warm place until doubled in bulk, 1½ to 2 hours, or let rise in refrigerator overnight (8 to 12 hours).

Turn dough onto a lightly floured surface and roll about ½-inch thick. Using a doughnut cutter, cut out rounds. (Reroll doughnut centers and recut to make 1 or 2 additional doughnuts.) Cover with a damp towel and let rise until slightly puffed, about 30 minutes (45 minutes if dough was refrigerated). Heat oil to 350°F in a heavy 4-quart pot. Fry 2 doughnuts at a time, turning once or twice with a slotted spoon, until golden brown and puffy (about 2 minutes). Drain. Reheat oil to 350°F before frying the next batch. Cool and glaze.

**GLAZE**

¼ cup milk
1 teaspoon vanilla
2 cups confectioners' sugar

Heat milk and vanilla in a medium saucepan until warm. Sift confectioners' sugar into milk and whisk until well mixed. Remove from heat and place over a bowl of warm water. Dip cooled doughnuts individually into the glaze. Drain on a rack over a cookie sheet.

## *Aunt Hetty Little's Stewed Okra with Corn and Tomatoes*

*Okra* (Hibiscus esculentus, *a member of the same family as the Confederate rose) grows well in the heat and humidity of the South and is a staple of Southern gardens—and Southern cooking. The plant seems to have originated in Ethiopia, then distributed to the eastern Mediterranean, Arabia, and India. A Spanish Moor visiting Egypt in 1216 wrote one of the earliest accounts of okra's use as a vegetable, reporting that the young seedpods were cooked with meal to reduce their gummy texture. In the American South, cooks follow something of the same practice, dipping the sliced pods in cornmeal and frying them.*

*During the Civil War, okra seeds were dried, parched, and brewed as a coffee substitute. This recipe is from the*

Southern Banner, *Athens, Georgia, February 11, 1863:*
*"Parch over a good fire and stir well until it is dark brown;*
*then take off the fire and before the seed gets cool put the white*
*of one egg to two tea-cups full of okra {seed}, and mix well.*
*Put the same quantity of seed in the coffeepot as you would*
*coffee, boil well and settle as coffee."*

3 to 4 strips bacon, diced
½ cup diced onion
3 to 4 cloves garlic, diced
8 to 10 pods fresh young okra, sliced
1 cup corn kernels
½ cup diced green peppers
1 cup diced tomatoes
1 cup tomato sauce
½ cup water
¼ teaspoon red pepper flakes
½ teaspoon dry thyme
½ teaspoon salt
1 teaspoon black pepper

Sauté diced bacon, add onion and garlic, and sauté until
onions are transparent. Add all other ingredients and bring to
a boil. Reduce to a simmer and cook, stirring occasionally, for
35 to 40 minutes or until okra is tender.

## *Mildred Kilgore's Southern Coleslaw*

*No Southern celebration would be complete without a big bowl*
*of coleslaw. The word comes from the Dutch words,* kool sla
*(cabbage salad, usually served hot). This recipe, which features*
*a sharply sweet-sour dressing, is picnic-perfect, a vinegary foil*

*to a platter of fried chicken or barbequed ribs. Celery seed was a favorite Southern flavoring, especially recommended for use with cabbage.*

1 pound finely shredded cabbage
1 medium red onion, quartered and finely sliced
1 cup toasted pecans, chopped

**DRESSING**

1 cup sugar
1 teaspoon salt
1 ½ teaspoons dry mustard
1 teaspoon celery seed
1 cup vinegar
⅔ cup vegetable oil

Combine shredded cabbage with sliced onion and pecans. Combine dressing ingredients and bring to a boil. Pour over cabbage and toss. Serve warm or chilled.

# Resources

Blackman, Ann, *Wild Rose: Rose O'Neale Greenhow, Civil War Spy.* New York: Random House, 2005.

Farquhar, Michael, " 'Rebel Rose,' A Spy of Grande Dame Proportions." *Washington Post*, September 18, 2000.

Greenhow, Rose O'Neal, *My Imprisonment and the First Year of Abolition Rule at Washington*, London: Richard Bentley, 1863. Also available online at http://docsouth.unc.edu/fpn/greenhow/menu.html (Accessed July 22, 2011).

Ross, Ishbel, *Rebel Rose*. St. Simon's Island, Georgia: Mockingbird Books, 1973.